Founded by the wealthiest woman in London, an unconventional crime-solving club brings together single lords and overlooked ladies from every rung of society. It's a perfectly scandalous match . . .

As London's most sought-after bachelor, the Duke of Leomore stuns society when he announces his engagement to a woman who has just been branded a thief. Yet as his painfully shy "bride-to-be" understands, it is merely a ruse until The Society for Single Ladies apprehends the true culprit—and a ploy to further delay Leo's obligation to wed. For him, marriage will be a purely practical affair. Still, why does a stolen kiss with his faux fiancée conjure such tempting visions of romance?…

As if being falsely accused weren't mortifying enough, Phoebe North is now the talk of the town. And while she knows Leo did the honorable thing to protect her reputation, she can't help but long for more. It would be an impossible match given their unequal stations, and Leo has made his view of marriage quite clear. Yet his kiss and flirtatious ways say something else. If only she could persuade him of how delightful it would be to thumb their noses at convention—and become fools for love…

Visit us at www.kensingtonbooks.com

Books by Lynne Connolly

The Society of Single Ladies
The Girl With the Pearl Pin

The Shaw Series
Fearless
Sinless
Dauntless
Boundless

The Emperors of London Series
Rogue in Red Velvet
Temptation Has Green Eyes
Danger Wears White
Reckless in Pink
Dilemma in Yellow
Silk Veiled in Blue
Wild Lavender

Published by Kensington Publishing Corporation

The Girl With the Pearl Pin

The Society of Single Ladies

Lynne Connolly

LYRICAL PRESS
Kensington Publishing Corp.
www.kensingtonbooks.com

LYRICAL PRESS BOOKS are published by
Kensington Publishing Corp.
119 West 40th Street
New York, NY 10018

All Kensington titles, imprints, and distributed lines are available at special quantity discounts for bulk purchases for sales promotion, premiums, fund-raising, educational, or institutional use.

Special book excerpts or customized printings can also be created to fit specific needs. For details, write or phone the office of the Kensington Sales Manager: Kensington Publishing Corp., 119 West 40th Street, New York, NY 10018. Attn. Sales Department. Phone: 1-800-221-2647.

Lyrical Press and Lyrical Press logo Reg. U.S. Pat. & TM Off.

First Electronic Edition: September 2019
eISBN-13: 978-1-5161-0952-4
eISBN-10: 1-5161-0952-X

First Print Edition: September 2019
ISBN-13: 978-1-5161-0955-5
ISBN-10: 1-5161-0955-4

Printed in the United States of America

To Jennifer, Michelle, Martin, Helen, Renee, and all the wonderful staff at Kensington who have helped me so much.

Author's Foreward

Writing a new series is a mixture of terrifying and exciting. A lot of late nights and research have led to this new venture, and at last, it's ready for you. May the SSL prosper!

Chapter 1

April 1750

Phoebe North was about to experience the most romantic episode of her life. Quite unexpectedly too. The Duke of Leomore, "Call me Leo," leaned into her with the evident intention of fastening his mouth to hers. And Phoebe, surprised but completely in agreement, prepared for the onslaught.

Then merry hell exploded outside the secluded grotto they were sharing. Screams and the sound of running feet interrupted them.

The duke jerked back, gray eyes gleaming in the moonlight, and took her arm, urging her to retreat. Phoebe shook him off. Somebody out there was in trouble. This was no time for discreet withdrawal.

She took a couple of quick paces to the pillared entrance and went down the two steps to the main path, lifting the skirts of her new ball gown in a graceless manner her hostess would definitely not approve of. The sound of running came closer, and the ground under her feet trembled with the coming onslaught. Around the corner hurtled a man dressed in drab street clothes, his cocked hat pulled down low over his forehead. Something glittered in his grasp. He was too large for Phoebe to block with her body, but as he raced past, trailing the aroma of well-used clothing and body odor, she grabbed at his hand, trying to wrest away whatever he was carrying. The sounds of shouting and "Stop thief!" grew closer.

The bully shoved Phoebe, and she caught her heel in her skirt, tumbling backward.

Strong arms hauled her up, and she found herself drawn close to a hard, male chest. Her breath gone, she needed a moment, but she should really pull away.

A woman's shrill cries centered on her. "There she is, the thief! Look what she has in her hand!"

A soft male voice from behind her countered her ladyship's words. People crowded around, abandoning the brightly lit ballroom beyond. "I fail to understand how you draw that conclusion, ma'am. My betrothed and I were merely snatching a few quiet moments together."

Betrothed?

* * * *

Earlier that same evening, Leo's grandmother glared at him over the dinner table. Leo wouldn't have been surprised if the delicate china and gleaming silverware had turned to stone, followed in short order by himself. "You must not marry to oblige me. You must do it for the title and estate. You cannot be the last Leomore in the direct line." She tapped the crisp linen tablecloth twice to emphasize her point. She spoke with a vigor that belied her seventy years, but the walking cane propped within her reach told a different story.

"Pay heed, Leomore, if you do not make a decision for yourself soon, I shall do it for you."

He tried for frozen hauteur, although trying that with a woman who had personally hauled him out of trees on the estate and punished him for it made ducal reserve difficult to assume. "I will find a bride, Grandmama, never fear. I'm fully aware that you deserve rest and comfort, not to be obliged to act as my hostess and work for the family."

A smile curved her thin lips. While his grandmother barely topped five feet, every inch counted. Nobody overlooked her delicate form, nobody turned away when the Dowager Duchess of Leomore entered the room. She had all the dignity and grace of a queen and deployed it to great effect.

She softened her tone. "I know that, my dear, but you should also be aware that I will prevent it, if your selection is not suitable. I failed to do that with your father, but I will not shirk my duty a second time. While I cannot force you on to your knees in front of an eligible female, I can arrange matters to make it impossible for you to go ahead with an engagement to an unsuitable candidate." Her expression gentled, her gray eyes revealing more than most people saw. "Indeed, I regret the necessity, since you are content with your bachelor state. If your heir had lived, I would have remained content to let you take your time. Now the insufferable Erasmus has become your heir, you must do something to prevent him taking the dukedom."

Leo knew she was right. His cousin and heir up until the end of last season had died in a boating accident. John would have made a very good duke, had Leo died, without issue. On the other hand, John's younger brother, Erasmus, had absolutely no interest in family obligations. Not his own, at any rate, although he cared passionately about the Caesars. He would have the estate, its employees and dependents bankrupt in no time, despite the wealth the title carried, by buying the contents of Rome, and probably Athens, too. That must not happen, not after the depredations of Leo's parents.

His father had married for love. She was from a good family with a reasonable portion, but after Leo's birth they set about ruining the estate with their high living. The duke gave her everything, and then they had died together. Smallpox had taken both of them in a week, and because of the risk, Leo hadn't been allowed to see them.

They left a wrecked inheritance and a small, bewildered, half spoiled, half wild boy to carry on the venerable dukedom. Leo owed his grandmother more than he could ever repay. But that didn't stop him trying.

Leo picked up his glass of wine, watching the dark liquid glimmer before he took a sip. "I know it, ma'am." He would not keep her in suspense. "I intend to look about me this season. Did you compile the list I requested?" He would not have his grandmother upset, so his first criterion was to find someone the dowager liked, or at least could tolerate. The omissions would tell him what he needed to know. Nobody knew society better than his grandmother, even though she rarely ventured abroad these days. She did not need to. Society came to her.

She flourished a sheet of paper. "Here."

Silently he perused it until he got to a name near the bottom. "Miss Angela Childers?" He glanced up. "That's long odds, to say the least."

His grandmother lifted her chin. "The woman said she would never marry, but have any dukes asked her before? Dukes of your consequence?"

"Apart from the title, I can offer her nothing she cannot get for herself." He liked Miss Childers, the daughter of what society haughtily referred to as a mixed marriage. Which was to say, her grandmother had been a duchess, and her grandfather on the other side a wealthy City man. Leo had not seen the beautiful banker since the autumn of last year, but he recalled his pleasure in her company. And her rejection of any man who tried to get closer to her. "She refuses to marry, and I cannot imagine she will change her mind." But his grandmother had a point about the title, and he could not deny he liked Miss Childers. "I daresay everyone who is in town will be at her house tonight."

"She cannot hold the ball on her own," the duchess said, her lips primming in disapproval. "Asking men to her house when she lives there alone is not done."

"Her uncle reluctantly serves as host on these occasions, I believe."

Stuffy rules. As if Miss Childers would ever behave in a way to draw opprobrium. In a few years, society would consider her an old maid, and then she could do as she wished, or so she had declared last year. Protecting women was one thing, but the ridiculous unwritten rules society lived by irked him excessively. "I will have a chance to look over most of the women on your list." All the people his grandmother considered "everyone," at any rate. "Do I escort you, ma'am?"

His grandmother reached for her cane, her hand trembling. Old age had hit her hard the past few years, and now her hands were twisted with arthritis. Leo would marry the devil himself if he could get her the rest she deserved. "I received an invitation, but the event will be a sad squeeze, and I am in no mind to go. However, you may give the lady my warmest regards."

The dowager duchess's regards were hotly sought after. Leo duly promised to pass them on. He glanced down the other names. His grandmother had listed ten young ladies who would no doubt be eager to receive his attentions. A few weren't there. He would not trouble them, not caring enough about any of them to make a fuss or defy the dowager's wishes.

He knew what he wanted for himself. A sweetly amenable woman of good character and high birth who would not expect the close intimacy that had no place in a rational marriage. He allowed a certain measure of affection from his mistress, but his wife should be aware of her position in the world and behave accordingly. Recent family history made that requirement even more important.

He would do everything in his power to give his grandmother a tranquil old age.

"Leo, you must not marry without affection," his grandmother said, "but ensure your feelings for your bride are no more than that."

Leo nodded. He and the dowager agreed on that point. "Liking will be enough."

"Indeed, you may lavish affection on your mistress," Her Grace said. She shifted a little, enough to make the footman standing behind her chair hurry forward to help her stand. Not that she needed it, but she appreciated an attentive servant.

"I did." Leo shuddered, recalling La Coccinelle's final tantrum. Final for him, that was. He had sent her the deeds to the house he'd bought for her, and she could consider their affair at an end. He would certainly not return there.

Getting to his feet, Leo tossed his napkin down on the table before making his bow. "I will uphold the dignity of the dukedom, never fear."

"I know you will. You always do."

* * * *

"You look lovely," Angela said. "You'll do well tonight, Phoebe, mark my words."

Phoebe let her mouth tilt up in a doubting smile. "I'll d-do well enough." She flourished her fan. "At least I m-mastered that part." Her relatively plain gown marked her as inferior, so she didn't expect any special notice. In fact, she'd positively dislike it. They were standing outside Angela's bedroom door, ready to go downstairs and greet her guests.

Angela took her hands in hers. "You've come a long way since you escaped from your odious suitor in the country. Now you may enjoy yourself."

Phoebe smiled back. Yes, she had. Sir Marcus Callow, a bold, handsome, overbearing man had set his sights on her in the provincial Assembly she regularly attended. He was unexceptional, except that he wanted his own way in everything. Phoebe had avoided him. When he'd tried to press his suit by forcing a kiss on her so rough that it split her lip, Phoebe had grabbed Angela's invitation to visit her and escaped. All the way to London. With any luck, when she returned, Marcus would have settled on somebody else. Having a retiring nature did not mean she was compliant or weak, as many people supposed. And she would not marry Marcus. Not if she had to remain a spinster for the rest of her days.

Phoebe waited for Angela to lead her down the stairs and into the brilliantly lit hall below. Angela's Uncle Harold, who acted as host at times like this, waited for his niece. He was, as always, austere in the darkest of blues, his fashionable white wig firmly in place.

This was Phoebe's first society ball. She'd attended a few affairs in the week between Easter Monday and today, and now she was glad of it, because this was society at its most glittering.

This spacious London house took her breath away every time she went down into the main reception rooms, although Phoebe knew enough by now not to gawk. She bobbed a curtsey to Angela's uncle. "Good evening, sir." He gave her a smile and a nod.

Phoebe followed Angela through to the main chamber, the biggest drawing room, which was acting as the ballroom.

Forced up to the highest echelon in society, she was still overwhelmed by the grandeur and sheer luxury everyone displayed with a carelessness that concealed their wealth. Everyone except Phoebe. She'd come from a small town in Buckinghamshire, where her mother was the resident queen of local society to—this.

This being hundreds of candles in glittering chandeliers, precious gems around the women's throats, expensive French lace at every elbow—three rows of it—the most sumptuous fabrics used in careless profusion and a plethora of liveried servants ready to attend one's every need. And the sound of chatter, noisy and loud, buzzing in her head. The ball had only just started, and already the rooms were full. At least Angela had decreed no receiving line. This was more a rout than a ball, apparently. Not that Phoebe was entirely sure she knew the difference.

People crowded forward, eager to meet Phoebe's cousin.

Phoebe's stomach swooped, and she slammed her foot to the floor as the other slipped forward, and she nearly lost her balance. She should have roughened the soles of these shoes, but in her haste she'd forgotten. Now it was too late, and the parquetry floor was polished to a high shine. The servants hadn't even put French chalk on the part of the floor meant for dancing. If anyone else had shoes with shiny soles, the result could be interesting.

Angela responded to everyone, and Phoebe curtseyed when people deigned to notice her. Which they did too often for her liking. Her head spun with the names of all the earls, dukes, marquesses, and Lord knew who else flocking to the house for this ball. They politely enquired after her welfare, but their gazes never rested on her. They drifted past her to Angela. She doubted any of them would know her if they passed her in the street if she was here on her own.

The humiliation of that careless disregard annoyed her, but she could do nothing. As she was stiffening her shoulders, someone stopped. Lady Hamilton smiled and met her gaze. "Good evening, Miss North." She'd even remembered Phoebe's name. "Are you well?"

"Tolerably, I thank you," Phoebe said, dipping into a token curtsey, warming to the lady. "Is your daughter here tonight?"

Lady Hamilton wafted her fan in the vague direction of the dancers. "I believe so. But my son has arrived from the Continent. Do you think Miss Childers would like to meet him?" Not would Phoebe like to meet him, because who cared about her?

A sigh threatened to escape. And she was actually thinking that someone wanted to talk to her! How foolish she was. "I daresay she would, my lady. I'm sure she will enjoy meeting him." She would have to warn Angela before Lady Hamilton trapped her.

Angela headed, as she always did, to the group in the corner. The women and girls who sat together for company, chattering and pretending that not being asked to dance was exactly what they wanted. She always said she was one of them, even though she could obviously have any man she wanted for her husband. She chose not to, that was the difference.

Phoebe followed her.

This was where Phoebe belonged, with the older sisters who had not taken in society, women of little fortune, or those who genuinely did not care for dancing and popularity. This was the natural home of companions, the employed, or poor relations. A few widows, wealthy and otherwise, were sprinkled in for interest. Phoebe felt more at home there than anywhere else in a fashionable ballroom. When Angela left the group, Phoebe would stay.

Angela spoke to a few women, then took a seat, ignoring the stares from the more exalted guests. Fans fluttered, enough to make the flames of the hundreds of candles flicker in their holders. "Ladies, it does my heart good to see you."

They didn't titter or giggle. The women here were beyond that. They sat, a phalanx of the rejected, keeping each other company and pretending they didn't care. Some truly didn't, of course, and scorned society. Others did.

The lady next to her froze, and Phoebe lifted her gaze. And also froze.

A dark shadow in male form loomed up. His Grace, the Duke of Leomore stood and waited politely for Angela to notice him. He always made Phoebe shudder, and she did not know why. She had seen him before, since he attended most society events, or the ones that would amuse him. This season, or so gossip said, he intended to find a bride, which explained his attendance at parties he usually avoided.

He wore his hair naturally, a raven's wing tied back in a black bow. His eyes were dark gray, his frame large. But it was the intensity of this gaze that gave her pause, the way he saw through everything to the person beneath.

As far as she knew, he'd never actually noticed her.

Her heart pounded when he came to stand close to her. He bowed, not making his obeisance too deep, as gentlemen sometimes did, intending their bows as mockery rather than gestures of true respect.

Angela turned her attention to him with one brow raised slightly and met his smile of greeting with one of her own.

"Madam, it is always a delight to see you looking in such good heart," he said. "Would you do me the honor of dancing with me?"

"I'm afraid my hand is bespoken, sir." Angela could beat anyone at elaborate courtesy if she wished, which she rarely did. "May I present my cousin, Miss Phoebe North?"

The duke bowed to her, his expression stony. Fobbed off on the companion!

Phoebe nearly burst into laughter but sealed her lips firmly until she had risen to her feet and curtseyed to the exalted being. Although her reaction lasted but a second, she had the disconcerting impression that he'd noticed her amusement. Why should she care when he evidently thought so little of her? She should not, but she couldn't prevent her reaction to him.

At least he hadn't turned his back on her, even though Phoebe had fully expected him to do so. She was perfecting her bitter laugh. Perhaps she could use it on him.

But he didn't turn away. He gave her a bone-melting smile. "Would you do me the honor of favoring me with the next dance?"

A duke wanted to dance with her? Angela had adroitly turned him to her, but Phoebe was not sure this counted as a favor.

"Do you feel quite well, Miss North?" he enquired gently as she stifled her amusement.

Good Lord, this man was observant. She forced a smile. "Quite all right, th-thank you, Your Grace." The highly polished marquetry floor slid under her feet.

"I saw that," he said. "When you came in and you slipped. Take care, Miss North."

He'd noticed her faux pas? Who else had seen it? Were they already laughing at her?

He held her hand properly, that was to say, barely at all, and led her in the first steps of the country dance. Phoebe took her courage in both hands, finding his manner daunting. The perfection of his moves, the way he stared down his nose at everyone, marked him as the kind of person she preferred to avoid. "May I call you sir, or d-do you prefer that I use your proper title all the time?"

"Leo will do," he said carelessly. Of course, he would not care what she called him. She was well below his notice.

"I cannot c-call you by your first name," she said. While she was mindful of the correct address, she knew young ladies did not refer to gentlemen by their given names. "I c-cannot p-possibly call you something so familiar." She would call him "sir," as was proper.

"My given name is George. Nobody calls me that, or I might be confused with a dozen or more other men here tonight. My title is Leomore, and since I inherited, people call me Leo."

"Of c-course. L-like the lion. But I would not presume."

He cleared his throat—or was that a laugh? "Perhaps when we're in private you might consider doing so." Was that a gleam of answering challenge lighting his gray eyes?

Before they separated in the dance, she had time to reply. "I feel c-convinced that will n-never happen, sir." Curse it, her stammer had broken in once more. She thought she had overcome that burden. It was the bane of her life. She rarely stammered in private, but in London, where she did not feel comfortable, it had started up again. The harder she tried to overcome her stammer, the worse it became.

As the dance demanded, she moved on to her next partner.

Well, if she'd seen interest in him, she had certainly doused it now. An awkward, stammering woman, dressed in one of the plainest gowns possible and wearing a ribbon around her throat instead of jewelry—he wouldn't be interested in anyone like her. Moreover, one who could not keep steady on her feet.

Country dances involved little skips and hops. Every time her foot left the floor, Phoebe held her breath and prayed she would land safely. She managed very well, even though when they changed partners, the men looked over her head or to one side, as if she was not good enough to meet their gaze. She wasn't imagining the way they didn't look at her. Their unspoken snubs only made her straighten her spine and dare them to meet her gaze. If they wouldn't look at her, she would stare at them. Dare them to continue to ignore her. Which they usually did successfully.

Did she feel excluded? Yes, because they meant her to. For that reason, she would never show them how deeply the treatment affected her.

Eventually this torture of a dance would end. With relief she faced the duke once more, because that meant the dance was drawing to a close. He gave her his hand with no hesitation, his manner impeccable. His expression was warm without condescension. Leomore had such perfect manners that he quite cowed Phoebe, whereas she felt only defiance to those without such address.

After the dance he would return her to the corner of the room from where he'd collected her, thank her for her company, and never give her another thought. Women glanced at him, sending him flirtatious glances, but he took no notice. His manners were far better than most other people in the room, despite him being a duke, which meant he could probably strip naked in the middle of the dance floor and everybody would treat it as a mild eccentricity. Or that he was setting a new, amusing fashion.

She should not have brought that image to mind because now her cheeks heated, and her breath came shallower. He was tall, broad-shouldered and with no trace of padding in his clothes to make up for a lack of muscle and shape. He was wonderfully good-looking. With the excuse of the dance, Phoebe could examine that blade of a nose, the flashing steel-gray eyes, and surprisingly full lips. His cheekbones were as high as his station demanded, and he moved gracefully for such a large man. His clothes, while dark in color and sober compared to the popinjays here tonight, were nevertheless of the best quality. The buttons marching down his waistcoat and coat were probably real gold. Disdaining the fashionable wig, he had adopted the new style of gentlemen wearing their hair naturally, but most did not draw it back so simply. The black velvet bow behind his head absorbed the light from the chandeliers.

Thinking about the duke naked had fatally distracted her. Phoebe hit the floor awkwardly. Her stomach opened into a bottomless pit as she skidded, more like a skater on a frozen lake than a graceful dancer. The sickening sound of ripping fabric rent the air, piercing the melody of the quartet in the corner, quickly followed by a clatter and a crunch as she dropped her fan and promptly stepped on it. Someone sniggered, but she was too busy trying not to fall to discover who.

The duke's hand slid from hers, and Phoebe's heart plummeted along with the rest of her. She would land with a decided thump and have to leave the floor ignominiously on her own, running the gauntlet of amusement.

He was as bad as everyone else, and she was mistaken thinking him a gentleman.

Except she steadied when he grabbed her lace-covered forearms and simply lifted her off her feet. He set her down so gently she hardly felt it and had to force herself not to flail as if she was falling once more. The next moment, he touched her elbow. "Come with me," he said softly.

Phoebe glared down at where her feet peeped out from the hem of her gown. Those new shoes had let her down at last. The rest of the season loomed in front of her, terrifying and ominous. She would be known forever as the clumsy stammerer who could not keep her feet in a simple country dance.

He supported her, one hand firmly under her elbow. "Keep your head up. Smile."

His voice was so low she hardly heard it, but automatically she responded to the command inherent in his tones, and she did as he bade her, even though her ankle hurt like the devil. Doors either side of the ballroom opened to stone staircases that descended to the garden. She counted every one and ensured her foot was well planted on them. Her care did her no good, because on the second to last, she stumbled.

With a curse, the duke swung her into his arms and carried her off, as if she was some kind of princess who couldn't walk.

She squeaked in alarm. "I can manage."

"Be still," he commanded as she struggled.

"This is ridiculous. I'm not hurt. Please, sir, put me down." She could not call out. Someone might hear.

"If you stumble again, we will never get that ruffle repaired. It's early in the evening, and a chilly night. Nobody will see you. Don't you think this is better than people watching and speculating?"

Chapter 2

Leo surprised himself by his behavior toward Miss North. He did not usually go around carrying respectable women into deserted gardens, but this one was so keyed up that he could feel the vibrations coming off her body through her layers of clothing. He should have escorted her upstairs and handed her off to a maid in the room set aside for ladies, but he could not bring himself to do so. Where was the fun in that?

He'd seen her slide when she came in and had been alert for another. He hadn't been wrong, but her evident distress affected his tender emotions in a way he was not used to.

The small, unobtrusive Miss North interested him. She wasn't a professional companion, an assumption confirmed when Miss Childers introduced her as her cousin. She wasn't from the City, didn't have the superior air of the wealthy merchants or the town polish, so she must be from the other side. That would make her gentry, someone who had a settled life in the country and whose social life circulated around the nearest large town.

In an odd way he felt responsible for her, from her visible shock at being asked to dance. She intrigued him, and he did not know why, so he used her accident as a way to snatch her away and discover more about her. If she had allowed it, he would have taken her into supper and discovered more about her and her relationship to Miss Childers.

The indifferent attitude of her partners in the dance raised his ire. They didn't look at her or converse with her, a display of appalling manners he would never have allowed in himself. Country dances were supposed to be social. Miss North was isolated by her inexperience and their superiority. That kind of boorishness could drive him to violence. If any of them appeared in the fencing studio he attended, he'd be sure to challenge them to a bout. And be equally certain to beat them soundly. Let them see what being laughed at felt like.

Would it kill the men she danced with to exchange the time of day with her? Thank God none of the men he considered his particular friends had taken to the floor and treated her in such a way. He would have cut them too. There was no excuse for such appalling manners.

The woman who had laughed? Leo knew who it was, and she would suffer for her cruelty. He would personally attend to the matter.

He never paused to wonder why his fury was so extreme. He'd barely met Miss North and he was already her champion.

Miss North was trembling in his arms now. At least she was wearing one of those new collapsible hoops, so he didn't have to tangle with a circular piece of whalebone springing up and threatening her modesty. He did, however, have to manage the yards and yards of silk that constituted her skirt and petticoat. He lifted a swathe of it and dumped it on her lap to stop the silk trailing on the ground. They'd had a shower of rain earlier this evening, and the path would still be damp. At least they had a full moon, so their progress was reasonably well lit.

Thank goodness. He'd come here on instinct, and he'd been proved right when a small grotto came into view, half concealed behind a few ornamental plants. These gardens often had secluded summerhouses or the like. This place would work well to mend her ruffle and her spirits. Oh, now her fichu had come loose and was flapping around as he carried her. What had possessed him to play the part of chivalrous knight? He must be mad.

Mad or not, he had to get to the grotto soon, or all that silk would slither out of his hold and the lady with it.

These places were built apurpose for lovers. Not that he was a lover, merely a concerned friend. Acquaintance, perhaps, or her escort. No, damn it, he'd stick with friend. After the behavior on the dance floor, that was the very least he could offer her.

He placed Miss North gently on the bench running along the back of the building. The space was lined with pebbles and seashells, a folly more often seen in the countryside. Pretty but painful, should one tumble against it.

Miss North kept her head down and behaved modestly, as he presumed a companion should.

He knelt at her feet, ignoring her faint protest. "Do you have pins?"

"Y-yes, sir—L-Leo." She pushed a paper packet into his hand.

He should not have felt that twinge at his groin when she faltered on his name, revealing her vulnerability. Valiantly he ignored it, telling himself that all she evoked was his sense of chivalry. "Miss North, you should not concern yourself with the opinions of those lower than you."

She laughed. That was better, even if somewhat harsh-edged. "Nobody is l-lower than me, sir."

"It depends whether you are talking of character or rank," he snapped, still out of sorts.

"The young ladies are well educated, fashionably dressed, and accomplished," came the bitter reply. "I cannot compare myself to them."

He found the torn ruffle. That would have tripped her up for the rest of the evening. "They certainly think so. They make you aware of that every time they look in your direction." Even if he had been seriously considering furthering his acquaintance with one of them, he would not do so now. His grandmother had given him a list of a dozen likely candidates for his hand. What he'd seen in the ballroom had halved that list.

He looked up into her face. She appeared tranquil, but on closer inspection, the lines around her mouth were deeper than they should be, as if she had firmed it against displaying her distress. He admired her bravery, but his anger on her behalf was surely more than the situation deserved. Leo considered himself a thoughtful man, but the women sitting at the side of a room or propping up the walls had completely passed him by. They would not do so again. The slow burn of anger settled in the bottom of his stomach. He could do with a brandy.

Recalling his task, he opened the paper. Several pins were stuck through it. Every woman usually had a small packet of pins, but Miss North had obviously been carrying them for some time. "They're somewhat rusty," he observed, gazing at them. "They'll ruin your gown."

"I'll cope," she said firmly. "I can probably cut that part out when I repair it."

Leo shook his head. Even he could see she'd already skimped on the flounce. It was not half as, well, *flouncy* as it should be. Losing even more of the fabric would worsen the effect.

He dropped the useless pins and plucked out the pin from his folds of linen and lace at his throat.

"Oh, sir, you c-can't!"

Her protest made him smile. "My cravat will manage very well without it."

"But that pearl!"

He regarded the item in question indifferently. "It will manage well, too."

She swallowed and met his gaze. "It's huge." Her eyes gleamed when she turned her head, the light of the moon catching them. This was the strangest assignation he had ever had, but also the sweetest.

He chose to take the remark flirtatiously. "Why, thank you, ma'am. I cannot think it more than ordinary."

"Oh!" Miss North covered her cheeks with her hands. His slight innuendo had not gone unnoticed. Interesting. Did she have brothers? That was where ladies often learned what they should not. "I beg your p-pardon." She had responded to him with spirit, despite her obvious discomfort with his behavior.

Since he'd picked her up and carried her here, he had behaved with indecent intimacy. Something in her drew him, something beyond social situation and circumstance. He felt close to her in a way he never allowed with society ladies. Yet she had tried no artifice on him, nor coquettishness of any kind. And yet she appealed to his baser nature too. He was too honest to deny that, and so was his body, which had reacted with predictable enthusiasm to his close proximity to a woman.

Ignoring her protests, he threaded the long pin through the rip in her gown and capped the end. "That should do for now," he said.

"I will ensure you have the p-pin back as soon as possible."

He got to his feet, dusting his hands. "Take your time, my dear."

The small endearment, mild though it was, brought her color up again. He found her response charming. She was dainty and pretty, and he liked her.

He should take her back to the ballroom, but he couldn't converse with her properly there. Instead, he took a seat next to her. "They behaved appallingly to you during that dance. I shall ensure they do not do so again."

"Oh no!" Her horror provoked a short, tense laugh. "I b-beg your p-pardon, sir, but if you show me any particular attention, that will s-serve to make matters worse."

"How does Miss Childers treat you? Is she hard on you?"

She could not have feigned the way her pretty eyes widened in shock. "Goodness, no. She is very k-kind."

He detected no subterfuge in her reply. So the problem lay outside, with the way she was subtly cut by the more affluent and fortunate members of society.

Her bosom heaved as she sucked in a deep breath, gathering courage, or so he guessed from her heightened color. She should tuck her fichu back into place because he found the sight most distracting. "Sir, I appreciate your help. However, I must not impose on you any further." She clasped her hands tightly until the knuckles turned white. "I c-cannot accept more of your k-kindness. If anyone believes you are m-making any particular advances toward me, my situation will only worsen."

Righteous anger was a cleansing emotion sometimes. It certainly gave him a purpose now.

He got to his feet and held out his hand. "I will not allow the ignorant of society to pursue you and castigate you. I cannot understand the way these people think, and I will make that clear." When she softly put her hand in his, he murmured, "I would take great pleasure in driving you around the park tomorrow. Could you be ready at, say, two?"

She froze. "That would not be a good idea, sir."

He was not above using the trinket as an excuse. "How else are you to return my pin?"

"I would not t-trouble you so. You could send a trusted servant to the house to collect it."

"But I insist, ma'am. I shall call on you at the correct hour."

"You might run into the society, sir. I do not think you would wish for that."

He frowned. "What society?"

"You have not heard?" When he shook his head, she continued. "The cartoonists have certainly found amusement in it. Miss Childers has opened a suite of rooms for the use of single ladies such as she was conversing with tonight."

"Single ladies?"

Her pretty mouth twisted. "The Society for Single Ladies. A literary salon, if you will. A place for us to meet, like the clubs men are so eager to set up."

"Ah!" Now he understood her meaning. He was the natural quarry of single ladies. To arrive during a gathering of such people would be to put his head into the lion's mouth. Especially now that he had promised his grandmother he would marry and breed an heir. He might as well have a target on his back for all the toxophilites who would produce their bows and arrows especially for him.

"These young women deserve somewhere of their own. They are overlooked and some are used hardly by their families."

"Are you?" he asked abruptly. He watched her carefully.

"Oh no," she assured him. "I am merely a visitor in her house, acting as her companion while her usual duenna is ill. Our mothers were cousins."

"You are far too young to be a companion, ma'am," he declared indignantly.

"Indeed, so people keep telling Angela. But she takes no notice. She always ensures she has a strong footman or two when we are abroad."

Something troubled her. He would ask. But she had lost that hesitation in her speech, for which he was glad. He should take her back inside.

After he'd claimed his kiss. She was skittish, but he wanted his reward. Close up, she had the most remarkable skin, as if it glowed softly from the inside.

Slowly, waiting for a sign of resistance, he drew her closer. Her eyes wide, she came to him, making him ridiculously pleased. He didn't want to startle her, but this lovely woman was like a bird in his hands, soft and delicate. No more than a kiss, and that despite his better judgment, but he longed to feel it, to know what those lips felt like against his own, and how she tasted.

Before he could take his reward, a commotion erupted from outside the grotto. Shouts of "Stop, thief!" rang around the previously quiet garden. The sound of feet pounding against the gravel path sped toward them. Were it not for the firm foundation of this building, they would have felt the vibrations.

Aiming for discretion, Leo stepped back, drawing Phoebe with him, but she slipped out of his grasp and went forward instead. Concerned with her safety, he lunged after her, cursing under his breath. His heart almost stopped when he heard a pistol discharge close by, the explosion rocking the quiet garden. The report hammered in his ears, shocking and unexpected.

When she screamed, he snaked his arm around her waist, but the damned silk meant she got away. Pulling out of his arms, she picked up her skirts and ran down the steps of the grotto.

"No, you fool!" he called, pursuing her.

She held out her arm as a man hurtled toward her. Considering the relative mildness of the evening, he was dressed unusually, bundled in a heavy cloak in some dull material. He struck her, shoving her aside. Phoebe spun, her skirts tangling around her feet, and she tumbled to the ground, crying out. Leo roared her name, but by now more people were upon them, pursuing the man who'd knocked her down.

Ignoring the escaping man, Leo got there first. Scooping her up, he set her on her feet, still holding her around her waist in case she was overcome and could not stand on her own. She blinked, but called out, "He went that way!"

He groaned as Lady Latimer ran up to them, followed swiftly by other people. The greatest gossip in London *would* have to be the first guest to arrive. But he was more concerned with Phoebe's welfare. "What did you think you were doing?" he demanded.

"He was absconding at speed, so I thought to stop him. I was n-not thinking."

"Evidently." His heart was regaining its normal rhythm, but when she'd run into the men's path, Leo's heart had missed a beat. What if they'd had another pistol or a dagger to hand? "Did you not hear that shot?"

"My bracelet!" Lady Latimer snatched a glittering object from Phoebe's hand. Her eyes gleamed as she turned her head toward him. "Did you catch this little thief, Your Grace?"

"They ran past us," Leo said, sparing the lady a glance.

Her mouth curled. "Your sense of chivalry is delightful, sir, but someone stole my jewels. This lady!" Dramatically she pointed at Phoebe. Her elaborate powdered hairstyle quivered along with her finger. Half a dozen people stood around, enjoying the display. Enough to spread malicious gossip, that was for sure.

Hard on the heels of his determination not to allow her to be ignored, this was too much for Leo. He assumed his best ducal manner, glaring down his nose at the woman. "Miss North needed air."

"I'll wager she did after she snatched my jewelry. Where are my earrings and necklace, you hussy! These are family pieces, the diamonds presented by Queen Elizabeth to my husband's ancestor! Give them back at once!"

Phoebe was trembling. "I d-d-d-d-d-d—" She could not speak, trapped in a circle of stammers.

"Hush." Leo touched his fingers to her mouth. Her lips quivered against the pads. He kept his voice soft and unthreatening when he spoke to Lady Latimer. "Precisely what occurred, ma'am?"

"Ask her!" Her ladyship thrust an accusing finger at Phoebe, her voice rising dramatically. "But since you insist—the jewelry is old and heavy. I went to the ladies' retiring room to rest for five minutes, and removed the pieces, putting them in my lap for safe keeping. I must have fallen asleep, because the next I knew the jewels were gone and I saw only a flicker of blue silk as the thief left. She must have met her accomplices outside. After all, who knows this woman?"

"I do," Miss Childers said calmly. "She is my cousin and companion."

Leo had not seen her arrive, but he heard her voice with relief. Miss Childers was a sensible woman, but unfortunately she was not here with the thief. But her word would mean nothing without corroboration. Some sectors of society would love to see the wealthy Miss Childers brought down. He had to corroborate her story or two women would suffer.

There was no avoiding the inevitable. His grandmother would kill him, cut his heart out with one of the elegant knives they'd used at dinner tonight, but he had to do it.

"You are mistaken, my lady," he told Lady Latimer, who was glaring at Phoebe. "Miss North has been with me for some time." He took Phoebe's hand in his. It was cold and shaking. "I had just asked her to do the greatest honor a woman can bestow on a man and accept my hand in marriage."

He ignored the collective gasp and gazed down into Phoebe's face. The torches brought by two footmen flickered, making her eyes glitter. "She had only just given me her answer. I had not expected such a crowd to arrive to share what should be a private moment."

His statement had the desired effect. Nobody spoke.

Liquid warmth flowed over his hand, where it clasped hers. Only then did he notice that she was bleeding.

* * * *

Phoebe could not process what had happened in the last hour, or how smoothly His Grace had handled the disturbance. He'd escorted her to Angela's private sitting room and dressed her wound himself, despite her protests that she was fine. Her thoughts were reeling.

When Lady Latimer had snatched her bracelet back, Phoebe had felt a sharp sting but thought nothing of it in the confusion. Not until His Grace noticed the long cut slashed up the side of her hand. Heavens, she had nearly stained his beautiful lace cuffs.

Angela took care of Lady Latimer, taking her to another room and plying her with enough burgundy to sink a battleship, as she privately told Phoebe later. And the ball went on, only a slight stir in the supper room disturbing the tenor of the evening. No doubt the gossips would be busy tomorrow.

"You should go," she told the duke. For all his kindness, she could not think of him as anything but a gentleman who had taken her breath away with his calm statement. The great ruby he wore on his finger glittered in the candlelight as he gently wound the bandage around her hand. "T-truly it is not a s-s-serious injury. I s-s-swear I will not d-die from it."

"Ah, but we must be sure." He tucked the end of the bandage neatly underneath the result, a feat she had never achieved without the whole thing coming undone. "In the morning when you have rested, you must remove this and bathe it again. Have your maid clean it at least twice a day."

Phoebe snorted, and at once his features froze and a dark eyebrow winged skyward.

"Did I say something amusing?"

"A maid," she informed him. "I b-b-borrow one when necessary, like t-tonight, but for the m-most part I shift for myself."

"Do you indeed?" He eyed her curiously, as if he had never heard of such a thing. "But a maid saves so much time. I fear my wife-to-be must appear in public with some style."

"N-no, sir." As her anxiety rose, her stammer grew worse. It still returned at times of agitation, such as that mortifying moment outside when she could not get one word past her lips. "You are joking me. That is foolishness. S-society will have forgotten by the m-morning. It is of n-no m-matter. I will be g-g-gone soon enough. N-nobody will remember m-me."

He folded her good hand in his and met her gaze. He had the most beautiful eyes, clear and pure, changing in depth of color depending on the light. She felt as if she could trust him with anything. "Draw a deep breath." When she did, he said, "Now another. Take your time. Think what you are about to say and then say it."

"Oh." She did as he bade her, his steady gaze helping her to calm her thoughts. That was how she generally coped with her stammer, but he had behaved as if she hadn't spoken in anything but a normal tone. He understood. How startling.

When she was ready, she tried again, putting care into enunciating her words and taking her time. "I do not think you c-can have thought about what you were s-saying. A b-betrothal between us is preposterous." Her mouth quirked. She'd managed a whole sentence with only slight hesitation. "How did you know?"

"About what?"

"C-Coping with the s-stammering."

"You are not the only person who has had to overcome that problem." Her eyes widened. "You?"

He nodded, smiling. His smile was as wonderful as his eyes. In a different way, of course. "It affected me after my parents died. However, mine did not last long. My grandmother would not allow it. I gave you the advice I received, that is all. Passing along the knowledge I have learned. Of course," he added, his voice becoming reflective, "if I had continued, people would have declared themselves charmed, and perhaps even imitated me."

"Why would they d-do that?"

His smile broadened. "Because I'm Leomore. The title is more important than the person holding it."

"Oh no, I would never say that."

His expression hardened, and his eyes became colder, the color of a bleak winter stream. "Most people do, and it is only the truth."

What was he thinking of, this man who had the highest privilege and the greatest title of the peerage? Dukes were at the top of the aristocratic ladder, although the thought of all those dignified people standing precariously on the rungs almost made her smile.

She stood—or rather sat, considering their relative positions—in awe of this man. She did not find the task at all difficult, even though he was kneeling before her with a bowl of warm water at his side. He had just tenderly cleaned her cut and kept her amused with the utmost grace and charm.

Phoebe must not find herself caught in the snare of his kindness. That would never do.

He got to his feet in one smooth movement and held out his hand. She laid her own in it, and he drew her to her feet. Although she knew she was a mess, her gown creased and soiled, her hair straggling down from its pins, his warm gaze made her feel like a princess. "You're extremely g-good at that."

He raised a brow. "Good at what?"

"Making the p-person you look at feel b-better. I know I'm in a state." She flicked the silk of her gown. "This is ruined. But you m-make me forget that. Did you have to p-practice?"

He laughed shortly. "I wasn't aware I was doing anything out of the ordinary."

"You n-noticed me. That is unusual." She did not know why she'd said that, only that he drew the truth from her. She would have to take more care to control her emotions

He retained his grip on her hand. "I fear you will find more attention aimed your way in the next few weeks. We must keep to our betrothal."

"B-But it's f-f-foolish. Surely nobody will b-believe you. I thought I would j-jilt you t-tomorrow, or we would say it was a m-misunderstanding."

"I have conceived a violent passion for you." Not by a twitch did he betray the foolishness of that remark.

She burst into disbelieving laughter. "M-Me? N-Nobody will b-believe that."

When he lifted her hand to his lips and kissed the back of it, she snatched a breath. He affected her in a way she hadn't experienced before, and his gaze on her face—she could almost believe him.

"If you wish it, we may part at the end of the season. Let our association fade away, and if anyone asks, we may merely say that we did not suit. But for the foreseeable future, you are mine."

"Y-yours?"

"Indeed so." He drew her closer. "And this time we must seal our bargain. I meant to steal a kiss before, you know, as a reward for stopping you falling on the dance floor, but now I claim one merely because I want to know how you kiss."

Not at all, she would have told him, but she could not, because he pressed his lips to hers.

Phoebe had been kissed before but not like this. The black pinpricks of his incipient beard that she'd noticed earlier now abraded her tender skin, teasing it delightfully. He smelled wonderful, of a no doubt costly cologne and of warm male. She detected no lavender or camphor, both scents she was used to when meeting people in their Sunday best, products to deter pests when the garments lay in storage. He probably had best clothes for every day of the week.

Her mind flung itself in all directions, panicking at having a man so close. He drew away slightly. "Do not concern yourself. I'm kissing you, that is all."

"How did you know?"

He chuckled, his warm breath brushing her cheek. "Every muscle in your body tensed. Now let's try again, shall we?"

To her mingled horror and delight, he suited deeds to words.

This time Phoebe heeded him. Instead of studying him, she closed her eyes, the better to savor the experience. She even dared to touch him, brushing her fingers against the soft cloth of his sleeve. He made a small sound in the back of his throat and tilted his head, sealing their mouths together more securely. His fingers bit through her sleeves into her upper arm, but not enough to bruise. She felt them like small brands, marking her forever.

When she parted her lips, he took possession, sweeping his tongue around her mouth, claiming it as he had claimed the rest of her, touching her tongue and teeth, before gently finishing the kiss.

Phoebe opened her eyes and gazed up at him, unwilling to move. She didn't know what to expect, but not the warmth in his eyes when he gazed at her, and the smile that slowly spread as he watched her. Putting a hand to her cheek, he smoothed an errant curl back into place. "You really are quite lovely, you know. We shall have to ensure society does not miss that."

As a spinster—one, moreover, from a different stratum of society—Phoebe was completely unaccustomed to such remarks. Heat surged to her cheeks and she stared, not daring to speak. She'd never get a single word past her lips.

He ran his thumb across her skin before he stepped back and bent to retrieve the china bowl. "I will leave you now, but I'll return tomorrow at the proper hour to take you driving in the park."

"Oh, should we…" She bit her lip.

His attention went to where her teeth indented her delicate skin. "We most certainly should. I will return to the ball and bravely bear the brunt of the congratulations. I shall tell them you have retired early, to recover from the distressing events. Unless you wish to accompany me downstairs? I will wait while you change."

The thought of all those people smiling and wishing her well made Phoebe feel sick. "Certainly not. They never n-noticed me before. Why should I notice them now?"

That bark of sharp laughter returned. "You are perfectly right. I will tell Miss Childers that you have retired to bed. Good night, my dearest one."

Fortunately, he turned to leave, otherwise he'd have seen her decidedly gauche response. Her mouth dropped open, and she wildly tried to think of an appropriate reply. Her murmured "Good night, sir," would have to suffice.

Chapter 3

Hurrying downstairs the next day, Phoebe heard the murmur of feminine voices from the club room and smiled. For once she felt at home, with friends. That happened so rarely that—goodness, she had felt like that with Leo last night. Surely that wasn't right.

"Phoebe, a moment!"

Phoebe turned around to face her cousin.

Angela wafted a handkerchief. "Truly, Miss Helmers can talk! And her isolation after her illness is pushing her to more. I swear she could talk the hind leg off a donkey."

"You should allow me to see her. I could keep her company."

Angela's companion, currently recovering from a bout of influenza, only saw a few people, for fear the sickness would spread. Angela, having caught the illness a month before, declared herself immune. "Nonsense, my dear. I wish her to rest, and she will do so." She patted Phoebe's hand. "Besides, I am thoroughly enjoying your visit. You suit me so well, I am sorry you are not available permanently." She tucked the lace-edged cloth up her sleeve, where she could produce it with a flourish if necessary. "Before we go into the club, I'd appreciate a word in private."

Phoebe could guess what that would be. She followed Angela into the small, pleasant parlor at the front of the house. Angela closed the door behind them. "I heard you telling Watson to inform the duke you were indisposed when he called."

Heat rushed to Phoebe's cheeks. "I'm sorry, but I c-can't face him. Not after last night."

Angela frowned. "How so? He behaved perfectly. I have to admit I didn't think he would come up to the mark, and I was already devising some tale to appease the gossips, but I didn't need it."

"He says that we c-can let the engagement d-drift away at the end of the season."

"Did he say he would do it?" Angela asked sharply.

Phoebe shook her head. "He says I must. Of c-course I will, but with my p-parents coming to London..." She shrugged. Her mother would love to see one of her daughters marry a duke. Unfortunately, not Phoebe. Her family had planned to spend a few weeks in town, mainly to allow Phoebe's younger sister, Lucinda, to make her curtsey, but they would not arrive yet. And with any luck, her parents wouldn't hear about this latest start.

"I have told Watson to show your suitor in when he arrives," Angela said firmly. "If you really cannot bear to go driving with the duke, he deserves a personal explanation."

Yes, he did, and Phoebe was being cowardly not to give it to him. But she found his presence overwhelming, and she wanted time to control her reactions. She doubted herself more than him. "He made me st-stammer."

Angela tilted her head. "Did he indeed? I have found your stammer only makes itself known when you are agitated. Does he affect you in that way?"

Miserably she nodded.

Angela tutted. "Familiarity with him will help. Eventually you will discover a fault in him, and he will lose the rosy hue you have enveloped him in." Angela left the desk, her sense of order finally satisfied. She picked up a leather pouch from the desk and went to the door. "In the meantime, the Society for Single Ladies awaits us."

So it did.

A footman leaned in to open the door to the green drawing room, a large space on the ground floor. Inside, the chatter halted as attention turned to them, then started up again.

A sense of familiarity and comfort settled on Phoebe. She was among friends, people who knew who she was, who noticed her. These were the ladies who went disregarded and unnoticed, the older sisters passed over in favor of their prettier, younger siblings, the respectable but poor, the companions and duennas. The ones she'd seen at the ball last night. The room contained about twenty women, the average for such meetings.

Declaring herself one of their number, despite possessing more wealth than they did, Angela had started the society and provided the drawing room for their use, whether she was available or not. More of a club, she'd said. She'd provided a sanctuary where the companions, widows, and overlooked sisters could meet and be themselves. The single women, especially the unmarried ones rather than the widows, had unenviable futures. No home of their own, at the constant beck and call of more fortunate members of their families, they were shuffled around from place to place where they would be of the most use. And the worst, or so one had mentioned, was the loneliness.

Ostensibly the club was a literary society, of which there were many. They made the text they were reading as obtuse and tedious as they dared, to deter others from asking to join.

Phoebe slipped into a comfortable chair, receiving a few nods and smiles, which she returned, and took a dish of tea handed to her by one of her colleagues.

Angela glanced at Phoebe as she took her seat. "The news of the theft of Lady Latimer's jewels is all around town this morning, so I assume you ladies have heard of it."

"As well as Phoebe's betrothal," Miss Manners, a poor relation of the great family of the Duke of Rutland, commented with a smile.

"The betrothal is one of convenience," Phoebe confessed. "The duke saved me from ruin, but that might still come. He has been most kind, but neither of us expect a lasting connection."

"He's not known for his kindness," one lady commented. "I have heard he is a stickler for the proprieties."

Phoebe could not reconcile the man she'd met last night to a stiff-rumped aristocrat. He had kissed her, he'd treated her with consideration and kindness, but he had not struck her as a man who depended on his rank to command respect.

Angela got to her feet and waited for quiet. It wasn't long coming. "Ladies, the affair of the necklace brings forward an idea I had. I have a proposal for you all. The Society needs an occupation, something to tie us together, and I have come up with a scheme. The bank occasionally develops problems we cannot solve in-house. Pieces of jewelry without owners, inheritances without heirs, mortgages with doubtful applicants. We handle a lot of delicate business. I would appreciate your help on occasion. Of course, there would be a reward for successful work."

The ladies glanced at one another, murmured.

"The rooms are open to you all, no matter what you decide. But if you are interested, please let me know. You have access to society. We move unobtrusively, we're barely noticed, so why not use that to our advantage? The bank definitely needs people prepared to undertake difficult and confidential cases. When I was discussing the matter with my managers,

I came up with this idea. But you are the first I have told." She looked around the room. Almost everyone was smiling.

The opportunity to earn money of their own, the chance to have something useful to do, struck Phoebe as brilliant. As was Angela's point that the ladies here were uniquely situated to help.

"I have a gift for you all." Pulling apart the strings of a leather purse, she spilled a stream of silver onto the table. Plucking one item loose, she held it out. "Pins with our insignia. We may use these as identification and communication. And decoration, if you will."

"Why, this is marvelous!" Miss Manners got to her feet and accepted a pin, taking more to hand around. "We are the people who notice while nobody notices us. We see it all. I have longed for something useful to do."

Angela continued. "I shall open accounts for you all at the bank if you do not have one already and pay your rewards into that. If you have no male sponsors, or you do not wish them to know, my managers will oblige. Finding lost objects, lost people… Which brings me to our first case." She beamed at Phoebe. "Lady Latimer's lost jewelry."

The ladies murmured, and some sent Phoebe smiles. Phoebe turned her new pin over in her hand, stroking the smooth surface. The pin consisted of the three letters SSL entwined, but flat, so the pin could be worn discreetly. Rather look at that while she blinked the tears of happiness away. These people thought of her as a friend. If her stay in London achieved nothing else, she would have new friends to exchange letters with.

"Lady Latimer is saying that Phoebe had something to do with the theft, placing her prominently in her account of the incident," Miss Manners said. "She has spread the news all over town. She claims that Phoebe was waiting in the garden for the thief, who was to pass the goods to her. If he was caught, he'd have nothing. I was shopping with my great-aunt this morning, and everyone was talking about it."

Angela's brows drew together in a frown. "The accusations are of course false, but Phoebe will have no peace until we discover the true perpetrators. Lady Latimer will settle for nothing less than her jewels back, and she will continue to cast aspersions on Phoebe until the matter is resolved." She pursed her lips. "I do not scruple to tell you that Lady Latimer is a spiteful woman."

"Then we must find them," said Miss Hansen brightly. She appeared much more approachable here, without her customary stern frown and steely glare.

Angela finished her tea and put the dish back down in the saucer with a decided clink. She rarely lost her temper, but small signs like that showed she was on the edge. "Her ladyship claimed she saw the corner of Phoebe's gown as she was leaving the room where she was resting. If not for the duke, Phoebe's reputation would be ruined."

"That means there was a woman, as well as the man I saw," Phoebe said. "A conspiracy, not an impulsive theft."

"We will stand your friends, Phoebe, you may be sure of that," Miss Manners said.

Phoebe felt strangely humbled. "Thank you."

Angela gave a triumphant smile. "We are the single ladies that society ignores at its peril. We will make our mark. And we will start by solving this mystery."

* * * *

When the doorbell clanged, Phoebe jumped in alarm. From her seat opposite, Angela grinned. They had repaired to the small upstairs parlor to wait for the Duke of Leomore to call.

She spread the skirts of the modish carriage gown Angela had lent her, trying to make it appear she was wearing a hoop, and consequently, not expecting to go anywhere. The full skirts of the dark blue stuff gown were in the latest mode, masculine in style, plain but beautifully made and obviously of the finest quality. She would return it to Angela when she was done, but her surreptitious smoothing of the folds gave her great pleasure and helped to calm her tingling nerves.

Lifting her chin, she pasted on the gracious smile she'd been practicing in the mirror. Angela had advocated it as a way to recover from her social awkwardness. And that damned stammer. Phoebe hated her stammer. The more she tried to overcome it, the worse it grew, and to have her problem reemerge at the worst possible time made everything worse. Thinking of the times when she'd stood before someone, trying to push out the words and only succeeding in embarrassing herself, made her cold with guilt and embarrassment. Maybe she could smile instead of talking.

The footman opened the door, and both ladies stood. Phoebe firmed her jaw and lifted her chin. And kept smiling.

As he entered, her tension spiked. He wore dark green, a cloth coat that had to have been tailored to his form, so closely did it fit to the waist, before flaring out into full, stiffened skirts that reached nearly to his knees, the open front framing strong thighs clad in buff breeches. The cut-steel buttons on his waistcoat caught the light from the bright spring day outside, and his tall black boots were polished to a blinding sheen.

He paused a few steps inside the door. "Ladies." He bowed first to Angela, as was only proper, but after he made his bow to Phoebe, he lingered a fraction longer, and when he rose, his smile was warmer. "I am fortunate to find you ready to leave, ma'am. Not every lady is so punctual."

"Will you not stay for tea, sir?" Angela asked.

"Thank you, ma'am, but I am anxious not to keep my horses waiting," he said in reply to Angela's question. "I have been smitten by the desire to show Miss North my new grays. They were an extravagance, I admit, but they are beautifully matched and delicate high-steppers." His easy smile made Phoebe smile back. How he could make her comfortable and nervous at the same time passed her understanding. "Miss North is probably acquainted with the basics of horsemanship, and she will undoubtedly know a good carriage horse when she sees it."

Phoebe's breath stopped. She had finally admitted the truth to herself, that she wanted this. For once in her life, she would be the person other women envied. She had this one time, this chance to shine, and she would take it. She'd dreamed of it, all the time knowing it would probably be better left as a dream unfulfilled.

And with this man, of all men. He sent the tiny hairs prickling along her body. But he was a duke. She couldn't have him. She was from a different world with different expectations, her dowry was modest, she had no powerful connections, she stammered…any number of reasons. But none of them were enough to stop her wanting it.

She picked up the little velvet box she'd found for his pin. She'd had to sacrifice the container for one of her few pieces of jewelry, but she couldn't bear to press the pin into his hand without any wrapping. That would be taking gaucherie to its extreme. Nobody would know that she had pinned it to her pillow last night.

To safeguard it, she'd told herself, but in the dead of night she'd reached out and stroked its smooth, bulbous form.

"Sir, this is yours. I thank you s-sincerely for your loan. It saved me when I was in d-dire need."

She closed her mouth, shocking herself with her eloquence. She'd just said the words, not even thought about it, and usually she had to work out what she would say and practice it a few times before she could get it out without faltering.

He took the box from her and laid it aside. "I would rather collect that another time. I don't want to wear two pins in my neckcloth, so I prefer for you to take care of this one a little longer."

Phoebe had no answer. She could hardly ask him why he couldn't slip the box in his coat pocket.

After bowing to Angela, he led her from the room and down the stairs. "May I say how lovely you look today, ma'am?"

Caught in the act of taking her dashing cocked hat from the footman, Phoebe nearly dropped it from nerveless fingers. It wasn't that she didn't know how to accept compliments, it was the way she accepted them from this man. He affected her far too deeply for her comfort. "Th-thank you, s-sir," she managed to get out.

She concentrated on pinning the hat into place and putting on her gloves. As usual she did not have her hair powdered, and even if she said it herself, she had to admit that the rich blue of the gown suited her better than her usually insipid colors, enhancing her looks rather than making the mousiness appear even worse. Unfortunately, most of her wardrobe was purchased with her blond sister Lucinda in mind. They were of a similar size, and Phoebe was fully aware that Lucinda would adopt most of her new gowns. And probably ruffle and furbelow them to death, since Lucinda was fond of embellishments.

Phoebe braced herself to face the world.

He held out his hand, and she laid her own on top of it. Even gloved as they both were, his heat and sheer vitality thrilled her, as if she were a young girl facing her first season. And yet she could not stop herself reacting this way to him. Perhaps familiarity would breed contempt. She would try to work toward it.

When she saw the carriage, Phoebe caught her breath. She'd expected an open vehicle, since riding in a closed carriage alone with a gentleman was tantamount to declaring herself a wanton hussy, but not *this.*

He had brought a curricle. It was built along fairy lines, so delicate it looked as if it would not take much before it fell to pieces. Phoebe knew better than that. Although the vehicle had only two wheels, they were large and strong, their yellow spokes enhancing decorative qualities. This was a vehicle built for speed and by a master of his craft. "It's m-magnificent."

"Thank you," he said dryly. "My carriage does not fill you with dread?"

"No, why should it?"

The horses snorted as she approached, but the smartly liveried youth at their heads spoke to them and calmed them while Leo helped her up. Phoebe had to gather her voluminous skirts tightly to step on the small iron ledge that gave her access to the seat. Concentrating on climbing up as neatly as possible, she did not miss his small groan, though what had caused it passed her understanding.

Taking the seat, she disposed her skirts as he climbed to the perch next to her and took the reins. He nodded to the youth, who stepped back. As Leo clicked the horses into action, the boy swung up behind them in an agile move that spoke of long practice. Although in theory Phoebe knew they could do this, she was alarmed to discover the boy had to cling on to a narrow position with no hope of rescue if he fell. "Aren't you concerned he might hurt himself?"

The duke flicked a glance at her and then behind at the boy. "No. Jem's been working for me since he was a small boy. A smaller boy," he corrected himself. "He's never fallen off."

He turned his attention back to driving long enough to take a corner at considerable speed and without hesitation. Phoebe resisted the temptation to clutch the seat to steady herself, but her stomach swooped at this display of driving.

"You've gone very quiet," he said once he'd navigated several streets.

"I did not want to ruin your c-concentration," she said softly.

He glanced at her, his gaze sharp. "I beg your pardon. I know these streets well. Besides, I wanted to display my prowess. I will be more circumspect, I promise."

"Oh n-no! This is utterly thrilling." And it was. Bowling through the streets behind two highbred horses was a new and enjoyable experience.

But he slowed the steeds to a walk anyway. The smart equipage attracted the attention of all passersby. Some raised their hands in greeting, but at least Phoebe knew not to acknowledge them. A lady in a carriage in the street should not do that, Angela had informed her. Leo, however, nodded to a few select acquaintances, but then dukes did not follow the rules of good behavior. They made them.

She had no doubt her presence was remarked on, and she could even guess what they were saying. "You can go f-faster if you want to."

He chuckled. "Perhaps I want to show you off instead of my driving."

"I c-cannot imagine why." She primmed her mouth.

A particularly pleasant smile curved his lips. He appeared genuinely amused. "I know you cannot, but I do. Much of the attention we are receiving is because of you."

"You're very kind, sir. I daresay we have helped not a f-few s-scandal-sheet hawkers earn their livings today."

She liked his laugh, too.

It occurred to her that although they were passing over cobbles she wasn't jolted. The suspension on this vehicle must be particularly good. "Aren't s-sporting vehicles m-meant to be sensitive?"

"Oh, it is. It can be adjusted though, and I do not wish to rattle the teeth out of your head. Of course, at this pace, we are hardly likely to rattle anything at all."

"I think I can manage." Having the wind blown from her lungs was better than being stared at, and she had loved the speed and the elegant, skillful way he'd handled the ribbons.

She could see the park gates. They didn't have far to go.

"They're envious." The amusement in his voice annoyed her.

"Of me, of c-course they are. You're at the top of every invitation list." She had not meant to sound so waspish, but there, it was done now. "And they think our b-betrothal is real."

"Oh, it's real all right. Never question that."

Mindful of the tiger behind them, Phoebe sealed her lips. They had to keep up this pretense. "I should not have said that."

"You must say whatever you wish to me." He cast a glance over his shoulder. "If we keep our voices at this level, Jemmy cannot hear us. He is extremely loyal, however, one of the few servants I can completely trust. His father has served my family all his life. Jemmy Linton is likely to do the same. So do not imagine that I said our betrothal is real for his sake. It is the truth."

He shot her another glance, eyes glittering. Every time he did that, she fell further under his spell. Did he know he was enthralling her? Of course. Someone in his position rarely did anything without thinking hard and long about the effect they had on others. "Why would you n-not let the matter rest, sir? S-say our betrothal was a m-misunderstanding?"

"I knew exactly what I was doing. No misunderstanding was involved. Besides, I'm bringing you into fashion," he said calmly, as finally he drove through the open gates.

Hyde Park was the place to go to display one's wealth. Although she had none, for today Phoebe was part of the cream of society. She might as well lean back and enjoy it.

Well, perhaps not lean back. This seat did not seem fashioned for that particular activity. Her stays helped her to remain ramrod-straight in any case.

People stared as they bowled up Rotten Row, and continued to stare. This time she had to acknowledge them, although they were not giving her more than a slight nod. They wanted to make themselves known to him. "You're managing very well," he murmured, as he touched his whip to his hat. A lady and five younger women, presumably her daughters, all dressed to the hilt, made their curtseys.

"What does one call a group of simpers?" she wondered aloud.

"If I'm not mistaken, at least three of them are in society, or shortly to make their debuts. I am suitably warned." He bestowed one of his genuine smiles on her. Already she could tell the difference; when he smiled properly, twin indents appeared at the corners of his mouth. His polite smile didn't produce those. Neither did it show the wicked gleam in the depths of his eyes.

Perhaps she should be glad she didn't see him smile more, because she found the expression disturbingly attractive.

He nodded to another lady, who appeared eager for him to stop, and continued along Rotten Row for a good fifty feet. "I think we should get out and walk," he said.

"Won't that take longer? I thought this was a duty drive."

A crease appeared between his brows when he turned to her. "Don't do that."

"What?"

"Make the assumption that I don't want to be with you. I much prefer you than those people back there." With a jerk of his head he indicated the lady they had nodded to, now far behind them on the Row. "You are more amusing and interesting than they could ever be. You answer honestly, and you do not agree with everything I say. You have no idea how tedious that can get."

"No, I don't," she said dryly.

Neatly and efficiently he drew the horses to a halt. He helped her down himself, but unused to such precarious steps, she stumbled and fell into his arms.

His hold tightened. Startled, she gazed up into his face. The world closed in around them, and she knew nothing other than him. Sounds receded, the background blurred as she concentrated on his face. He seemed transfixed on her. She ignored their shocking proximity but waited. His eyes grew slumberous, darkening as his pupils widened and he parted his lips. He was going to kiss her, and she wasn't about to stop him.

Someone close to them laughed, high and shrill. His nostrils flared as he drew in air, and he stepped back, keeping his hands lightly on her elbows. "Can you stand on your own now?" His voice roughened, as if uncaring of society and its strictures.

"Of course." Clearing her throat, she stepped out of his grasp and straightened her skirts. "The ride was m-merely a new experience." She shook her head slightly. "I am not usually s-so unsteady."

"Are you ready for another new experience?"

The members of society would not be so crass as to hurry, but it was obvious that people were anxious to speak to him or be with him. Before any could reach him, he offered her the support of his arm and nodded to his groom. "Take them around and come back."

That would take forever at the snail's pace the horses were forced to adopt here. He gave her no chance to object, but struck out along a relatively secluded path, moderating his pace to hers.

"We are fortunate in this fine day," she remarked.

"Yes, it has rained rather a lot recently," he responded immediately. "Of course, at this time of year we must expect inclement weather."

He blandly responded to her remarks in the same tone. She stifled a snort of laughter. Her mother had told her she had an unfortunate laugh. Perhaps she did, but she did her best to control it. He brought that out of her, too. "I saw a number of light, fluffy clouds this morning. They had no rain in them."

"Perhaps they are gathering together to create a storm another time."

"Or fending off the rain c-clouds, like champions f-fighting for their honor."

"Or their lady."

Before she could stop herself, she said, "Clouds do not have ladies!" Laughing, she took her attention from the sky and turned to him. "Truly, sir, you should not lead me into such foolish n-notions! I c-cannot imagine what you think of me."

"When poets make epics to trifles like locks of hair, I do not see why we should not speculate on the behavior and chivalry, or otherwise, of clouds." He was smiling too.

She had found someone who shared her absurd sense of humor. Until that moment Phoebe had not understood how alone she felt, adrift in unfamiliar territory. She would hold this moment precious, whatever happened next. Could she have found a friend?

Surely not in this resplendent specimen of masculinity, this leader of society. She wet her lips. "Such nonsense we are speaking."

"Indeed. But if you recall, by discussing the cutting of a maiden's hair, Pope managed to bring the affairs of nations into his epic. Have you read the poem?"

Eagerly, she nodded, scarcely aware of the people passing them, eyeing them curiously. "But that poem caused the ruin of one young woman."

"The poem merely drew the public's attention to the lady's scandalous behavior. She caused her own ruin."

"I was n-nearly ruined last night. You saved me."

His lips curved tenderly. "It was my privilege to do so."

Guiding her gently, he turned her back to the path. He halted. They were facing each other, his expressive eyes taking her in. His hand moved, but he did not touch her, as she'd thought he was about to do. "You look charming today, Phoebe. Quite lovely."

She shivered at his use of her name. That was such an intimate thing to do. "Th-thank you, sir."

He clicked his tongue in exasperation. "What did I tell you? Call me Leo." He gave a tiny shake of his head. "You are lovely, especially in these rich colors. Do not denigrate yourself. And don't listen to foolish gossip."

"That's easy for you to say." Indignation fired her words. "I have no d-defense. They may say whatever they like about m-me with no reperc-cussions. And they do."

"They will *not*," he said firmly, and drew her hand back through his arm as they looped around a group of trees, preparing to return to Rotten Row. "I will behave, I swear." He touched his free hand to his chest to emphasize his promise. "But I enjoy your company, Phoebe, and I will not allow cheap gossip to deprive me of it." He paused and shot her a lightning glance, as if he'd startled himself, or she'd surprised him. "I will take care of you, never fear."

The arrogance of the man! "And I do not appear well in s-s-s-s-s-s-s..." The worst happened. Phoebe did not often get stuck on words these days, but the sight of the cream of society watching them landed on her with the force of a ton of bricks. The words remained trapped in her throat. Like a garden songbird stuck on one note, she tried the word again, determined not to let it beat her.

He did not finish it for her. Of all the tactics people took with her, that one infuriated her the most and tended to make matters worse. Instead, he slowed down, guiding her into the shade of a nearby tree.

"Society!" She finished what she'd meant to say with a flourish, spitting it out as if it intended to do her harm. "It's my p-problem with speaking, which you have noticed. They consider it a lack of b-breeding."

"Some members of society consider breathing demonstrates a lack of breeding." His tone was not complimentary.

"P-People never t-talked about me before yesterday."

He shrugged, an elegant lift of one shoulder. "Jealous cats aren't worth paying attention to. I do not mean you harm, Phoebe, and I will do my best to ensure that none comes your way." His eyes darkened. "I will care for you, I swear it. You will come to no harm with me."

When he leaned over her, she knew what he was intending. Tipping her head back, she parted her lips in time to receive his kiss. All her lectures to herself, all the danger disappeared as if it never was.

When he kissed her, the world melted away and ceased to matter. While aware her response to him was dangerous, it was too powerful, too seductive for her to take heed. Kissing a person in public, even someone betrothed, could lead to damaging gossip. But Phoebe had temporarily ceased caring.

He touched her chin, guiding her to him as he thrust his tongue into her mouth. She sucked on it, hearing his gratifying groan, feeling the vibrations the sound caused all over her body.

He drew away, gazing down on her. "See? Perfectly acceptable. Nobody can see us here." He grinned. "I checked. I made you a promise I will keep. No scandal. But that doesn't mean I won't try to kiss you when it's safe to do so."

Reminded forcibly of their situation, she gasped and jerked away, nearly dislodging her cocked hat. He replaced his, tugging it down with an impatient gesture.

She could not spend too much time alone with him. That would cause her ruin for sure, for she had no self-preservation where he was concerned. That kiss had drawn them into their own world, one where nothing else mattered. Just for a brief few seconds, she'd known what passion felt like.

He held out his arm in unspoken command. She laid her hand on it, and they commenced their stroll back to the carriage.

"You appear perfectly well in society," he continued, as if they had only been exchanging pleasantries. Was he not as rocked by the kiss as she was? Clearly not. Perhaps he kissed every young woman he drove around Rotten Row. He had certainly selected a clever place to kiss her, where nobody could see them. "The only speculation I heard was that you were a paid companion, but Miss Childers soon put a stop to that nonsense. Even if you were, what of that?" He pulled her in to his body again, a gesture she found subtly exciting. "Now, madam, are you ready to brave the perils of my carriage once more?"

He led her across the rough surface to where the groom stood waiting with the horses, now less restive since they'd had some exercise.

"More than ready," she said. "In fact, I enjoyed the experience."

The stammer had gone.

He noticed too, and as he courteously helped her back on to her seat, he murmured, "So that's the cure. I will try to kiss you more often."

Before she had time to answer, he walked around to his side, climbed up, took the reins and set the horses into a slow walk.

Phoebe recalled what she meant to say to him and now, when she desperately wanted to move the discussion away from her feelings for him, seemed like a good time. "My friends have decided to help discover the thief."

"Thief?" He shot her a puzzled glance, then his face cleared. "Oh, the diamonds."

"The diamonds are the reason we are in this mess."

"Not a mess." He sounded quite stern. "Never call it that." Catching the reins expertly in one hand, without even watching what he was doing, he turned his head to regard her. Not a trace of humor marked his features. "I mean it. I'm content, and I trust you are, too."

"Oh." She wasn't sure what to say, except for a feeble, "Thank you."

"You are an interesting woman, Phoebe, and a cozy armful. I am happy to further our acquaintance. In fact, you interest me more than any woman has for a long time." He paused to turn at the end of the Row, which he did with a deftness she was forced to admire. "You do not toady to me, and you answer me honestly. You are evidently intelligent, and I value your opinion." He nodded to someone passing by but didn't stop the horses to talk to them.

Phoebe didn't know what to say. His statement had entirely taken her breath away. This was not a duke, it was a man, a person she could talk to, someone who listened to her. And a friend. "I-I like you too."

They exchanged a warm smile. No more than that, but the connection between them strengthened.

He turned back to the horses, since the traffic was increasing as they approached the gate. "I would counsel you and your friends not to take action on your own. The thieves could well fight back. I do not wish you to be hurt."

"We're aware of th-the dangers. We won't take any unnecessary chances." She sat up straighter, folding her hands neatly in her lap, then relaxing her hold a little as she pulled on the bandage beneath her gloves.

Of course, he noticed. "How is your hand?"

"Much better, thank you, sir. I've given your handkerchief to the laundress. I thank you for the loan."

"Thank you. But I am more concerned about you. You washed the wound and changed the dressing?"

"Of course." She'd seen what happened to people who left wounds to fester.

When he drove through the park gates, Phoebe felt sorry that her treat was coming to an end. She would never have assumed she would feel that at the outset of the drive.

"I expect you to take the greatest care of yourself," he continued, "until I am able to assume that task myself."

"Sir!" Phoebe exploded indignantly. "That is not what we are doing here. You know it isn't, and it is cruel of you to lead me on in such a way."

"Is it not?" Since traffic was considerably more varied and thicker here than in the park, he was forced to keep his eyes on the vehicles in front of him. From fashionable carriages to battered hackney carriages, with drivers of varied skill, he could not take their passage for granted. Phoebe was relieved. "Who can tell what will happen? What if we fall helplessly in love, and act on our impulses?"

Her delighted gurgle of laughter needed no words. She didn't stammer when she laughed.

Chapter 4

Leo left the carriage at the mews and made his way to his house, where his grandmother was holding court. Today was one of her "at home" days, so he tried slipping upstairs in an effort to get to his room and change without her noticing him. If the wind was in the right direction, he could get out and to his club without her knowing he'd returned.

Sadly that was not to be, as she had left a note requesting he attend—although "request" was a polite euphemism in this case. But he could use the excuse of being in all his dirt, and so earn twenty minutes' respite before he had to go down to the drawing room and confront her and her cronies.

Although breakfast had been uncomfortable, he was glad he had broached the subject of his betrothal with his grandmother at the first possible opportunity. She had lectured him severely, accusing him of impulsive behavior. "How do you know this woman is not a fortune hunter? She is fresh from the country, and her family is, by your admission, of slender means. Snaring a duke in her first season? Is she very beautiful?"

He thought of the plainly dressed, outspoken Phoebe and smiled. "She is not accounted a society beauty, but I think she is. She does not. Indeed, Grandmama, there was little I could do. I could not stand by and hear her wrongly accused. And although our mission was innocent, she could have been labeled a hussy or worse."

"The torn ruffle excuse is the oldest in the book," the dowager said. "I am surprised you allowed yourself to be trapped by it."

"Her ruffle was truly torn. And it was so because through the country dance, all her partners did their best to ignore her. I will not stand by and allow such appalling behavior. She was distressed, although she tried to tell me she was not. She needed a place to recover."

"Are you telling me that you initiated retiring to a garden pavilion?" his grandmother demanded wrathfully.

"I did," he confessed, "and I would do it again."

"I see." She regarded him through narrowed eyes. "Then I will have to venture into society. Truly, Leomore, I thought I could trust you at your age!"

Leo should have expected a reception like this. His grandmother would never allow the grass to grow under her feet.

Once suitably attired, he went back downstairs.

The drawing room was comfortably full. At least, his grandmother would think so, though he was not sure he would define it that way. Heaving at the seams was more like it.

He was marked prey, and nothing could have expressed that clearer than the number of eager young women crammed on the various sofas and armchairs, most of whom had attended Miss Childers's ball last night.

As usual his grandmother occupied the wing chair by the fire, the gilded one he privately named her throne. Without doubt she was holding court this afternoon, inserting herself into the middle of the situation he had initiated last night.

Flicking back the skirts of his crimson coat, Leo sat, accepted a dish of tea, and prepared to be charmed. He knew exactly what his grandmother was doing. She wanted to persuade him that his unfortunate alliance was misguided.

The ladies who attended were not deterred by his betrothal. Most women, learning he was betrothed, might send their congratulations, but they would not flirt the way these did, nor would they drop gentle disparagements.

While his conversation with Phoebe on the nature of clouds and their habits was utterly charming, his efforts to reproduce the whimsy was met by disbelief.

"Clouds do not think," Lady Mary Devon pointed out. She was a lovely creature, an accredited beauty of the season, and quite determined to win the hand of a duke. Unfortunately, that put Leo squarely in the running. Her golden hair and cerulean-blue eyes were much admired.

In a few words she'd hammered his flight of fancy to the ground, forced it into submission. However, he wouldn't give up without a fight. "Are you sure? Because they do know when rain is coming with a great degree of accuracy."

On Lady Mary's other side, the dark-haired Miss Caroline Spencer-Marshall trilled with careful laughter. "Indeed, sir, clouds have no thought. They merely carry the rain, don't you know."

"Indeed." Lady Mary flicked open her fan. "More to the point, sir, do you think the weather well enough for a drive in the park tomorrow?"

And there was the hint. Leo refused to take it. "I have lately returned from a charming hour escorting my betrothed in the park."

Lady Mary wafted her fan, the brilliants along the edge catching the light.

Miss Spencer-Marshall's lip lifted in a sneer. "Ah yes, you were with Miss South."

Leo's ire rose, but he kept the easy smile in place. "Miss North, I think you'll find. She is staying with her cousin, Miss Childers."

"Your generosity and egalitarian attitude is remarkable," Lady Mary said smoothly. "I commend you on it, sir. Not everyone would be so kind to a person barely on the fringes of society. I believe Miss North is employed as her cousin's companion."

He was beginning to understand what Phoebe was forced to face on a daily basis. With effort, he kept his temper. "Miss North is a relative of Miss Childers, paying a visit while the lady's paid companion is indisposed."

"We have an aunt who lives with us," Miss Spencer-Marshall continued. A gleeful silence accompanied her words. "She is extremely useful. I don't suppose she will ever leave us. Mama says she has a remarkable capacity for endurance." She smiled, expecting amusement in reply. She got it, but Leo remained silent. He felt for the woman with the remarkable capacity for endurance. She had little choice, he guessed.

"Miss North has done me a great favor in accepting my offer. I consider myself the most fortunate of men." Never more than now, when he had a glimpse of what he could have had. Until they had unveiled their true natures, he might have been taken in. They had been carefully well-behaved with him, mildly flirtatious, agreeing with everything he said. He should have known better. If he had cast his lure to any woman, it would not be to any woman here today, eager to disparage Phoebe and take advantage of her weaknesses.

Shortly after, they took their leave, all sending Leo sly, smiling glances. Oh Lord, he was so sick of that discreet flirting. When the last one had left, his grandmother let out a long sigh. "Ring for fresh tea, will you, Leomore? And do not leave. I want a word with you."

Several, if Leo knew his grandmother.

When she was settled with fresh tea and a cushion behind her back, which she declared was aching, Leo took his tea and sat in his favorite chair. The furniture in the drawing room might have the appearance of high fashion, but it was built for comfort, something Leo insisted on when his grandmother decided on refurbishment a few years ago. Now the upholstery was a rich green instead of the ridiculous ivory color that had to be laundered every time someone breathed on it, much less sat there. The furniture wasn't gilded to within an inch of its life, either, except for the one his grandmother used, but had a pleasant mahogany sheen.

The dowager broke into his comfortable contemplation. "Leomore, what were you thinking? You will not marry that girl, it is unfair to both of you. She is from a modest background, and I have heard she is remarkably reticent. You must consider someone else. I am speaking of a lifelong partnership, not something unwisely conceived in the heat of the moment."

"I intend to fulfill my obligation to Phoebe."

A small smile curved his grandmother's lips. "That does not sound very lover-like."

He curled his lip. "You and I know that love is not what I require in my life's companion. We have had too much of that in recent years, and it has led to disaster."

The duchess sighed. "She will not settle to her rank. Leomore, I want you happy, but do not allow yourself to become carried away with dreams. If it is possible for you to withdraw from this arrangement, I pray you do so. How do you think this woman will cope with becoming a duchess if you force her to it?"

"She is intelligent and lovely. She will manage." That was only the truth, though he wisely kept his unaccountable desire to see her naked to himself. He really had to get his hunger for her under control. Truly, their union was destined to be fleeting. He had rescued her from an unfortunate predicament. And his grandmother knew it. But she had used this situation to force him to think about his future.

"Can you see her at court? Or in charge of the estates, poring over household accounts? Interviewing housekeepers and butlers? Controlling a staff of fifty servants? Sitting for her wedding portrait?"

The disconcerting thing was that he could. "Yes. All of that."

The dowager studied him for a full minute. Leo met her gaze steadily, waiting for her to respond. He never underestimated her. She had controlled the household during his parents' wild years, and preserved the estate for him, rearing him single-handedly. Despite her increasing frailty, she still did. "Well, I have to say I have been severely disabused in the characters of many of the young women on the list I gave you. I request that you remove Lady Mary and Miss Spencer-Marshall from it. Their behavior in rushing here and then disparaging the woman you have chosen was vulgar and insensitive. I expect better of the next Duchess of Leomore."

"Indeed. I agree with your judgment." Although he agreed with his grandmother, the thought of Phoebe losing her impulsive quirkiness saddened him. However, he would rid her of that stammer before the season finished. He almost smiled when he recalled her shock after he'd confessed the hesitation in his own speech as a child.

"We will weather this. You must be happy in your rank, because you cannot avoid it. So must she. I will send your Phoebe and Miss Childers an invitation to dinner."

Leo's mind drifted to the one woman who had not lost her dignity today. The challenge she presented fascinated him, and her luscious form, displayed to such advantage today, drew the baser part of him.

He could not think of it, though he foresaw a torrid season ahead, while he quelled his more basic instincts. Lord, he'd made a tightrope that he had to concentrate to remain on. If he fell, he was lost.

After excusing himself, he went upstairs to freshen up. He would pay the long delayed visit to his club.

Before he left, he sat at his desk and picked up his pen. After chewing on the end for a moment or two and staring out the window onto the vista of his tranquil garden, he scribbled a few words of thanks to Phoebe for accompanying him today. She deserved that, at the very least.

* * * *

Three hours later Leo returned to his room to find a note awaiting him. The curtains were closed and the fire lit, making his room a cozy haven. Although he was due to attend two balls this evening, he was sorely tempted to remain. After allowing his valet to help him out of his coat, he drew back his desk chair and opened the note.

He had expected it might be from a friend, since it smelled of nothing but paper. A lady would have drenched the cream-laid parchment with some flowery scent. Of them all, he found lily of the valley the most cloying. His last mistress, famously known as La Coccinelle, had insisted on drenching herself with the stuff, and he could not break her of the habit. So he had broken her of another habit; him.

He nodded when the valet held up a velvet coat with gold braid and buttons. He'd chosen the dark blue because then he would not have to change the ivory waistcoat he already wore. His ennui was spreading to his wardrobe.

Lord, he was tired.

The note was sealed with an undecorated wafer. Breaking it, he found the same handwriting from the outside of the envelope. Children were taught the slanted, copperplate hand in the nursery, but there were always differences. This writer enjoyed adding flourishes to her y's and g's.

For it was a her. Skipping forward to the signature, he saw she'd signed it *Phoebe North* with pretty flourishes under her name.

He settled to read.

"Dear Your Grace,"—that made him chuckle.

"I assure you, you have no reason to thank me for anything. Rather, I should thank you. Now society knows my name, and I am sure to become the center of attention. Such a delightful prospect."

He could hear her voice, dryly reading the words to him, but with that slight hesitation he found extraordinarily sexy.

"I will no doubt receive everyone's approval and be the toast of the season, whatever becomes of our betrothal."

His smile broadened.

"Your vehicle, while initially alarming, provided a great deal of amusement. I can honestly say that I have never had an experience like it. The nearest was the old gig my mother is fond of castigating as a cart, which she sneers at but drives anyway."

That was interesting. She had not mentioned her family before. Comparing his phaeton to an old gig made him smile. Who else would write to him in such terms? He could think of no one. Smiling, he read on.

"Truly, I should have waved more often. I did think of it, but I was too busy holding on for dear life. I can truly say the drive is one I will never forget. Unfortunately, we don't have much call for it in the country, or the roads, otherwise I would order one straightaway. I daresay I will be riding in my old gig or another very like it for the rest of my days, but you have given me the dream I needed to fire my fancy. As I drive, I will imagine it as the equipage you generously allowed me to share for an hour. The fine upholstery, the way you handled the ribbons, and the beasts whose power drove us on to greater heights were unsurpassed delights.

"Thank you for the ride, sir. I would wish that you take no other woman up in your chariot, but I fear I will be disappointed, so I will learn to bear my chagrin. I am fortunate to have held your attention for so long."

Dropping the paper to his desk, Leo burst into laughter. The undertones, the clever double meanings of the letter, hit home. Miss North wasn't so innocent after all. She had said nothing anyone could object to, but the meaning remained. They had spoken about Pope's epic "The Rape of the Lock," wherein a young woman was ostensibly ruined by a man cutting a strand of her hair, but that act had hidden the unsavory underworld and the secret lives beneath.

Oh yes, Miss North knew about secret lives.

Picking up his pen, he waved off his valet when he returned, and started to write.

Chapter 5

"Goodness, two pages!" Angela flicked her fingers at the letter Phoebe had dropped next to her breakfast plate. "Judging by your smile, I assume that is not from your family."

"You're quite right. It is from Leo—the duke."

"I've never thought of him as droll before. May I see?"

When she reached out, Phoebe snatched the letter away from her reach. "It is mine." With a sigh, she picked up the other letter. "This is not so welcome, I fear. My f-family is arriving in town soon. Mama wrote to m-me and said because of my news they are bringing their visit f-forward. She is hiring a house on Harley Street."

"She is not," Angela said indignantly. "They will stay here. All but your brothers, of course. They must lodge elsewhere. Proprieties, you know. I will write and tell them so."

"Are you sure?" Phoebe asked anxiously. "That will p-put them at the center of s-society. And Mama is determined to snag a d-duke for Lucinda. 'For if you can do it,'" she quoted, referring to the scrawled letter, "'your sister c-can do it easily.'" She couldn't suppress her groan. "Let them go to Harley Street, and I will j-join them. That way my betrothal may slip into the background. If I am not seen in society…" She ignored the pang of sorrow that hit her when she said it. After all, her dream had to come to an end sometime soon.

Angela held up a delicate hand in an unmistakable gesture of command. "Stop. You are staying here because I wish to have your company for a while longer. So your family must come, too. I will not have them take you away from me. Or remove you from your duke."

Phoebe loved her family, but she saw them clearly. Where she was quiet, her mother was positively raucous. Where she dressed soberly, Lucinda had never seen a ruffle she didn't like. "My f-father hates Whigs and will not hold back when c-condemning them and their Frenchified behavior." She could hear the arguments that made her shudder already.

Angela leaned her chin on her hand, a lock of gleaming blond hair sliding forward to touch her shoulder. She looked nothing so much as a mischievous fairy. "Why should it end? Don't think like that, Phoebe. You are as good as anyone else in society, and better than most. True, your portion is not large, but your birth is respectable and your manners exquisite."

Phoebe was an ordinary woman in a family with not a smidgen of influence in London. She must restrict her wishes to the realistic, and she could not afford to lose sight of that, although the task was growing more difficult with every day that passed.

Angela cast a roguish glance at the paper. "Won't you read the duke's letter to me? Do I not deserve a reward?"

"Of course." To do anything else would put connotations on it that she didn't wish to arouse, not even with Angela, but Phoebe wondered what was going on here. She'd written her thank-you note in a spirit of mischief, knowing she should not but unwilling to end their flight of fancy.

She tried to read the letter in as light a tone as she could. Not knowing the notes that had gone before, Angela would probably not understand the flirting going on underneath.

"My dear Miss North, it was very k-kind of you to remember me in the midst of your hectic social life. I pray I find you well and that our little outing did not discommode you in any way. Your n-neck must be quite s-s-trained. I w-would send you some embrocation, if that is the c-case."

Angela frowned. "Did you hurt your neck?"

"We s-spent some time discussing the w-weather, l-looking into the s-sky." Warmth crept into Phoebe's cheeks, but she chose to ignore it.

"I won't pry. You like him, don't you?"

Closing her eyes, afraid of what they would reveal, Phoebe nodded.

"I have always considered him a dry, handsome stick. But I am wrong. He has hidden depths, it appears."

Recovering her composure, Phoebe opened her eyes and smiled. "Yes, he has." Although not so hidden, to her, at least. Their effortless conversation gave her great joy.

Angela kindly did not mention the return of the stammer, though from that alone she would know Phoebe's tension. She could say no more. Her heart was pounding, fit to burst from her chest. Her stammer was growing worse, and in a few moments she'd come to a full stop and turn into a wreck trying to get out one word.

Angela covered her hand with her own, the touch warm and comforting. "Know I will always stand your friend."

Phoebe knew she would. Whatever it cost her.

"My dear, Leomore has the whole town in a spin."

"But when he m-m-m-meets my f-family..." She could say no more. For the second time in her life, an eligible male had paid attention to her. The first, Sir Marcus, had been unwelcome, and she had told him so, but Leo had an entirely different effect on her. And she wanted more, before she had to give him up. Quite badly.

"He is too well-mannered to say anything." After patting her hand, Angela leaned back again. "He will not comment, I swear." Her family would make their mark in town, but Phoebe feared it might not be the right kind of mark.

Overcome, Phoebe nodded. Having friends like Angela meant a great deal to her.

Later, when she went upstairs to wash and change out of her loose morning sacque and into something more appropriate for meeting guests, Phoebe scanned the letter again.

When she read silently, she had no stammer.

"I am determined to give you that treat again. I am flattered my poor vehicle should be the cause of such pleasure. I cannot, in that case, deprive you of your enjoyment.

"I must confess my own pleasure was far more than is perhaps seemly on such occasions. I have the greatest respect for your lively turn of mind, and I would wish to experience it again, in as close quarters as possible.

"While we are upstanding members of society, we must strive to prevent our friends from gossiping, but I feel that such innocuous pleasures should be enjoyed to the full. We may find our own enjoyment somewhere between childlike innocence and full-blooded riot, though I understand your reticence, as a lady of honor."

He was talking utter nonsense, but she loved that he had picked up her inner meaning and did not treat her as if she knew nothing. Even respectable virgins had some understanding of the other life they were supposed to be ignorant of.

And the delicate referral to their kiss—she loved that, too. She brushed a finger across her lips, recalling how delightful it had felt.

As if she could be ignorant, when gentlemen spoke openly of the insalubrious details that made this city such an enthralling place. With all her heart Phoebe wished to visit the places only spoken of in an undertone—the notorious rookeries of St. Giles and Seven Dials, where anyone with a full suit of clothes and a guinea in their pocket stood to lose their lives in an instant; Tom's Coffee House, where ladies of the night met their clients and then took them somewhere more private; and the taverns of the City, tucked down one of the narrow alleyways that had sprung up in the wake of the Great Fire, or even despite it, where thieves and cutpurses congregated. London teemed with life, and Phoebe wanted to experience it all before she was forced to return to the village she called home, where everyone knew everyone else's business and nobody transgressed so much as to speak ill of anyone. But talk to a neighbor a minute too long and local society would have them wedded and bedded before the month was out.

The letter ended in a frank confession, one Phoebe treasured.

"To be truthful, Miss North, I found great pleasure in your company. You have a liveliness of mind and a boldness of spirit that calls to me. I would wish we could be friends, and at the very least continue our correspondence. It will give me something to look forward to."

Phoebe carefully tucked the letter away in the third drawer down of the tallboy where she kept her shifts and night rails.

She stroked the little velvet box that held the pearl pin. She would never wear it, but she loved being its custodian, having that reminder of him.

The seed pearls would do for today. The guests they were expecting had seen them before, but that mattered little. That wasn't the purpose of today's meeting. Phoebe slipped into her gown of green-and-white stripes, fastened the bodice at the front, checked her lace cap was on straight, and looped the pearls around her neck. She dropped a handkerchief into her pocket, picked up her fan, and she was ready. A last glance in the mirror assured her she would do, and she left the room just as the maid assigned to her use on this visit entered.

The girl was a waste of time. Phoebe rarely waited for her, unless she was attending a ball or some other event where she had to dress more elaborately. At home she shared a maid with her sister, but Lucinda never gave her any time, so she was accustomed to getting herself ready.

She glanced out the window. "Speaking of which…"

An equipage Phoebe knew well drew up outside the house. The duke leaped down from his phaeton and tossed the reins to his groom.

Phoebe gave an uncomfortable laugh. "What is he doing here?"

"He's come to see you." Angela shot Phoebe a smiling glance. "By all means, see him and tell him you are merely enjoying a quiet afternoon indoors. Take him into the breakfast parlor. That's far enough away from this room. Leave the door open, mind, I won't have your mother accusing me of risking your reputation."

Phoebe laughed. "She won't care." Picking up her skirts, she hurried from the room and ran downstairs to prevent the butler sending him away.

The duke glanced up as she hurried down the stairs. His warm smile took her breath.

He swept a bow. "Good day, ma'am. I had hoped you might accompany me once more."

"To the park?"

"Precisely."

"Oh!" Flustered, she dropped her skirts and tried to put them in order. "I'm afraid I am not d-dressed for c-carriage-driving, but my—Angela says I might speak to you in the small p-parlor if I leave the door open."

"I see." He handed his hat, gloves, and overcoat to the butler, without taking his gaze from her. "Then pray lead on. Jemmy may walk the horses."

Trying not to reveal her state of nervousness, Phoebe took him to the room at the back of the hall on the right.

She liked the breakfast parlor. It was one of her favorite rooms in the house. The table, a round one, stood by the window, so the diners could enjoy the vista beyond. Angela's garden was generous and at this time of year bursting into bloom, splashes of color appearing among the lush green plants and lawns. Recent showers had enhanced the generosity of the colors. She could watch it all day, except that she had something much better to look at inside the room.

He put her on edge in a way she'd never known before. Not the kind of situation that brought her speech impediment into play, but something else that made her body ache.

Even being in his presence sent her senses rioting. It took all her acting skills to conceal her lamentable state and turn to him, smiling. "May I offer you some refreshment?"

He shook his head. "No, I thank you. I am content. Or rather, I am not. Madam, I wonder if you will be attending the Everett ball tonight?"

"I-I think Angela intends to go, so naturally, I will accompany her."

"Then may I request the first minuet?"

"Oh!" She cupped her cheeks with her hands as they heated to a boiling point. Tears sprang to her eyes. That would be a declaration of his intent before the whole of society. She could never live that down, once their connection had died.

"If I danced with anyone else, gossip would be rife, you know," he said kindly.

She swallowed. The news from her family had given her pause. "Yes, of course. But we may have to c-curtail our arrangement sooner than I had imagined."

"Why?" His voice was steady, but she had put a crease between his brows.

"My f-family will arrive sooner than I thought. I wrote to my p-parents, telling them of our arrangement, b-because as Angela p-p-pointed out, they would probably hear of it from another source. They have brought their visit to town forward."

When he took a step closer to her, she had to draw a sharp breath and force herself to stay where she was, instead of retreating. He touched her elbows, tucking his fingers under her single lace ruffle, grazing her skin delightfully. "I see no reason why that would put an end to our betrothal." He'd used the word she'd hesitated over. "Are your parents likely to refuse their permission? I collect that I should have hot-footed it to their home and formally requested it, but the situation being what it was, I had no opportunity to go through the usual procedure. Do your parents harbor a deadly secret?" As he smiled, his frown smoothed out.

"Oh no." Her mother had never kept a secret in her life.

"Then I see no problem." He was so close she could smell him, a tantalizing citrus aroma mixed with pure male. If anyone asked her what he smelled like, her only answer could be, "Heat." Not that she would say that aloud, of course.

Heat radiated from him where his bare skin touched hers, the palms of his hands sending sensation shooting up her arms and into the rest of her. Her awareness of her own body overwhelmed her, the way she wanted to move closer, to let him do anything he desired, so long as that included her.

The world shrank to her and him and nobody else.

His eyes darkened, and the lines around his mouth deepened. His light touch tightened. He used his hold to draw her closer, and with a muffled, "Oh, hell!" brought her into the shelter of his body.

He slid an arm around her, pulling her closer. Using one hand, he lifted her chin, holding her in place while he brought his head down and kissed her.

As his lips touched hers, her tension snapped. Although no man had done this to her before, instinctively she knew what to do now. Leaning her head on his broad shoulder, she kissed him back, opening her mouth when he touched his tongue to her lips.

He devoured her, and she devoured him right back. He caressed her with his mouth, sliding his tongue against hers, claiming her. His hands burned against her skin, even through the layers of clothing they wore. She wanted them gone. The plethora of buttons on his waistcoat bored into her front, above where her stays kept her captive, impressing her in a way she'd never forget, even if he left marks. Why should she care? She couldn't if she tried.

Leo drew away, murmured something. "We shouldn't."

"Yes, we should." She dragged him back. When he groaned against her mouth, she sighed, melting into him. Her breasts pressed against him. What would it be like to touch his bare skin, to smooth her hands over his chest and discover the muscles she felt flexing against her palms? She had one hand behind his neck, and the other on his arm. When he moved, they swelled and changed shape, revealing powerful muscles.

He dropped tiny kisses on her throat, working down to the valley of her breasts, nudging aside the folds of her filmy fichu.

She might be a virgin, but she wasn't entirely innocent. She knew what was happening to him, and when she pressed against him, desperate to get closer, she imagined she could feel the thick shaft between his legs rising and pressing against the part of her that was made to accept it.

She pulled him close, widened her legs and groaned.

Cold air whooshed between them as he forced her away and stepped back. Bewildered, she clapped her hand to her mouth. She wanted to keep him there, but as awareness surged in, horror replaced the passion of a moment before. This was how men were trapped into unwelcome alliances, and a man of his rank must have faced this potentiality before.

Propping her hands on the table, she sucked in a breath, then another, letting the cool air do its job.

"My fault," he said roughly. "All my fault. I would beg your forgiveness, ma'am, but I cannot. Not yet. Give me a moment."

He dragged a hand over his hair, some of which had come loose from the neat black velvet bow that confined it at his nape. Abruptly, he turned around.

The strands of silky dark hair that had escaped made a mockery of his usually neat appearance. His waistcoat buttons were half undone, gaping over his crisp linen shirt, now creased where her hands had stroked it. His lips were plumper, their color heightened. What must hers look like?

A concave mirror hung on the wall behind the sideboard, but she ensured she would not catch her reflection. She'd use it before she quit the room, but not now. Lifting a hand, she touched her lips. They were hot.

His avid gaze followed her revealing movement as he lifted a hand and roughly dragged the ribbon out. His hair floated free, strands touching his shoulders, making her glad he didn't wear a wig and powder, as other men did.

His hair made him resemble a member of one of the ancient hordes that stormed Rome, the barbarian showing from the veneer of respectability.

"Why are you smiling?" His soft voice held a hint of menace, an edge of exasperation.

"I was thinking of you as a Visigoth."

He barked a short, humorless laugh. "I deserve that. I should never have behaved in such a manner toward you, treated you with such disrespect. Whatever the provocation, I should not have done it."

"What p-provocation?" Indignant, she straightened and faced him. "I am no provocation for a man."

"You are for this one." Planting his feet firmly on the polished marquetry floor, he met her gaze fearlessly. "Whatever you may think of me, you shall not call me a liar."

Belatedly, she glanced at the door. It was closed.

He kept his attention on her but smiled grimly. "When you said you had to leave the door open, I decided we were past such childish strictures. It appears we are not."

"No." That much was true. "Is it childish, then?"

"Being unable to resist is. Losing control is."

The swell of emotion she had experienced had been new and overwhelming. But how could she discuss that with him? Her awakening awareness of her own desire, the way he had evoked such a shocking response from her, shocked her. Even at the remove of mere moments, Phoebe could not imagine why she had done such a thing. "What would you c-call this? What is h-happening?" Why did her carefully developed control melt away when he touched her?

He must have read the bewilderment in her voice, because his own tones gentled, the harsh note melting away. "Lust. It makes fools of men. It has led to the downfall of nations." Gathering his hair in one hand, he turned to the mirror and swiftly tied the ribbon around it.

At least now she did not have the almost irresistible temptation to sink her hands into the dark mass and run them through the strands, just to feel the intimacy of the caress. She'd touched his cheek and felt the prickles of his incipient beard, the power of the man beneath the fine clothes. He'd made her aware of him as she had been of no other man before.

With sure hands, he refastened his waistcoat and twitched his neckcloth. He wore an emerald pin stuck through the folds today, green fire glimmering against the snowy linen. That reminded her of something. With relief, she recognized her escape path.

"I will fetch your pearl p-pin." She moved toward the door.

He stepped in front of her, preventing her escape. "Tidy yourself instead. If you do not, the servants will carry the news to their mistress and then to the house next door and so around the square. Tidings of our meeting will be all over town by nightfall."

Seeing the sense of his remark and hating him for being right, she grabbed her cap and took his place at the mirror, pushing her hair into its bun at the back of her head, and fastening the fine piece of linen and lace over the top. The lappets draped behind, fluttering to her shoulders. "There, will that do?"

"It will more than do. You look lovely."

She clicked her tongue in annoyance. She was anything but lovely. Had he taken her acquiescence for granted? "Was it the letters? Is that why you th-thought I would...?"

"No!" His violent response shocked her enough for her to turn to face him. "It was not the letters," he insisted in a calmer voice. "You must not think that. If you choose not to write to me again, I will understand, but our correspondence was the high point of my day. I would miss them."

He liked them? Even as she'd written them, she'd considered them perhaps too suggestive, but she never went over the bounds of propriety, and carefully ensured that the conceits she used could easily be the innocent comments they appeared. She enjoyed contriving them. But surely she could do that no more. She would have to reconcile her heart to what she had told Angela earlier; they did not have a future, at least not one together.

Even though she had forgotten his status, as she did every time she was with him, his clothes and the careless way he dismissed what was obviously a valuable treasure reminded her he was wealthier than was decent and carried more influence than her whole county.

In short, George, The Duke of Leomore, was a powerful man, and it would behoove her to remember it.

"Keep the pearl pin for a little while longer," he said softly. "I would prefer that you care for it for me. It gives me a link I have no right to think of, after the way I mauled you today. But I want to." He swallowed. "Let us be good to ourselves. A few careless kisses, that is all."

"You speak from experience?" So he had done this to other respectable women? Was he a rake in disguise?

He shook his head. "No."

She appreciated the opportunity to regain her composure. He was right; if she'd flung herself upstairs, people would have noticed her disheveled clothing and heightened color.

He stepped forward. Gently, he took her hands. The thrill she'd felt before coursed through her anew, the desire to move closer. "You see?" he said. "We are aware of our mutual attraction, but we do not have to do anything, if we do not wish. I will swear by whatever you like not to distress you again."

"It was n-not stress exactly...." She wasn't sure how to describe it. With his kisses, Leo had unlocked a door. Before, she would have remained content, ready to live her life as a single woman. If she refused her first suitor in favor of another local man, he would have taken offense and done his best to make matters difficult for her family. She knew that when she had made a choice to refuse him, and accepted the consequences.

Now, she wasn't so sure. She'd successfully resisted the few attempts that had come her way to fix her interest. Now, she wanted something else. A whole new world had opened up for her, and he'd done it.

"Would you take that drive with me? We could both do with some air." One corner of his mouth lifted in a wry smile. "I swear I'll be good."

She still had the carriage dress from yesterday. And she had loved riding in that curricle. "Very well, I would love to. If you wouldn't mind waiting for ten minutes while I change?"

Phoebe lifted her skirts and ran up the stairs to her room.

But this had to be the last time. With the imminent arrival of her family and her continued lack of self-control with Leo, this affair could only end in disaster. She could not allow Leo to end in a situation he could not want. And she would never forgive herself if she forced him into a marriage that could only be a misalliance. From now on they would drift apart, and so she would tell him. No more letters, private meetings, or rides in the park.

She would be kind to them both and sever their growing intimacy.

Her buoyant mood melted away, and determination took its place. This would happen today. It could not go on like this.

Phoebe occupied an elegant bedroom at the end of the same corridor that contained Angela's room. She had a few days yet, perhaps as much as a week before her family arrived and her dreams were crushed.

If Leo could change places with Sir Marcus Callow, her suitor from the country, the reason she had been so eager to come to London and stay with Angela, she would be truly happy. But he could not, and so matters between them must end today.

When she opened the door to her room, numb shock made her stand stock-still and stare at the mess inside, blinking as if that would clear the devastation before her. Recalling her senses, she raised her voice, screaming her distress. "Help! To me!"

Chapter 6

People came running. First a manservant, who took one look at the room and ran to the staircase, calling for help. Then a couple of housemaids came rattling down from the floor above, and two footmen.

Phoebe's room had been ransacked. Clothes lay strewn about, slashes leaving gaping holes in the fabric. The sheets had been torn off the bed and the mattress upended. Every drawer in the tallboy had been dragged out and tipped over to empty its contents. Phoebe waded across the floor, staring at the mess in wide-eyed horror.

Angela came up from the ground floor. "What is it?"

"Good God!" Leo must have followed her upstairs. "What happened here?" Immediately he strode to Phoebe, and heedless of the witnesses, folded her into his arms.

After one indulgent moment when she pressed her face into the warmth of his waistcoat, Phoebe drew away. She must not give way to tears. Not yet. "What would anybody want with my things?"

A footman arrived. "I've checked all the other rooms on this corridor, ma'am. Nothing is disturbed. This is the only room that shows any sign of intrusion."

"It was fine when I left half an hour ago," she said numbly. "How could anyone do this in that time?"

"With determination, easily," Leo said, meeting her gaze. Then he turned his attention to the wreck that had once been her bedroom, but he kept his arm around her waist, holding her firmly. Phoebe didn't have the strength to draw away. She was shaking in shock, near to tears at the thought of someone pawing through her things.

Leo narrowed his eyes, examining the scene closely. "The intruder did nothing that would make a noise and attract attention. Nothing is smashed. What sounds he made could have been excused as a housemaid doing her work."

"And how is it that nobody heard and investigated?" Angela swung around, demanding the information from the servants.

"Nobody is here at this time, ma'am," a housemaid ventured. "We do the bedrooms in the mornings, when you're at breakfast. We change the sheets on Mondays. Miss North does not use a personal maid every day, and your woman is out, ma'am."

Angela's eyes filled with wrath as she turned to the footman. "I want everyone downstairs in the green drawing room. Everyone, do you hear?"

The room slowly cleared, except for the housemaids and footman Angela tasked with clearing the mess.

"You must take another room," she told Phoebe. "The one next to mine. I should not have put you here, so far away from anyone else."

"But I asked you to," Phoebe reminded her. She'd loved this room, with its windows on two walls, the airiness and solitude she could find here. The privacy was so delightful after the crowded rooms she was used to. No more.

Leo lifted his gaze to hers. "There is wanton destruction here, but I see a method, too. This was not done from spite alone."

"I will get to the bottom of this if it is the last thing I do!" Angela said, her eyes sparkling with fury. "Come, we can do no more here. Let the servants clear the mess."

The attacker had upended her jewelry box, its miserable contents lying in a small heap. The ribbons and lace ruffle she wore around her neck, her coral necklace, the pearl one, its tiny pearls sprinkled over her linen, and a few other trinkets lay forlorn on the sliced-up clothes.

Before she left, Phoebe swept up the letters from Leo and the small velvet box she'd stroked earlier. Had the thieves taken the pin? She was too shocked to cry, and by the time she came out of her initial shock, the urge to weep had gone, replaced by seething anger.

Downstairs, the green drawing room was crammed with people. The servants huddled at one end, talking in hushed voices, and Angela and Leo at the other. Phoebe went to stand between them. On her way downstairs, she had gone through the questions she wanted to ask. This was her problem, and she had every intention of solving it.

"We saw nobody unusual," one of the liveried footmen volunteered.

"That doesn't mean nobody came," the cook said. A tall, thin woman, she was rarely seen outside her domain. "The only thing different was the man delivering a new piece of furniture. He brought it through the kitchen." She tutted. "Upsetting my maids."

"That was it," Phoebe said. "Which stairs d-did he take?"

"The servants' one. Taverner went with him."

Angela took her part. "I had ordered a new side table for the second bedroom, so nobody would have objected. Where is Taverner now?"

The servants looked around as if expecting him to step forward. "Find him," Leo demanded, then shot a glance of apology at Angela. She nodded briefly.

In the hiatus that followed, Phoebe plucked the small case from her pocket. "They didn't take my j-jewelry, but that isn't entirely surprising. I don't have much." She paused, recalling something. "I did have a small paste brooch that my sister gave me for my birthday last year. I don't remember seeing that. But this was with the jewelry." Opening the case, she revealed the pin, still there. "That's worth a l-lot, isn't it? So wh-why is it s-still there?"

"It certainly is," Angela answered. "That pearl is huge."

Leo pulled the pin from the case and twirled it in his fingers. "So why, if these people were thieves, didn't they take it?" He tucked the pin back in its case and closed it, but he made no attempt to take it from Phoebe. "And why did they not go to your room, Miss Childers? I have seen you wearing some magnificent jewels."

Angela nodded. "I have a few good pieces, yes. Most are in the safe, but I have more everyday jewels than Phoebe, and my room is close by."

Phoebe blinked hard. Why hadn't she seen that before? "They were l-looking for something l-larger than a p-pearl pin. They were searching f-for a n-necklace. Th-They wanted one particular piece."

Beside her Leo went still. "The Latimer necklace." He groaned. "But you don't have it."

"L-Lady Latimer thinks I do, and she's been shouting about it all over t-town." Phoebe stroked the soft velvet on the box, her senses calming. "Why are they still l-looking for it if they s-stole it?"

Leo turned to her, realization dawning in his gaze. "Because they don't have it. You don't have it, but the thieves don't have it, either. So who does?"

A footman hurtled into the room and drew up short, nearly colliding with a side table. "Ma'am, I found Taverner. He was in the small powder room nearest to Miss North's chamber. Someone knocked him on the head.

There's a bit of a mess." He shot Angela a sheepish look. "They used the washbasin, broke it over his head."

"How is he?" Angela demanded.

"He came around when I shook him a bit. He has a headache, so I sent him up to bed, ma'am, but I don't think he'll come to any lasting harm."

Angela nodded. "I will go and see him at once. Poor man!" At the door, she waved. "Go back to your duties, please. I'll talk to you all, and anyone who has any concerns, come straight to me."

Phoebe and Leo exchanged a glance, in accord. Once Angela had quit the room, Leo stopped the footman before he left with the others. "How long has Taverner worked for Miss Childers?"

"Twenty years, Your Grace," the footman who found him answered. "He's been with the family since she was small. He'd never do anything to hurt her or betray the family."

Phoebe sighed. Taverner must be the older man who was putting on weight. She hadn't recalled his name. "He'll be fine," the footman assured her gently. "He's got a hard head, has Taverner."

"But you will be one footman down for a while," Leo said thoughtfully. As he turned away, the footman left the room.

Immediately Leo drew her into his arms. His heart was pounding, as she nestled into him. In a minute she'd pull away, but he felt so good. She couldn't deny the shock she'd received. "You should not have gone into your room," he said, his voice rumbling through her body. "The intruder could still have been there."

If she weren't so close to him, she'd have missed his shudder. Only slight, but it was there. His concern for her warmed and comforted her. Having a stranger rifle through her belongings had made her feel as if she'd been violated. Not that she would admit that to anyone, even the man holding her now. "With Miss Childers's permission, I will loan her one of my staff. Jemmy's father, Linton, to be precise. He will be your footman, Phoebe, for you to send on errands and to take with you when you go out."

Phoebe understood his meaning immediately. "You're worried about me?"

"That I am." He leaned back, gazing down at her. "Let me do this for you, Phoebe. I won't rest until this affair is cleared up, and I thank my good fortune I was there with you that night. Someone wants those diamonds badly."

"Lady Latimer, for one."

"And whoever has that necklace."

Chapter 7

"I am to be your companion tonight instead of the other way around," Angela said, an amused smile curving her lips.

"Oh no!" Phoebe whirled around from where she had been enjoying her reflection in the mirror.

Despite her protests, Angela had insisted on providing Phoebe with a new wardrobe. Most of the gowns had been made over from Angela's discards, or so she claimed, though Phoebe was skeptical. However, the butter-yellow and cream gown she was wearing tonight would not have suited Angela in the least.

"You can't allow people to say that. I came to London to act as your companion, so if you think I'm putting myself forward too much, you must say so."

Reaching around her neck, Phoebe made to remove her pearl necklace, which she'd painstakingly restrung after the thieves had broken it. She had no need of it tonight. The gown was of watered silk with a cream petticoat and robings down the front, embroidered with gold cord and tiny images of birds. It was the most glorious thing she'd ever seen, and on Angela's advice she'd left her hair unpowdered, the better to show the gown to advantage. But she did look far grander than she was.

"Don't remove that necklace," Angela instructed her. "And I think it's delightful that you are blossoming. Why you always refused to dress well before, I do not know. Your parents would not object."

Phoebe sighed. "No, they would not. My m-mother would not notice. But I determined to b-behave with the greatest propriety when I came to London, and now look at me! Every time I enter a room, people l-look."

"Because you're lovely. Not an accredited beauty, not yet, but you could be."

Angela should know; she was certainly an accredited beauty. "I do not w-wish to be feted in that way." Truly she did not. Such admiration as she was receiving made her feel like a fraud. She was not beautiful, she was just the same person as before tricked out in grander clothing. And a little more confident, she had to admit. Phoebe picked up her fan from the dressing table, and after taking one final peep at her appearance, left her room in Angela's wake.

The last thing she wanted was to draw attention to herself, but she could hardly avoid it now that she was betrothed to a most eligible bachelor, however temporary that was. But perhaps they could continue as friends when her adventure was over. She wrote to Leo at least once a day, and he wrote back. They exchanged views about books, plays, even politics, and no subject escaped their notice.

Climbing into Angela's extravagantly appointed town carriage was almost normal. They had not dined out tonight, although invitations crowded the mantelpiece in the breakfast parlor. Both ladies had agreed that a quiet dinner a deux was the perfect start to what promised to be a long evening.

After the opera, they were to go to no less than two balls, both at unexceptionable places. Phoebe didn't know how long she could keep up this pace, but she was game to play a few more rounds.

A footman in Leo's livery waited for them at the door to the opera house and took them to Leo's box. This was Linton. Like Taverner, he was a little older than the average footman, but burly enough, and with a countenance that would scare most would-be attackers away.

Leo had brought a friend, another duke. Dukes were rare, but there were at least seven here tonight. This opera had been hotly anticipated, and in any case, the theater was a place society frequented, to see and be seen.

Resplendent in peacock blue and gold, Leo lifted Phoebe's hand to his lips. So used to Angela being addressed first, Phoebe nearly botched the exchange, but Leo grasped her hand firmly and raised a dark brow as he straightened. The sardonic gleam in his eyes told her he had not missed her hesitation at the entrance.

The two rows of seats provided plenty of room. Her quick survey showed her the footman at the back, waiting to do their bidding, the elegant seating, so unlike the benches in the gods way above them, and the attention of the people all around the theater. Nobody was watching the first piece being performed anymore. Spyglasses were turned in their direction.

Then she was introduced to the Duke of Colston Magna.

Even Leo's peacock blue paled compared to His Grace's magnificence. His white wig was fresh, elaborate, and at the height of fashion. The pair of curls above each ear were neatly done. He wore brocade, bright green with flowers woven into the pattern, as if they were scattered carelessly over a field of summer blossoms. His breeches and waistcoat were a gleaming ivory, the buttons glittering with either brilliants or diamonds. She didn't want to speculate which. Leo's friend was a complete dandy.

But nobody would mistake His Grace of Colston Magna as anything but essentially male. One of the two small swords propped at the back of the box belonged to him, and the expression in his dark eyes promised heat between the sheets.

Not that Phoebe would know anything about that, although she'd had a few strange dreams recently.

The duke bowed over her hand in the approved manner, not touching her bare skin except with the tips of his fingers. When he straightened, his warm gaze turned to cool intelligence as he gave her a brief but thorough visual scan. She returned his scrutiny until he smiled. A broad, jaw-cracking grin that transformed him completely. Plucking out a spyglass, he surveyed their audience below. "Lud, but they must be bored. It appears they find our little scene more riveting than what is happening on the stage. I admit I thought the forepiece a dull thing, but the opera promises well. Have you seen *Rodelinda?*"

Phoebe answered in the negative, not bothering to admit that she had never seen any opera, although she understood it involved a lot of singing.

"You will enjoy yourself, I am certain, especially this new version. Allow me to help you."

"That, my dear Col, is why I am here." Smoothly, Leo inserted himself between them, at the same time turning. "You know Miss Childers, of course."

"Naturally." His smile turned smoothly on to Angela. He bowed over her hand with a grace Phoebe had been unable to observe the first time. She could have sworn he actually kissed Angela's hand, but Angela showed no sign if he did, merely greeting him and allowing him to seat her on the outside of the front seats.

Leo allowed Phoebe to sit first, which meant he had the outside seat, neatly trapping her. But with several hundred people watching them, she could hardly demand he let her out. Or that she enjoyed the attention he was paying to her. But she was.

And she loved the opera. The performance barely grazed the attention of some of the people in the audience. The audience in the gods ate its oranges, fought and yelled encouragement to the singers, who loftily ignored the comments and raised their voices. The gentlemen in the box on the stage continued their game of cards, laughing and passing around wine as if this was an extension of their gentleman's club.

But the singers had good lungs, particularly the musico, Cellini. This opera had been revived especially for him, at least she had read that in that morning's journal. He was a large man, with the pale skin, long limbs, barrel chest, and receding chin typical of so many of his kind, but his voice was an angel's. A pity he could not act, as the king in the play went through a gamut of emotions, none of which he displayed adequately. Against him, his counterpart, the arrogant Italian Maria Barnadotti, showed more range, but the crowd had come to see Cellini.

"I've never heard a musico before," she said at a pause between scenes. She turned her head to find Leo watching her, a smile putting creases into his cheeks. "It's very enjoyable."

"Then I am delighted to bring you this treat."

"Do you think he m-misses it?" Flicking open her fan, Phoebe covered her face. She should not have said that, but she found talking to Leo so easy she could almost be conversing with herself.

Leo answered her anyway. "Many castrati come from poor households, so perhaps the loss of their male parts is compensated by the enormous sums of money they may command."

"Oh." She hadn't thought of that. "But however poor, they must find certain functions difficult…" She tailed off. She'd done it again. With Leo she found sharing her thoughts far too easy. That could not continue. "Oh n-no, how d-dreadful! I should not be talking to you in such a w-w-way. I'm s-s-s-s…"

He put his hand over hers and squeezed gently. "Do not. I prefer you always your sweet self with me. You have brought me much pleasure with our meetings and our correspondence."

"Sorry!" But the word was no longer appropriate. Ignoring the magnificent aria being poured out onstage, she turned her head to meet his gaze. The warmth she saw there could surely not be feigned. "Thank you."

"Don't mention it." His lips twisted in a wry grin. "And I look forward to tomorrow's letter. Your comments on tonight's entertainment should be untrammeled, especially since this is your first experience of a castrato." He used the word few people enunciated in public. Most preferred the euphemism of musico, but he had not concerned himself with such niceties. He had flattered her by using the correct term. He must have known she would not protest or go off into a faint.

Swallowing, she turned her attention back to the stage. The soprano was about to launch herself into a heart-rending declaration of love, at least going from her anguished expression and the way she clasped her hands over her heart.

"Would you like to use this?"

Leo gave her a lovely eyeglass, similar to the one Angela owned. It was a gold tube with inset enamel pieces, a lovely object. She smoothed her fingers over the glossy surface. "Is this your c-coat of arms?"

"It is." The small, relatively discreet image at the base of the instrument was more for identification than as part of the decoration. The glass collapsed into a single ring-shaped cylinder, which was decorated with rims of chased gold, and at the center, a black-and-gold enameled design. The object was exquisite. When she held it to her eye, it brought everything into clear detail.

She watched the opera, fascinated by the details she could now see.

Leo passed Phoebe a glass of wine. She sipped it and let her attention rove over the audience, which had returned to its previous pursuits of gossip and flirtation. And gambling. Everywhere people existed, so did betting. Gentlemen in the pits swept their opera glasses everywhere except for the stage. They lingered on the boxes, blatantly ogling the ladies and the other kind of lady, the lady of the night. This was one of the few places all members of society, including the female section, shared a space with the courtesans. And the common whores, if the activity in the gods was anything to go by. Phoebe averted her gaze, but if she was here on her own, where nobody could remark on her interest, she would have taken a closer look.

Phoebe stored up the experience for future consideration, but then a glint in one of the boxes opposite caught her attention. Fumbling for the spyglass, she lifted it to her eye and peered through it.

A lady sat there with a collection of other people. The glint came from a magnificent necklace that caught the light every time she moved.

At her strangled cry, Leo touched her arm. "Is something wrong?"

"No, sir." She handed him the spyglass. "At least, yes, perhaps. The lady in the b-box opposite, do you know her? For she is wearing something that appears remarkably f-familiar."

He peered at the box. "She is masked. I cannot say if I know her."

"But that l-looks like the necklace. Lady Latimer described it in d-detail, and I did n-note it b-before it was stolen. If it is the necklace, we may clear this matter up tonight."

And then there would be no need for her betrothal to the Duke of Leomore. Phoebe pushed that thought aside.

If she was not mistaken, the second act was about to come to a close. "Will you take me to walk outside? We may make our way across to the other side and discover the identity of that woman. She could be the thief."

Leo leaned across the space between the two sets of seats and murmured to Angela. On her other side, the Duke of Colston Magna lifted his own spyglass. "Good Lord," he murmured, but Phoebe only knew that by the movement of his lips. She was too far away to hear him properly.

At the close of the second act, His Grace got to his feet. Both Their Graces, to be more precise. Colston Magna helped Angela up as if she were a delicate piece of porcelain. Phoebe sprang to her feet, eager to chase down the woman who could end her nightmare.

"Not such a tender flower, then," Leo remarked, evoking a glare from his betrothed. "Do give the impression you cannot do anything without my support, or I fear my reputation will suffer."

Phoebe snorted inelegantly. "I do not believe that for one minute, sir."

"Then at least wait for me," he complained plaintively, so much like a child that she could not hold back her laughter. But she did as he asked, and when he emerged from the box, she placed her hand on his arm. He wore woolen cloth tonight, but so fine her fingers sank into the fabric and paused on the evidence of hard muscle beneath.

He glanced down at her. "Are we for the chase, then, or would you prefer a gentle promenade?"

Behind the boxes were relatively broad passageways, and doors into who-knew-what, but probably more staircases. Theaters burned down on a regular basis, about once every thirty years, so these days the architects provided the patrons with ample routes of escape.

"D-Do you have to ask?" Phoebe demanded before she belatedly realized he was teasing her.

"We will accompany you," the Duke of Colston Magna said, easily keeping pace with Leo and Phoebe. "Suddenly the evening is full of promise."

At his other side, Angela clung to the duke's arm and lengthened her pace. "If I had known hunting was planned, I'd have worn boots, not shoes with punishingly high heels. However, never let it be said that a Childers was not game."

"I always knew you were a good 'un, ma'am," her companion answered, "even though I had no sure evidence of it. I have every expectation that you will live up to your name."

"Ha!"

They quickened their pace, passing through the doors at the end and along the corridor behind the auditorium. Well-dressed people stood and conversed there, but Leo effortlessly wove his way through them, heading steadily for the door beyond. It seemed miles away. They kept moving although several people appeared in their paths. The dukes were adept at working their way through without actually stopping, and Angela proved herself no mean practitioner of the art, as well.

Phoebe's anxiety rose. Her throat tightened, and her heart increased its beat, thumping against her chest. Leo virtually dragged her along, but anyone watching would have seen very little out of the ordinary.

He seemed as eager as Phoebe to bring this tawdry affair of the necklace to an end. If he had any sense, he'd be keen to end his betrothal to her, too.

And then what? After that she'd have nothing to do but retreat and mark the whole adventure down to a memory.

Finally they reached the end door. People still thronged, but as the footman opened the door and bowed them through, Leo's hand brushed against Phoebe's. Momentarily she froze, tingles spreading over her skin from the contact, and she barely managed to keep up.

Angela had lagged behind, finally snared by an acquaintance, so of course her escort remained with her.

Leo showed no hesitation. Although this corridor was as crowded as the previous one, he plowed on. "I can see her," he told Phoebe. Being a head taller than most people here, he had a better vantage point. Phoebe could only see expensively clad torsos.

A cry of "Ah, Leomore!" was met with a polite, "I haven't seen you this age, madam! Do give my compliments to your husband," but he didn't stop.

The crowd was thinning now as people were reassembling for the next act, but a glint of light showed Phoebe where they were going.

Leo stopped stock-still, abruptly enough that Phoebe cannoned into his broad back. Peering around him, she saw what had brought him to such an abrupt halt. The lady was no longer wearing her mask, but Phoebe still didn't recognize her. This close, Phoebe marked the flamboyance of her clothes, the extravagance of her neckline, and the fact that she was standing in the midst of a throng of men, not a companion in sight.

Trying to turn, she got into a mess, and lost her balance.

Chapter 8

Whimpering, Phoebe grabbed a handful of material and prevented her headlong tumble, but her hoops crushed against him until he spun and steadied her, his hands around her waist. "Dear me, Miss North, we'll have to get you out of this crush!"

People were headed for their boxes, but a few wanted to speak to them. Confused, Phoebe gazed up into his face. "But…"

With a firm hand, he half-led, half-dragged her to the side of the corridor, then glanced around, opened one of the doors and pulled her inside. Dexterity and smoothness prevented others noting his retreat. Plus, the remarkable beauty of the lady had attracted most eyes.

"We can't…" she began.

"Nobody saw us, thank the Lord." He dragged one hand over his hair and tugged at the black velvet bow at the back. It fell away, and he closed his eyes, resting his forehead on the edge of the mantelpiece and uttering a frustrated groan.

They were in a small parlor, a space dimly illuminated by a window high up. A cozy retreat, it held a side table furnished with a decanter, a pair of wine glasses, and a large, comfortable daybed covered by a signature white and gold cloth, proclaiming the flashy, though meaningless, coat of arms of the opera house.

In short, a room where lovers might tryst.

Then Leo turned the key in the lock.

"Sir!"

"She and her lover were heading in this direction. No doubt this room is laid out for *her*."

"Who?"

"La Coccinelle. The woman we were trying so hard to speak to. This is typical of her tricks."

He turned to face Phoebe. With his hair flowing around him he resembled nothing more than a warrior from the old days, wearing fashionable clothing for a jest. A murderous gleam glinted in his eyes. The smile turned dangerous.

With a gasp, Phoebe took a step back and fumbled for the door.

"No!" he cried. "Don't go, please!"

* * * *

When he'd seen who was wearing that necklace Leo knew Phoebe shouldn't be within the other woman's orbit. The sight had enraged him, forcing him to seek sanctuary anywhere he could. His protective instincts had impelled him to drag her with him. He should have left her outside. If anyone saw them leave this room, they'd suspect the worst and then they would be truly trapped into marriage, because he would not dishonor Phoebe.

His only compensation was that he suspected this situation was the last thing the woman had wanted. He saw her plan in a flash, and had done his best to avoid it, only to get them into this mess.

He lowered his head and took some deep breaths.

She was still in the room. He felt it, he didn't have to see the hem of her gown to know that.

Eventually he lifted his head.

"What's wrong?"

Absurd pleasure warmed him when he noted no trace of hesitation. Her impulse to leave had been mere instinct, nothing else. She trusted him.

"I'm sorry. If I had taken more notice of the woman rather than the necklace this could have been avoided. I was wrong. I do know her."

A frown creased her brows. "What do you mean? Who was that woman?"

Ah, now they reached the sticking point. "La Coccinelle, otherwise known as Lisette. Of course, that isn't her real name. Lizzie Fisher she is, born near the Pool of London. Her father worked in the docks, her mother was a laundress, so good that her skill gave her the entrée to the best houses in town. Now Lizzie is the most feted courtesan in London."

She understood. "And your mistress." The sparkle dulled, and she looked away from him.

"Yes. But I dismissed her months ago." He sighed. "She dislikes me because I left her before she had the chance to leave me. I tired of her behavior, and her extravagance. I will not allow my people to be discommoded by her."

"What do you mean?"

Sighing, he went to the decanter and poured two glasses of the excellent brandy he found there. He handed her one and took a fortifying sip from the other. "I need this."

She swirled the liquid around the glass before taking a sip. No hesitation there, either. "What did she do?"

"She acted like my wife, not my mistress. She called at my house, demanding to see me, behaving like a lady of fashion, not a member of the demi-monde. I still don't know why she did it. She knows the rules. I had no choice, but I think she knew I was already tiring of her. She does not lack for suitors, so I suggested she moved on to one of them."

"I see. Do you think Lord Latimer is one of them, and that his how she obtained the necklace? And would he really give her a family piece?"

He paused, thinking. La Coccinelle was nothing if not encroaching, but would Lord Latimer be infatuated enough to give her a family treasure? "I don't know." He gave her a wry glance as his temper subsided. "Come and sit down."

She glanced at the daybed, then at him. He sat, leaned his arm on the back of the wide sofa in an inviting gesture.

She came and sat at the opposite end of the piece of furniture. His fingers barely grazed the tip of her shoulder. "Do you think that is the real necklace?"

"I don't know. It would explain a great deal about this mystery. She is avaricious, and to show herself in such a piece would be to thumb her nose at the society that rejected her. Including me. Perhaps that is what she wants. I will find out, I promise you. She could even have been the mysterious lady in blue who stole the jewels."

"If she exists."

He raised a brow and she carried on. "L-Lady Latimer would have s-said anything, to detract from her own behavior. D-Did she really see someone? After all, if she had not b-been careless, they jewels would n-not have been taken."

She was perceptive, his betrothed. And she was right. They only had Lady Latimer's word as to how the theft took place. "Real or otherwise, wearing the necklace tonight was unwise. If Latimer gave it to her, it would be as a deliberate insult to his wife."

"Would you do that?"

"Not even if we were living at opposite ends of the house and not speaking to one another."

"I d-didn't mean me."

He loved the flush that rose to her cheeks. La Coccinelle did not hold a candle to Phoebe North. Phoebe had an intelligence and lively interest Lisette would never have imagined. He remained completely still. Either that, or lunge for Phoebe, and she wouldn't welcome that. He had never felt more like the savage warriors in his ancestry. He'd read about them as a child, now he knew what they felt like. He liked to think he was more civilized than that, but perhaps he'd been fooling himself. Instead, he put his mind back to what they were supposed to be discussing in the time they had to wait in this horribly intimate room before they were safe to leave. "When I told Lisette—La Coccinelle—that we were done, she vowed vengeance on me. Perhaps this was it."

"It was the theft that brought us together, so she could hardly have caused that."

He nodded. "But to flaunt the jewels before me, when she knows you are living in their shadow, that would be like her. That could be the necklace she is wearing, but I cannot allow you two to meet. Do you understand?"

She nodded. "I might be p-provincial but I am not ignorant of the way the w-world works. My father—" She stopped, biting her lip. But she glanced at him and continued. "My father had a m-mistress. The woman c-caused my mother not a little distress. Being my mother, she t-told him so. Then she d-dismissed his mistress, who was not a courtesan, but the wife of a friend." A reminiscent smile curved her sweet lips. "In the middle of a p-public assembly. Quite c-comprehensively."

"Could you imagine what would have happened if I'd allowed you to meet Lisette?"

She took a sip of brandy. "Only too vividly. She would have l-loved the encounter, wouldn't she? And it would have ruined me. That's t-twice you've saved me."

He finished his drink and put the glass aside. "I have every faith in you. You would have extricated yourself, I'm quite sure. For all your quiet demeanor, you are a formidable woman, are you not?" He discerned strength in her quietness. She was not abashed, she merely appeared that way, but she had an inner strength he would dearly love to see her display. Phoebe North had iron in her soul.

"You are too good." He regarded her, enjoying the sight. "Far too good for me, I fear." Because she was. He could not use this woman, but he would do everything in his power to save her reputation. Even if he had to marry her.

The notion that came so easily jolted him once he'd recognized it. But it wouldn't come to that. She should have someone she could rely on, who would devote the rest of his life to making her happy. He couldn't do that. He had never remained true to one woman for more than a year at a time, and what did he know about fidelity and goodness? He had watched his parents tear the estate and each other apart and turn on him if he wasn't fast enough. He had no stable family life to take strength from. No idea what fidelity looked like. He didn't know if he had it in him.

The expression in her eyes if she discovered he had betrayed her would kill him.

On the other hand, he had to marry someone, and he had met nobody he wanted more than her. But he would not humiliate her, would not treat her carelessly. And how could he be sure he wouldn't do that? What experience did he have of fidelity and honor in an intimate relationship?

"Would La Coccinelle have made matters d-difficult for me?" she asked, seemingly at ease now, sitting there, taking delicate sips of her brandy.

"Undoubtedly. She would have crowed her triumph to anyone who would listen. Indeed, I fear she took that box to flaunt herself and present the comparison."

"I could not compare with her b-beauty."

He shook his head. "Do you truly believe that?"

"Of course. I am not an accredited b-beauty, nor like to be. I don't have that d-dazzling attractiveness."

"Do I detect some wistfulness?" Lifting a hand, he stroked his forefinger down one cheek, emboldened when she did not draw back, but watched him through those rich brown eyes of hers. "You should not. You are quite lovely, you know, but in a delicate, exquisite way rather than the kind of flashy beauty that attracts the uncouth."

"I would have c-come off worst." She kept her gaze on his. "You know I would. And you know why."

He would not point out that she had not stuttered once, bar a few slight hesitations. A ridiculous sense of pleasure suffused him, that she would treat him as a friend and relax in his company. Except he wanted more than friendship. If she were in the same position as La Coccinelle, he would not have hesitated. She would be sharing his bed before the night was out. The mental vision that evoked went straight to his groin.

"You would not have come off worst. Your wit would carry you through. And you are far more alluring."

She scoffed, made a sound of derision he would not accept.

No more. He could take only so much of her gaze, the feel of her skin in his hand and her sweet perfume. Closing the few inches between them, he kissed her.

She responded immediately and gratifyingly, opening her mouth so he could slide his tongue between her lips. Slowly, so as not to startle her, he moved close enough to curve his arms around her and tighten his hold on her waist. Still in the kiss he lifted her, enjoying the little gasp she made into his mouth, and settled her across his thighs. Her hoop was the new kind, and obligingly folded up as he pressed closer.

Her hand cupped his face, then she traced lines against his skin with her nails, before threading her fingers into his hair and toying with the strands.

He would have done the same, but although she wasn't powdered, she'd had her hair put into an elaborate style he doubted he could begin to recreate if he destroyed it now. He had just enough sense left to realize that before he deepened the kiss.

At first he supported her back with his outspread hand, but that wasn't enough. The pleats at the back of her gown teased him, and he followed one up, tracing the center of her back where her spine would be, drawing up, seeking bare skin.

At the top of her gown he found it. The prominent bone above her spine moved under his seeking fingers, then he explored what he could. He lifted his lips from hers, but only to kiss her cheek, and nibble his way across to her ear.

With a sigh, she settled into his arm when he curved it around her back. She leaned her cheek on his coat, giving him tacit permission to continue. She gazed into his eyes, her own soft and accepting. Completely unable to resist, he kissed her again.

This time she spread her hand on his chest. Even through his layers of clothing he felt that touch like a brand, inciting him to continue. He obliged, stroking her skin with more purpose, seeking a way in.

Her evening gown did not have the fichu ladies generally sported in the daytime. Only a small frill of lace lay between Leo and paradise. But it might as well be an iron gate because she was properly laced into this gown. However, he knew his way around ladies' clothing. He slipped his finger into the cleft between her breasts, watching a sweet flush rise in her cheeks. He kissed them, nuzzling down to her mouth once more, lingering to draw her sweet taste back. But he kept this kiss tender, slow and exploratory. He could not get too carried away. They had to leave this room somehow and face the world outside. They would have gone in for the next act by now. Col would have the sense to disguise their absence, perhaps ask for the lights at the back of the box to be extinguished. That was what he would have done.

With regret, he finished the kiss.

Phoebe aroused was quite a sight. The lovely flush was enhanced by the sultry gaze from heavy-lidded eyes. Her lips were plump and pink, tempted him to take more, to go further. But he could not.

Even though they were betrothed they had not taken any steps that would make marriage inevitable. He did not want this lovely creature forced into doing anything she didn't wish. More than that, if they ever came to a time where they would marry in truth, he wanted her choice to be untrammeled by anything but need.

The notion gave him pause, brought his thoughts to a juddering halt. That was the second time since they'd entered this room that he'd found himself assuming a marriage to her, instead of accepting the match was out of the question.

When had he considered a real marriage? Looking forward to her letters every day, letters that had gone from a polite exchange into something more intimate in a matter of days? He had considered their regular correspondence a way of discussing the affair of the necklace without too much closeness, but now he looked forward to seeing her with keen anticipation and the letters were becoming part of that need.

"We should go," she murmured, her voice throaty.

"We should," he agreed, but he made no move.

"What will we do about the necklace? Shouldn't you find out if it's the real one?"

Her question brought him back down to earth effectively, but he kept her on his lap, enjoying the closeness. "Are you suggesting that I visit her?" His mouth quirked.

"Indeed I feel you must. If it's ineligible for me to meet her, then you should do so."

Carefully, he lifted her away, and settled her back on the daybed. That small taste of her had left him trembling. He was hard, but he did not think she had noticed, so many layers of fabric had been bunched between them. "You are suggesting that I visit my former mistress? What if she wants me back?"

A slow movement of her hand on the silk of her gown attracted his attention. He watched as she smoothed the folds into place, and resettled the robings at the front, drawing them back against the fabric. "You must do as you see fit. I am in no case to dictate your desires."

He caught her hand in his, holding it captive. "Oh, but you do. You dictate my desires quite thoroughly, my sweet. Or did you not know?"

Still not looking at him, she stared at her lap, where their hands were joined. "I had thought it the normal behavior of a man. At least one who found a woman he could entice into such situations."

A rough laugh escaped him. "Indeed not. Many women have tried to trap me into situations like these, with one purpose in mind…"

She shook her head. "I c-could hardly lay claim to you when I will be returning to B-Buckinghamshire soon."

"I see. And my interest matters so little?" Did she care for him at all?

"No." Finally she raised her chin and met his eyes. "But I know the w-way the world works. You m-may amuse yourself with me, but you will marry a lady who knows how to b-be a duchess."

Indignation rose in him. Why should she not? "I fail to discern how you consider you would not. You have a fine sense of responsibility, and I have never heard you disparage those you consider under your notice. Moreover, you have a sense of the ridiculous I find utterly enchanting. And you are beautiful."

She sighed. "I w-wish you would stop saying that."

"It's the truth. All that is needed is for you to believe it." Lifting her hand to his lips, he kissed the knuckles. "The greatest beauties are the ones who hold themselves gracefully and believe in their beauty. Not necessarily the ones with perfect features."

"But…" She tailed off as he kissed her again, this time a soft kiss of affection.

"I will visit Lisette in the morning, no doubt discommoding her greatly since she doesn't get up until noon. Then I'll come to you. I will not linger, and believe me, she has no appeal to me any longer."

His smile was genuine, full of mirth. This innocent, sweet woman was sending him into the arms of one of the most notorious women in London. Except that Lisette wouldn't get her arms anywhere near him. He was determined on that.

Chapter 9

As Leo walked into his club after a fraught meeting with La Coccinelle, he was met with a shout from the end of the room. "Ah, here's the hero of the hour!"

Wineglass in hand, the Earl of Marston toasted Leo as he crossed the room. Gentleman sat in the chairs set around small tables or grouped informally. The walls now held shelves, containing a collection of books and a stand at the end displayed the day's journals. Leo glanced at the stand, wondering what had driven Mars's accolade. No doubt he would find out. Still sore from Lisette's outrageous demands and denials, he had wanted peace and quiet for an hour or two. That seemed less likely now.

He lifted a brow in query. "What have I done now?" Had anyone seen him leave that assignation room with Phoebe last night? He had taken the utmost care, sending her ahead, and allowing her to return to the box a good ten minutes before he arrived, as if they had been in different places. But someone could have seen them.

Mars poured him a glass of rich red wine, which he accepted gratefully. He took a healthy gulp, then curled his hand around the glass, threading his fingers on each side of the air twist stem and curving them around the bowl. The smooth glass felt comfortable and reassuring, which was what he needed.

"You put La Coccinelle back on the market." Mars grinned. "She was seen at the opera with a number of suitors. A sign she is available."

He suppressed his growl. News traveled fast. "As far as I knew, she was never off the market. I ended our connection two months ago, but even then she was not exclusive. She has never restricted herself to one man at a time."

"She was with you." Mars gave Leo a mock toast before draining his glass. "Didn't you know? You must have known. She declared she was devoted to you, that you are the love of her life. She has sworn she will get you back."

Leo took a seat. "I don't care. She was available when I wanted her, and that was sufficient. She's a very demanding and temperamental woman." Extremely so. He shuddered. Having two parents who fitted the same mold, Leo had a deep dislike of that kind of disruptive behavior.

"But beautiful and accomplished. With a different background she'd have made someone an excellent wife."

Leo shrugged. "She could still do that. Just not in society." And not his. "Courtesans have made marriages before. I heard a rumor that La Perla is the wife of a country vicar these days." Why hadn't he chosen someone like La Perla? An intelligent and reasonable woman, unlike the infuriating Lisette, with her moods and petulance. But she was enticing, wicked in a delicious way, and witty. None of that had been enough to keep him, her tantrums and demands eventually driving him away.

Mars sighed. "La Perla was a prime 'un. I never had the pleasure, but I would have enjoyed mounting her. It was not to be." He brightened. "But now I have a chance with La Coccinelle."

"I would advise against it. She insists on so much attention, it is hardly worthwhile. Since I disposed of her services two months ago I have not employed anyone."

Mars leaned forward. "You've been *celibate?*"

He shrugged. "I've been bored. Nobody took my fancy." Discussing the women he bedded was nothing new in male company, but he preferred not to be as indiscreet as some. Although Mars was one of his dearest friends, he would not discuss the intimacies of his private life with him. He took another sip of the excellent wine, his mood calming. "We did well, employing Marchant to run the club. He's been busy."

He glanced around. The St. James's Club had been started with a subscription, which gave the founding members useful privileges. Clubs were all the rage at the moment, but most were men-only. Not all, though. He gave a reminiscent smile when he thought of the SSL and Phoebe's excitement about it.

"So have you, by all accounts. Been busy, I mean. The news of your last encounter with the lovely La Coccinelle is all over London. She is heartbroken, she declares. She needs consoling."

So much for his attempted change of subject. He gave an appreciative grin. "Truly? I have to give her credit for making profit off the back of

our discussion. She must have another keeper by now, if not several."
Reluctantly, but yes, she had not been born with the benefit of a respectable
family or a competence. The woman had to make a living.

"And you were seen going into her house this morning. Have you
reconciled with her?" Mars demanded.

Leo closed his eyes and groaned. "Gossip runs faster than an arrow
from a bow. No, I have not reconciled with her. Quite the opposite. We
parted on bad terms."

Mars leaned back and crossed his feet at the ankle. "Old news. The
people in the street heard the row. What was it about?"

Damn. "Merely a piece of jewelry."

Mars perked up. "The Latimer diamonds? We all saw what she was
wearing last night. Did Latimer have the effrontery to bestow the real
necklace on her?"

Leo could only wish that were true. Then Phoebe would be absolved
from suspicion. But he'd needed to be sure before he could confirm that.
And sadly, although she'd taunted him with the necklace, Lisette had not
produced it or offered to show it to him.

Although the groups of men around the room appeared to be engaged in
their own conversations, Leo would bet his best pearl pin—which Phoebe
still had in her possession—that he had an avid audience. He waved his
hand languidly in denial. "Not at all. Another one I gave to her."

He doubted that would keep the gossips busy for long. They knew he'd
gone after the necklace to clear his betrothed's name. At least they would
not say he had gone back to his mistress.

Lisette's beauty had not drawn him today, even though she had tempted
him with her best tricks. Dressed in a loose morning gown fastened by
a mere row of satin bows, the top one left undone, leaving her gleaming
hair unbound and wearing the enticing perfume he'd had made for her had
not worked. Then she had pleaded with him to take her back, promising
him exclusivity, but he'd refused. His interest had been well and truly
doused the last time he'd seen her, when her temper, petulance, and
appalling misjudgment had finally driven him away. She'd wanted marriage.
As if he could walk into court with her on his arm or take her to the
ballrooms of his peers.

She had ended by screaming at him, throwing a dozen ridiculous
threats at him. "She claimed the necklace was real, but then confessed it
was not, although Latimer tried to tell her that it was. Naturally she had it
assessed. Giving even a copy of a famous piece like the Latimer necklace

to a mistress was in appallingly poor taste. One would imagine her ladyship was considerably disturbed by the news." To say the least.

If she had proof that Lord Latimer had not only been consorting with one of the most notorious women in London but had presented her with a copy of the famed Latimer necklace, her ladyship would no doubt fall down in a dead faint in the center of the largest public gathering she could find.

Leo looked forward to seeing it, or at the least, reading about it.

"One would. One will be. I'm sure society will wallow in the news," Mars drawled. The tidings would be all around the city by this evening. It added another twist to the tale.

La Coccinelle was not stupid, and she could spot a paste necklace in a second. But she would use it to get her revenge on Leo, flaunting the piece his betrothed was accused of stealing.

He raised his voice slightly to make eavesdropping easier. "Lady Latimer has visited Bow Street, too. She very loudly accused my betrothed of theft in the presence of witnesses, something I do not take kindly. I trust nobody will repeat *that* particular calumny in my hearing."

If he heard that again, he would personally go to the Latimer residence with his father's cavalry saber. But he didn't say it aloud. There was little need. The men here knew him, and he had hardened his voice on the last notes. If this affair caused a rift between his family and the Latimers, he would gladly take the challenge. And win.

One thing was for certain: the affair of the Latimer diamonds would not go away any time soon. He would have to break the news of the scandal to his grandmother, but knowing the efficiency of her spies, she had probably heard already. Already doubtful about his engagement, she might not take kindly to it, so Leo kept his peace. Holding fire, in other words.

The dowager preferred to take the season at her own pace, and this early would not attend too many gatherings, but she had invited Phoebe and Miss Childers to dinner. Her health had not been wonderful recently, her arthritis troubling her more than she cared to admit. Her hands were cruelly twisted with it, and her maid had informed Leo that the pain frequently kept the dowager awake at night. Not only did he owe her everything, he adored her, and he would protect her at the cost of his life. But now another woman was disturbing his peace. If the two women clashed, then he would take his grandmother's part, no question, but he would miss Phoebe.

Every day he met Phoebe was another when he was becoming increasingly convinced that she would make him an excellent wife. Her letters showed wit and intelligence, as well as a sense of humor he deeply appreciated. What had started as a gallant move was fast becoming reality.

Now all he had to do was persuade Phoebe. If he decided to go ahead with the betrothal. Although a man could not withdraw, there were ways, mostly involving procrastination, to end a union.

What more proof did he have of his interest than the shocking way he behaved around her? He craved her kisses, and for a grown man accustomed to more involving liaisons, that was saying something. That, of course, must stop. He had no intention of setting society on its ear as his parents had consistently done. If he took her into many more private rooms in public places, the gossip would damage both of them.

Mars refilled his glass and offered Leo another, which he accepted. He had a feeling he would need it. "Do you go to the Berminton rout this evening?"

"I believe so."

"Good. Her ladyship has several eligible daughters. Three I think, and I do not wish to face them alone."

"Perhaps." But Mars was not in particular want. Col might be glad of such a healthy infusion into his recently depleted funds, due to long-lived and profligate parents. If Leo's mother and father had not died when they had, he might have found himself in the same case. But they had perished, leaving Leo and his grandmother to make what they could of what was left. Since Leo had been a boy at the time, the burden had fallen on his grandmother for many years. He owed her for that.

But to give up a woman he wanted for a duty marriage to some society miss? Would he go that far?

* * * *

That evening found Leo dining with his grandmother and a selection of superior guests.

Phoebe attended in company with Miss Childers, both resplendent in blue silk, but Phoebe wore a darker shade than her pale and fair counterpart. They looked to advantage together, Phoebe with her gleaming dark hair and eyes, next to the ethereal Angela Childers. Leo knew which of the pair he preferred.

Although aware the duchess was watching her keenly, Phoebe behaved with a great deal of grace, with only one unfortunate incident marring the evening, when she got stuck on a word.

An appalled silence fell over the table, before the murmur of quiet conversation started up again when Phoebe abruptly stopped her attempt. Flushing, she stared at the food on her plate. Under the gimlet gaze of his grandmother, Leo could not cover her hand with his. Her Grace would consider such behavior gauche and be more likely to blame Phoebe than himself. So he asked her if she needed more food, reaching for the creamed carrots, which he knew she liked.

She shook her head. "I am c-content," she mumbled, her voice so low he could barely hear her.

The impulse to spirit her off grew stronger, as did the desire to protect her. But knowing Phoebe as he did now, he was aware that she would not thank him for it. He should give her a little time.

Phoebe lifted her chin when the duchess addressed her, and met her hostess's eyes. "No, Your Grace, we have no need of three course, twelve remove dinners in the country, but my mother would dearly love to do so."

Not a quaver or a hesitation. Leo felt inordinately proud of her. She had rehearsed that answer in her mind, gone over it and ensured she could get it out.

That would appeal to his grandmother, who had bravely faced a lifetime of pain and coped. That was the word the best women gave to dealing with the deepest problems. They coped.

"Are we to have the felicity of meeting your parents soon?" the duchess asked sweetly.

"They will b-be arriving in London sh-shortly," Phoebe answered. Only Leo saw her breast move in a regular pattern as her heart beat hard enough to cause the slight quiver. "M-My sister, Lucinda, is to have her c-come-out. I have written to m-my mother." She closed her mouth with a snap but kept her smile.

Leo found the hesitation adorable, although he felt for Phoebe. His brief struggle with the same affliction had given him an understanding he might not otherwise have. But after his parents died and his grandmother informed him that he was the new duke, in default of anyone else, he had developed the halting way of speaking. Sheer determination had worked for him, but he was fully aware it did not work for everybody. He doubted Phoebe had any lack of determination.

"I see. They do not wish to celebrate your betrothal?"

"Of c-course they do. But L-Lucinda's visit has b-been planned for a time."

"Were you brought to London for your come-out?" The duchess's eyes were shrewd. Already she had worked out something Leo had taken longer to understand.

"N-No. M-My mother s-says I am the b-brains and L-Lucinda is the b-beauty. Men do not b-beat a p-path to the d-door of clever women."

Leo could hold back no longer. "I wonder who told you that? Believe me, it is a fallacy, which Miss Childers for one can attest is false."

His grandmother nodded. "Women who are expected to occupy a great position need women of intelligence to match them. Or to run the estate in their absence. Without that, great estates can fall, to the detriment of us all."

She was talking about his parents. Neither had been of more than average understanding, and neither had taken any interest in the dukedom except to spend what they could and gamble the rest away.

"I d-daresay. But I am not in a p-position…" Phoebe tailed off and shot an anxious glance at him.

He sensed the anger in her, or was it frustration? Whatever, it had worked to clear the stammer and leave her with that sweet hesitation.

Miss Childers added her mite. "Naturally Sir Frederick and his family will stay at Grosvenor Square. I wrote to inform them today. I rattle around that house like a dried pea if I have no guests." Placing her knife and fork neatly on her plate, she reached for her wineglass.

"Do you not have different ways in the City?" the duchess asked.

"I wouldn't know." Miss Childers took a delicate sip. "I do not live there. The house my father occupied has been given over to offices. The bank is expanding its interests, and we need the space. I prefer to live in Mayfair."

"Your husband will have a great deal to take on." The duchess shot Leo a pointed glance before returning her attention to Miss Childers. "Only a few men are capable of controlling a large bank, as well as running an estate and other investments."

"I do not intend to have a husband." Miss Childers, seemingly calm, repeated her assertion. "I have not met a man I can trust to care for my legacy. In any case, I have no desire to give up my interests."

"But one day you must," the dowager said, as calmly as Miss Childers.

The two women would not back down. Lazily Leo watched them. They were both far too controlled to make a scene. But while he admired Miss Childers's mettle, he did not have the same measure of interest in her as he had in her companion. Phoebe aroused him, tempted him beyond bearing sometimes. Around her he behaved like a reckless, lovesick swain. If he was known for anything, it was proper behavior and stiffness of manner, but Phoebe wouldn't believe that if he told her.

He couldn't work out why he was behaving in such a manner.

After a spirited but icily polite altercation, the duchess nodded and turned her attention back to Phoebe. "If this betrothal is to take, we must ensure you are seen in the right places, and in my company. I will take you to my mantua-maker's tomorrow; then we will attend Lady Porter's musicale on Thursday. Leomore will accompany us, naturally. When your parents arrive in town, we may entertain them."

He did not have the opportunity to speak to Phoebe privately until later in the evening, when he contrived to get her alone in the carriage on the way home from the ball. Miss Childers had given him a glare when he'd asked her permission, but reluctantly gave it, on condition they took the ten-minute journey directly. "I am an uncomfortable duenna, but if you create many opportunities like this, your marriage will have to happen, and fast."

Although a betrothed couple had some leeway, they were taking too much. Disturbingly, Leo didn't care. Once in the carriage, he dragged down the blinds and pulled her into his arms.

"You can't do that!" Phoebe gasped, but she could say nothing more because his mouth was on hers.

Only when he'd taken what he'd been longing for all evening and received her eager response did he draw back. "I can't?" Her responding delightful flush and smile almost enticed him to go in for more, but they did not have much time. "I ordered the crest on the doors covered, in case you had not noticed, and I sent the liveried footmen away. We have a driver and one attendant."

"Oh. But Grosvenor Square?"

"Miss Childers will be waiting. My sweet, I needed to speak to you." If he did not, he might lose his nerve. He, who had nerves of steel was concerned about her response. Lord, he was a prime catch, or so he'd been told repeatedly. Losing his address, he spoke hastily. "I would like you to consider making our false betrothal into something more long-lasting."

Her eyes widening, she swallowed. "You mean until the end of the year?"

"No. Longer."

But he couldn't say more.

"But we are only engaged until m-my name is c-cleared. Until we find the n-necklace."

"The search may take more time." Truly, she was a cozy armful. "I suspect La Coccinelle's necklace is the copy, not the real one. She refused to let me see it when I asked her."

Pursing her lips, she made a rude noise, but such a sweet, small version of it that he was forced to kiss her again.

When they parted, she spoke, but now her hand was spread over his heart and her hair distinctly tousled. "D-Did Lord Latimer t-take up with La Coccinelle to spite you?"

He frowned. "Why on earth would he do that?"

"You are admired and imitated. Did you know that g-gentlemen have taken a quite f-foolish interest in me? And it is only b-because you have done so."

That didn't sound good. "Then they must desist. You are mine."

"For now."

"Perhaps not. Think about it, Phoebe. We will talk more about this."

The carriage came to a halt, but her stunned gaze remained on his until the attendant opened the door and let down the stairs.

Chapter 10

He had not said that. Surely she had misheard. Leo had not explained his final words but hurried her out of the carriage to where Angela waited.

Phoebe lay in bed half the night staring at the canopy, wondering what on earth he meant. Not what her vivid imagination had told her, surely. But what else? Her mind completely engrossed by the possibilities, she forgot the information he had given her until the next day, when the maid drew the curtains with a rattle and a cheerful, "Good morning, ma'am! Your mother is below."

So soon?

Once she left her bedroom, Phoebe wouldn't have needed to be told her family had arrived. With a sinking sense of familiarity, she followed the cacophony down to the breakfast parlor. She loved her family, but their arrival must herald the end of her dalliance with her ducal suitor. Once he met them, he would understand why a connection between the two had to end.

Her quiet, civilized breakfasts with Angela were over. The servants had put extra leaves into the circular table, making it a long oval, and around it sat a group of people she was only too familiar with.

Her father got to his feet, and after a glare from him, so did her two brothers.

Phoebe didn't hesitate. She flung herself into his arms, and as they closed around her, she felt home.

"I declare!" her mother said, in the voice that could be heard over a hunting field of thirty riders and a set of hounds. "You do look fine, my dear!"

Phoebe extricated herself and embraced her mother, careful to do it when the lady was drawing a breath, because she could deafen a person close up. "I am delighted to see you all." Even Lucinda, who was pouting. But

Lucinda was convinced her best expression was a pout, so no conclusion could be drawn from that.

Phoebe took her seat next to an amused but rather stunned Angela. Although Angela had met her family before, she had not done so for a few years. Having her parents, her two brothers, and her younger sister around the same table could take some getting used to.

Her mother wore her usual dazzling palette, with a gown of emerald green and a butter-yellow petticoat. Very fine, and not one Phoebe had seen before. "Did you travel in that?" she asked.

"No, silly puss! We stopped overnight at the inn by St. Paul's and sent word we were here first thing."

Considering Phoebe hadn't got into the house until the early hours of the morning, she might have crossed her mother's messenger on the doorstep. Morning to her mother meant up with the birds. In London they went to bed with them singing outside the window.

"I am delighted to welcome you all," Angela said. "You must of course stay with us."

"Except for Freddie and Thomas." Lady North frowned at her sons. "They will remain at the inn. It's not proper for two unmarried men to stay under the same roof as a single young lady. And about this young man?" Phoebe's mother was never afraid to come to the point. "When are we meeting him?"

"I-I do not know. He is here f-frequently. He is s-sensible that he sh-should have spoken to you first."

Sir Frederick humphed. "We'll see about that. I assume he'll want to speak to me now."

Phoebe could not hide the truth from her family. "It happened s-so f-fast. Y-You know I wrote to you last week. It was when Lady Latimer's j-jewels were stolen at a b-ball, and she accused me of taking them."

"Good Lord! I know you didn't do that. If you wanted a new necklace, we would have bought you one." That was one reason Phoebe loved her mother. She believed her children without question. Even if her mother's attention was taken by her sister, the pretty one. Lucinda was her surprise baby her darling, and she had turned out to be a beautiful child, so naturally the baby had garnered all the attention.

"Not this necklace," Angela said firmly. She picked up her butter knife and grabbed the last fresh bread roll. Obviously, despite being an only child, she understood the necessity to take one's opportunities when they occurred. "This is an heirloom necklace, with a great diamond at its center. The jewel was supposed to have belonged to Queen Elizabeth."

"I daresay they can say that about any jewel. Who knows where it's been? But I take your point." Lady North picked up the teapot and helped herself to another cup. She could drink tea until it took root inside her. Already the footmen were coming in with more supplies of tea, bread, and everything else. They deposited their burdens and, at a glance from Angela, left the room, closing the door behind them.

While Phoebe went to the sideboard and helped herself to what she wanted, beating her brothers by a matter of seconds, Lady North listened to Angela's succinct but discreet account of the events that fateful night.

"So naturally the duke had to say he was betrothed to Phoebe," she concluded. "Otherwise Phoebe would have been in a great deal of trouble."

Lucinda, busy watching everyone else, shot her sister a sharp look. "You mean it's not real?"

"Oh, it's real," Phoebe answered her. "But it w-will not last. W-We agreed to wait until the end of the s-season and then allow it to slip away." She would not tell them about Leo's shocking volte-face and his decision to make their betrothal a real one, meaning leading to marriage. Once he met her family he would see how impossible the connection was. Phoebe loved her family, but she wasn't blind. Or deaf, for that matter.

"What's he like, this duke?" her father demanded. "Is he honorable?"

"Completely," Phoebe said stoutly. "It was k-kind of him to rescue me, but I have no hold on him."

However much she wanted to answer otherwise, her family deserved the truth. Her father would enjoin her brothers to keep their peace, and as for Lucinda—she had no reason to spread the news. Her family, county to the last inch, was not impressed by Leo's title. Perhaps the man would impress them. County and Country were at loggerheads, and had always been, Tory versus Whig, but sometimes the two intersected. She'd come to town with no expectations of furthering herself, and she could not afford to expect it now. The plunge back down to earth would be far too painful.

Lucinda had whined for days when her mother had decided to send Phoebe to London. "You think I can trust you out of my sight?" she'd said to her youngest child. "Phoebe will behave herself. She's a good girl."

Except Phoebe had not exactly behaved very well recently. When Leo kissed her, she kissed him right back. When he held her, she gloried in it. Took what she could get while she could get it. She was as bad as the flirtatious Lucinda, who regularly set the neighborhood on its ear with her coquettish behavior.

Worse, because she was engaging with a duke at the heart of society. People watched. The journals contained new gossip every day, and the print shops teemed with scurrilous cartoons. Sometimes about them. Phoebe had learned not to look. Lucinda would have adored the attention, probably sent a few things home, and definitely kept them.

The noise was comforting. Phoebe could lose herself in it, let the busy chatter go on over her head, and devote herself to her own thoughts. Until Lucinda broke into them, as usual. "You're wearing a new gown." It sounded like an accusation, and probably was.

"Yes." She glanced at Angela, who grimaced. "Someone ransacked my room. They destroyed most of my clothes."

"No doubt if they were not interrupted they would have continued in mine," Angela put in.

Phoebe glanced at her, halted in her narrative. Angela gave her a minute shake of her head.

She was right. Of course people knew of the incident, but they didn't want to spread any more rumors concerning the necklace. She hadn't told her family about the break-in, judging it better to tell them when they were together.

She'd have been forced to apply to her father for money, had Angela not provided extra pieces. And they were in the latest mode, since Angela's maid had fitted them to her. She'd kept the dashing riding habit, and Angela had insisted on buying her more clothes with the excuse that she could not allow a future duchess to go about in rags. Compensation for having her belongings destroyed in her house. Since Angela was deeply distressed about the incident, and she had money to spare, so she wouldn't deprive herself, Phoebe had allowed the purchase of half a dozen new gowns and petticoats. Of course, a dozen had arrived.

Lucinda eyed Phoebe with a jealous eye. "I must have gowns in the latest style, must I not, Mama?" She turned a particularly sweet smile to Angela. "Could you recommend us to a mantua-maker, ma'am?"

"I would advise you to purchase gowns that are half-made already, for speed," Angela said smoothly. She shook her ruffles back as she reached for the coffeepot. "I can certainly accompany you to several fine establishments. Then we may find a maid to alter them for you, and you will be ready for society in a trice."

Lucinda pouted so effectively that Angela promised to take them that very day. "But you are to ride out with the duke, are you not?" she asked Phoebe.

Not that Phoebe knew, though she took the excuse eagerly and made it her own. "Indeed, yes. I should go and change."

"And do not forget that the SSL meets this afternoon."

Indeed not. Phoebe loved those meetings, where she felt most at home. "Oh really?" Lucinda said. "What is that, pray?"

"Spinsters, widows, and other single ladies," Angela said. Phoebe enjoyed her sister's wince. "We have a literary society that meets at least once a week. We are discussing Niely's *Sermons on the Rock* at present. Would you like to join us?" Her voice couldn't have been sweeter.

Lucinda held up her hand. "Oh no, I think not. But thank you. I believe I will be too busy."

"You can't keep your betrothed waiting," her mother said. "That would never do. I'm sorry we'll be away from home when he calls, but we will meet him soon, will we not?"

The very thought of that meeting brought bile to Phoebe's throat. How could she introduce them? Especially now she'd told them the truth about their connection. She had to tell him, before he found out for himself. Although she loved her family, she knew how they affected other people. The meeting could well bring her betrothal to a premature conclusion, and she found she disliked that notion intensely.

* * * *

The afternoon's meeting had brought no developments in the search for the jewels, but the ladies were extremely interested to hear the news about La Coccinelle.

Phoebe dressed with care, in a bronze-colored gown in heavy taffeta, decorated with pinked ruffles and with a matching petticoat. Clasping her modest pearls around her neck, she thought of the pearl pin still in her possession and opened the drawer containing the small box. Opening it, she ran her thumb over the smooth surface of the pearly globe and let herself dream.

Then the door opened, and Lucinda strode in. Lucinda never knocked. "My, you are fine, Phoebe. You've even powdered."

Phoebe touched her hand to her hair as she closed the drawer. "Sometimes I do."

Lucinda had also dressed with care, in a turquoise gown that outshone the candles set in the sconces, with a blindingly white petticoat heavily embroidered with violets and daffodils. Society might see her differently, but Lucinda was not the only person addicted to bright colors. She would find her place. She always did, and it would not be with the overlooked women at the edges of the dance floor and the back of the supper room.

"You never did before." Hands on hips, Lucinda glared at her. "You've grown very grand in a whole month. How did you catch him, anyway?"

Phoebe chose not to answer her sister's impertinent question.

A smile spread over Lucinda's face. "Oh, I see. That story about the jewels. Very clever. You have him running around town on your behalf. What will he do when he discovers it's all made up? You always did have a vivid imagination. Making up stories about me when I was little. Do you remember?"

"I n-n-n-n-never did."

Phoebe clamped her mouth shut. She would not embarrass herself by stammering her way through an argument. Lucinda was perfectly capable of sneering and deriding her. She was, after all, only eighteen, a foolish age of overconfidence and lack of consideration. At least it was in Lucinda's case.

All she could do was stand mute and listen to Lucinda's torrent of words, not all of which made sense.

As she did, she descended into her morass of despair. She could not force herself out of the pit, and if she opened her mouth now she would only embarrass herself and make everything infinitely worse. Putting up her chin, she ignored her sister's chatter as she prepared to go downstairs, ready for the ball they were to attend that evening.

"Mama says Lady Latimer is a gracious countess. She met her once, she said, and she wouldn't have believed she had made such accusations. The lady must have been distraught. Mark my words, when Mama speaks to her, she will understand. She has an eligible son, or so Mama says. I could charm him into persuading his mother not to persecute you. She is still accusing you all over London, you know. It is only your connection with the Duke of Leomore that is stopping her making it worse. Mama says you are very clever to have caught a duke, and she is sure I can do the same."

She picked up a comb from Phoebe's dressing table and curled a ringlet around it, posing in several fetching attitudes. Dropping the comb, she found Phoebe's fan and used that instead, peering at herself over the top in a coquettish manner a woman might use, but a girl fresh out of the schoolroom should not. "I think I can easily get myself a duke, don't you? After all, if you can do it, I will do it in half the time! And none of it is real, so I could even take your duke off your hands! You don't want a duke, Phoebe. You'd never be able to cope with what is expected of you. I've been studying the subject for years. Much better than French or the stupid globes."

If Phoebe could trust herself to speak, she'd have pointed out that most duchesses were expected to have a certain degree of intelligence and education. But a familiar tightness of her throat warned her against it.

Leo had sent her the fan earlier that evening, a pretty trinket she'd planned to take with her.

Unfortunately, Lucinda was posing with the pretty affair of ivory sticks and painted parchment. Delicate too. The way Lucinda was handling it would shorten its life considerably. But if her sister realized Phoebe wanted that fan, she would not relinquish it.

So she dug in a drawer for another and found a lace and bamboo one that would serve. Unfortunately, Lucinda retained the fan as if she had forgotten she was holding it. Which was far from true. She had purloined many of Phoebe's possessions and claimed them for her own. Phoebe usually took them back when her sister had tired of them. Tonight she would not. Snatching the fan from her sister's grip, she gave her the other one instead. Lucinda squeaked in alarm, but Phoebe took no notice, leaving the room and heading downstairs, gratified at the disdainful swish of taffeta. She didn't have to speak to make a point in this gown.

She got by on mutters and low-toned murmurs, giving herself time before she tried a full sentence. But the family spoke enough for her. They crammed into the carriage usually occupied by just Phoebe and her hostess, although when the men saw the four women filling the vehicle with their skirts, they backed off and said they would walk and wait outside.

"It cannot be but twenty minutes," Angela said.

"If they arrive at all," her mother put in. "There must be clubs and inns on the way."

Phoebe groaned. Of course there were. Perhaps Angela should send a footman with them, but what could he do? He'd probably end up as one of the party of men on the town. A London footman would know the places to go.

As it was, the ladies had misjudged the gentlemen. When the carriage rolled around the corner of Sycamore Street, there they were, waiting outside the house. The shiny black doors were flung open, and two footmen in maroon and white, with silver trim, stood haughtily either side of the door. The people they knew went straight through—others had to produce invitations.

Angela ensured the Norths got inside. The boys gave one another brief grins before Freddie quickened his pace and gave Phoebe his arm. "Got to escort my favorite sister," he murmured, and shot Phoebe a knowing smile. "Proud of you, my girl. Very proud. Papa says we shouldn't tangle with the nobs, but I don't take no notice of that. People are people, aren't they?"

"And all men like a g-good b-b-boxing match or c-c-cock fight," Phoebe managed.

Unlike her mother, who didn't have the patience to hear her out, or Lucinda, who spoke straight over her, Frederick tended to wait for her to finish, which sometimes helped, and sometimes did not.

Tonight it helped her regain her voice.

Freddie's eyes brightened. "Indeed you're right, and most likely I'll find someone who knows exactly where I should go."

They climbed the stairs at a stately pace. The walls were festooned with portraits of ancestors, mostly from the Cavalier era, when the family had supported the Crown. And suffered for it, by all accounts. This house was witness to the seesawing fortunes of the family that owned it. Her own had been solid country gentry for hundreds of years, never deviating from the straight course from birth to death. "I'm sure they will," she assured her brother, patting his arm.

Entering the ballroom with her family came as a new experience to Phoebe. Now society would be able to place them. Their good but plain clothes, the slightly outmoded fashions, and their confident demeanor marked them out for what they were. Pure county, salt of the earth, the backbone of England, her father would say, and no doubt repeat in the course of this evening. But she belonged with these people, and she felt at home with them.

Phoebe watched as her two worlds collided. Angela definitely belonged to the upper echelons, so that left Phoebe effectively in the middle.

She would have made her way to the ladies in the corner, but someone else was approaching.

Leo bowed, and Freddie acquitted himself creditably as Phoebe performed the introductions. "You will forgive me if I escort Miss North for the next dance," Leo said smoothly, and Freddie gave way, grinning.

"Gladly," he said.

"P-people are w-watching," she murmured, trying hard not to clutch Leo's sleeve.

"They always do." He glanced down at her, smiling warmly. "It is good to see you, my dear. And now for our first minuet."

Perhaps their last. But she had to take her pleasures while she could. Soon she would go home with her family. She doubted that Leo would follow her there. Phoebe, who had always been good at facing reality, found the task difficult tonight. Because she wanted what she could not have, what she had allowed herself to dream about for a few weeks.

But she had this minuet.

The dance brought courtship to life. Unlike the country dances, the partners remained with each other throughout, and the bows and curtseys conveyed elegant regard. At the very least. But the way Leo's gaze burned into hers, everyone who cared to look could tell more than that was happening here. He was making his desire for her blatant.

She could not respond, should not, but when his fingers touched hers, she shivered with awareness, only suppressing it with an effort. What had begun as a convenient lie was fast turning into reality. At least, it was for Phoebe. She gazed into his eyes, turning her head at the last moment, as the dance demanded, but she meant every coquettish gesture.

And people were watching. Flushed with heat, and not because of a consequence of a hundred people and as many candles crammed into this space, she lost awareness of the world around them and watched Leo, only Leo.

And yet, this had to come to an end.

All through the dance, he held a slight smile in place—warm for her, colder when he gazed out at the crowd watching and the other dancers. She'd have to ask him how he did that. Not a muscle twitched as his expression changed, but the transformation emphasized his regard for her. Or his seeming regard. She could not afford to take him too seriously. Or he'd break her heart. His recent hints that he would like the betrothal to last a while longer was nothing serious, she was sure of it.

When the minuet came to an end, he was bowing over her hand, and she dipped into a deep curtsey. She rose without a wobble, but that was partly because however flimsy his hold might appear, it was anything but slight. He held her steady while she rose, and his smile broadened. "My lady, you put others to shame," he murmured so that nobody else could hear.

Despite her determination to keep her head, pleasure swept over Phoebe. "I only know the steps. I'm not at all graceful."

She flicked out her fan, and he followed her movements, noting his gift to her. "I'm glad my poor offering finds favor with you."

That made her laugh. "Pooh, I d-don't have another so grand. I would be foolish if I didn't make use of it." But she spoiled her gentle teasing by adding, "Indeed I l-like it very much."

"Then I am learning your tastes. I am glad of that." He led her to the edge of the dance floor. "Now I should make the acquaintance of your parents."

All Phoebe's awkwardness returned in full measure. "I-I, yes, of c-c-course."

A small crease appeared between her brows as he paused and turned to face her, still retaining her hand. "Now what have I said to discommode you? It would be an honor to meet your parents. You must know that, Phoebe."

No, she didn't. "We're only provincials."

"And I have no idea what you mean by that. You are Phoebe, that is all. We are never provincials, my dear. It's just a word, it means nothing."

"But it d-does. You're a Whig, Papa is T-Tory. He is a m-magistrate at home, and you sit in the House of Lords. He rides to hounds as often as he can, and you attend a fencing s-studio. He's a c-country squire. You are not."

His eyes twinkled, and he smiled. "I have been known to hunt. And I live in the country too." He glanced around, and his gaze halted. Right at where her family stood. Freddie had gone, probably to scout out what was happening, but miraculously her younger brother Tom still stood there. Oh no, not miraculous. Lucinda was clutching his arm, probably holding him in a death grip until she had the ballroom in the palm of her hand.

Although Lucinda had undergone a spectacular come-out at home and was now the toast of the neighborhood, she had far stiffer competition here in London. But Phoebe wouldn't put it past her to try. As long as she didn't flirt. *Dear God, no, not the flirting.*

"Goodness," Leo murmured, or she thought he did, although he might have used a stronger expletive.

Phoebe's family was a stunning sight. None of them believed in becoming shrinking violets. They nailed their colors to the mast in no uncertain manner. Phoebe's sister's regalia rivaled but did not exceed her mother's dazzling green creation. At home their dressmaker indulged them, and they had set a fashion. Where Phoebe preferred subtler colors and a judicious amount of ruffles and furbelows, her mother and sister wondered, Why have one ruffle when you could have two? Or three?

Fortunately her mother had the figure to command such magnificence. Phoebe did not.

Leo did not so much as twitch a muscle by his mouth as he bowed over Lady North's hand, and then Lucinda's. Lucinda flourished her fan and peered at him over the top of it. Lady North declared herself delighted to meet him. "Miss Childers will no doubt ask you to dinner one night, and I can't wait to find out all about you. My husband wishes to discuss portions with you." She wrinkled her nose. "Tedious stuff, but let me tell you, Your Grace, we are more than ready for the discussion."

"I must insist that you dine with my grandmother and myself," Leo said without a qualm. "She will be delighted to meet you. Her health does not permit her to attend as many functions as she would like, but I am sure she will want to meet you."

"Why, that's very kind of you," her mother answered, her smile broadening. "I am sure we'd love to meet her. Are your parents out of town?"

"They are no longer on this earth," he said gravely.

Leo carried the question off with aplomb, particularly considering his parents' reputations. Phoebe had been in London long enough to understand that people never referred to his parents in his presence.

Lucinda nudged her mother, and Phoebe wanted to sink into the ground. Nudging? Lord, what next? Poking?

No, what followed was Lucinda's sharp trill of a laugh. "Really, Mama! I have read their stories to you this age! The duke was brought up by his grandmother after his parents died."

"Oh yes, of course." Phoebe's mother tended to retain what she needed and let the rest slip. So she hadn't considered the story of Leo's upbringing particularly relevant or interesting. "Silly me, I forgot. Your grandmother did not marry again?"

Beside her, Phoebe's father snorted. "Will you remarry when I'm in the earth?" Another snort, as if he'd said something funny. "I'd reach out of the grave to stop you."

Her mother laughed uproariously. Not something society appreciated. Glancing around, she saw people turning away, and her soul shrank inside her.

Phoebe had a terror of standing out, of being seen as different, not a sentiment she shared with her family. People did not bellow with laughter in a society ballroom.

Leo took everything in his stride until Lucinda opened her mouth. "Phoebe only came to London as a duenna, but look at her now! Cousin Angela has been so kind to her. I declare, once her regular companion was back, we thought Phoebe would come home, but instead we came to her."

Ignoring Leo's frozen silence, Lucinda deployed her fan, flicking it out prettily and wafting it before her face. "We are enjoying ourselves vastly, sir, Your Grace." Lowering her lashes, she paused before flicking them up and gazing into his eyes, her expression of eager desire unmistakable. The flirting was too bold, too blatant for a young girl not yet twenty. A maiden without a sure footing in society would do better to behave more circumspectly. The problem was, having Lucinda as a sister would draw unwanted attention to Phoebe, and by association, Leo. She'd be lucky if he didn't cut the connection there and then.

Phoebe flinched.

But Lucinda was not yet finished. "And this is the most beautiful house, truly. I daresay London is full of them, but I only made my come-out last year, so I have not seen many of them. Would you show me your house one day, Duke?"

That was going too far.

Phoebe had heard of society masks, but she had never seen one as effective as the one Leo donned now. His face gained a stillness, and his eyes fixed in cool orbs, holding Lucinda in a ray of chilly attention. "It would be for my grandmother to invite you. Since you are the sister of my betrothed, I daresay you will be invited." The implication—that left to him, she would not see his house—remained hanging in the air.

Phoebe's mother drew a sharp breath and, before Lucinda could reply, asked him a question. "Your main seat is in Derbyshire, is it not, sir?"

His smile thawed a fraction as he turned to her. "Yes, it is. But I own other properties, and I do not like to ignore any of them."

"That makes me glad we only have one," her father said, and led Leo into a discussion about houses and their upkeep which was totally innocuous.

Phoebe stood there, mortified, unable to think of anything to say. When Leo turned to her and asked her if she was hungry, she kept her gaze downcast and spoke before she thought. "I-I-I c-c-c-could n-n-n-n-n-n-n-n…"

She was stuck. She only stopped when he lifted his hand and touched her lips, very gently. "Let's go to the supper room. I'm sure we can find something to tempt you."

After bowing to her parents and brother, he led her away. Tears pricked her eyes.

She tried to pull away, but he clamped her forearm to his side. "P-p-p-p-please, l-l-l-l-let me go." She wanted to find a dark corner to hide in until this nightmare had ended. What was she thinking of, dreaming that this man would even consider being her husband? He'd been a gentleman, that was all, helped her out of an awkward situation. She was doomed to marry Sir Marcus Callow, or stay a spinster. She was foolish to think of anything else.

Once she was through this evening, she'd sit down and think how she could escape.

"I don't recall getting a letter from you today," he said softly.

Whipping her head around, she stared up at him, meeting his amused gaze. "I didn't have time."

They stared at each other. "You see, you are fine. Now what put you in a pet? By the way, I won't hold you to a letter every day, though I have to admit that I've been looking forward to them."

"When we s-separate we c-can still write, can't we?" It was magic. She was talking to him like any ordinary person.

"What's this about separation?" Leading her to a corner of the busy room, he took her hands and turned her to face him. "What brought that on?"

"My p-parents. Or not them exactly. Lucinda, perhaps. I d-do have a suitor at home, and she reminded me of him."

"I see. Was anything said between you and this suitor?"

He meant promises. She shook her head. Marcus worried her, and he was far too overbearing for her liking. "I never promised him anything."

"In that case, he is irrelevant. You are betrothed to me." He tucked her arm under his once more and strolled to the long table at the end, where a number of dishes were being uncovered. "Do you like oyster patties?"

His smile didn't invite argument, but now she'd found her voice again Phoebe wasn't about to settle down. "I c-cannot imagine why you are s-saying these things. You know what we d-discussed. And now you have m-met my p-p-parents, you know how impossible this is."

He kept his society smile in place. "Eat, drink, and I will take you back to your estimable parents."

And just like that, Phoebe wanted to die.

As they were about to sit at a small table, he said, musingly, "I cannot wait for my grandmother to meet your parents."

Chapter 11

Phoebe's days of quiet enjoyment with Angela had gone. Since her involvement with Leo, society took notice of her, and now it appeared more people would be watching her. This morning's *Journal of London Life* had contained a poorly disguised account of her recent public appearances with Leo, or rather, the other way around. They were concerned with Leo, not her. They accused him of making a fool of himself with a provincial miss of no address or particular beauty, and drew cruel pictures of them all, depicting her parents as country bumpkins and Phoebe as a schemer, gazing up at Leo with a sly smile. She had thought she could accept such attention, but she was wrong. They were hurtful, unkind, thoughtless, and she wanted none of it. And yet she kept reading them and studying the prints when Angela wasn't fast enough to destroy them.

Journal in hand, she wandered through the hall, preparing to go upstairs to freshen her appearance, preparatory to a visit to a dressmaker with her mother, Lucinda, and Angela.

Her thoughts froze as she looked up.

"Just look who's here, Phoebe!" her mother cried brightly.

Standing in the hall, staring at her with a smile wreathing his handsome face, was the reason she'd begged her mother to come to London. Sir Marcus Callow. The son of friends of her parents, he had assumed she would be there for him when he had finished sowing his wild oats, which he did with little regard to discretion. His one attempt at courtship was so forceful, so distasteful that she had avoided him ever since. But she had not told anyone about it.

Marcus didn't ask, he assumed, and when Phoebe's throat locked up, which it did around him, she found him completely overwhelming.

Marcus's square-jawed, beetle-browed face swam into her vision. She blinked. He was still there. "Sir M-Marcus," she managed.

The broad smile was so familiar. "Oh, don't do that, Phoebe, nothing so formal. Marcus is fine."

Before she could stop him, he embraced her, a hug that temporarily knocked the breath out of her body. "Now where is this upstart duke? I'll teach him a thing or two!"

Phoebe shuddered. "I'd r-rather you d-d-did not."

As usual, Marcus rolled straight over her objections. "Nonsense! Your champion is here."

Her mother strolled into the hall. "Ah, I see you have arrived, Marcus. Do not forget that Phoebe is betrothed to the duke."

For once her tone was frosty. She liked Marcus and viewed him as an excellent match for Phoebe, who had, before she left for London, begun to accept the inevitable. Before that kiss, and the realization that a lifetime of such treatment might well kill her. It was either that, or remain unwed, which was a fate no woman would actively pursue, unless she had the funds to live high on the hog. Like Angela.

Other men in her district with lesser prospects appealed to her more, but Marcus had scared them all away, standing before her like a sheepdog protecting his precious flock. But she wasn't a sheep or a lamb, and she'd have preferred to make her own choice. She would rather remain a spinster than marry him, but she might not have much choice.

She wouldn't surrender without a fight.

Filled with resolve, she stepped back. "I believe I'm expected in the club." When Angela nodded, she curtseyed and made good her escape.

The club room was situated in the west wing of the house. It had its own private entrance. Very useful for some of the members, who had demanding relatives and employers.

"Good morning." She chose a journal and took her place in an exceedingly comfortable chair with a sigh of contentment.

The ladies responded quietly, seven of them today. They all had keys, and they were invited to enter whenever they wished, just like a gentleman's club. The pins Angela had given them were displayed proudly on their person. Angela had thrust hers into the fabric of her bodice.

Angela had wanted to provide a refuge, but the SSL was turning into something else. Together with the regular newspapers were others, more specialist to help them fill their new self-appointed roles—parliamentary reports, accounts of trials and books on the law—most of which were tedious reading but necessary, if the ladies were to become effective in their chosen activity.

"I have some news," Miss Collinge, a tall lady, announced.

Half a dozen sets of curious eyes turned in her direction.

Miss Collinge cleared her throat. "Ahem. Well, I was talking to Lady Stuart's personal maid the other day—you know how she gossips. Well, maybe you don't."

Miss Collinge, the genteel daughter of respectable parents, worked as a governess. Betwixt and between, she referred to herself, but here in the club, they were all equal. It was one of Angela's few rules. "In any case, she told me that when her ladyship's best enamel watch went missing last year, a footman found it lying in the street and returned it for the substantial reward. But that had happened before, to the same watch. Her ladyship's suspicions aroused, she spoke most particularly to that footman. Not one of hers, you understand, but he belonged to an establishment further up the street. He denied anything, but the household was left with the strong suspicion that a group of the Stuart footmen were working with others. It is a slight possibility, but it is worth discussing, is it not?"

A murmur of agreement went up. Phoebe's recollection turned back to that night. A man in a cloak had knocked her off her feet. Had she seen the flash of livery braid? She had certainly seen something, and at the time she assumed the flash had been struck off the jewelry. Then the sting of pain from her cut had distracted her. Livery was flamboyant, its purpose to display the wealth of the family it belonged to. It often employed gold or silver braid.

"The m-man I saw who had Lady Latimer's j-jewelry was well-set and wearing a heavy c-cloak. The night was not c-cold, merely chilly, and the cloak far too thick for that weather. C-Could he have worn it to cover something up?"

"It's possible," Miss Hansen said slowly. "Ladies, I think we should look into this. A conspiracy of footmen? We know servants talk and mingle. That is why scandal spreads so fast in this city."

"But to go from servants g-gossiping to a p-planned conspiracy is a stretch," Phoebe pointed out. She found the theory a little far-fetched. Barely possible.

"We need to look into it." Miss Hansen reached for the law journal she'd been perusing. "It is not altogether impossible. That would explain why they could find no trace of the jewels. They vanished so quickly. Handed to another conspirator, who made away with them, or gave them to someone else. The thief could then return to duty, and people wouldn't associate him with the theft."

Damn, she was right. "Angela had the house s-searched, but obviously the j-jewels had disappeared." Phoebe recalled the fuss Lady Latimer had made. The woman was a nuisance, but since she had lost a family treasure, nobody could blame her for it.

However, Lady Latimer had continued to screech in the most public places that the harridan, Miss Phoebe North, had likely done away with the jewels before her paramour, the Duke of Leomore, had aided and abetted her. Why would she continue to do that? Why did she even believe that in the first place?

Miss Hansen rubbed her hands together. "I do believe we are finally getting somewhere," she said.

Once they had solved the mystery, Phoebe should be glad to have her name cleared. But she wasn't, because that would be the end of the strangest interlude of her life. And the best.

* * * *

If that damned girl hit him with her fan once more, he would not be responsible for his actions. Sitting next to Lucinda North had proved far more of a trial than even he had imagined. Leo braced himself for another strike. Her playful taps were a good deal more than that.

His grandmother had insisted he amuse the youngest girl that evening. Dinner had been enlivened by Phoebe's company, but somehow, mostly by pushing, her sister had taken Phoebe's place at the musicale his grandmother was holding. When the soprano sang, Lucinda giggled, as if the lady was making a great joke. Phoebe sat next to her sister, her erstwhile suitor on the other side.

Lucinda gave a light laugh as the singer came to the end of a poignant folk song. "Indeed, I would never stand for such treatment. I am no mewling miss. Mama says I will be a match for any man."

That was one way of putting it. For Phoebe's sake, he would put up with her family. He gave the girl a halfhearted smile. True, she was pretty, and with a little care could be beautiful, but her looks were nowhere near enough compensation for the irritating manner.

Leo prided himself on his evenhanded approach to all walks of life. Tonight tempted him back to the dark side. He could squash this girl with an attitude so superior she'd believe clouds hung around his neck. But he would not. For Phoebe's sake, he *would* desist.

To his relief the soprano began again, and Lucinda had to pause, but not for long. While people tended to chatter all through theater appearances, private performances demanded more polite attention. But Lucinda did not appear to notice the distinction. Nobody would tell her to be quiet—the guests were far too refined for that. But what he would give for a carefully aimed orange from the upper stories to hit her on her delicate nose. Anything.

Her voice grated on him. "I have had the most careful education in musical appreciation. I play the harpsichord, and I can sing. This lady performs most delightfully, does she not? My word, that was a high note!"

"Indeed," he said frostily, but either she did not notice his attitude, or she did not care.

The professional artist ended her performance and took her leave. Leo would send her flowers as an apology the next day, but of course, that might be misconstrued. Perhaps his grandmother would consent to put her name to the offering. The poor woman had valiantly struggled through Lucinda's chatter and the occasional snort from Tom North, whose choice of entertainment evidently did not include the opera.

Now the amateurs could show off their talents. Leo had no idea if Phoebe had a musical bent, but before he could ask, Lady Coniston took the platform and his heart sank. While he enjoyed her playing, she did tend to choose the longer pieces to demonstrate her skill on the keyboard. That meant he was stuck next to Lucinda even longer. He glanced at Phoebe, who sat stiffly, hands resting over her fan on her lap, staring straight ahead. As he watched, Callow leaned over and murmured something to her.

Claws of quite inexplicable envy pierced Leo. True, the man had pretensions toward Phoebe, but while he, Leomore, was in her life, he determined no other man should be. And yet, if she liked Callow, that would be the perfect excuse to end their engagement. She could jilt him to marry her childhood sweetheart.

From the way she held her body so rigidly, that solution would not be welcome to her. But Leo could be mistaken. Callow was a brawny, bold man, the kind ladies often flocked to. Was Phoebe one of them?

Her brothers were more amenable, despite Tom's lack of interest in the music. And while her mother was flamboyant, Leo had a grudging admiration for her. She knew who she was and where she belonged and was happy there. Similarly, when he had engaged her husband in a mild political debate over dinner, Sir Frederick had answered readily enough and with the sound understanding of a man who represented his part of the world.

But the older brother, known as Freddie, and the sister were beyond bearing. Freddie had tried to patronize Leo, kindly talking about the pleasures of hunting as if Leo had never heard of the sport, explaining the proper way to do it.

He should not judge, and he was trying very hard not to. But the way that man was engaging Phoebe in conversation made his blood boil, when he actually saw Phoebe recoil from him. What had the blackguard said? Perhaps he needed to invite him to a fencing match at the school he frequented. Or better still, call him out...

What on earth was he thinking? Just because Phoebe had moved away slightly, he wanted to maim a man? That was ridiculous.

Tonight had convinced him of a few things, but most of all that regretfully, he would have to draw back in his courtship of her. Not end it, even the thought made him shiver, but he must consider the original plan of letting it die. Or prolonging it for longer than he'd planned.

Her family would not fit into his world, and both sides would be unhappy. Phoebe clearly loved her family, and any division would distress her. That, despite Lucinda's vaunting ambition. If she found a partner during this visit, it wouldn't be in the echelons of society. One or two ramshackle dukes existed, the kind living off their uppers and not invited to the most influential functions. They might take an interest in the flashy Lucinda. The girl was eighteen and not yet settled into herself. But her vanity was deep-seated.

Even though personally, Phoebe drew him like a magnet. In her presence he wanted to kiss and touch, guard her like a dog ordered to protect his master's most precious possession. That was even more reason to make the break clean. Who in society was married to a woman they had fallen in love with? Hardly anyone. True, in some situations love had grown after marriage, but that was not what marriage was for. A purely business transaction, to benefit both families and foster closer ties. He should be looking at the Howard women, or perhaps the Manners ladies. Not the Norths.

But he was still looking.

More obviously, his grandmother would not be happy to be associated with the Norths, and he would not for anything make her unhappy. He owed her everything, from preserving and rebuilding the title and estate after his parents' deaths, to protecting and loving him. Without her love he would not have known what love was. He owed it to her to find a bride with a family she could be comfortable with. Sometimes a duke had to think of more than himself. More often than not, actually. Employees, duties, relatives—the list went on. Leo had never considered that part of his position painful before. That was a shock.

But then, every holder of a prestigious title had relatives they barely acknowledged. He could not, he must not, lose his head over a pretty face.

Usually he enjoyed musical evenings, but not this one, but at least the performances gave him time to consider his next move.

Striding down the stairs after the guests had left and his grandmother retired to bed, he wondered what Phoebe had that none of the other women in his life had even approached. Perhaps familiarity would breed, if not contempt, then boredom and satiation. That burning desire he felt for her would fade.

As he clapped his hat on his head and left the house, he let his memories roam, as he rarely did. They were too painful, for the most part, and his memories vague and patchy. One vivid memory haunted him, typical of many in his young life. Dressed in lace far too fine for a young boy, gossamer linen and light colors, held fondly by a beautiful woman who smelled of lavender and roses. His mother. Then she got to her feet, and he fell to the floor. She'd totally forgotten he was even there. Her words, "Take this away," held no affection, merely boredom, and referring to him as "this" had scored his heart.

The memory was typical of many scenes with his parents, but he remembered that one most of all.

He had not wanted for affection, but he could never trust the women who crowded around him. He grinned. Maybe he should have gone away somewhere and passed as simple Mr. Cavendish, his family name, to see if he could attract a woman on his own. The nearest was Phoebe. Perhaps that was her secret, she gave the impression she didn't care for his position or his riches. Women had done that before, of course, and for the most part he'd seen right through them, but Phoebe—she was honest and true.

All the more reason for him not to hurt her by putting a burden on her shoulders that she might not be able to sustain. She was a sensitive soul, and her stutter grew worse when stressed. He would have to put her under a lot of that, and she'd have to accustom herself to meeting strangers on a regular basis.

Despite his doubts, Leo had a vision of Phoebe greeting his guests at his London home, discussing political affairs or the latest literary sensation, and after they had gone, joining him in bed. Where they would share a passion only they would know about.

He could almost taste her most intimate flavors, hear her cries of fulfillment.

Even walking through this quiet London street, his body stirred. And wasn't that why he was reluctant to let her go? He wanted Phoebe with a wild passion that made no sense but didn't abate. Their kisses and caresses only served to stoke the flames of his desire, but he could not stop it. He could not take her without marrying her. She was a lady, so he had only one recourse to her. But she had never held that prospect before his nose, as other women had. "Marry me and you can have all of me." That wasn't her way. Despite her modest appearance, she had an excellent understanding—their letters were testament to that.

No, it could not be. But first he would resolve the matter of the necklace.

Tonight he would trawl the worst of the hells, the places he avoided where his contemporaries went for a thrill, a glimpse of the sordid side their lives rarely afforded them. If the necklace was sold, it would be in those places. He couldn't enter the rookeries of Seven Dials and St. Giles without being murdered for his purse, but he'd get as close as he could. The shacks propping up the piazza in Covent Garden, the gaming hells in crumbling cellars, the brothels. Even the notion made him shudder, but as long as he had guineas to spare, they'd welcome him there.

That attempted theft at Miss Childers's house had given him a clue. Before that, he was convinced the necklace was long gone, broken up and sold on, but if someone thought Phoebe had it, that meant *they didn't.* It had been mislaid, or lost, or stolen from the thieves. They might believe that Phoebe had indeed snatched the necklace from the thief.

But if they did not have it, who did?

He turned a corner into the Strand. Sticking his hands in his pockets, he set his course for Covent Garden.

The diamonds still existed. They could be found. Leo would not share his supposition because he had no proof, only a slim chance that they did. If he could trace them before the hue and cry went up, he would purchase them, whatever the cost, and return them to her infuriating ladyship.

It was worth trying. And he was spoiling for a fight. He didn't want to give up. The male in him, descended from the savages who had slashed and burned their way to power, wanted Phoebe, roared for her, but the rational aristocrat told him something completely different.

But if he found the necklace, he could clear her name. Then they would be free to make their own future. Phoebe would not be compelled to do anything she did not want. And he could walk away, knowing he'd done his best for her.

He could not consider the prospect of a real marriage between himself and the luscious Phoebe. He would not be treating her fairly if he expected it.

So why was he still thinking of it?

Chapter 12

Preparing to enter the carriage on their way to yet another ball, Phoebe couldn't believe the idea did not fill her with thrilled excitement. But apart from the prospect of seeing Leo there, the notion held nothing for her.

On the other hand, her family was excited.

Angela had hired another carriage to supplement her own, so they were thankfully alone, at least on the journey. Her parents and Lucinda crammed into the new vehicle.

Phoebe spread the skirts of her sky-blue gown, letting her hands linger over the flowers embroidered in raised work on the robings and flounces. They were done so well they almost appeared real. She loved it, but this time she had to pose a question. "You must render the cost of at least some of my new gowns to my father."

"I wouldn't dream of it."

"But Angela—"

Angela held up her hand, the sapphire adorning the middle finger flashing in the dim twilight. "No. Consider it a wedding present, if you must. If you are to become a duchess, then you will have to expand your wardrobe, and I will enjoy helping you do it." A teasing smile quirked the corner of her mouth. "Unless you mean to cut me, of course."

The carriage jolted around a corner, and Phoebe grabbed the door handle to keep her balance. "Why on earth would I c-cut the richest woman in England?" she asked, teasing in her turn.

"Many people do." Angela glanced out of the window. "Lord, we're nearly there."

The way she cut eye contact told Phoebe her remark went deeper than her light tone would suggest. "Who did that?"

"Nobody important." Angela sighed when Phoebe kept her gaze sternly fixed on her. "Very well. The Latimers. Since that incident with the necklace, she is making life more difficult for all of us."

The news infuriated Phoebe. Her fist clenched on the fine material under her hand. "How dare she!"

"She is commenting on your people. No wonder you stole the necklace since you come from such a vulgar family."

Angela turned back to Phoebe, her gaze fulminating. "She forgets it is my family too. We will find that blasted necklace and the earrings she is whining about and announce the fact publicly. I am determined to do it. Either that or pay her the value. But she is claiming the compensation from an insurance company, and I cannot interfere with that. My name would be mud in the City." A small smile curved her fine-cut lips. "She has forgotten something else, too. I own a bank. We are running a few checks on her and her husband."

"Angela!"

Her cousin dismissed Phoebe's concern with a wave of her hand. "Oh, we do so on all our customers from time to time. This is not out of the ordinary."

That was how people got a reputation for being superior. Apart from actually being superior, that was.

The confidence had buoyed Phoebe's spirits and encouraged her in her friendship. But she refused to accept anything further. "I don't belong here," she said. "I will be b-back soon in my rightful place." Leo wouldn't want her now, not after he'd seen her family. She would give him his freedom whenever he asked for it. Perhaps before that.

"And will you then marry Sir Marcus Callow, as your family expects?"

Phoebe repressed a shudder. "I cannot like him. For all that he behaves like a gentleman. Just not the kind of gentleman I like." He had demanded kisses in the past, but when she drew back, he had laughed and told her she would welcome them in time. He had taken a few anyway, and she was right. She found his embraces unpleasant.

When Leo kissed her she melted into him, and he was not gentle either. He held her as if she was precious but ravaged her mouth. And she ravaged him right back.

When she went to sleep at night, she'd pretend he was with her, lying just out of reach, so that she could touch him any time she wanted. She still stuck his pearl pin into her pillow sometimes, too. The notion gave her comfort, and she slept far better than usual. She would keep that secret close to her chest. Nobody would discover her dreams, least of all the man who had inspired them. She knew how pathetic her little fantasies were. While she could, she'd enjoy what she had. Give herself memories she could fall back on when life became too tedious.

By the time they reached their destination the sky had dimmed, the velvet thickness wrapping around her like a blanket. A footman helped her down, avoiding her gaze, but unlike Angela or Leo, she always noticed them. At home they lived closer with their servants and knew them by name, instead of referring to them by a generic "James" or "Jane." She thanked him by name.

Home seemed so far, although it was in reality a mere day away. Her cozy, comfortable life in a place where everyone knew everybody else, where she didn't have to introduce herself or suffer strangers staring at her, seemed so different to this. People watched her, talked about her, published her name in journals and print shops. They took notice of her.

But not for long. If she was to accept reality, that meant Marcus or spinsterhood. She would do well not to forget that. She constantly reminded herself, in an effort to keep her feet firmly planted on the ground.

By now she knew how to make an entrance. As her family climbed down from their carriage, she held back just long enough to allow Angela to lead the way, then lifted her skirts the bare inch she needed, climbed the stairs and swept inside without stopping. The footmen stationed at the door stepped back to let her through.

Her family had the invitations they needed to get in, and they had to show them.

London houses in Mayfair had very similar layouts. The serried rows of white stuccoed town houses, made to look like one great mansion, had replaced the palaces and mansions over the last fifty years. Owners of those great houses had, for the most part, moved the treasures to the country and either sold the property or had the house demolished, and a square of houses put in their stead, which provided useful unentailed income. The smaller, elegant buildings were all most families needed for the three months or so they spent in London every year. And Lord knew they were still spacious enough.

They had a layout she could probably navigate without having set foot in them before because they were so similar. Upstairs they would find the reception rooms, the largest room set aside for dancing, and the others for card playing, refreshments, and general gossip. There might be a terrace, the gardens built up so the guests only needed to go down a short flight of stairs to outside. Sometimes she wasn't even sure whose house she was in until she saw their hostess at the top of the stairs.

Next to Lady Comyn stood one of her daughters. Her ladyship was blessed with what seemed like a plethora of daughters, but Phoebe had made the acquaintance of this one, and they got on well. She had visited the SSL, although she was not in possession of the precious silver pin.

A shock went through her. She was beginning to belong here. She could walk into a ball without showing her card, knew enough members of society to be comfortable, and nobody raised eyebrows when they saw her. Goodness, who would have thought it? She'd been in town for six weeks now, and already she had found a niche.

When she left, the space she occupied would disappear with few people missing her. Would Leo? Would he want to write to her when their betrothal was at an end? He said so, but he had the most exquisite manners she could not be entirely sure he meant it when he said he wanted her to write. She so enjoyed getting his letters. Writing to a gentleman was allowed, under the rules of gentility, so she could continue to do so. But he might not have time. Or he might lose interest in her.

Her mother's voice floated up the stairs, stridently declaring this house was very beautiful, and she would take note of the flooring in the hall when she got home. "You can probably hear that woman's voice across a forest," their hostess muttered.

Phoebe made her curtsey. "Why yes, you can," she said brightly. "But my m-mother is well aware of it. I b-believe she has met others who enjoy hunting."

Lady Comyn flushed, but Phoebe chose not to see it. "Ah, Miss North. Of course, she's your mama, isn't she? Her presence has livened several affairs recently. We will no doubt miss her next year."

When the Thames flowed on and would continue to do so.

The air stirred, and she turned her head to see Leo approaching her. His smile warmed her, and her confidence built. "Your Grace." She swept into a curtsey, but he caught her elbows and gently raised her up.

"My dear, I'm delighted you arrived in good time." He nodded to Angela. "Miss Childers, well met. I believe Col is here somewhere. The last I saw of him, he was heading for the card room."

"Indeed, I have no interest in knowing where the Duke of Colston Magna might be," Angela declared, but her color was up, her lightly powdered cheeks clearly revealing her blush. "I shall ask Phoebe's brother Tom to escort me to the main room."

"I would be delighted, ma'am," said Tom, who knew his manners.

Smoothly, Leo caught Phoebe's hand, brought it to his lips, and then placed it on his maroon velvet-clad arm. Automatically, she curled her fingers into the soft, silky material. "You look wonderful," he said softly.

"Thank you." She would be in possession of a collection of gowns too magnificent to wear once she got back to Buckinghamshire. Most of her female acquaintances would suspect her of having high-and-mighty airs. And they wouldn't be shy about saying so.

For now she could enjoy her grand clothes and the way some members of society accepted her presence. That was balm to her soul, especially since nobody felt that way at home. The rivalries were closer and more personal. Society in London was larger and had room for more people to move in and out. Phoebe liked that.

"I want to take you somewhere quiet and kiss you," Leo murmured. "Very much. In fact, I doubt I will resist."

"But you can't."

He turned to her, a broad smile wreathing his face. "Is that a challenge?"

"No!" Or he would find somewhere. "But I know how you feel," she admitted, color rising under her cheeks.

He groaned low in his throat. "So you torment me. Come and dance. Then I will greet your parents and even dance with your sister, if she wishes it."

"Lucinda is very pretty. She will have admirers, so you had better ask her now." Although she didn't want to see her sister with her betrothed. Sometimes she forgot he was a duke. He was just Leo now, and she had to recall his exalted rank. That was not the first thing she thought when she saw him.

That fantasy sometimes closed in on reality, and tonight it certainly did so. Hastily, she put her mind to something else. "If we could walk instead of dancing, I have a little news for you."

"Hmm." As he led her into the large salon where a quartet played, he glanced at the dance floor, and then nodded. "Very well. Although I might ask you to accompany me into the garden later." He sighed. "Unfortunately, her ladyship's garden is not as spacious as one would wish, and it has a severe paucity of neglected grottoes."

Recalling the night they met she smiled, even though that was also the night her reputation was tarnished. They walked, and although they bowed to people who acknowledged them, Leo led her firmly on.

"Tell me. Then we can dance. It's either dance or disappear," he said.

"People would n-notice, Leo."

"I do not care, especially when you say my name in that breathy tone. I want to feel that breath on my face and have your lips under mine."

He was in a flirtatious mood tonight. Much more difficult to cope with. Glancing at him, she swallowed. She loved to feel the soft, silky strands of his hair between her fingers. If he kissed her, she could indulge.

No. She must speak to him of other things, not allow him to distract her. "The SSL met yesterday. We discussed the necklace, of course."

"Do your mother or sister attend?" he asked sharply.

She started at his harsh change of tone. "No. They believe we are a literary discussion group. Neither my mother nor my sister read a great deal."

His short laugh showed her his reaction. "Then discuss away."

Phoebe frowned and tapped his arm with her fan in mild reproof. "They are my family, whom I love."

"There is love, and there is blind love," he said. "I love my grandmother, but I am sensible of her faults."

Phoebe felt suitably chastised, but she would still have spoken up. She would not have her family discussed with any lack of respect. "Indeed." She had to admit his point. But that would not stop her loyalty. "We spoke of the jewelry today. Some ladies think there is a conspiracy of footmen."

He swept two glasses of wine from a tray carried by one of the people she was talking about. He handed her a glass of the ruby liquid, and she accepted it with a smile. "That sounds dramatic."

"It does, doesn't it? But they must wish for the opposite, to keep this very quiet. We know that servants spread gossip better than anything else. This seems to be a more organized version, passing stolen goods rather than chatter. So items will be purloined and immediately passed to another person in the chain, and to another. Then someone completely unconnected with the first person will sell the treasures, and the money is divided."

Twin creases appeared between his dark brows. "I have suspected something such for years. How else could valuables disappear without a trace? However, to call it a conspiracy is surely taking the theory too far. Footmen carouse together, they spend their free time in each other's company. I have seen them in the coffee houses in the City, and the inns. But that is different to a deliberate plot. Are you sure of this?"

Phoebe had to shake her head. "It is as yet only a rumor. We have nothing to show for it, except a strong suspicion and a vague idea of who was involved. That night, when the n-necklace went missing, it was passed on."

At the end of the room, they did not stop, but passed through to the next, where people were sitting around card tables, their concentration intent on the pieces of pasteboard in their hands. Candles flickered as they set up a slight breeze when they passed by. A few people glanced up and nodded to Leo and Phoebe, nobody surprised at seeing them together. As if they belonged with each other.

Which, she told herself sternly, they did not. Or only temporarily. If she did not constantly remind herself of that hard fact, she would become carried away. And then she would crash to earth with a bump.

"But if that is true," he continued, covering her hand with his as if he had always done it, "the necklace is long gone."

"Not necessarily. They could be holding it until some other scandal sets society alight. Then it would be safer to get rid of it."

"I fear that any thief would set about breaking up such a treasure as soon as they got it." He spoke regretfully. "After they have disposed of the jewels, they will melt down the setting."

Alarm rose. "B-but if that is the c-c-case, we will n-n-never f-find it."

"I do not believe the necklace is gone."

"You do not?"

He shook his head. "If it is, why would someone still be searching for it? Why search your room? I saw that mess. Someone was methodically hunting for something, pulling out drawers to search behind, looking for hiding places. And they were careful not to make any undue sound."

At the end of the card room, she stopped and turned to face him, meeting his eyes directly. "But they cut up my c-clothes."

He nodded. "Looking for hidden pockets, or perhaps to make us think it was impulsive and mindless."

Not spite, then. Her spirits rose. "So there's a chance the n-necklace is still intact."

"And that we may find it and return it to Lady Latimer."

Goodness. She had quite given it up.

When he began to walk again, she had to go with him. He led her out of the card room, and they entered a corridor. There would be a place for quiet discussion here, perhaps a ladies' room.

"We will find it," he said. "Even if I have to have it remade myself."

"You can't do that!"

"Of course I can. I don't want you to worry, my sweet."

She loved the endearment, bathed in it. But showed nothing. "I have p-put you to far too m-much trouble already. How can I ask that of you? I can never repay you for replacing that necklace." She continued talking before he could interrupt her. "I forbid it. That is all. You will *not* replace the necklace. If it has d-d-d-disap-p-peared, what of that? I w-w-w-will g-g-g-go home soon, and…" She tailed off as she took in her surroundings.

They were alone, in a small room. Candles were lit, but the fire was dead, and nobody sat on the sofa or leaned against the table by the shuttered window. "We sh-sh-should g-g-g-g—"

He cut off her agitation by the simple expedient of kissing her. Swinging her into his arms, he nestled her close as his lips came down on hers. Phoebe couldn't resist. She sighed into his mouth, and he groaned, the sound reverberating down her throat. When he tasted her, he did it leisurely, sliding his tongue between her lips. She met it with strokes of her own, sucking gently as her body became more attuned to his. She pressed her breasts against a remarkably hard chest, evident even through their layers of clothing. Spreading her hands over his upper arms, she dug her fingers into the soft velvet, meeting pliant masculine muscle.

When he finished the kiss, it was only to change his angle of approach. His eyes were heavy, slumberous with desire, and hers must have been the same. She would not deny her need for him. It would not be fulfilled, but that did not stop her recalcitrant body reaching for him.

He lashed one arm around her waist as he explored her, stroking the bare skin of her lower arms, before sliding his hand around the column of her throat and tickling the tender skin behind her ear.

Continuing to kiss her, Leo touched her everywhere she showed skin, down her bosom, making her gasp in delight, as he traced the line of her décolletage, his touch gentle but insistent.

He laid a trail of kisses from her mouth to her temple, and then to the rim of her ear. "I would take you now, and if we were anywhere else, I would have to struggle to remember I'm a gentleman. What you do to me, Phoebe. You rouse me to near madness, sweetheart." Delicately, he traced his tongue around her ear, then took the lobe between his teeth. "I told you I wanted to kiss you. Now I want more." His low groan vibrated through her.

His honeyed words dropped into her senses, soothing and arousing her at the same time. She could trust this man. He would guide her into loving. And she wanted him. She would not deny that when the evidence was there, in the way her nipples were so hard and sensitive, by the dampness between her thighs. Innocent she might be, but not ignorant. "I want to feel your hands on me. I want to touch you."

"One day you will touch me all you wish," he murmured, continuing his journey of exploration, by dropping kisses down her throat. "I want you, Phoebe." He groaned. "I was determined to let you go, to follow our original plan, but you drive me insane with desire. I want you so much."

She was playing with fire. He was so close to sending her far past the place she should be. And yet she was aware of the perilousness of their situation. A betrothed couple might steal a kiss or two, but any more would arouse condemnation, especially when the match was as uneven as the one between a duke and a daughter of the gentry. But a cat may look at a king. A cat could tuck her hand under his coat, curling it around to his back, where his waistcoat was shorter, and she could get at his shirt. She pushed her fingers between the silk and the linen. "You're so hot."

"For you, Phoebe. Only for you."

If he had said that without the accompanying passion, she'd have denied him. Put what he was saying aside as pretty but meaningless words. But they meant everything to her now. "Leo, I wish you were not a d-duke. Or that I were not a c-c-country girl."

"There are no ranks here." He drew back, gazing into her eyes. "Only you and me, a man and a woman. Nothing else. This passion between us is honest and true. But I swear to you, Phoebe, I will not dishonor you. However much I want to lay you down on that sofa, push up your skirts and make you mine, I will not."

"But—"

He laid his finger across her kiss-swollen lips, stopping her telling him that she wanted him to do that. If they could, perhaps they could get past this desire consuming them both.

"No. But there are different ways we can indulge each other. I can touch you without taking you, hold you without making that final step. I would not dishonor you, sweet Phoebe, but you drive me to the edge of control."

"I know we are to p-part, that we can n-never b-be."

He gazed at her, not giving her the insult of denying her words. "I thought I'd be relieved to hear you say that. I'd come to that conclusion earlier today. But I don't want this to end, and that's the truth."

Was he feeling the desperation she was experiencing? Their association had an end in sight, a matter of weeks. Could they take some time to themselves beforehand? If she learned nothing else from her duke, it was that she could make a man desire her. His gaze, his heat, the way his hands touched her bare skin as if he couldn't stop, all told her that she was truly wanted.

"Can it be d-done? Can we snatch a few hours together?"

Lifting her hand, she cupped his cheek, feeling the slight prick of his incipient beard on her palm. He turned his head and kissed her, softly, reverently, holding her hand in place. "Madness," he murmured, "but so necessary. I brought you here to give you a place to breathe. Instead, I've lost mine."

He gazed at her as if she held all the secrets of the universe, and when he looked at her, she felt that way.

Without warning, the door burst open, hitting the wall behind. Leo spun around with a curse on his lips, stepping in front of her, but not before she saw her mother, flanked by Lucinda and Marcus, standing in the space.

"Phoebe! How could you!"

* * * *

The dramatic exclamation, performed, as usual, at the top of her mother's lungs, shocked Leo into instinctive reaction. Shoving Phoebe behind him, he spun around to confront the intruders. Fury simmered inside him, but he had long ago learned to control himself. Swords were not welcome at balls, but he would have welcomed one now, if only to get rid of the smirk on Callow's face.

Briefly, the thought crossed his mind that Phoebe had a hand in this. Men had been forced into marriage for less, and this was not the first time they'd been caught alone together.

Whatever was it about this woman? He had desired women before, but not as powerfully, not with the feeling that if he didn't have her he would die. Perhaps he'd been playing with fire, wanting the situation where he could not turn back, wanting someone else to force him to make the decision that had been driving him demented over the last few weeks.

Last night he'd decided to say a reluctant farewell, to return to their earlier arrangement, agree that any idea of her taking on the burden of high rank was wrong. But he could not do it. Even if she had arranged with her mother for them to be caught.

As the thought crossed his mind, he dismissed it. The way she was clutching the back of his coat did not speak of conspiracy. His Phoebe was as shocked as he was. And yes, she *was* his. Without trying, she roused his protective instincts to the point of fighting for her.

She must have been in a high state of shock, which meant she would not be able to speak properly for a while. "Would you mind lowering your voice, madam?"

Lucinda's high-pitched squeal echoed around his head. She followed her dramatic exclamation with, "How could you do this to Marcus?"

That made no sense until Leo recalled that Sir Marcus had claimed Phoebe. He could not imagine anyone less suited to her. Callow had no awareness of Phoebe's needs, or if he did, he did not appear to take any notice. She needed someone who would cherish her.

Leo had never considered himself the cherishing type before. Even that notion did not stop him standing between her and her family, legs spread, anger arcing through him.

"Phoebe, get into the main room," her mother said. "What were you thinking, to go into a private chamber alone with a man?"

While he understood her mother's concern, Leo did not appreciate her way of speaking to her daughter, or her reference to him as "a man." Accordingly, he reached behind him, finding her hand and gripping it.

He drew her out to stand by his side but did not release her hand. "Your intrusion is not welcome," he said softly. "If you will leave us now, I will bring Phoebe to you directly. However, I will not have you speaking to her in such a fashion."

Lucinda stamped her foot. "Who are you to say how Mama can speak to her daughter?"

Leo merely met Lucinda's gaze with a cold one of his own. The girl looked away, wincing as if he'd struck her. Rather a dramatic response, but everything Phoebe's sister did appeared *con brio*.

"Yes." Putting up his square jaw, Callow stepped forward. "Phoebe and I have had an understanding these many years. I will not let her go without a fight."

"I suggest you moderate your tone," Leo continued over the sound of a scoff. Not Col's, although there he was, shoulder propped against the doorjamb, toying with an enamel snuffbox. "While I am fully prepared to meet you at a place of your choosing with any weapons you wish, I will not bring Phoebe's name into the argument." Gentlemen did not do that. A lady could be ruined that way, married or not.

The man had enough sensibility to flush. Red did not become him, especially with the russet shade of his coat. "I beg your pardon."

"Accepted." He moved into full duke mode, staring haughtily at the man. "Do you honestly believe I would traduce the good name of my betrothed?"

"She's not your betrothed. I am." Now the man sounded sulky, like a boy thwarted of a favorite toy.

"Do you have a signed contract in place?"

Sir Marcus didn't answer, but Lucinda did. "They don't need such formalities. Marcus and Phoebe are childhood sweethearts."

"Phoebe, come here."

He felt her instinctive movement to her mother as she tugged at his hand. Braving an undignified tussle, he held on. She glanced up at him, and desisted, but he saw a spark in her eyes. She was not pleased. Still, he refused to give in. Her mother should speak to her with more address, and by God, one day she would.

A few people were "accidentally" passing by the door. He had to close this uncomfortable scene down, make it into something less gossip-worthy. "Madam, I believe Miss North is past her temporary weak spell. She was feeling faint. We may return to the ball." He turned to her, fixing his gaze on her. "You will do me the honor of dancing with me?"

That would at least keep her with him.

"I will speak to my husband," Lady North said, her tone moderated to close to normal. "He will visit you in the morning."

"I welcome the opportunity to speak with him."

He led his betrothed out of the room. They were well and truly betrothed now, and Lady North had just ensured everyone knew it. If he analyzed the situation, he had played into their hands, if they had meant Phoebe to hang out for a wealthy husband. But what else could he have done? If she had gone with her mother, she'd have been convulsed with stammers, and if he guessed correctly, the lady would have demanded that Phoebe explain herself. Callow might have bullied her into going with him, and Leo would not stand for that.

The country dance afterward gave him a chance to settle down, and more importantly, soothe Phoebe into a calmer mood. She said very little until they had finished, but then said, "Thank you. Nobody did that for me before."

A quite unrealistic gratification took hold of him.

* * * *

Resigned to his fate far more happily than he wanted to examine, Leo called at the Childers house the next day.

Awkward family members could be handled, and they would have to be, since it appeared he wanted Phoebe more than was advisable. Last night only confirmed his desire for her. He would not go back on this decision. The scene still confused him, but he would get to the bottom of it.

He went one step further toward committing himself to her, by discussing the marriage contract with her father. He proved of more sense than he had first supposed and took his duty of care to his daughter seriously. Leo was impressed. Afterward, he obtained permission to wait in a parlor upstairs where he could see Phoebe for a precious half hour. With the door open and a footman outside.

But after he was shown into a comfortable parlor, the first person to enter the room was Lucinda. Alone. Suspecting trouble, he backed away, but she kept coming. Today she wore yellow, a gown he vaguely recognized. Had she borrowed something of Phoebe's? He could have sworn he'd seen her in that gown. But sisters often shared, so perhaps that was the case. He would be charitable and believe that. But not charitable enough to entertain this girl for long.

She dipped into a low curtsey. "Your Grace, Papa asked me to tell you that he will be with you directly. He is sorry he wasn't here to greet you."

"I have seen your father, thank you. Where is Phoebe?"

"Mama took her out shopping. She should return very soon. I had a sore throat, so I stayed at home." She touched her fingers to the hollow at the front of her neck. "Should you like something to drink? Refreshments?"

He glanced at the brandy decanter. "I am not in need of anything." Too late, he recalled that if he had asked for tea or some such, she'd have had to leave the room to find a servant. What a rag-mannered family this was! And he was seriously allying himself to it? Saddling himself with constant headaches for the rest of his life? Perhaps he could find someone willing to marry Lucinda. She was pretty enough, after all.

When he thought about it, his main objections lay with the younger sister. She was a young eighteen, indulged and without the manners or intelligence that made her acceptable. She needed polish, but he would not be the person to give it to her.

He made a perfunctory bow. "I will return later, since I have called at an inconvenient time." Except that he had not. Phoebe had known he was coming, so why had she gone out? He quelled his irritation. Having stated that he would visit, would it not have been incumbent on someone to have waited for him? Even Phoebe?

Hastily Lucinda moved to stand in front of the door. "No, pray don't go."

Since he had the choice of forcibly putting her aside or staying where he was, he would wait her out, unless she tried to close the door or otherwise compromise him.

Lucinda moved farther into the room until she was standing before him. She glanced up at him, then down again, as if she could not bear to meet his direct gaze, a trick he had confronted many times before. Tedious flirtatious ploys that he disliked intensely. "Sir, I would like a private word."

He glanced at the open door and sighed. "Yes?"

"I have to tell you that Phoebe and Marcus have been quite devoted for many years now. Everyone expected them to make a match of it, and Marcus came to London on the expectation of completing their union."

Did he indeed? Would Phoebe have encouraged Leo if that was the truth? No, she would have told him so at the earliest opportunity. "Did Phoebe know of this devotion?"

Her mischievous smile said so. "Of course she did. But she was completely overwhelmed by you. I have to admit I understand that, having seen you in person…"

Another worshipful glance at his face followed, but this time she kept her celestial gaze fully fixed on him. "I mean, I can believe it. But Marcus is incensed. He feels hurt and angry. I only warn you of this, because he will come to you again, and dear sir, I would not have you hurt for the world." Lifting her hand, she spread her palm over his chest. Leo resisted the urge to step back and rid himself of her touch until she had shown her play. But this far and no further. "I have developed quite an…interest in you myself. I have rarely met a man so handsome." Her voice lowered to a seductive purr.

Not a trace of a flush marred her soft skin. Phoebe would be pink with embarrassment by now. "Marcus will press his suit, and I am sure he will prevail. He knows, and Phoebe does too, that they belong together. But you must not be left with a broken heart, dear sir, or humiliated by a country squire. To counter that, I thought perhaps we could pretend we were interested in each òther. But it would not be pretense—would it?" Her expression spoke of complete devotion, if not adoration.

Basically, she was making a move to supplant her sister in his affections. Apart from that grisly fate being completely impossible, Leo felt sorry for Phoebe, to have such a scheming sister. A suspicion crossed his mind. Had she deliberately rid herself of her sister and her mother?

Lucinda had planted a seed of doubt in his mind. If Phoebe honestly preferred Callow, then naturally he would let her go, despite his desire for her. But she had never shown a preference, indeed, quite the contrary. After all, how much did he truly know about her? With most of the young ladies he'd been linked with, he knew them well, had grown up with them.

No. That was foolish. He dismissed the suspicion without a qualm. With this girl gazing at him as if the sun rose in his eyes, he recognized her tawdry appeal. She was pretty, but she was by no means tempting. He knew what he wanted, and it wasn't this minx.

He placed his hands over hers and plucked them off his chest, immediately releasing them and then moving away so she could not replace them.

Time he put her straight, but he would not assume his ducal air to tell her. He did not need it. "I have tried to give you the benefit of the doubt, Miss North, but I find that only straight talking will give you the answer you need. My dear girl, I would not marry you were you to change places with Miss Childers, with all her wealth. You have nothing that appeals to me, or my requirements for a wife."

Her face fell and tears glimmered in her eyes. But that would not deter him.

"I look for graciousness, intelligence, and beauty. I found those in Phoebe, but you have some way to go before you come anywhere near her. If you ever do."

He had also found a woman he could lose himself in, but he would not tell this girl his innermost feelings. She did not deserve that. He glanced again at the brandy. It was even more tempting now.

"I thought you would have more sympathy than that." She began crying in earnest. Thank goodness she had a handkerchief. Any moment he expected her irate father to stride in and demand that he did the right thing, a ploy he was particularly bored with by now.

Again, that niggle when he recalled how he and Phoebe had met. Impatiently he cast the notion aside. Phoebe was made of finer stuff. "Well, I have not. If you care for Callow so much, perhaps you should marry him. But I take leave to tell you that you are unlikely to find a man of true quality to marry if you continue to deploy every strategy you can think of. You do not have the skill to carry it off."

"Oh, like Phoebe?" She glared at him over her now sadly crumpled handkerchief. "She did it to you, did she not? Waylaid you privately and forced you into announcing the betrothal?"

He recalled that evening vividly. "No, she was falsely accused of stealing a valuable necklace. Or had you forgotten that part?"

She flapped her hand. "Oh pooh, that was nothing! A ploy. She could have just denied it and left it there. With Angela's support, she'd have recovered."

Considering Lady Latimer was still accusing Phoebe to anyone who would listen, he doubted it. More likely her ladyship would have dragged Angela Childers down with Phoebe. She had never liked Miss Childers's wealth or her position in society. Did Lucinda care so little for Phoebe?

"Besides," the girl continued, "you could have bought her ten diamond necklaces."

"But not that one," he snapped. "It was—is—a family heirloom."

The tears continued. "I swear, Duke, it was when I first set eyes on you. I knew you were mine, that we should be together. I do not know how

Phoebe persuaded you, but I will not hold it against you when you come to your senses. You are *mine*."

Now she was rambling. However, she had moved away from the door. He eyed it like a lion spying the open door of its cage. He took his chance and deftly reached his escape. His business with Phoebe's father was done, so he'd call back to see his betrothed later.

He would spend the rest of the time at his club, the only refuge he trusted anymore.

* * * *

Phoebe had allowed her mother to take her out on a shopping expedition on the understanding that they would return after Leo had completed his conversation with her father. "You know what that entails," her mother said as they rattled away in Angela's town coach. "We must give him and your papa a chance to have a *proper* discussion. Women have no part in that. Come out for a few hours, and we will return in time for you to see your duke before he leaves."

Phoebe saw the sense in that, although she disliked the assumption that she would not want a part in the discussion about what would be her future. The practical considerations concerned her. She did not want her father demanding a settlement or providing too high a dowry.

If this was continuing. For the first time, she dared think about a future with Leo. The public attention would be a true trial, but if that meant she got him, it would be worth it. She would not shame him by any hint of poor behavior, and that included her stammer. She would conquer it once more. It had been well on the way out of her life when she had arrived in London, but the change in her circumstances had brought it back, and she was fighting a battle she had thought she'd conquered.

What she had done once, she could do again.

Could she be a duchess? As she followed her mother out to the carriage, she pondered her fate. When she arrived back at this house, would she be one step closer to her dream? Not to be a duchess, but to be Leo's wife. She refused to deny the truth any longer. He was the one she wanted. Nobody else. If she could have him, she'd take him, and cope with everything else later. If she wasn't in love with Leo already, she was well on the way to it. She had no way of knowing. Was this how love happened?

Her shadow, the footman Leo had assigned to follow her, swung up behind. Linton was a man of a certain age, but of a powerful build. Every time she went out, so did he. His presence was almost unnerving.

As the carriage rattled its way over the cobbles of a side street, she barely noticed the jolting as her mother grumbled. "I had meant to visit some of the places Angela told me of, and fit Lucinda with a few new gowns. Her sore throat makes that difficult." She brightened. "But you have excellent taste, dear Phoebe. Perhaps I am better with you by my side. I have to admit that Lucinda has the most *blinding* taste in clothes. Between us we may contrive to find her a few more suitable outfits for a young girl just making her come-out."

"She always had a lively taste," Phoebe admitted carefully. Since Lucinda tended to rip up at any aspersions she perceived, Phoebe had grown into the habit of avoiding giving her opinion. "But only if you say that you chose the garments, Mama. Because if she knows I had a hand in the selections, she will most likely refuse to countenance them."

Her mother sighed. "That is true. But yes, I can say I chose them for her. Then if we can persuade Angela's maid to take a hand in the fitting and alterations, she will no doubt be flattered by the attention and a lot less trouble." She patted Phoebe's hand. "I cannot imagine why you would take Leomore over dear Sir Marcus. He truly wants you, you know. Although I cannot deny you have made yourself a brilliant match. Lucinda is far more the duke's style."

She had indeed, but not in the way her mother meant. Comparing Leo with Marcus was almost laughable. She had been a playmate to Marcus, which meant she had done his fetching and carrying, until she'd learned to avoid him. At first his looks attracted her, but they held every girl in the neighborhood, and he was not fussy which one he paid most attention to. He was too full of his own importance to care about anyone else. While Leo knew what he was and what his rank demanded of him, she had never once seen that superiority and condescension some people had warned her about. Not directed at herself, anyway.

Leo would make her happy, so if he and Marcus could just change places, she would be content. But then, Leo wouldn't be Leo, he'd be somebody else. The conundrum made her smile, and her mother smiled back. "We will ensure you don't disgrace the family, my dear. But let us get Lucinda outfitted first, then she will stop demanding quite so much. She covets the clothes Angela gave you, which I have to say would not suit her at all. We will naturally compensate Angela in some way."

Phoebe found her mother's habit of thinking aloud restful. She could lose herself in her own thoughts while her mother rattled on. But when they arrived at the Oxford Street drapery shop Angela had recommended, Lady North was all business. Leading the way inside, she imperiously demanded to see what the draper had to offer, contemptuously waving away the first partially made garments offered by the fawning shopkeeper. "None of those will do. These are for my other daughter. She is a lovely fair blonde, and eighteen years old. This is my oldest daughter, soon to become the Duchess of Leomore."

That did the trick. An acutely embarrassed Phoebe watched the man fetch more sumptuous garments, and then offer her gowns and petticoats that were admittedly attractive. But she had learned from Angela in her short stay in London. Phoebe wouldn't have accepted any of them. She'd far rather have one very good gown, made of top quality fabrics and decorated with perfect embroidery and trim.

Keeping her counsel, she helped her mother choose six gowns, which would keep Lucinda happy. They were half-made, left so the buyer could adjust them to their size, so Angela's maid would be busy. Bright colors, shiny fabrics and plenty of brilliants scattered over the surface. Clothes Phoebe would never have accepted, because of the plethora of decoration, but Lucinda would love them.

"She may choose the hats herself, but I would like to buy her some more gloves and stockings," Lady North observed, watching through narrowed eyes as the assistants carefully wrapped her purchases in tissue paper.

"Will you not choose something for yourself?" Phoebe asked.

Her mother shot her a darkling look. "I have sufficient. I will supplement my lace. That will do." She paused. "And then we must find your bride clothes. I will not have you going to the duke with borrowed clothing and old lace."

Phoebe demurred. "I have plenty."

"Indeed? Allow me to differ. We will make a start on the items you need."

"I do require some underwear and perhaps a new pair of stays," she admitted, "but do we not have to return to the house?"

Pulling out her gold watch, Lady North consulted it and tutted. "I fear you may be right. One more shop and we will return." She patted Phoebe's hand. "You will see your duke before he leaves."

Was she so obvious? She must have been, for her mother to notice. As the visit had gone on, Phoebe had become more agitated, but she had thought she kept control, as always. Evidently not. Her mother, never a perceptive woman, had noticed her simmering irritation. She was deliberately havering, taking her time, and Phoebe would go back if she had to walk.

The shop assistants were taking an age wrapping everything. "I will go outside for some air." The shop was airless, the top of the shelves dusty. Outside the sun was shining and the clouds had cleared away. The day promised to be fine. Perhaps she could persuade Leo to take her into the park tomorrow, where they could be relatively private. She enjoyed his company so much. And she had not yet written today's letter to him.

Their carriage waited outside, but Phoebe waved the footmen away when they snapped to attention. She would not go out of their sight. She merely wanted a few moments to compose herself and return to the draper's with her serenity restored.

"Phoebe!"

A male voice, one she did not immediately recognize, had called her name. Someone within the carriage a little farther down the street. Cautiously, she moved along the road, keeping her distance.

Linton followed, but Phoebe waved him off when she saw who it was.

Marcus sat inside the vehicle. She breathed out in relief, although some tension remained. "Good afternoon, Phoebe my dear. Well met!"

She had to converse, and she couldn't do it shouting across the six feet that separated her and the carriage. A plain traveling vehicle, hired, most likely. Was he leaving? Her heart lifted a little at the thought, which made pasting a smile on her face easier. "Good day, sir."

"Oh no, Marcus, please."

"Rules are different in the city."

His mouth flattened. "But not between old playmates, surely? I merely wished to pass the time of day with you."

"What are you doing at this end of Oxford Street?" Few establishments were here that would appeal to a man.

Marcus leaned back into the relative dimness of the carriage. Surely he should get out and speak to her? However, she would not cavil at that. "I had occasion to visit someone," he said.

Phoebe allowed herself an internal smile. "Then I should not keep you."

"On the contrary, it's so good to see you. Are you shopping?"

"Yes. My mother is finishing our purchases. She will be out directly." Phoebe would have crossed her fingers.

When he moved, she caught sight of a jewel on his coat. A pin. "Where did you get that pearl?" she asked abruptly. Surely there was only one of those pearls in all London.

"This?" He tweaked the pin. "Lucinda gave it to me. It is nothing, a fish-scale pearl, I have no doubt. But I didn't want to upset her by saying so." He laughed. "Lord, if it was real, it would be worth a fortune! Where would Lucinda get that kind of jewel?"

"From my drawer," she said bitterly. She had not checked the box's contents this morning. With her light-fingered sister around, she should have changed the hiding place, for surely her sister had seen it when she'd interrupted her the other day. "You should return it to me. It was not hers to give."

How ironic, to be accused of stealing a diamond necklace and then being actually responsible for the loss of such a piece as this.

He glanced at it again. "Is it yours? A strange jewel for a lady to have. Too short to be a hatpin, more the kind of thing a gentleman might use in his cravat."

"Exactly. It isn't mine. It belongs to the Duke of Leomore."

His eyes widened. "Dear me." He leaned back. "You'd better come and get it, then." He tsked. "What was Lucinda thinking?"

Sighing with annoyance, Phoebe lifted her skirts and scrambled into the carriage. It had the kind of mechanism where the steps were let down when the door was opened, so she didn't need help. She would take it and go to her mother's carriage. No doubt he would try to tease her for a kiss or some such. Marcus was never so happy as when he was taunting someone, usually her. She would loftily ignore it.

From behind, she received a hard shove. Losing her balance, she tumbled into Marcus's waiting arms. The door of the carriage was slammed, and at the same moment the vehicle began to move.

"Spring 'em!" Marcus shouted, and the carriage jolted into action.

Phoebe emerged from folds of cloth. "What on earth are you doing?"

"What I should have done to start with. You, my sweet Phoebe, are coming home with me. You are mine. You always were."

She lunged for the door, but before she could reach the handle he had her around her waist.

"Oh no, dear one," he murmured into her ear, a triumphant laugh in his voice. "You are well and truly compromised, Phoebe. You belong to me."

Chapter 13

Leo should really not feel as good as he did, considering he was all but trapped in marriage. Although this time he did not feel trapped. He looked forward to starting his new life with Phoebe. After calling at Doctors' Commons to pick up the license he'd applied for yesterday, he took a chair to Pall Mall. The day was still young, and he had some time to kill before he could go to Miss Childers's house for dinner.

He had a spring in his step as he climbed the narrow stairs to the upper floor where his club was situated. The rage for clubs was in full swing, and now the new fad for gentlemen's clubs, where only members were allowed and they could take their ease, was in full swing. This was a smaller example, the St. James, but it suited him well.

A porter inclined his head to Leo as he passed through the small lobby. He smiled back. Every time he entered the establishment, a bit more had been done to improve it. He'd already performed his part, paying his subscription and arranging for a good supply of spirits from his contact in the City. The club was developing so quickly that obviously it was filling a place that should have been occupied some time ago.

The large room he entered was comfortably full, but his particular friends were not present. Never mind, he would relax, read the papers, and have a drink.

"Leomore!" A call attracted his attention. Several people sat around a small table, playing cards in hand. "Shall we deal you in?"

He shook his head, smiling.

"Come and have a drink anyway," Cavanaugh urged. "We're not playing deep, only a guinea a point."

One of his companions groaned and tossed his cards facedown on the table. "Not even that," he said, disgustedly. "Perhaps when your betrothed brings you the diamonds you can liven up the gaming tables with them."

Fury erupted in Leo. He sprang to his feet and put his hand on his sword hilt. "I will not let that stand."

Leigh held up his hands in a placating gesture. "I do beg your pardon, Leomore. It was a poor jest in bad taste. I meant no harm by it."

Leo took a deep breath, then another before he released his grip on his sword. "Very well, I accept your apology. The lady is my future duchess, and I was with her when the diamonds went missing. Proposing," he added grimly, realizing that in fact he had not proposed to her yet.

"That's not what the Latimers are saying."

Leo took his seat once more and reached for the brandy decanter and an empty glass. "The Latimers can go hang. If they say it in my presence, I'll give them the same response." He had not seen the Latimers for a while, but if he did, he would have no hesitation confronting them. Perhaps he had let them get away with too much and he should seek them out. "They should spend their efforts discovering who stole the jewels, not persecuting an innocent woman."

Perhaps he would take a hand of cards. When Cavanaugh gave him a querying glance, he nodded to be included in the deal. An hour here, then he would pay his visit to Phoebe. They were one step closer to marriage, with the settlement agreed upon. He could be a married man by the end of the month.

Fool that he was, the thought made him smile.

But he'd heard the talk. Just because Phoebe was with him didn't mean she was not involved in the theft, the gossip went. Had she gone to the grotto in order to receive the stolen goods from the thief, and he, Leomore, had interrupted her? He could hardly refute that piece of nastiness without admitting he'd carried her there.

"Your wife-to-be has an interesting family," Cavanaugh remarked. "I had the pleasure of meeting Lady North at the theater last night. She is a most…remarkable woman. She informed me that she had no desire to remain in town much longer. I would have thought that finding oneself at the center of society would have pleased any woman, but apparently not."

"My wife prefers the country," Leigh put in. "She sighs every time I suggest a visit to our London house. In fact, she is going home this weekend, barely halfway through the season." He wrinkled his generously built nose. "The country stinks. But her absence will give me more time to visit the lovely Pauline. I have her installed in St. John's Wood, in a cozy little house. Much more to my taste." He discarded a nine of spades.

Leo picked up the card and added it to his hand. "Mistresses can be too much trouble."

"So you're settling down with your wife?"

Yes, yes he was. But he would not give them the pleasure of calling him a dead bore once he'd turned his back on other women. "I don't have a wife yet."

He could hardly believe he was going ahead with this. However, if he had to choose between losing the woman who had made his life a delight recently and claiming her, he would take the latter. He had, earlier today, and he was still wondering what he was doing. He was not in love; he was incapable of it. His grandmother had shown him cool affection; his parents changed their minds every other moment. He had not learned how to fall in love, or what it was. Surely he would have to understand it to undergo it?

Men in love lost their heads, committed foolish acts, and he had not done that. Apart from seeking her out to steal kisses, but surely he was allowed that indulgence. Love was for mistresses, a fleeting emotion that had no place in the longevity of marriage. With a little training, Phoebe would make an excellent duchess. She had intelligence and beauty. The rest, the things she'd have to know, would come in time.

He discarded the nine. It wasn't as useful as he'd supposed. His mind was not on the game.

A disturbance by the door made everyone look up. Newspapers rustled as Lord Marston entered the room in a state of high agitation. His hands were tightened into fists, and his neckcloth was decidedly askew. As he neared their table, Leo became aware of the beads of sweat on his brow and the wide-eyed expression of, what—horror? Shock?

When he reached them, he did not mince his words. "It's La Coccinelle. She's dead."

A murmur set up around them, with a few shouts of "What!" and "You don't say!" as the news spread.

"Lisette? What happened?" Shock arced through him, galvanizing him into action. Once more he rose from the chair.

"Isn't she your mistress, Leomore?" Cavanaugh asked.

Leo spared him a glance. "No. I cast her off weeks ago." He turned his attention back to Mars. "What happened?"

"Murdered," Mars said. "I've come straight from her house. I found her."

Abandoning the dish of guineas at his elbow, Leo took Mars's arm and dragged him from the room. "What did you do?" he asked as they strode through the lobby.

"You think I killed her?" his friend demanded indignantly, his thick black brows drawing together in a frown.

Leo made a sound of exasperation as they clattered down the stairs. "No, you dolt, I mean what did you do when you found her?"

"Notified Bow Street and came to find you. Left a key with the servant. Recalling that scene at the theater the other night, I thought you should know."

The necklace. Was it, after all, the real thing?

Outside, Mars had a hackney waiting. Leo flung himself inside and onto the nearest street, rapping the roof with his knuckles when it did not immediately start into motion.

Mars slammed the door as they set off.

"Where is the house?"

"In the City, the one she uses for business. She has another residence further out of town."

"I know," Leo said. "I bought that one for her. What happened?"

"I turned up, rapped on the door, her servant let me in, and I went up to see her. She was dead. It's not a pretty sight, Leo. Someone shot her." Marston sighed and shook his head. "Such a waste."

"Nasty." He winced. "Any idea why?"

Mars shrugged. "She wasn't exactly talking to me. This was my first appointment with her. And my last."

They arrived in fifteen minutes. The house was in the City, one of a line of houses built after the Great Fire, and as was usual in the City, crammed next to shops, businesses and residences. It was easy to spot because a crowd clustered around the door.

After tossing a coin to the hackney driver, Leo shouldered his way through and rapped on the door. Mars arrived at his side.

The door opened, and a small man in a russet coat stood there, glaring at them. "I found her and sent for you," Mars said, and the man moved aside just enough to let him through. Leo didn't give the man a chance to block his entry.

Mars was already halfway up the stairs. With tension rising to his throat, Leo followed him to the second floor, where he pushed open a door. These houses were not built for men to stand side by side, but Leo managed it.

The stench of fresh blood tainted the air, mingling with the acrid stink of ignited powder. His stomach churned, but he forced his bile back down.

Lisette sat on a sofa set before a huge, gaudily draped four-poster bed, wearing a silk-and-lace confection that barely covered her naked form. Her head was tilted to one side, slumped in an ungraceful way she never affected in life. Lisette had been full of energy, elegant, and witty. Not now. Her long blond hair was stained with blood where it dangled over the wound in her chest.

At least she hadn't been shot in her face. She would have hated that. But the lovely features were forever at rest now. Her eyes stared at him, sightless and dead.

He couldn't bear to look at them. On silent feet he crossed the room and gazed into her sightless eyes. So beautiful, so lifeless.

He stepped back, rubbing his shoe against the carpet to get the blood off it.

"Sir, I must ask you not to touch the corpse." The little man had followed them up.

"Who are you?" Leo demanded.

"Cocking from Bow Street."

Leo spun around. "Cocking?"

The man scratched his neck. "Cocking," he confirmed, meeting Leo's gaze defiantly. "And I know you, Your Grace." He cleared his throat. "You were the lady's protector, were you not?"

"I was once, but I haven't been so for some time."

The room was draped in sumptuous fabrics, but beneath them was bare plaster, damp and cracked. Leo turned his attention back to Lisette. "She was difficult and temperamental, but she didn't deserve this." Had a lover killed her in the height of passion? Or when she refused him? Or was his first instinct right, and someone had come for the necklace?

"She could have done it herself." Mars had noticed what Leo had missed; too engrossed in the lady, he hadn't spotted the weapon lying by her left side.

"She had no reason to do that." He glanced at the pistol, which had definitely been discharged. Ordinary enough, but he'd never seen it before in Lisette's company. Something was odd. Ah yes, he had it. "Lisette was right-handed." He added the extra information. "She damaged her left hand as a child, and her grip was poor. Not strong enough to pull a trigger."

The small man in the russet coat cleared his throat. "That is useful information. Then we are looking at a murder, are we not?"

"It appears so," Mars said slowly. "Who would do that?"

"A spurned lover?" the little man said.

"Doubtful," he said. "She had men flocking around her. But don't discount it."

Mars came around his other side, the old timbers of the floorboards shaking under his weight. These houses in the City had been thrown up after the Fire, not all of them as sturdy as they should be. The walls were thin. "Did nobody hear the shot?"

"A couple of neighbors," Cocking said. "But they didn't raise the alarm. This area is a bit…colorful."

So many things had happened since he'd given Lisette her congé. "I cannot tell you where she has been or who she entertained recently." He marked the scene again. Her neck bore a red mark. If she'd lived, that might have turned into a bruise. Did people bruise after their deaths? Damned if he knew.

"She was wearing the necklace," Mars said abruptly. "Or at least, a necklace, and the thief tore it off her."

"A burglary?" Cocking rubbed the back of his own neck, as if in sympathy with the woman. "A man was seen leaving the house hurriedly. Nobody heard the shot, or so they claimed, but a few saw the man. And they identified him."

Mars clicked his tongue, frowning at Cocking. "Well, don't keep us in suspense, man! Tell us his name!"

"His name was Forrester, and he's a ruffian of the first order. Been up at Bow Street before now, but he's a slippery one." He paused. "Buys himself out of trouble. Pays other people to do his dirty work. He must have seen the necklace and assumed it was the real one. Gone after it and took it."

"Interesting that he did this himself, then," Leo remarked.

"Maybe he doesn't want to share," Mars commented.

Leo's mind raced. "Or maybe he did share to start with. That would explain much. If his original conspirator betrayed him in some way, perhaps ran off with the necklace, that would explain why he is still in pursuit."

"Interesting."

Leo could almost see the Bow Street man's mind working. His thick brows drew together, and a deep frown creased his forehead. "The Latimers have been creating a great to-do about the diamonds they have lost. But did Lord Latimer give the necklace to his mistress, and then arrange the theft to cover up his transgression?"

That would make sense, especially if this was the real necklace. It would be just like Lisette to flaunt that she had it. But would Lord Latimer be so besotted as to hand over a family treasure?

After considering the point, reluctantly Leo shook his head. "Lady Latimer would have known the real jewel from paste and would hardly create such a fuss if she knew the piece was not real. And if her husband had taken the necklace, why would she create such a fuss when the copy was stolen? On the other hand, why would someone steal this one if it was paste?"

"Either someone thought this was the real jewel, or they killed her for another reason," Mars put in. "Or it was the real one."

Leo determined to pay a visit on Latimer the first chance he got. He needed answers rather quickly. "It might not have been the Latimer necklace that was stolen. Her lovers gave her some pretty pieces," he said, but his gut told him that it was. He moved closer and saw something glint under the lady's tumble of hair.

Before Cocking could order him to move away, he tweaked the hair aside.

Well, that answered his question. She was wearing the matching earrings. Or rather, earring. The other must be lost in her clothing. No, there it was, on the sofa, half covered with fabric. Picking it up, he turned it over on his palm. "These are the earrings that accompany the necklace." Lifting the article up to the light, he sighed. "Look, there's a chip on the central stone. That doesn't happen to diamonds. It's as paste as the necklace was."

He glanced down. Under the frill of lace on her arms, he saw the gleam of a bracelet. Lifting the obscuring lace, he confirmed his supposition. "My betrothed returned the real bracelet to her ladyship, so this is a copy."

Mars crossed the room to look at the earring. Leo handed it to him.

Someone wanted the necklace. Which led Leo to a few suppositions, none of which pleased him. The matter had become urgent. His blood ran cold. Would the thief have killed Phoebe, if she'd been in her bedroom when it was ransacked?

She was in danger, at least until the necklace was found. His instinct to settle Linton by her side was correct.

Silently, he bade La Coccinelle farewell. She had been a magnificent example of a courtesan in her prime, and she had led the male half of society in a merry dance. Unfortunately she would never pass her prime. "People will remember her for this. A shame her death will surpass her life," he murmured as he stepped back.

He could do nothing more here. He needed to speak to Latimer urgently. Then go to Phoebe, who would be safe inside Miss Childers's house by now. Or as safe as she was anywhere. Forewarned, Miss Childers would ensure Phoebe was safe. And he had sent one of his most trusted men, whose sole duty was to care for her.

Chapter 14

Leo tracked Lord Latimer down in a City inn, where he was partaking of a meat pie and ale in company with several other gentlemen. He had to call on Latimer's London house and liberally grease the palm of the butler, but the price was worth it.

Normally he'd have partaken of something himself, but after seeing poor Lisette, he was still feeling queasy. The full impact hadn't hit him until he left the house, but the stink of scorched blood remained in his nostrils even now. He'd slept with that woman, laughed with her, argued with her, and now she would do none of those things ever again.

The walk to the inn on the Strand had blunted the sting, but it remained embedded in him. Now he had a personal stake in finding the murderer. And since the killer and the thief of the necklace appeared to be intertwined, his quarry was also Phoebe's.

Without his wife, Latimer was an unpretentious fellow who enjoyed life, but Leo did not allow that to stop him doing what he wanted. Greeting the man affably enough, he asked for a word.

"Charlotte said I was not to talk to you," he answered, while his friends watched with not a little interest. He visibly brightened. "However, my wife is not here."

"In private, if you would," Leo said.

They found a room. Small, and furnished with two scarred wooden benches, black with age, but the place served its purpose. "Have they found it?" Latimer demanded. "The necklace?"

"No." Leo kept his eyes trained on His Lordship, waiting for any telltale signal. If Latimer knew anything about the jewels, Leo wanted to know it. "What did you do with it?"

"Me?" his voice spiraled up. "I let my wife wear it to that confounded ball. Then I watched as she chased the woman who ran off with it and the man she passed it to."

Leo got straight to the point. "But was the real necklace stolen? Or did you give the real one to Lisette? Men were vying for her attention once I cast her off. She was auctioning herself to the highest bidder. The necklace would have suited her nicely."

He needed to be absolutely certain that the piece stolen was not the real one. If it was, then the thieves might be satisfied. But that would leave Phoebe still accused of the theft, if the item did not turn up.

Latimer emitted a strangled cry. "What kind of a man do you think I am? I might give Lisette a pretty piece of jewelry, but the Latimer necklace? My life wouldn't have been worth living if I'd done that. Of course the real necklace was stolen from my wife!"

Exasperated, Leo spun around and took two steps one way, and two steps back, all he could achieve in this confined space. He needed information, not an argument, although he was spoiling for one right now. He wanted to hit out at somebody, and the perfect candidate was standing before him.

Latimer had a tendency for protruding eyes and a receding chin, rather like a frog. Leo tried not to hold that against him. And failed. "Did you give her the paste necklace, or did Lisette have it copied herself?"

Latimer avoided Leo's eyes. "I gave it to her. We always had copies of the thing, to put thieves off. I gave a good copy to Lisette, with the earrings and bracelet."

"Did you tell her it was the real one?"

A telling pause followed before Latimer shook his head. "But I didn't tell her it wasn't, either. Why, did you think it was the original?"

Leo turned his shoulder in a shrug. "Men have made idiots of themselves for less. And she was fascinating."

"Was?"

Leo let the pause grow for a few seconds before he gave his answer.

"La Coccinelle was found earlier today with a bullet through her chest. I believe she was wearing the jewelry when she was killed, because she also had the matching earrings and bracelet. But the murderer took the necklace."

Latimer stared at him, pale blue eyes so wide that Leo feared they might pop out of his head. "What?"

"She was murdered," he repeated slowly, as if he didn't understand the words.

"Lisette?"

Leo recognized the confusion in Latimer's eyes; not so long ago he'd felt exactly the same himself. But he was coming out of his shock, while Latimer was entering it. That was why he'd kept the news back until he had the information he needed. Latimer was not an actor. His shock was real. He had not known, so he was probably not involved in the murder. Even if he had ordered someone to retrieve the necklace, he had not told his agents to kill anyone.

"A man called Forrester was seen leaving the house." He ventured a theory. "Did he work for you at any point?" As a footman, perhaps?

Latimer frowned and swallowed. "No." A pause followed. "But another man, a footman called Chapman, disappeared the night of the theft."

The man who collided with Phoebe?

"Was he there at Miss Childers's house the night the necklace was stolen?" Leo snapped.

"Yes." Latimer helped himself to a brandy from a decanter on the mantelpiece. Leo wasn't so far gone that he would have partaken of the doubtful substance. But Latimer knocked it back.

"Why did you not tell anyone?"

"I didn't know until yesterday, when I sent for him. Then my wife told me he had disappeared." He growled the words, obviously reluctant to admit them. "She runs the household. I keep out of the way."

Leo could almost feel sorry for him, except that Phoebe was involved in this mess. He clapped the man on the back. "Go and get drunk. I wish I could. Lisette was beautiful, she was clever, and she was a pain in the backside. But she didn't deserve what happened to her. The magistrates will no doubt send someone to see you."

Latimer covered his eyes and groaned. "And if I don't get home immediately, my wife will see them. Then my life won't be worth a farthing. She refuses me her bed, so what did she expect me to do? Dear God, the woman is impossible."

He dropped his free hand, and it fell to his side with a slap. "Don't marry anyone you cannot share your life with, whether it is as a friend or a lover. Be sure before you tie the knot. Or don't marry at all." Sticking his hands in his pockets, he shook his head. "I must go home. Thank you for telling me. If I had the choice, I'd far rather have had a woman like La Coccinelle, who was honest and affectionate, if a handful, than a cold fish like the one I'm married to."

Leo could promise His Lordship he would not make that error, if he cared enough to tell him.

He needed to see Phoebe before the news reached her from another source. He had to tell her himself. And he had to ensure she was safe, even if he had to stay by her side day and night. They had not found the diamonds yet, so Phoebe was still in danger. Besides, he felt a need to confide in someone who understood his concerns. And he wanted to hold her, to feel a live woman in his arms.

* * * *

The Childers household was in turmoil. The usually well-ordered mansion held an air of fierce activity. As Leo walked through the unlocked, unguarded door into the hall, he was nearly knocked off his feet by a maid, who was running, no, hurtling, through the space at breakneck speed. "Oh, Your Grace, sorry!" She did not stop to greet him but continued on her way.

Judging from the confusion in the hall, he'd arrived too late. The footman on duty glared after the maid but stepped forward. "Miss Childers is not receiving visitors today, Your Grace."

"I'm not here for Miss Childers. I want to see Miss North."

"She is not receiving visitors either, Your Grace."

Like hell she wasn't. "Then I'll wait."

"I'm afraid—"

Leo tired of arguing with him. When the man showed signs of blocking his way, Leo tossed his hat to him, which he was forced to catch. He wasted no time racing up the stairs. At the top he would have hovered, but a maid stood outside the doors to the drawing room. "Miss North?" he enquired. Blushing, she opened the doors, and Leo went inside.

"Ah." He turned around, but the maid had closed the doors. He was alone in the room with the wrong Miss North.

Lucinda executed a flourishing curtsey. She wore another gown that seemed familiar, in deep blue, and now he knew why. The last time he'd seen it, Phoebe had been wearing it. Lucinda was much slighter than Phoebe, but that was taken care of by tight-lacing. *Very* tight-lacing. Her breasts swelled above the neckline, which he could see because she had no fichu covering her curves. The lace at her elbows was fine, delicate French lace. Probably also belonging to Phoebe.

"Your Grace." She swished forward, holding out a limp hand, which he presumed he was to take. He did so, but only briefly, giving himself enough time to bow over it. But he dropped it as soon as he could.

His senses tingled. There was danger here. "I called to see your sister." He had no time for niceties. "Would you tell me when she will be down?"

She didn't answer immediately but flicked out her fan and turned to the window, staring out before she turned back to him in a swirl of silk, flashing him a glimpse of her ankle and lower calf. Admittedly they were shapely, but they drew him not at all.

"She has gone!" Lucinda stretched her arms wide, the fan dangling precariously from her fingers. She drew them back and clasped her hands. "I am so sorry, sir, but she has gone off with her lover!"

Leo's heart missed a beat. "Explain."

If he hadn't crossed his arms, she might well have flung herself at him. She showed alarming tendencies to do so, but halted before she reached him. Only just in time. "Phoebe has been in love with Marcus forever, but he never regarded her as more than a playmate until recently. But when he came to London, they saw themselves differently. I am afraid that shortly after they met here, they became lovers." She paused.

Leo did not reveal his shock. "Where is she?" He kept his voice steady, quiet.

"She has run away with him. They left this morning, just before noon. Mama took her shopping, and Phoebe stepped out for a moment. When Mama came out of the shop, Phoebe had gone. The footmen told her she had met Marcus outside and left with him in his carriage. Unfortunately one of the men tried to reach her, and he was injured, but apart from that, nobody was hurt. She did not leave a note, at least we did not think so until I found this."

Diving into her pocket, she produced a folded sheet of paper and handed it to him.

"Dear Leomore," it began.

"I cannot bear to be without my Marcus any longer. Please forgive me, I know you saw my father about our marriage, but I cannot go through with the ceremony. The union would not be fair to either of us, when I love another. I have always loved him, and we were always meant to marry, but I allowed myself to become carried away by your rank and my prospects as a duchess.

"By the time you receive this, I will be long gone. My home is but a day away, and having obtained a special license, Marcus and I will be married as soon as we arrive home.

"Look at my sister. Lucinda is beautiful and refined. She would make you a wonderful duchess. I will leave her in my stead.

"Yours etc,

"Phoebe North."

Could today get any worse?

Leo heaved a great sigh of pure exasperation. After folding the letter very deliberately, he lifted his head and confronted Lucinda. "What have you done?" He was weary rather than angry. She didn't deserve his anger.

She opened her mouth, no doubt to protest her innocence, but at that moment the door was flung open and Lady North stormed in. She had her skirts gripped tightly, an indication of her tense mood. "I am sorry, Duke. I sent word, but you obviously have not received the message."

He hadn't been back to his house. He should have changed for dinner, but he'd had no opportunity to do so. Drawing out his watch, he checked the time. It was a repeater, but he wanted visual confirmation. Phoebe had been gone nearly four hours.

Leo could barely control his fury, driven by an underlying fear for her safety. This minx of a sister had caused more trouble than she knew. Ignoring her ladyship's precipitate entry, he kept his attention on the daughter. "Answer my question."

"Nothing!" Her indignation echoed her stance. Really, Lucinda should be on the stage. She'd studied the attitudes and had them off pat, even to the angle of her head when she struck a pose. "I am the messenger, nothing else! How could you think otherwise?"

"Of course he does not think that, my love. But for Phoebe to do this passes understanding. Why should she?" Her mother was obviously impressed by her daughter's protests, her tone conciliatory. "My dearest, I know that Phoebe taunted you in the past, and you have shown a great deal of Christian forbearance to act as her messenger in this awful business."

Lucinda blinked fast, enough to bring tears to her eyes. "She always did. And she knew I wanted Marcus, but she refused to leave him alone."

In one sweeping motion she was by his side, and before Leo could stop her, she had his hand cradled between hers. "I know what she's like, my dear duke. She will lead you on, and before you know it, you are agreeing to do whatever she wants. She's encroaching, and I am so sorry she treated you in this way."

Leo would let this play out, but not for much longer. "In what way?"

Lady North answered. "Leading you on, getting carried away by a handsome face, and a title," she said. "Phoebe is a good girl, but she does not always behave in a way I would prefer. Lucinda has caught her out before. I thought sending her to London would be good for her."

"Good of you," he said dryly.

The lady missed the harsh note in his voice. Lucinda took up the conversational ball. "I know. We try. But she does play fast and loose with men. She and Marcus have always belonged together. You should let them be, to be happy. Meantime," she continued, her voice brightening, "I am a Miss North. If you are afraid of losing face, I will gladly step into the breach. Society will expect you to marry a Miss North, will they not? And here I am. I will make you the best duchess, I swear I will."

Leo had never been proposed to before. He found he did not enjoy it, especially from this scheming child.

"You will be much more comfortable with Lucinda, will you not?" Lady North beamed. "This is the perfect ending. Then Phoebe will be able to get on with her marriage, and she will be far more comfortable too."

"Allow me to differ." Leo allowed ice to creep into his voice. "While I am sensible of your offer, I have a few points of my own to make. First, that I am not in the habit of passing one sister over for another. I have never considered women interchangeable." Pulling away, he gave Lucinda a hard, cold bow.

He would be far better dusting his hands of the whole family. How could he introduce these two to his family and friends in the country? Society would laugh at him, for allowing these bumpkins to fool him.

But he would not, and he could only use one word to describe why. Phoebe. She deserved better than a mother who constantly favored her younger daughter. Better than being passed over in favor of an obviously pretty, spoiled child who thought nothing of taking her sister's clothes.

Marcus Callow was a bully, and if Leo knew anything, it was that Phoebe deserved better, even if that was him.

"I have come to an agreement with Sir Frederick, which I intend to comply with."

"But Lucinda is a Miss North," Lady North cajoled. "She would make an excellent duchess."

"Enough!" came a new voice from the door. The stentorian tones silenced the women, but not Leo. He turned around slowly, confronting Phoebe's father. "This is foolish talk. I have allowed you your own way for too long, and all for the sake of peace in the household."

Tight-lipped, he faced Leo. "I am deeply sorry that you had to face this, but in one thing, the women are right. By running off with Marcus Callow, Phoebe has sealed her fate."

He shot his wife a hard look. "You will go to your room and prepare to leave London as quickly as possible. Both of you."

Lucinda's protesting wail made Leo flinch, but her father must have faced this before, because he did not move a muscle. "I have sent a note to our hostess, outlining the events and begging her forbearance."

"And she is here." Miss Childers's soft tones cut through the short silence. "I would not have had this happen for the world." She had evidently come from her work, because she was dressed plainly, and her face was clear of powder or other artifice. Her brow furrowed. "Has Phoebe truly run off with her childhood sweetheart?"

Leo could stand no more. He snorted and flourished the letter. "No, she has not. I believe she has been abducted, and I am seriously concerned for her safety. This is not her handwriting."

Miss Childers took the note from him and scanned it, her lips tightening.

"How do you know she did not write this?" Lucinda demanded. "Phoebe's copperplate is much like any other." Did the girl never learn?

Leo kept his voice steady. It was either that, or fling every ornament in the room against the wall, and there were not enough of them to assuage his fury. His training served him well now, helped him to remain in control of his temper and thus the situation he was facing. "I know her writing and her signature. I also know her style. Phoebe did not write this. I assume you and Callow were in cahoots."

He forced ice through his veins.

Lady North's mouth dropped open. "Is this true?" she asked in a failing voice, the quietest Leo had ever heard her. The woman who could bellow across a hunting field had gone. Her face had paled, and for once she looked old and confused.

Well, she might. At least she had known nothing of the scheme, her expression told him that.

Leo took the initiative. "Perfectly true. Moreover, I do not appreciate scheming, especially when it concerns me. Watching it can be amusing, but not this time. I am far too old a hand for this to fool me. I will find her and marry her."

"But how can you if she marries Marcus?" Lucinda demanded.

"If I kill him she'll be a widow." Although his murderous mood definitely stretched to Callow, he was also afraid for Phoebe. The man was big. He could hurt her, use her foully. If he did that, then Leo *would* kill him. "I would not marry an ingenue in any case, especially one who could construct a scheme so clumsy. I expect more of anyone I associate with." He scanned her from head to foot. "That gown suited Phoebe better, I believe." He prepared to verbally tear the child to pieces.

Before he could say more, Miss Childers cleared her throat. "I heard about La Coccinelle," she said to him. "I was already on my way here when I got my uncle's note." Ignoring everyone else, she turned to face Leo. "Has it occurred to you that Phoebe could be in danger?"

Leo closed his eyes. "Yes. If someone thinks she has the necklace, you mean?" Specifically the man Forrester.

Miss Childers nodded. "Precisely. Someone wants that jewel, and if they think Phoebe has it, they will pursue her. She only has Callow to protect her, and neither of them know what happened this morning."

"What happened?" Sir Frederick asked quietly.

"A woman of the night was murdered because the thief thought she was in possession of the Latimer necklace," Leo told him, to a chorus of gasps.

"What happened to Linton?" Leo demanded.

"He's upstairs. One of Callow's footmen knocked him on the head, rather than let him get to her. I sent him up to bed."

Leo nodded. "Linton is a family retainer. That is another score I have to settle with Callow."

Fear clutched Leo's heart, forcing him to suck in a few deep breaths to steady himself. Whoever wanted the necklace would have had time to study it. If it was not the real thing, they would continue their pursuit. If they found out she had left town, that would be a gift to them, and an invitation to follow.

"I must go."

Miss Childers caught his arm. "I thought you'd say that. I took the liberty of having a horse made ready for you. It is furnished with what you will need. I can order someone to accompany you, if you wish."

Leo forced a tight smile of thanks. "I will travel faster alone. I am inordinately grateful to you."

Miss Childers waved off his thanks. "Go. I will take care of matters here. There's a map in the saddlebag, and the route to Phoebe's home is marked."

Such efficiency made him sorry he was not more attracted to her. He liked her enormously, admired her for her business acumen, but felt little desire for her. Certainly not the roaring flame when he was in Phoebe's presence.

"I will be eternally grateful." After bowing briefly, he was done, shaking the dust of this family off his heels. Except that he would not forbid Phoebe from seeing them, if she wished.

Unless he was hanged for killing her abductor.

Chapter 15

Once Marcus had her in the coach, Phoebe pretended to faint clean away. Deeply worried that he would try to seduce her—or worse—she took matters out of his hands and copied Lucinda's favorite tactic, by letting her eyes flutter closed and going limp in his arms.

The plan could redound on her if he decided to molest her anyway. But Marcus was not quite that low. He laid her on the seat opposite to his, and let her be, although she felt his gaze on her and had to fight hard to keep her demeanor that of an unconscious woman.

Through half-closed eyes, Phoebe watched the countryside pass the carriage window, and regretted her lack of chances to get away. The door was locked, but she would have created a fuss that nobody could have ignored, given the chance. In the country, she had far less opportunity to escape than the city. What was she to do?

She could not remain in that state forever. Eventually, she let her eyes flick open. Marcus stared at her, a sinister smile curving his thin lips.

"Let me go."

He ignored her demand. "Are you feeling better now? Do you need anything?"

"I w-want to go b-b-back to Angela's house." Phoebe fought to keep her temper and her self-control. Every hair on her body stood on end, and her throat was tight with anxiety.

"One day we will visit." He glanced out of the carriage window. "We have had to go the long way around, because we were at the wrong side of London." He frowned. "Irritating. If I had taken you from Grosvenor Square, we could have taken the faster route. Unfortunately, the delay will make our journey longer, but I think we'll still be home by nightfall.

We'll marry tomorrow." He watched her, eyes glowing. "I will make you mine tonight."

Phoebe remained stretched out on the seat, her head pillowed on a spare cushion. If she sat up, he might try to join her. Her stays were pinching, her cane-hooped petticoat uncomfortable under her, but at least it had fallen the right way. It didn't feel good, though, one side heavier than the other. No doubt he'd snapped one of the hoops. The way he'd dragged her through the carriage door, she was lucky to escape with no broken bones. "How c-can we marry tomorrow?" Apart from the fact that she would kill him first.

Brightly, he patted his chest, where the inside pocket of his coat must lie. "I have a special license."

"What if I tell the v-vicar I d-d-d-don't want to m-marry you? You c-c-c-can't make me."

"But, my dear, after you've spent the night with me, it is me or nobody. You understand that, do you not?"

Nobody then. In ten years' time she'd be looking after Lucinda's children, living off her sister's charity, as a despised, single member of the family. She would never have a home of her own, never have a family or children. She didn't have the resources for that. Or she could run away and become a governess. She'd still be looking after someone else's children, but at least she'd be paid for it.

She would rather do that than marry Marcus.

"Besides," he said thoughtfully, crossing one leg over the other, "you're better off with me. At least I don't spend my nights in the City, visiting the most disreputable dens I can find." Although she tried not to react, he must have seen something in her eyes because he pursued his advantage. "Have you not heard the gossip? Your duke visits whores in the worst, the filthiest of sordid rooms, and goes to the gaming hells where people are stabbed to death nightly at the turn of a card. I won't do that, not when I have you all right and tight!"

Leo had too much honor. "You're lying." Of course he was.

"I do not expect you to believe me, but you may ask anyone you like if we ever return to town. Everyone in London knows that."

"No. And I will not m-m-marry you."

He lifted his shoulders in an exaggerated shrug. "Our vicar holds me in high regard together with the rest of the district. You must know this. I will remind him you are shy and retiring. Everyone knows you are, you've cultivated that opinion for years." He grinned, a nasty, no-humor curve of his lips. "Your natural reticence does not allow you to walk boldly into marriage, and you can barely get a word out without stuttering. Why? Would you rather I had you and left you?"

"N-no." *Yes, but she'd rather he didn't have her at all.* She had no doubt he would tell anyone who would listen what he'd done, and her reputation would be destroyed.

Her gaze dropped from his face to the pin carelessly thrust through his coat. The pearl was fine; she had never come across one so pure or so large before. The slightly uneven shape only drew her attention to the flash of tiny diamonds set at its tip and on the base, where the pearl met the gold pin. "That pin was in my room."

"Lucinda gave it to me." He touched the smooth surface of the pearl. "She said it would persuade you to join me. And it did, didn't it?" He pulled the pin out of his coat. Somewhere it had lost the gold cap that stopped it pricking the skin or slipping out and getting lost.

"Yes. It d-doesn't b-belong to me. It is the property of the D-D-Duke of Leomore."

"That fool?" Uncrossing his legs, he spread his thighs and leaned forward, resting his elbows on his knees. "Don't think of that man any longer. He's not in your life anymore. I'm sure he'll breathe a sigh of relief when he hears our news."

Would he? The doubts that constantly niggled at her returned in force now. Trying not to fidget, to draw attention to her body, she concentrated on what she was going to say. Stopping the dratted stammer. But the more she thought about it, the worse it got, and after an abortive line of n's, she gave up.

"Oh dear, that sounded awful." His mouth framed his words, but his eyes said something else. The dark depths gleamed. He was looking forward to having her, and he didn't care how he did it. Oh, she did not doubt that was part of his plan, to make sure of her before they reached home. What might be excused as reckless but understandable behavior in a woman on the eve of her wedding day would be utterly condemned in a spinster.

What was she to do?

Fight, perhaps, get away at the first inn they stopped at to have the horses changed. But in that case, he could restrain her in the carriage, or even take her here. Fear curled through her like an old flame, slow, wily, waiting for its chance to flare up and conquer her. If she gave in to it, she'd lose her mind.

Unexpectedly, he twirled the pin in front of his face, watching it before he leaned forward and tucked it into the fabric of her green gown.

"It looks better on you. It's too feminine for me."

She failed to see that. He wanted it gone, though, and that was good enough for her. She would care for it until she met its owner or had a chance to return it to him. Or she could plunge it into Marcus's black heart. It wouldn't make much of a hole, but she'd feel better for it.

Could she create a bigger hole in his chest? She closed her eyes and then opened them again, letting her attention drift. Carriages usually contained pistols in holsters high up, but the ones in this vehicle were empty. No doubt Marcus had taken the precaution of removing them.

Her heart plummeted the rest of the way. Whatever the outcome of this madness, her ducal suitor would not want her now. He was the recipient of enough opprobrium already, but to marry a woman who had run off with her lover would be the outside of enough. And even a duke could not afford to turn his back on his network of contacts and friends. Leo was not in love with her—at least, she didn't think so—but he desired her. Desire was a transient thing. It died. So all they had to do was wait it out.

Why did that sound so hard? Why did despair hold her captive?

Because she loved Leo, that was why. And to her dismay, she thought she always would. Certainly she couldn't imagine anyone else in that part of her life. Not the man before her, that was sure and certain. Even if he ruined her, she would not marry him willingly.

He might force her. She could do little about that. With marriage such a transient thing, when men and women could hold hands and declare they were married, how could she deny it?

Forcing down her panic, she set herself to thinking and planning. Trying to devise a way to get away from him and save her reputation.

Despair caught her in its claws yet again, and this time she let it have its way. Whatever happened to her, she was doomed. Spinster or married to a man she was growing to actively dislike rather than tolerate, she would not have the future she had dared to believe was hers.

She would get away, and she would defy Marcus. That was all she had left. To that end, she took a mental inventory of what she had at her disposal, and what she might have if they stopped at an inn.

First she'd have to ensure they did stop at an inn before they reached the area where Marcus would be recognized and tolerated. And her. Being seen together in these circumstances would wreck what reputation she had left. Better to stop at an inn and take her chances on escaping.

She started to heave. If she did it enough, she could make herself sick. Then Marcus would have to stop.

* * * *

If they kept to the main roads, he should catch up with them before nightfall. Heedless of his own safety, Leo sent Linton ahead, to scout out the inns and roads. Unfortunately, major highways near London were rarely empty, so enquiries about recent carriages passing by only received disbelieving sniggers from the occupants of the houses along the route. Linton had insisted on accompanying him. He felt he had let Leo down, despite receiving a knock on the head that would have felled lesser men for a week. Dressed in plain clothes with a bandage wrapped around his head, he'd rejected all requests for him to get down and go inside the house. But secretly, Leo was glad to have him. He could trust Linton. His son served as Leo's tiger, and his wife was the head housemaid. Leo took care to keep the little family intact, not separating them to work at different houses, and they responded with their loyalty. Whatever happened next, Leo could trust the man implicitly.

Miss Childers had furnished Leo with ready money, and after scrawling her an IOU, he set off, letting no dust settle under his horse's hooves. He found food in the saddlebags and a plain coat, which he would change into at the first staging post. The woman was indeed most efficient. His town coat would stand out like a beacon once he got twenty miles outside the city, and he did not want his progress marked. Sending to his house for one of his steeds would have added to the head start Callow had on them.

Linton rode ahead and had fresh horses waiting at the staging posts. He cajoled the landladies into providing saddlebag food, the kind that could be consumed on the road, rather than wasting time at an inn table.

Linton had a weathered face, brown and lined. He didn't have a bit of fat anywhere Leo could see, and his hands were sinewy and skilled.

And Leo had the opportunity to question Linton, to see if he had discovered anything during his sojourn at Miss Childers's house. He chose his moment, just as they left an inn on fresh horses. They walked them while they ate their princely repast of bread and cheese. "Tell me about the conspiracy of footmen." He dragged another chunk of bread from his pack, giving his companion a chance to invent a lie.

"Oh, that rumor's been around for years, sir. Everybody's heard about it below stairs, but it's like the Masons. If you belong, you don't talk about it."

"I see." That made sense. "So what are the below stairs rumors?" He glanced up, a piece of bread in his hand, and took a bite, taking the time to steer his horse around a deep rabbit hole. "Considering this is a major thoroughfare, the road is in a terrible state."

"A lot of the roads around London are like that," the footman responded. "Too many carriages, not enough maintenance." He accepted the piece of cheese Leo handed him with a word of thanks. "I've seen and heard things," Linton continued. "Not anything definite, but there are a lot of stories around. Gossip is good currency. If you have a lively tale, the other domestics will look up to you."

Leo continued eating, letting the groom fill the pause.

"I've seen them come and go. Footmen are usually big and brawny, and they fill out a suit of livery well. In London they move around a lot from house to house. London servants don't have the staying power of country domestics." Linton stared ahead, watching the road. "Like other people, they're ambitious and very different. But the ones out for the main chance will keep the honest servants away. If there is a conspiracy of footmen, that's how it would start. And you know staff gossip, especially in London. People hear things."

"If this conspiracy existed, how would it be done? How could they steal something, say a necklace, and get away with it?"

Linton threw the heel of his bread away. A couple of birds landed on it and tore off pieces. Society attacking an outcast couldn't be more enthusiastic. "Easily, sir, especially in London, where people live close together. They just need to know who they're operating with and where the goods will end up. The footmen have families in London, who could possibly help them get rid of whatever it is. Once they have handed the goods to the next person, it can travel up the chain and be lost. No amount of searches will find it, and the faster that's done, the better."

"In theory, of course."

He had never considered, not for a second, leaving Phoebe with Callow, or not going in pursuit. He never believed her sister, and the ludicrous plan of taking Lucinda in exchange would have made him howl with laughter if the situation weren't so serious. If her sister had not put Phoebe right into the eye of the storm. Taking Phoebe from her abductor was a given, but if he could avoid the scandal of her abduction, she would find society much more comfortable. He wanted her so badly he'd consider estrangement from his beloved grandmother. That had never happened before; his grandmother was always paramount in his considerations. Not this time.

The news that the buffoon Callow had taken her rather than the more dangerous jewel thief was a relief, but even now Forrester could be in pursuit. Phoebe was the most vulnerable she'd been for weeks.

He'd left a message for his grandmother, which Miss Childers had promised to deliver, telling her he was gone unexpectedly out of town. Although usually he went out of town to visit a mistress, or to attend a sporting event, so his grandmother would accept the message. But his errand was different this time. This time was serious.

The afternoon wore on. They could expect dusk to fall at around half past seven or eight o'clock, but Leo had no intention of stopping. They must have made good time in the carriage. If they continued at this pace, he and Linton could expect to catch up with them before they arrived at Phoebe's home village.

As far as Leo was concerned, the time depended whether he would let Callow live or not. If he'd forced Phoebe into marriage, he would die. If not, Leo would let him go. Probably not without fisticuffs, because Leo badly wanted to hit him.

He could not give up. He would *not*.

* * * *

Phoebe's attempts at being sick did not work. She couldn't do it. But as Marcus lunged for her, his intent obvious, the world spun around them and a sickening sense of inevitability filled her mind.

Plenty of people died in carriage accidents, but at this moment, she didn't care. That kind of end might be the easy way out for her. She was ruined, she had lost the man she wanted above all others, and her life dragged before her in a series of miserable events.

Sounds of crunching wood and metal, and the higher-pitched noise of shattering glass crashed around her as she threw her arms up to protect her head.

The carriage lurched to one side, throwing her against the end of the vehicle, driving a few prickly splinters into her exposed skin. Screaming might not help, but she felt the impulse down to her soul and threw herself into her cry. If this was the last sound she made, she would make it worthwhile.

Cries from the driver and footmen, and curses from her traveling companion, added to the cacophony. The coach creaked and groaned as it settled into its new position, threatening to collapse around them. Phoebe found herself lying in an undignified heap against the door of the carriage, which was now the new floor.

Strangely, now it had happened, she didn't want to die.

A heavy weight lay on her leg. The weight moved, so instead of her leg, Marcus was pressing on her stomach. He levered himself off her using his elbows, clambering on the back of the seat. "Are you all right?"

"I don't know." Cautiously she moved, shifted her weight, starting with her feet, rotating them to see if anything hurt. Working slowly, she moved her limbs. She'd bruise for sure, but nothing indicated broken bones. And she wasn't bleeding much, only a few cuts and scratches. Starting at her toes, she tweaked every part of her body, bit by bit. So far, so good.

Marcus shook off the debris scattered over his body, scattering bits of wood everywhere. "Damn, I liked this coat," he muttered at the sound of ripping fabric. "New this season."

Paying Phoebe little heed, he climbed up the coach to the door at the top, using the seats as steps.

"Oh, leave me here. I'll be fine," she commented, injecting as much sarcasm as she could into her tone.

"I'll get you out," he said, as someone from the outside wrenched open the door, letting in a flood of cool air. Marcus hauled himself up.

"You got to get out of here, sir," a footman called. "We're on the edge of the ditch, and it's a deep one. If this carriage falls into it, you could get killed."

Oh good. Just what she wanted to hear. A lugubrious fatality took hold of her.

Her fashionable straw hat had broken, and the top half of the broad brim flapped over her face. She shoved it aside impatiently and caught her hand on a spur of shattered wood. "Ouch!"

Ruefully she sucked at the gash. Not serious, but she'd gained a few more splinters and it stung, adding to the myriad small aches and pains she'd suffered. But she wasn't badly hurt. It just felt that way.

Maybe they'd forget her. Marcus had never been the most attentive of men, his concentration mainly on himself. Perhaps, especially if he found he was hurt, he'd forget to have her rescued. If she stayed here, very still, she could scramble out when the commotion outside had stopped and find help. Because this inn was so close to her home they rarely stopped here, there was a chance the proprietors wouldn't know her or recognize her in her present bedraggled state. Maybe she could walk home or find a farm where she could hire a horse.

If the carriage didn't tumble into the ditch before she escaped.

Since she'd been shopping with her mother, she had a few guineas in her pocket, enough to get her on the stage back to London, or to hire a room somewhere else for the night. She had a chance to get away. Otherwise her future was looking bleak, and since nobody was here to help her, she had to help herself. And control that damned stammer, lest somebody recognize her through it.

A heavy thump sounded on the side of the coach, which was now its roof, and a broad masculine face appeared above, blocking out what little light there was. "Here we are, missus! Your husband asked us to get you. Said you weren't badly hurt."

"N-no, I-I'm not." So much for controlling the stammer. If only it responded to her command!

"I've got a sturdy rope here, and I've made a loop in one end. If you can catch hold, we'll haul you up."

She had little choice. Only then did the implications of that one word hit her. *Husband?*

Her exit from the wrecked carriage was not graceful. She paused to untie the tapes of her shattered hoops so she could climb out of them. The cane had split, the resultant sharp edges threatening to pierce her skin. They were of no use now. After catching the rope, Phoebe scrambled up. She couldn't arrange her skirts or smooth them down to hide her modesty, because there wasn't room, so she had to step and trip and hear the fabric tearing as she worked her way out.

At the top, two men, evidently ostlers or other workers at the inn, pulled her out, by dint of one man tucking his beefy hands under her armpits and the other grabbing what he could and dragging up the remains of her clothes behind her.

Sitting on the top of the coach, Phoebe went to pull off her broken straw hat, but then paused. The way the front flapped down over the side of her face might help to disguise her. After all, she was not far from home now, and someone might recognize her.

"Come on, missus. Your husband has bespoken a room for you. We can look after you there."

That blackguard Marcus Callow had used the accident to his advantage before she could. At least she still had her pocket strung around her waist firmly, even if she'd lost a lot of the gown she'd been wearing. "I'll need a change of clothes."

She'd have to go along with the husband masquerade for now. As long as Marcus had not used his real name. Then she'd deny him. Lord, what a tangle!

The men lifted her down onto solid ground, and Phoebe surveyed the carriage, noting that her supposition had been correct. It had lost a wheel. The rest of the vehicle was in a sorry state. Perhaps Marcus would have to pay for its repair. That was a bright thought that sustained her as she limped the half mile to the inn.

Phoebe mustered all the rude words she knew and said them deep inside. He would *not* turn her into a hoyden. So now everybody in this place would think they were married, and because they were so close to home, word could spread. Sir Marcus Callow arriving with a new wife would not go unremarked. When she had clean clothes, she fully intended to take to the road and go somewhere else. There had to be another inn, and she could call herself a widow, or a farmer's wife or any damned thing. Because as sure as her name was Phoebe North, she wasn't going to fall in with Marcus's plans.

Pausing at the side of the road, behind the improvised shelter of a large oak tree, Phoebe tore away at her gown until she could walk without tripping up. Without her hoops, a lot of the fabric trailed on the ground. Her fashionable high-heeled town shoes were no help either, but they were all she had.

The inn was substantial, its whitewashed walls standing foursquare to the road. Not one her family customarily used, fortunately, so with any luck she would not be recognized. Although it wasn't a cold day by any means, Phoebe shivered. Her ordeal was catching up with her. Ideally she'd want food, warmth, and sleep, but she was some way away from that yet.

The landlady fussed over her and took her straight up to the best bedroom. "Your husband has ordered the best for you, my lady. I have put some fresh clothes up there for you. Nothing as good as your own, of course, but you might be glad of them."

Should she deny Marcus now? Tell this woman she'd been abducted? Not yet, because if she could get away without fuss, that would be better. A shame this inn was isolated, although she'd caught a glimpse of a few rooftops not too far away. If she could make herself decent, she might still have a chance to escape.

The landlady opened the door and ushered her inside but didn't enter with her. The squat, old-fashioned four-poster was turned down, crisp linen sheets invitingly on display. The room also held a desk and chair, and a washstand stood just behind her.

Marcus sat in a tin bath in front of the fire, and he was stark naked. Turning his head, he gave her a beaming smile. "They'll bring more hot water up for you."

Her first reaction was to turn and run. But she needed the clothes she saw on the other side of the room. She edged to the far side of the bed, glaring at him.

Now they were alone, she could let rip. "How c-could you d-do this, M-Marcus? What on earth m-made you think I would w-want this?"

His smile faded, and his mouth took on a mulish pout as he leaned his arms on the white towels draping the tub. "You will, Phoebe. This is right. We were always meant for each other, you know that."

"I know n-no such th-thing."

"Maybe this will change your mind."

With what Phoebe regarded as a distinctly sinister smile, Marcus pushed up, the muscles cording on his neck. Unashamedly, *disgustingly* naked, he stood up and stepped out of the bath. He didn't even try to reach for a towel, although there were plenty available. Instead, he put his hands on his hips. "Not so sorry now, eh?"

Phoebe's blood boiled as, after one appalled glance, she kept her attention firmly on his face. "You're not the first naked man I've ever seen." Although very nearly the first. A brief glimpse of one of her brothers darting into his bedroom one night, and an equally brief sight of a farm worker disporting himself with his sweetheart was all. And neither of them had flaunted his...masculinity so blatantly. On both previous occasions Phoebe had averted her eyes and made her departure as fast as she could. This time she didn't have that option. She couldn't go anywhere like this; she needed the clothes draped out of her reach.

She emerged from behind the bed, firmed her jaw and headed for the clothes. She would not look.

Marcus lunged for her, and before she could escape, he wrapped his arms around her. "Let's start our married life now, dear Phoebe. We will be married tomorrow, so I will not dishonor you." He kissed the side of her neck, a wet kiss that left snail-slime on her skin.

She couldn't move.

Chapter 16

Leo's spirits rose when Linton headed toward him after another scouting expedition, though he had to wait until the footman had looped around him and drawn his horse up on his other side. They had to coast this stretch of road carefully, as it was riddled with cracks and holes, far too risky to go fast. They were getting closer to the village Phoebe called home, about fifteen miles away now.

"I'm sure we've found them," Linton said as soon as he got within speaking distance. "A carriage lost a wheel. It's around the next bend. Two people were inside, the man claiming they were married, but one of the ostlers at the next inn told me they were no more married than he was. He said she cringed when he referred to him as her husband."

Leo closed his eyes for a second, trying hard to control his reaction to the information. He had to keep a clear head now. "Did they describe the couple?"

"A big brute of a man, and a dark-haired woman with a gown much the worse for wear." He paused. "Her speech was halting."

Leo's heart missed a beat. "We have them." While he would have preferred to storm the inn and slash Callow from neck to groin, he was realistic enough to know he wouldn't get far. Not, at least, until he was in the room with him. "I will claim to be pursuing the man who made off with my wife. I'll use my family name, Cavendish, rather than my title, to avoid notice."

Linton touched his forehead, then pulled his hat down firmly. "I'm your attendant then, sir. I didn't tell anyone our business."

"I warn you that if he has hurt her in any way, I will challenge him. If you would rather not become involved, I understand."

"I welcome it," was Linton's growled response.

"Nevertheless, I will not hold you to anything from now on, because I intend to get Miss North back at any cost. Do you understand? At any cost."

Linton nodded. "Any man who snatches a woman off the street deserves what he gets. I am at your command, sir."

Leo would ensure he received a fat bonus, whatever happened next. This man was rock-solid loyal, and he appreciated that. "You may return to London if you wish, or I'll pay for you to rack up for the night anywhere you choose."

"Then I'll stay at the Hare and Hounds, sir."

"Let's get at it, then."

Taking the two miles to the inn at a leisurely pace proved difficult, but if he kicked his horse into a gallop, he would likely arrive at the Hare and Hounds with a broken leg. The road was very poor here.

Around a bend, they came upon a scene of activity. A carriage lay on its side, straddling the ditch running alongside the road. Its precarious position sent bile into Leo's mouth. Another inch or two and it would have tipped right into the deep furrow.

A broken wheel lay a short distance from the vehicle, testament to the reason for the fall. Three men busied themselves clearing the road, and one loaded a piece of luggage into the cart standing nearby.

Leo felt sick. She could have been pierced with shards of glass, stabbed with a sharp piece of wood, fallen and broken her head. He slowed his horse. "What happened here?"

One of the men straightened, a piece of broken axle in his hand. "Nasty do, sir. Two job horses, spooked, but the coachmen stopped them before they dragged the carriage up the road. A man and a woman. Husband and wife. Not happy." He winked. "Not sure about the right of it. Both in a mess, Lord love 'em. But they walked to the inn, so they came off all right, bar a few cuts and bruises."

Leo let out the first breath since he'd seen the damage.

His imagination tortured him with visions of Phoebe abused and hurt, unable to speak because of her distress. He would kill Callow if he'd touched a hair of her head. His sweet Phoebe was only just discovering her inner core of steel. If Callow had damaged her burgeoning confidence, he'd kill him. Hell, he'd kill the man anyway.

An orange sky lit their way to the inn, heralding impending sunset. The fields ahead, lushly green, were beautiful in their extravagant colors. Cresting a gentle slope, they looked down into the valley below. Such an idyllic scene hiding so much potential unhappiness.

A village, a mere scattering of houses lit by glows from the kitchen fires, lay at a short distance from the inn. At this distance the tranquility would have provided an excellent scene for a painter, but people moved, small figures turning a still life into a place where people lived and had their being. Many of the occupants would not cross their parish lines in their lifetimes, and visiting the nearest substantial town would be the greatest excitement they knew.

Focusing his thoughts, he scanned the scene before he concentrated on the building ahead.

An inn with yellowed, whitewashed rough walls stood foursquare to the road. A yard separated it from another building, probably the stables, so this was a staging post, where horses were kept for wealthy owners, and carriages and hacks were held for hire. This close to London, business would be brisk. At least it appeared respectable. A few people went about their business, and as he watched, someone entered the taproom at the front. A straggling line of houses and cottages stretched down the road, enough to receive the designation of village.

As he rode into the yard, an ostler ran up to take the horse from him. Leaving Linton to deal with the niceties, Leo strode into the taproom.

The stench of beer assaulted his nostrils, mingled with the scent of baking. His stomach rumbled, but he ignored it. He'd thrust the contents of his town coat into the pockets of the borrowed one, and now he drew out a handful of coins and let them clink in his palm. They would have to be earned.

Glancing around, he met the stares of curious locals and fellow travelers. Touching his hat, he turned to the innkeeper, who bustled up, a relatively clean white apron wrapped around his considerable frame. "A word, if you will," he suggested softly, but with unmistakable command. "I am looking for my runaway wife."

* * * *

A judicious application of guineas persuaded the landlord of the necessity of discretion, and the urgency of Leo's situation. He indicated the room where he'd shown the couple. The sound of steps told him the faithful Linton wasn't far behind.

Leo needed no more. Taking the bare wooden stairs three at a time, he raced up to the next floor, where the best bedroom was situated. Not bothering to knock, he lifted the latch and shoved, nearly stumbling when it gave way at once.

Leo took in the scene at a glance. A naked Callow lay on the floor, blood seeping from a wound on his head. Not much blood, but it didn't take much of a blow to kill a man. Leo should not be so happy at that potentiality, but he would not deny his reaction. The stench of cheap brandy filled the room. Phoebe stood over her abductor, a mallet-shaped decanter in her hand. It had not shattered, the thick glass more resilient than Callow's skull.

He jerked his head, and Linton came fully inside the room, kicking the door closed behind him. The footman put the pistols on a nearby dresser and crossed the room to place his fingers on the pulse at the side of Callow's neck.

Ignoring the man on the floor, Leo lifted Phoebe and held her tightly, burying his face in her neck until he could control his wayward reaction, his heart pounding against his ribs, relief filling him.

He took the decanter from her lax grip and placed it gently on the chest of drawers under the window.

Despite her state of dishevelment, the smudges of dirt on her face, and her tousled hair, she was the most beautiful woman he'd ever seen.

"Did he marry you?" If Callow had forced Phoebe to marry him, he would die, if he wasn't dead already.

"N-no. Tomorrow he said." Although tears stood in her eyes, she hadn't let them fall. But she clung to him, and he liked that. "I hit him," she said.

"I can see that. I'm proud of you, Phoebe. You did well." He couldn't see himself letting go of her any time soon, despite the reek of cheap brandy. He addressed Linton. "Get him out of here."

Linton opened the door again to reveal the landlord. Two likely men stood with him. Having Phoebe in his arms wasn't only necessary, it was expedient. The way she nestled close to him validated the story he'd told the man.

"This is your wife?" the landlord asked.

"It is." No hesitation or doubt marked his voice. "I found this villain forcing himself on her."

"I would take a bunch of birch twigs to him," the man said disdainfully. "Do you want him locked up? I can call for the parish constable if you want."

"No," Leo said, regretting his decision, but he needed discretion. Involving more people would hardly achieve that.

Callow was beginning to move, his body twitching, moans rumbling from his throat. Leo nodded to Linton. Wordlessly, Linton got on with his orders. The footman lifted Callow, demonstrating tremendous strength. Callow was no lightweight. Tossing the man over his shoulder, as if Callow weighed no more than a bag of apples, Linton pushed past the landlord to make his way downstairs.

"Turn him loose," he said. All Callow's belongings were in this room, so Linton would toss the man out of doors naked and barely conscious. Good. He'd have the things parceled up and sent on, but Callow would have to find his own way back to his home. That should keep him busy.

Although he was proud of Phoebe for striking Callow, Leo regretted not being able to beat this man to a pulp. On the journey here he'd lived every blow and enjoyed them all thoroughly. The barbarians he was descended from were never so close to the surface as now.

With the biggest obstacle out of the room, he gave swift instructions to the landlord. In very little time, the bath had been removed, a new one ordered, and the staff sent about their duties, leaving him alone with Phoebe.

"Come." The room was too small for a daybed, although it was comfortably furnished, so he carried her to the bed. She sat up and he joined her, leaving a respectable distance between them but holding her hands. "Poor honey! You have been through the wars, have you not?"

She lifted her gaze to his. But instead of meeting a distressed, weakened Phoebe, he saw a woman with fire in her eyes. "The m-man is a c-c-complete idiot! And a blackguard. How dare he d-do this t-to me? He has r-r-ruined me! D-does everybody know?"

He was glad to reassure her on that score. "They do not." And if his plans came to fruition, they never would.

She sighed, her bosom threatening to escape what was left of her bodice. The accident had destroyed her delicate gown. Smudges and tears marked the once-pretty fabric, together with bruises and scratches. No doubt she had bruises beneath. The need to care for her overwhelmed him.

"Wh-What happened? How did M-Marcus know where to f-find me?"

"Your sister was in league with him. She gave me a letter intended to prevent me from coming after you, but it was not in your handwriting. I have reason to know the way you loop your l's and cross your t's, do I not?" Unable to resist the temptation, he lifted her hand to his lips and kissed her palm.

She did not flinch away, as he half expected. Undergoing such an ordeal might make her wary of his sex for a while, but she showed no signs of it.

"Yes, you know m-m-my handwriting." Then her expression hardened. "L-Lucinda? I am s-s-so sorry she did that to you! I c-c-cannot imagine what she was thinking, and I am deeply sorry. I w-w-will make her s-s-sorry for this, you see if I don't!"

"I'm sure you will. However, I believe your father has plans for her. He has ordered her to return home, in the company of your mother."

"F-F-Father?" Her eyes widened. "D-Did my m-mother know, too? I was out with her shopping when M-Marcus took me. L-Lucinda said she had a s-sore throat, so she stayed at home."

Her stammer was slowly becoming less pronounced, turning into a slight and, to his mind, adorable hesitation at the beginning of a few words. He felt honored that she felt easy enough with him to do so, especially since she was barely aware of the change. "I don't believe your mother knew until she returned to the house. But she did try to support your sister. They both tried to persuade me that since you had run off with your childhood sweetheart, I would be better off with Lucinda." He shivered, shaking off the prospect.

Phoebe sighed. "Yes, she would s-say that. Lucinda is Mama's favorite, and if there was a b-brilliant m-match to be made, she would have Lucinda do it. L-Lucinda is the b-beautiful one, she says."

He snorted in derision. "As if a man of taste would prefer her to you. You have intelligence, wit, and beauty."

"W-w-wit? B-b-b-beauty?" Her voice rose incredulously.

"Yes." He lifted her hand to his lips and dropped another kiss on the back of it. He daren't go further, not until they had talked, because if he touched her, kissed her, especially in these circumstances, their talk would have to wait. He wanted this part over with and put behind them. "Your letters are a delight. I would have you continue them after we are married."

He was sorry to see the tears return. "We c-c-c-cannot m-marry now. You must know it. I am a scandal. M-Marcus w-w-won't keep quiet. He'll t-tell everybody I was alone with him for a d-day, that we sh-shared a b-bedroom. All I can do is return home and live quietly. That is if M-Marcus does not ruin even that for me."

"He will not, but you will not be going home to live. Phoebe, you're mine. We're marrying as soon as possible."

He refused to let her out of his sight. Afraid for her safety, his alarm exacerbated by the news that Callow had abducted her, he would not let her go. And he wanted her under the same roof he occupied. The only way to do that was to be married to her. He couldn't be sorry about that.

"No!"

"You don't want me?"

She shook her head. "Not that. Of c-course I do. But you're a d-duke, and you c-can't m-marry someone like me. You were c-caught with me in a grotto. Half of society thinks I stole that b-blasted necklace."

Knowing her resilience and her straightforward honesty, he had to tell her about Lisette. She would not appreciate him keeping the truth from her. The road ahead was difficult enough without that. Leo kept his gaze firmly fixed on hers as he told her about the events of the morning, the murder of his erstwhile mistress. And why she was killed.

Phoebe swallowed but said nothing until he was done, only wiped away her tears with a handkerchief he gave her. He appreciated that silence. Constant interruptions would have made his task much more difficult.

When he had done, she asked, "Y-You are s-sure it was for the necklace?"

"She had it, and it was stolen. Nothing else was."

"Was it the real one?"

"Latimer says not, and I believe him. She was wearing a paste bracelet and paste earrings to match the missing necklace."

She nodded. "And L-Lady Latimer would know her own n-necklace from a p-paste one." His wife-to-be was no fool. He enjoyed the way she thought through every implication. "I-I am s-sorry for the lady, of course, but I n-never knew her." She paused, frowning. "And y-you d-discovered this when?"

"This morning."

"Oh." Her eyes widened. "And you c-came to me after that?"

Giving in to instinct, he tugged on her hands and drew her closer. Truthfully he wasn't sure which of them needed the most comfort. "I went out of my mind when I realized you were gone. You're connected with the necklace, and people in some quarters think you stole it. Who's to say the murderer wouldn't have come after you?"

Telling her the truth, not hiding it from her, was doing her all the honor he could. This woman had strength, far more than people thought.

"We have names, now. Chapman, a footman who worked at the Latimer house, was there the night of the theft, but he has not been seen since. Latimer told me he disappeared. I suspect he was the person who stole the diamonds. And Forrester, a ruffian from St. Giles, or so Cocking the Bow Street man says. He would have taken the jewelry and sold it."

"Then *why* are they still looking for the pieces?"

"Only Forrester is. Maybe Chapman made off with the piece. So when La Coccinelle appeared at the opera with it, he might have assumed Chapman was connected to her, especially when Latimer was seen in her company. Forrester is looking for that necklace, and he is a ruffian of the first order. When I heard you had been abducted, I lost a year of my life."

Lifting her head, she met his eyes, her own wide. "But you knew I w-was with M-Marcus. He isn't a m-murderer."

"You could have been pursued. Neither of you knew what was coming. Forrester wants that necklace badly, and he will kill to get it." He hugged her closer. "I would have come after you in any case, because you are *not* marrying Callow, but the thought that you were in danger gave me wings."

"Oh." When she licked her lips, he followed the movement hungrily. He wanted to do that. "And escaping from my sister?"

His smile broadened. "Indeed. She was wearing one of your gowns when I saw her."

"She always s-stole my clothes if she thought they were too g-good for me, or if she thought they would look b-better on her."

"She will do so no more," he promised grimly. "She will be fortunate if I decide to let her through the gates of my estate."

"Why would she?" Phoebe demanded. "Oh, I see. I appreciate your k-k-kind offer, Your G-g-g-grace, b-b-but you must know it is imp-p-p-possible."

Damn, the stammer was back. He would love to kiss it out of her, but he doubted that would work. He would kiss her anyway. But when she was ready.

A tap on the door indicated the return of the inn staff. When he bade them enter, four people brought in a bath, draped clean towels around it, and filled it with hot water, putting more hot water cans close by. Then they opened a folding table that was standing against the wall and laid several covered dishes on it.

Leo gave them all generous vails and thanked them. They filed out.

He pulled out a chair. "Come and eat. Unless you'd rather bathe first?" Steam rose invitingly from the tub. Set before the fire, it would keep its heat for some time.

"Oh, I'm so hungry." She was careful to use the washstand to clean her hands before she sat. As he pushed the chair under her, she glanced up at him. "I will bathe when you have gone to your room."

He was going nowhere tonight. He'd sleep on the straw-strewn floor if he had to, brave rodents and insects for her. Or simply get them to bring in a truckle bed. "Then I'll join you in the meal, because I am hungry too. And we can talk while we eat."

Sharing a meal eased the tension thrumming through the room. As they consumed a homely but well-cooked meal, they chatted about town affairs, his decision to redesign part of his garden, and the latest fashions. Anything but the subject that obsessed both of them. Leo wanted to ease her, get her to accept him as part of her life. Because he was fully determined to do that as soon as they returned to London.

The way they behaved around each other would set a pattern for their married life. And while he did not believe in love as part of a lasting relationship, he did want friendship and fondness. He would be making his heir on this woman, God willing. He wanted more than a mechanical act of baby-making. Friendship, accord, and passion lay in their future. All they had to do was take it.

She was finally losing the tension that had strung her up tight. The tendons in her neck didn't stand out so much, and her movements were becoming less jerky, more fluid. Deliberately he lingered over the simple meal, giving her time to accept what would happen next.

Her stammer was almost gone.

Placing her silverware neatly side by side on her plate, Phoebe lifted her head and gave him her full attention. "I would ask you one more f-favor."

"Which is?" He was prepared to listen, but he had plans of his own.

"In the morning, c-could you escort me to my home? We are but fifteen m-miles away. I am sure my father will reimburse any expenses when you return to town. If I am not in London, they will forget me the sooner."

Revulsion and total rejection of her question swept through him. He got to his feet, piling the used dishes on the large tray the maid had brought, giving him a chance to control his mood. "Do you think I will forget you?"

"You are aware that I'm t-totally ruined?" Her voice was quiet, but her eyes told a different story. They blazed with anger.

"Not necessarily."

She waved a hand dismissively. "Faugh! Do not try to reassure me with p-platitudes! I am right, sir, I know. People saw me drive off with M-Marcus. The news will be the t-talk of the t-town by now. Our understanding must be at an end. Lady Latimer still insists I s-stole her jewels. How much more do you need?"

By now he knew better than to try to soothe her with lies. "It's not as bad as that. You can recover from this. *We* can recover."

"You *c-cannot* continue with our betrothal. Your grandmother would dislike it intensely, and society will c-condemn you along with the rest of us."

He loved her passion. He could use that for any number of things, but the one he had in the forefront of his mind did not involve anyone but the people in this room. "Society will have to bear it. No, sweet Phoebe, I will not abandon you. What kind of man do you think I am?"

"If I go home and reside quietly there, I will b-be a n-nine days' wonder."

"No." He could not articulate how much the notion repelled him. How could he dump her at her home and walk away? He knew the answer to that, though it appeared she did not. He utterly refused to do it. And he was about to tell her so, when she spoke again.

"You know you must. B-but there is s-s-s-something else. P-p-please, let me speak."

He had finished stacking the crockery, so he opened the door and put the mess outside for the maid to collect. That way they would not be disturbed.

What had caused her stammer to return? What was she about to ask him?

After ensuring the door was firmly closed, he approached the table again. But he did not sit; instead, he came around the table to her side of it. "What is your question?"

As she met his gaze, she swallowed. "I-I know I am d-d-d-destined for a l-life of spinsterhood. I have f-f-faced this b-b-before, and I am sure I can become accustomed to it. I will." She firmed her jaw, the tiny muscles tensing. "B-b-b-but I d-d-d-d-do not want to become a virgin spinster. We are about to part." Her speech sped up, as if she wanted this part over. "B-b-but here, you c-c-c-claimed you are my husband, so you would s-s-s-save me. I appreciate that. C-c-c-could you not become my husband, j-j-j-just for this one night?"

He reeled. "You want me to make love to you?"

"Yes."

Did she not realize that if he truly intended to quit her for good after escorting her home tomorrow, he would never agree to such dishonorable behavior? But his exasperation with her insistence warred with desire so strong he doubted he could behave as he should.

All his carefully laid plans flew out of the window. "Come here," he demanded in the kind of rough tone that should deter a delicately reared female.

But not Phoebe. Placing one hand on the table, she got to her feet in one smooth movement. Barely an inch separated them. She lifted her face. "Then kiss me."

Chapter 17

She'd done it, told him what she wanted. She would not grieve until tomorrow. She had won a night, one night to live a life, one night to fulfill her dreams. She didn't intend to waste it.

Strong and vital, Leo didn't need his title or riches to make an impact. He was everything she wanted, especially now. Would he accept her offer? She had done everything she could to persuade him. She was not practiced in seduction, so all she could do was ask, plainly and honestly.

Leo appreciated straightforwardness, she knew that. And he wanted her, she'd seen that gleam in his eyes, the warmth of interest, and the heat of passion.

Just like the look now. If tonight had consequences, she would deal with them, but she wanted this so badly. Her reputation ruined, she would only be destroying it further, and ruined was ruined. Her father would not see her begging on the streets. Most likely she'd be pushed into the background, left to molder in the family home, the disregarded spinster sister who had once created a scandal.

After all, when she went to London, that was the fate she had thought she was heading for. But oh, before she accepted her future life, she needed this one night out of time.

Leo set his hands on her forearms. His breath heated her cheek. "Be sure, sweetheart, because if we do this, there is no undoing it."

She nodded. "I will m-m-manage." There were ways.

"You will do more than that. Here and now, let me make myself clear. If we do this, if there is any intimacy between us, we marry, and as soon as maybe."

She did not say yes. She would not give him her response until she'd had what she wanted from him. Because she had no intention of marrying him, allowing him to go through the fire with her. She could, single-handedly, ruin his title, his reputation, and his fortune. That would not happen.

But this would.

Slowly, as if giving her a chance to change her mind, he leaned forward and then his lips were on hers.

The welcome pressure opened her to such relief she let him take her weight, while she regained her equilibrium. He held her securely, with no hesitation. He caressed her lips with his, until she was ready to open further to him.

When she did, he slid his tongue inside her mouth, giving her his delicious flavor, all male and, for tonight, all hers. She responded, touching her tongue to his, moving closer, his clothes rustling.

As they kissed he spread his hand over her back between her shoulder blades, supporting her while he set his other hand to work unhooking her gown at the front where the hooks had not torn away. For the most part her gown had held together, but several rips to the skirt and grime from the accident had made the garment useless. Despite that, he unfastened it with care, as if it was the most precious of silk brocades.

Finishing the kiss, he opened his eyes and gazed at her as he slipped the gown off her shoulders and down her arms. She let it go, and it fell with a quiet *whoosh* to the floor, leaving her in stays and petticoats. She kept her gaze steady and smiled up at him. No doubt he was watching her so carefully to gauge any change in her decision, but he would not find it This night belonged to her, to them. Nothing outside this room mattered. If her life was to consist of hours instead of years, so be it, but she would allow nothing to spoil it.

"Turn around."

She obeyed, facing the tarnished mirror while she watched him behind her, unlacing her stays. The sound of tape pulling through eyelets audibly reminded her of the intimate service no man had ever performed for her before. Usually the maid loosened them, and she slipped the stays over her head, but tonight Leo pulled the tapes completely clear until the garment hung loose on her frame. She lowered her arms and let the straps slide down them, sending the stays to join her gown on the floor.

Before she dispensed with her pocket, she delved into it and found her handkerchief, unwrapping the contents. She offered it to him. "Here's your pearl pin. That was how he enticed me into the coach. He wore it on his lapel and said I could have it back if I allowed him to talk to me. I never imagined he'd drive out of London."

He took the pin from her, twisting it between his finger and thumb. "I will give you something to replace it. I expected you to wear it, to proclaim your possession of it for all to see, but you never did. You shall have something better." He tucked it in his coat.

She shook her head, feeling a hairpin come loose and tumble down her back. His gaze followed its journey, and he lifted his free hand, delving into her hair and discovering more pins. They fell in a shower now, her loosened hair falling to below her shoulders. "I've been wanting to do that for a while."

"Really?" The notion enchanted her, thinking of him watching her and her primly pinned-up hair. She rarely used lovelocks or ringlets, but tucked it neatly away in her cap. The cap had gone along with her hat, discarded. With, it seemed, her reputation.

He sifted his fingers through the fallen locks, gently disentangling the dark mass. "So silky," he murmured. His gaze snagged hers and heated in a second. Cupping the back of her neck, he urged her back for another kiss.

Since Leo had not even removed his coat, and she was in shift and petticoat, Phoebe felt decidedly, gloriously wanton. Without confinement, he could see her. The shadowy outlines of her nipples showed against the fine linen of her shift, and they stood proud. When he drew her close, she pressed against him, seeking to soothe the ache building inside her.

He kissed her as nobody had before, including himself, his intent clear: to prepare her for his possession, to feed her desire. He only left her mouth to kiss across her cheek and tease her earlobe, then her throat.

The tapes of her petticoats came loose under his deft fingers. When he pulled her forward, she willingly stepped out of them.

In a sudden movement, he dropped down onto one knee. After dragging his coat off, Leo bent to her shoes, unfastening the buckles so she could discard them. He ran one hand up her stockinged leg, over the calf, leaving trails of warmth behind him, and found her garter, just above her knee. He pulled that loose, too, then performed the office for the other leg.

No man had ever been that close to Phoebe, and very few women for that matter. She usually saw to dressing herself, unless for a grand occasion, and even then she donned her stockings and undergarments herself before the maid arrived. Now a man knelt at her feet, his head level with her most intimate place. If he breathed deep, he'd be able to smell her arousal.

With a small groan, he dropped his head, pressing his forehead against her stomach. "I can do this," he muttered. "I can take my time. You are divine, my Phoebe. I want you so badly." He slid up, then tilted his head so he was meeting her eyes, the mounds of her breasts in his field of vision. "I will not dishonor you. I will…" Pausing, their gazes met and clung, before he got to his feet.

His hands went to his throat, unfastening his neckcloth so the long strip of fabric hung either side of his strong throat, the Adam's apple bobbing when he swallowed.

He held out his wrists to her. "Here."

She had to concentrate on unfastening them, buttons on cuffs not being familiar to her. But she slipped the small horn buttons through the holes, releasing him so he could drag the garment over his head. It pulled out of his breeches, but he kept tugging until all the shirt was out and gone.

Her throat went dry. Leo seemed bigger out of his clothes, an impossibility that he was demonstrating as reality. His broad chest confronted her, sprinkled with dark hair, echoing the color on his head. Dark nipples punctuated the expanse. "Do I continue?" His voice had turned sultry.

Trying to moisten her throat, Phoebe nodded. She couldn't have spoken right now, but she wanted to see him. All of him.

Leo unfastened the fall at the front of his breeches, then the buckles at the knee. Kicking off his shoes, he dragged all his garments down and off.

Naked, he stood before her. "Now you can see how much I want you." She could indeed. His erection stood proud, grazing his stomach, primed and ready for her.

When he held out his arms, she went straight into them with no hesitation. They bound her to him. "Bed," he murmured and, without warning, bent and picked her up as if she weighed nothing, carrying her to the bed and laying her down on the sheets she'd eyed earlier when she feared what lay ahead for her.

But that was with the unlamented Marcus. Now she would be deeply disappointed if she spent the night alone here. As he helped her out of her last remaining garment, she let her gaze stray to below his waist, where she had not dared look before.

As she stared, a few drops of clear liquid emerged from the tiny opening at the top of his shaft. Greatly daring, she touched it, felt the moisture on her fingers, and licked them off.

He had gone still, watching her. Now he groaned. "Sweetheart," he murmured, so softly she barely heard him. "You honor me."

"It's a bit salty." She hadn't been aware she'd said it aloud, but that single taste had made her thirsty for more. He kneeled in the position he'd used to dispose of her shift, where she sat on her calves, at eye level with that magnificent—cock.

Her brothers had called it that when they thought nobody was listening, and they'd used other names, too. But she liked that one. Pressing her lips to the smooth surface, she marveled at the heat emanating from it.

"Touch it." He sounded hoarse.

She did, sliding her fingers up from the base, loving the softness of his skin covering the iron-hard muscle beneath. She traced around the rim, the indent where it flared out to the sensitive thin skin at the top. As carefully as a jeweler uncovering a treasure, she touched it.

"Harder."

Daring, she pressed.

He groaned. "Phoebe, you will be the death of me."

Discovering she could not encircle the base of his member with one hand, she brought her other hand into play, finding what he liked. He encouraged her, urging her on with soft words and instructions.

"Suck it."

She didn't need to be told twice. Holding the shaft steady, she opened her mouth and took him in. To have a man under her hands, making him helpless as she took him, gave her a new sense of power, a control she could not have imagined before tonight.

His balls tightened, and his erection stiffened even more, as if it might burst.

He grabbed her under her arms, dragged her away, and held her tightly, slamming his mouth down on hers as his shaft pulsed between them, his release erupting between them.

They stayed like that for a long time, until he pulled his mouth away from hers and gasped, tilting his head back to take greedy gulps of air. His heart pounded against his ribs. She moaned with the intensity of the moment.

He kissed around the rim of her ear before he separated them, cool air blasting down her skin as he guided her to lie on the bed. Her lips swollen with his kisses, her skin wet with his essence, she could do nothing but watch him as he climbed down from the bed and wet a cloth in the bathtub.

Coming back to her, he stroked the cloth over her stomach, cleaning it thoroughly before he rubbed it roughly over himself and tossed it over his shoulder, the small splash informing her it had met its target.

He gazed down at her, scanning her body with the kind of heat that made her skin prickle before climbing back up to straddle her. "You're so lovely," he said as he spread his hands over her waist and up to her breasts. "I didn't mean for that to happen, but it's probably for the best. I still want you so much, but some sanity has come back to me. Now it's my turn. Or rather, your turn." His wicked grin made her tingle right down to her toes.

A caress that spread sparks of arousal followed.

His touch made her feel delicate and precious, not a feeling she was used to. Cupping her breasts, he concentrated his attention there, lowering his head to take one nipple into his mouth, then the other, delivering wet caresses that made her shudder and push up to him, eager for more. He sucked, then licked, enjoying each pointed peak like a special delicacy. "Pretty pink." Phoebe loved the soft words as Leo took inventory of her body. He stroked her skin, caressed down to her waist, and farther. Where he paused and gazed up at her.

The flickering candlelight revealed eyes that were nearly all pupil, his concentration intent, and all for her. That gaze roused her, made her want him more than she could have imagined.

"I will keep my promise," he said. "We will enjoy one another, but I will leave you intact until our wedding night. I will preserve your honor if it kills me."

"You don't have to." In fact she would rather he did not. Tonight would not be complete if he did not make her his in every way possible.

"I do. I will."

And she would do her best to persuade him otherwise.

But for now, she let him explore, watching and learning. And heating her body to an impossible degree. "Leo."

"Shh." He was kissing her stomach, dropping feathery kisses over her skin, working his way down to the part of her she knew could deliver shocking pleasure. Of course she had explored herself, even found the key to her pleasure, but she would never admit that to anyone. But most women did that, didn't they? Either that or made their maids do it when they were helping them wash. At least she'd overheard one lady in London telling another. That kind of decadence lay beyond her experience, but it appeared she was about to undergo something similar. Something better.

His fingers slid between the lips guarding her innermost secrets. "So wet. Open for me, Phoebe. Let me in." His use of her name was more intimate than any endearment he could have used. He was with her, nobody else, and he knew it, acknowledging it while he touched his tongue to the tiny knot of skin at the front. He moaned. "Your taste is exactly what I imagined."

Phoebe licked her lips to moisten them. "You imagined this?"

He lifted his head, met her gaze. "Oh yes. Didn't you?"

"Yes, but my imagination is not this vivid."

With a chuckle he went back to his self-imposed task, the vibrations from his words adding to the thrills coursing up her body, claiming her.

Slowly he increased his pressure on that part of her and brought his fingers into play, dancing them down to her opening, then back, caressing and stroking her up. The sensations grew, and she gave up marking their passage, giving in to the powerful ripples invading her.

He built the storm inside her, pushing her with fingers and tongue, exploring every inch of her.

Almost every inch. But he didn't breach her opening. Instead, he stroked around the entrance with one finger, caressing, making the sensitive skin so responsive that Phoebe gave a cry of helplessness.

An impulse made her arch her back, push her body into him. Try to persuade him to take that final step. She wanted her virginity gone, so she could enjoy this man to the fullest extent. For tonight he was hers, and she belonged to him. And she would never forget.

When he hummed against her skin, she could take no more.

The sensations building in her body rose, joined together into one peak. Phoebe shrieked his name, her body convulsing, and only his restraining hand on her stomach prevented her tearing herself away from him. He tortured her to another, unrelenting in the intensity of her response until she went mindless, a soft explosion, senses tumbling, driving her to another place.

Phoebe had no idea if she had fainted or just temporarily floated in the air, but she found herself in Leo's arms, cradled next to his powerful body. Reaching down, he snagged the edge of the sheet and pulled it over them. Cocooned, she snuggled closer before realization hit her. "We didn't—you didn't…"

"No." The sound of his voice had a physical reality, too, rumbling through her, a delicious reminder of what he'd done to her. "That will not happen yet. Not tonight, sweet Phoebe. Although most of this house knows that I pleasured you."

She gave a small shriek and buried her forehead against his shoulder. "Oh God help me, I can never come back here."

"I don't see why not." He sounded amused, damn his eyes. "Everyone except your benighted abductor thinks we're husband and wife, and he is long gone."

"He is?" Lifting her hand, she cupped his cheek, made him look at her. But he only turned his head and kissed her palm.

"He is. If he tattles, we will gainsay him. I had planned that we would marry at the end of next month, but circumstances being what they are, I will bring that forward to the day after tomorrow."

"What?" Now she was fully awake. Pulling herself up, she sat on the mattress and drew the sheet with her.

He gave her a lazy smile and lifted himself to join her, slipping his arms around her waist. "Ah yes, that bath. The water in the cans will still be hot. We can salvage it."

"No!" She gave a small shriek as he climbed off the bed and scooped her up, disentangling the sheet to leave it on the bed. "Married?"

Ignoring her protests, he deposited her in the cool water and bent to pick up a can. "Scoot forward, sweetheart."

Automatically, she did as he bade her. Hot water splashed in, until she let out a sigh of contentment.

"Now lie back and raise your knees."

When she did so, he emptied the contents of the second can at the other end.

Bliss. Except she could not let him gloss over what he had said. But with her muscles warming and releasing any tension they had left, Phoebe found concentrating difficult.

He spoke, a soft river of words, not allowing her a chance to interrupt. Leaning his arms on the side of the bath, his skin a darker contrast to the white towels the maid had draped over the metal surface, he smiled. She had never seen Leo smile like that before, with wholehearted pleasure, not a trace of cynicism or sarcasm.

"A shame this thing isn't bigger, then I could join you. Inns always have such tiny baths." Picking up a cloth from the chair nearby, he dipped it in the water and picked up the cake of ivory soap, running it over the wet surface. While he spoke he washed her, so thoroughly he brought a blush to her cheeks. "I will brook no argument, Phoebe. I may not have taken your virginity, but I have taken your innocence. We are bound together now, more by what we have just done than what happened elsewhere today. We will marry, sooner rather than later."

"We can't." Why couldn't he see reason? "I am ruined."

"You will be if I take you back to London without a ring on your finger. You belong to this parish, do you not? Then we will travel to your home, and we will marry there. I have a special license in my coat pocket. We may marry in the church tomorrow, if the incumbent minister has the time. Believe me, sweetheart, he'll have the time. Then, after a night at your residence, we will return to London and the felicitations of our family."

"There is no need, truly. I never meant to trap you…"

Dropping the cloth, he grasped her hand and threaded his fingers between hers. "If I had not wanted to be trapped, I wouldn't have allowed it. Phoebe,

I know our betrothal began with a pretense, but it will end in reality. I spoke to your father yesterday, before I heard you had been abducted."

"I know, but I never thought you would agree…"

He nodded. "We are in agreement. We worked out the marriage contract then, and we will sign it when we return to London. You will be a wealthy woman, my dear. But that has not crossed your mind, has it?"

She shook her head.

"I thought not. Nevertheless, it will happen." One by one, he kissed her fingers, then dipped their conjoined hands in the water.

"It cannot! I cannot allow you to…"

His smile stopped her. "Answer me truly, Phoebe. Is the idea of marriage to me so repugnant? Do you not like me enough to contemplate spending the rest of your life with me?"

"I would love—"

He touched his fingers to her lips, stilling her response. "Not that. I have seen love tear holes in people's lives. I want us to be sure of our friendship, of the pleasure we take in one another, before we commit to this. But not love. Don't talk about love. You, Phoebe, are a delight. You have just proved how well we combine in bed, and our letters have revealed a side of you I admire. Your intelligence, your compassion, they all call to me. We are friends, and that is so much more than love."

As if he'd pierced her to the core, pain sliced through her side. She couldn't have spoken if she'd tried.

But he hadn't finished. "Once we are married, you will have a measure of protection against the accusations of theft. The Duchess of Leomore is someone who commands respect."

"So you are doing it to p-protect me?" She couldn't bear that, to be married out of pity or expedience.

"Partly." The corner of his mouth tilted in a wry smile. "But not entirely. We could have extricated ourselves from this crisis a different way. But I chose not to. You do not deserve the fate of the unmarried spinster, Phoebe, and I will not allow it. You have too many gifts to let them go to waste. I should tell you that my grandmother will be shocked by the speed of our union, and people will suspect we have anticipated our vows, but we will show the world how devoted we are to each other. We do not have to live in each other's pockets forever, never fear. But by the end of the season people will become used to seeing you. During the summer they will meet you at one or other of the estates I own. You will belong, I promise you."

"But my family, my s-sister…"

His smile turned into a grim line. "Indeed. Lucinda. Your father rescued me from that fate. Not that I would have taken it, but she could have created more trouble for you."

"My f-father did?" Phoebe hadn't seen her father act so decisively for years in the domestic matters he left to her mother. But then, he hadn't had to. So much easier to allow her mother to take the brunt of the decisions, and the blame for them. Her father liked to be liked, and this way he was a popular man.

"Yes he did. He told your mother and sister to pack and return home. Now, sweetheart, climb out of that water and let me dry you. Then get into bed and wait for me."

"Oh!" Her cheeks heated with anticipation of what would come.

He tapped her lips. "No, not that. Enough for one night. When I take you, it will be as your husband." He gave a wry smile. "Although if I had to wait longer than a day, I don't know if I would keep my resolve."

Chapter 18

If he had slept in that bed, Leo would have taken her. But he wanted to do this properly. Marrying this woman gave them a life together, and he wanted it to start as a marriage should. His parents had demonstrated the wrong way to do almost everything, including Leo being a "premature baby."

Enough irregularities were happening already. He did not wish for more.

So he found a clean shift for Phoebe from the pile of clean clothes left by the maid and gave it to her before sliding in with her and drawing her close. She was exhausted; he felt the heaviness as she rested her head on his shoulder. She felt right. She hadn't protested his decision very much, which was not like her. "Married," she muttered just before she dropped off. Unfortunately she said it with a derision indicating she didn't believe him. Not entirely.

At least she wasn't trying to run.

When he judged the time safe, he slid out of bed. Even then she moaned when he eased her out of his arms. His erection was already raging. It would have to wait.

Instead of a bath to ease the aches of a day on horseback, he made do with a thorough wash in hot water. He could not remain here and not make love to her.

He snatched up his shirt and threw it over his head, thrusting his arms through the sleeves with a vigor the action didn't deserve.

Good Lord, anyone would think he was a tyro fresh from the schoolroom, impatient to carve a swathe through Europe. That was the reason every parent who could afford it sent their sons on a long tour of the continent. They could sow their wild oats out of sight of society. Sadly, the theory didn't always work. Instead, the young men returned from Europe not only rampant, but practiced. Rome had some extremely skilled whores.

Leo climbed into his breeches, taking care when he fastened the fall because his erection had already developed to near-painful. What on earth did this woman do to him, and why? She was lovely, true, and he had a simpatico with her so rare he couldn't remember experiencing it before, even with his friends. She had upended his life to a point where he was ready to commit himself to one woman.

For the rest of his life?

He had no way of knowing for sure, but at present that was the way he felt. It couldn't be love; he wouldn't allow the distress that caused into his life. A glance to where Phoebe slept caught her sprawled on her stomach, head turned to one side, hair tumbled over the pillow, arm outstretched as if she was reaching for him even in her sleep. Nothing would please him better than to join her. But he *would not*. He had too many things to do. And a taproom to explore.

Normally the notion would give him some pleasurable anticipation, but not tonight. All his anticipation was elsewhere. Picking up his coat, he put it on and checked his pocket for the license. He checked his pocket watch. It was after midnight, because today was his wedding day.

He would go downstairs, order a pitcher of beer and a meat pie, and stand vigil. Nobody was coming close to her while he was around.

Perhaps he'd send a few instructions to London. He'd already left his factotum several instructions, but he wanted more. Everything had to be perfect for the woman he was making his bride.

Planning would see him through this long night.

* * * *

Leo sent the maid to rouse Phoebe at seven, with a tray piled high with food and a large pot of tea. When she returned, the woman reported that she was already up. Leo longed to go up to Phoebe, but he should give her some peace. He drummed his fingers on the scarred table before him until she appeared half an hour later. She wore the simple costume the landlady of the inn had provided, but to Leo's gaze she'd never looked so beautiful.

As she looked around, he rose, came forward to take her hand, and lifted it to his lips. Even the touch of her aroused him, so innocent and everyday. The sooner he got her into bed, the better. Last night was only a taste of what was to come, and he couldn't wait.

He'd hired a carriage from the inn to take them to her home, and it waited outside. He'd sent a servant from the inn to London, to collect his traveling coach, deliver the necessary messages to their families and generally prepare the way.

The landlord addressed him as "Your Grace" as they left the inn. He saw no reason to hide his identity, and it got him better service.

After he'd tenderly helped her into the vehicle, Phoebe faced him. "So you are t-trapping me into m-marriage by leaving this place in d-ducal splendor? They'll all know now. There'll be gossip a-plenty."

Leaning back against the squabs and repressing his sigh of relief, to ease his muscles against something that was actually comfortable, Leo addressed his betrothed. "I spent most of the night downstairs. The taproom was rarely empty, and I ensured people knew I was there. Besides, once Linton let slip one "Your Grace," the cat was out of the bag. And we are to marry today, in case you have forgotten."

"I still don't understand how you c-can expect to do that. Our v-vicar is an honest man. He won't be bribed."

"This is your parish, is it not, the place you reside?"

She nodded.

"Then we may wed. This license entitles me to dispose of the banns, although we must marry in the church where one of us resides. I see no problem. I sent Linton with a note to the vicar, warning him of the eventuality, and just before you came downstairs I had his reply. He will be pleased to marry us half an hour before noon."

Her jaw dropped. Leaning forward, he tucked his finger under her chin, and pushed it closed. The trouble in her eyes concerned him, but she spoke first. "I cannot m-marry you. You m-must know that. You did not b-b-b—"

For once he stopped her finishing her sentence. He kissed her, drawing her close, savoring her and giving her a taste of what was to come. She was panting when they parted. "No more of that. I am set on you, and I know you want me. Don't even try to deny it. No self-sacrifice, no foolish talk." He pressed another kiss to her lips. "If you really feel you cannot marry me, if I repel you so much, then say it now."

He forced himself to draw back.

She watched him, her face pale, but her lips reddened from his kisses. He gave her the time she needed, but after five minutes, when his patience was running thin, she gave him her answer. "Then yes. Yes, I'll marry you."

He couldn't resist another kiss, and this time he didn't release her but settled her head on his shoulder.

"I am to marry at home. I could not have wished for anything better."

He settled their linked hands on his thigh. "I will donate a tidy sum of money to the bell fund. Or the window fund or whatever the vicar prefers. There will be no scandal, I swear. I wanted you comfortable."

She waved her free arm, indicating the splendor of a well-sprung carriage and comfortable leather seats. "How could I not be? So what are your p-plans now?"

He smiled, not missing the sarcastic tones. "We'll go to your home and marry from there. Then leave for London in the morning. I fear we must bear the good wishes of our friends as well as we are able. We will show society how well matched we are, then, if you wish, leave for the country. My grandmother will want to see you."

"Sh-she won't be p-pleased," Phoebe observed sagely.

Leo was forced to agree. "She will not, but she will come around. She approves of you, dearest, so she will accustom herself to the speed of our union. After all, her main purpose in getting me to marry is to fill my nursery. I trust you are not averse to that?"

He was slipping. His bored duke act only raised a smile from her. A delightful blush spread from her neatly folded fichu to the top of her forehead, her cheeks rosy flags he longed to taste and kiss. But no, he would not have his Phoebe arriving at her family home in that state, even if the only people waiting for them were servants. The new Duchess of Leomore would be gracious and happy, not flushed with desire.

That would come later.

The fifteen miles between the inn and her home passed in less than two hours, and soon they were drawing up outside a comfortably sized manor, which reminded Leo strongly of his hunting box in Leicestershire. Since Sir Frederick found great enjoyment in riding to hounds, that comparison seemed entirely appropriate.

The front door opened, and a wizened male face peered out. A small man came through, careful to close the door behind him, but at the sight of the occupants of the carriage, a broad smile cracked his face.

Linton jumped down and smartly opened the carriage door, letting down the steps. Leo went down first and gave her his hand. He could have sworn she was preparing to jump down on her own.

Her attention was all for the small man who waited to greet her. "Robson! It s-seems an age s-since I last saw you! So much has h-happened!" She clasped his hands warmly before turning to address Leo, who stood by, smiling. He had family retainers too, but most of them remained in the country, except for the Lintons, who accompanied him everywhere.

Robson would not do as well in town. His black wool coat, shiny and too big for him, spoke of long use, and the way he met Phoebe's gaze directly spoke of long acquaintance. "Your mother and your sister arrived late last night," he said.

Damn. Perhaps they could marry and get back to town by nightfall, instead of staying the night. But Leo had to regretfully abandon that scheme. Town was a full day away. He could not rush Phoebe back to town and staying anywhere else would give rise to damaging gossip for the Norths.

Even so, he was tempted.

Phoebe turned to him, her expression mirroring his dismay. "Oh, I had no idea they would be back so soon. They must have hurried."

Leo smiled grimly. "Yes, they must." No doubt to encourage Phoebe's union with Sir Marcus. He glanced at Robson but felt sure he could trust the man.

He wasn't imagining the satisfied smile touching Robson's thin lips. "They said they had tired of the city, sir, and they had left Sir Frederick to finish his business there."

Leo humphed. "They would say that, would they not? However, it is because of my pursuit of the lovely lady here. Robson, Miss North has done me the greatest honor of accepting my hand in marriage. We are to wed today, so I would prefer her to be taken to a room where she may make herself ready."

"I can show you to Mr. Freddie's room, sir. I am sure he won't object, and there is no sign of the young gentlemen."

"They're kicking up their heels in the city. I appreciate the use of the room."

"We don't have too many spare rooms." Phoebe paused, biting her lip, and Leo wondered what she was about to say.

"This way, sir," Robson said, going back to the door.

Phoebe moved closer to Leo. Just where he liked her to be. "He's our family butler, but so much more than that. My father made him his land steward a few years ago, and he says he is excellent at his work."

"Thank you for that, ma'am," Robson said without turning around. "My ears might be old, but they're as sharp as ever."

Phoebe only laughed. Leo liked seeing her so at ease with a member of her father's household. Her brothers were rips, but harmless; her sister was pure poison. Stupid poison at that. Her mother always took the side of her youngest child.

Sibling relationships were a closed book to Leo, but he was learning fast.

* * * *

"There you are!" Lucinda stood in the room she shared with Phoebe, her hands propped on her hips. "You and the duke!" Her voice held a nasty, sneering tone.

Phoebe went to the bed and began to strip off her borrowed clothes. Checking her clothes press, she found something suitable to wear. From the look of Lucinda's clothes press on the other side of the room, her younger sister had availed herself of Phoebe's London wardrobe. She would leave it for her sister, compensation for losing the prize she really wanted.

Lucinda rounded the end of the bed. She was fit to burst with anger. "Did you stay with him at the inn? Did you seduce him? That is so like you, Phoebe, you always want what I have."

Strangely Phoebe wasn't at all inclined to answer. There was no point. She found a clean shift and pair of stays. Plain cream cotton, but they would serve. Fortunately they were already laced, because she could expect no help from Lucinda. She lifted the garment over her head and reached around for the tapes, expertly pulling them tight and tying them around her waist.

"I knew it! Mama agreed that he was for me, and when I told her that I'd given Marcus his heart's desire, she congratulated me."

That part deserved a response. Phoebe straightened and faced her sister, a fresh petticoat in her hands. "Your act d-did nothing but d-deprive you of a s-season in London. M-Maybe you should m-marry Marcus. I shall not."

Lucinda's lips curled in a sneer. "He wouldn't have you now. You're spoiled goods."

Phoebe met her gaze steadily. "B-Beautifully spoiled. Utterly and c-completely spoiled."

Lucinda flinched. "Well, if you get with child, don't come to me or Mama for help. Likely she'll have Papa cast you out completely."

If she told Lucinda of their plans for the day, she wouldn't give Phoebe any peace. Let her find out for herself. "I must ch-change. If you d-don't want to help, then please leave."

Grumbling, Lucinda helped her tie her petticoat tapes, but she didn't stop complaining. "It's all your fault. I could have had a duke, Phoebe. I was born for the London life, you know that. Look at me! I've always been able to charm any man I wanted to."

"C-considering the only men you've charmed are F-Frederick and P-Papa, that's n-not saying m-much."

But Lucinda had been balked of a season in London, one, moreover, at the center of society. She'd dreamed of it all her life, and an act of spite had deprived her of it. She was only eighteen, and a young eighteen at that. In a few years Phoebe would ask her back. But not yet. She had to establish herself yet, and it was that, rather than her upcoming wedding, that was turning her mouth dry and tightening her throat.

"And don't forget Marcus," Lucinda said silkily.

"He's a f-fool. A handsome, stupid one. T-Take him if you w-want him. I d-don't." She could say that with a clear conscience. Although Marcus had abducted her, he'd done it at Lucinda's bidding. Phoebe wasn't sure that Marcus would have tried to take her forcibly. Knowing him as she did, she would say not. Marcus was thoughtless, not violent, and as self-important as they came. He would have assumed that Phoebe would be an easy conquest.

But if she'd said no, would he have left?

That question remained unanswered, and she would always be profoundly glad that it would.

* * * *

An hour after their arrival, a rumbling sound announced a coach drawing up outside. A glance out of the window assured Leo his coach had arrived. His valet leaped down, carrying a large bag. A trunk was strapped to the rear of the vehicle. His valet appeared in his bedroom and got to work. They had to maneuver their way around a room considerably smaller than what they were used to, but between them they got him ready. His valet had packed the scarlet cloth coat and sewn on the gold buttons with his coat of arms. The waistcoat was ivory silk, and he wore ivory breeches, not a speck marring their immaculate, smooth surface.

A fresh black ribbon held back his newly washed and smoothed hair. As a final touch, he slid the pearl pin from the pocket of yesterday's breeches and pushed it into the folds of his neckcloth. When he held out his hand, his valet gave him his gold hunter watch, the snuffbox he carried but rarely used, a purse full of gold and silver, and the small box containing the ring he would give to Phoebe. It was the plain gold band he'd ordered. He would shower her with diamonds and rubies in the fullness of time, but he wanted the contract between them marked with something plain and honest.

When his valet approached with the pounce pot, Leo waved him away. "No powder." He glanced at the dark shadows under the man's eyes. "You made good time. It's a full day's journey to town."

"We set out as soon as we received the message, sir." The man turned, making light of his journey. "I had the best horses set to and told coachman to make haste."

They must have set out before daylight, as soon as they had received the message he'd dispatched from the inn via Linton. He did note that he'd ordered the footman to remain in London and take his well-earned rest, but he did not seem to have obeyed that order. He wouldn't call Linton out on it, although he would ensure the man took time off when they returned. Leo shuddered when he thought of the state of the road at the Hare and Hounds.

Although he appeared disappointed, the man bowed and took the powder away. He should be used to it by now. Leo kept wigs for the rare times he chose to use them. His valet could powder them all he liked.

He was ready. Gazing into the dim mirror, he tugged the edges of his waistcoat, his invariable act before leaving his room.

Going out of the room, he became aware of the sound of voices farther along the narrow corridor. Female voices. The windows lining the passage looked out over a pleasant, tranquil garden, hardly a breeze to ruffle the rose bushes below, but this house was not so peaceful.

He stood outside the door the voices were coming from and tapped. He would not eavesdrop.

The door was flung open, and Phoebe stood there, the figure of her sister behind her. The room contained one bed but two clothes presses, one bulging with so many items the door hung open, unable to close. He would wager his cozy manor house in Devonshire that one belonged to the girl standing behind Phoebe, a mulish scowl marring her pretty face.

Phoebe, dressed in a sky-blue gown he had not seen before, looked, as always, neat as a pin and to his eyes utterly desirable. But that did not blind him to the fact that the gown was relatively plain, and in the style of a few years ago. It had also been a deeper shade, as where the robings hid it from the light, there was a thin, darker blue line.

He allowed none of his observations to affect his expression. He gave Lucinda a cool nod. "You made good time."

"More than you did." Lucinda's mouth turned in a sneer before she dropped into a sketchy curtsey. "Your Grace." She wore a pink gown Leo knew he'd seen on Phoebe. Never mind, he would furnish his wife with many, much more beautiful clothes. Not that she needed them. She was lovely enough on her own. What he'd uncovered last night still amazed him—the perfect, silky skin, the mouth-watering curves. He couldn't wait to taste her again.

"Thank you for bringing her home. She must have been a severe trial." Lucinda glared at Phoebe. "She isn't made for a duke. And that stammer drives my mother and myself mad! Many a time has my mother told her to keep quiet, for fear she would disgrace us."

Keeping his attention on Phoebe, he held out his hand. She placed hers over his, in the approved manner. "We are about to leave for the church. Will we need the carriage?"

Phoebe shook her head. "N-not unless you w-want t-to be particularly d-ducal. St. M-Michael's is just across the g-green."

"Church? On a Saturday?" Lucinda said sharply.

"You did not tell her?"

Phoebe gave him a cynical smile. "In that room? I w-wanted to d-dress, not deal with a t-tantrum."

Then it would be his pleasure to tell Lucinda. "Your sister and I are marrying. Today. You forced the union by your reckless actions, and I am not prepared to leave Phoebe on her own for another minute. My delight and honor is to take her as my wife."

Phoebe returned his smile warmly, this one lighting her eyes with pleasure. Her sister responded with an ominous silence. At least the girl wasn't screeching. Perhaps she was learning.

Good. Her sister had not distressed her. Although Leo would wager that Lucinda had kept up her narrative while Phoebe was getting ready. She picked up a bergère hat and fixed it to the top on her head, then placed her hand in his. "I'm ready."

So was he. More than ready. At least Lady North had the sense to keep out of the way. He'd have enjoyed marrying Phoebe in front of her father and brothers, but not these two. In time maybe Lady North would come to realize which daughter had most value, but they would not be here to see it.

And he would not wait any longer to marry her. Would not risk losing her to her sister's spite and her mother's willful blindness. Rather than that, he'd risk scandal and marry her here and now.

Leo never rushed into anything, never. He hardly knew himself.

Lady North waited downstairs, her bright green silk a testimony to her taste. She had appeared uncomfortable in London, but here in the country, she fitted. As she gazed up the stairs to watch them descend, she smiled. A taut expression for sure, but she had more sense than her daughter. "I am so glad Phoebe is marrying from home," she offered. That was more tactful than Leo had expected. "Robson told me."

"Indeed, although you are aware the reason for the hasty union is expedience. I would rather have given Phoebe the wedding she deserved, although I daresay my grandmother will arrange a wedding breakfast on our return to London. If your neighbor had not taken a notion into his head, then we would be in London still."

The smile didn't waver. He had to admire that. "We won't speak about that, if you please. Ah, there is my Lucinda." Warmth spread as she saw the younger girl. "The vicar is waiting."

So they were to have the pleasure of Lady North and her daughter at their wedding, after all. He would not upset his bride-to-be, so he said nothing as they followed them outside.

They walked to the church, since Phoebe appeared to want that. He would have conveyed her there in style, but she told him she did not want to play the great lady here in her home. Nevertheless, although today was not a regular church day, the small, ancient place was packed. Word, it seemed, had got out, and this village was as efficient a conveyor of gossip as the city. From the moment his carriage had appeared outside the inn, the game was up.

For himself, Leo cared little. He'd played to bigger audiences than this. But Phoebe, already distressed from her ordeal, would not appreciate this.

Except his bride surprised him yet again. Her modest gown fitted in this company, more than Lucinda's finery, and he was proud of her, that she behaved so easily with her neighbors. No arrogance or superiority marred her pretty smiles and nods. For that matter, her ladyship greeted her neighbors with well-met bonhomie. Only Lucinda held herself apart, sweeping to the front pew and taking her seat with a graceful swirl of silk and a glare.

Leo went ahead, to allow Lady North to escort Phoebe to his side, in default of her father.

And in twenty minutes, they were married. He had not expected to find the simple ceremony so moving, and he had thought the church would be empty, but it appeared not. While he was not insensible to his rank, so many people came to smile and nod to Phoebe that he suspected they would have come to see her whoever she was marrying. A wry smile twisted his mouth when he considered the alternative. She might have been safe after all.

But married to a brute.

He allowed himself a kiss once they had reached the privacy of the vestry, to sign the parish register. "Not all my couples bother to sign," the vicar informed him. "But I have tried to keep the marriages here regular."

Recognizing a hint when he heard it, Leo handed over the license he had obtained in London. "The gentry mostly use these," the man said. "I have quite a collection of signatures. But yours will hold pride of place."

The formalities concluded, and the vicar out of the room, Leo took her in his arms. "I thought he'd never go."

* * * *

The Duchess of Leomore. Her Grace, the Duchess of Leomore. "Oh, Duchess…"

Phoebe repeated the variations on her new title in her mind as Leo took her out of the church to return to the house where she had grown up. Perhaps for the last time.

She paused to speak with her neighbors, people she'd known all her life. This community would grow distant. This was not the future she had foreseen for herself. She had expected to spend the rest of her life based in this district, married or not, but now a wider and more expansive future awaited her.

One that gave her pause. But she would do everything she could to be the best duchess she could. And she would never let Leo down.

His hand warmly tucked in hers, no formal parading, he spoke with the people on their way out of the church, giving no one the idea that he was in any way discommoded or that this marriage here had not been planned. "Unfortunately the pressure of business keeps Sir Frederick in town, but he will arrive in due course. I was delighted to have Lady North here to give Phoebe away."

He was indeed, because that meant they would not have to bear their company in London.

"I expected Lucinda to snag a duke," one woman said, nodding to where Lucinda stood chatting to a young woman.

Leo added his gentle nudge. "She did not show to advantage in London. Perhaps when she is a little older she may try again. Phoebe was ready to be plucked, and I was the fortunate man who got there first."

Phoebe blushed fierily. "Leo, I didn't…"

He brought their conjoined hands up and brushed his mouth over her knuckles. "Yes, you did. You should not contradict your husband, you know."

The woman laughed and moved away, leaving the way clear for Leo to begin to stroll in the direction of the house. "We shall sleep here tonight," he said, "and I will leave you for one more night with your sister, if you can bear that. If not, we'll climb into the coach now and stop on the way home."

"My mother would dislike that intensely."

"I already do, but only because I cannot have you with me. If I take you there, you will scream again. I'll make sure of it, and I would not have your mother and sister hear your cries."

The warmth of his eyes when he glanced at her left Phoebe in no doubt of his intentions. Her protests died on her lips. "Yes, I can manage Lucinda," she said instead.

As he kissed her goodnight outside the room she shared with Lucinda later that evening, he warned her that she would not go another night out of his bed. "Be ready to leave tomorrow, early," he told her. "We are not lingering here."

She had no intention of lingering.

Chapter 19

Phoebe slept most of the way to London. Leo gently woke her when they stopped to change horses, but otherwise ensured she had everything she needed and let her sleep. When she awoke, they were driving through a village, the road occupied by a good number of other vehicles, some of them, like the one she rode in, with crests on the doors.

They did not stop at the house in Grosvenor Square that was Angela's home. Instead, they went to the ducal London residence in Berkeley Square. Not far away, but the change in her life was telling. The sun was dying, casting a rosy glow over the white stuccoed front of the house, giving it a tranquility she suspected it rarely had.

Outside the house, servants sprang to open the door as soon as the carriage came to a halt. Phoebe swallowed. She would live here now and try to live up to her new rank. Only now, after the rush and a day's sleep, did her tension catch up with her, together with reality.

Leo handed her down tenderly and tucked her arm under his, leading her into the house. Phoebe would not deny her nervousness.

The servants were ranked inside, upstairs and downstairs maids and menservants, far too many to count. But she met them with a smile and a nod as they curtseyed and bowed when Leo introduced them. She caught most of their names and committed them to memory. At least the duchess did not insist on calling them by generic names.

But she would never live so close to these people that they were almost friends, as she had at home. The houses she would occupy from now on would have space for the servants to keep their distance.

They went upstairs, but her ordeal wasn't finished. The worst was to come. But to her surprise, he took her up another flight of stairs and into a large bedroom. A maid stood in the middle of the floor. She bobbed a curtsey.

"This is Hatch," he said. "Her family has served mine for centuries. I have asked her to act as your maid for now, but we must see to finding you a proper lady's maid in the morning."

His attention went to a small table, where a set of covered dishes were dispersing a delectable aroma around the room. "I'll leave you to your meal and to change, if you wish. We will attend my grandmother in an hour."

He left her.

Phoebe had never felt so alone. Fear rushed in on her, and she froze. After one glance at her face, the maid, a small woman of around forty, went to the table and pulled back a chair. "I would suggest you eat first, Your Grace."

Those two words. She would hear them a lot in the years to come. She took the seat offered and lifted the first cover.

An hour later she was ready to leave. Or rather, better prepared. The French clock on the mantelpiece had tinkled the time, nine o'clock, and right on time, he knocked on the door.

Having done her work efficiently with a friendliness that did not encroach, Hatch stepped back. Phoebe answered the door herself, enjoying Leo's appreciative gaze. Since she would not leave the house that night, she'd chosen a new gown, one of the few Lucinda had left her. Hatch had explained that she had unpacked what there was, and Phoebe had explained frankly that she had a thieving sister. After all, what loyalty did she owe Lucinda after the clumsy scheme her sister had entered into that had nearly destroyed Phoebe's future?

"You look charming," Leo said, and reached for her.

Her tension rose because she wasn't used to kissing him this blatantly. Anyone could be passing by.

But it didn't matter. This was Leo's home, and she was his wife. *His wife.* As he drew her to rest against his shoulder, he made the kiss thorough, and she responded with enthusiasm. "Soon," he murmured against her lips. A promise as sincere as the ones they'd made that morning.

He released her gently and waited for her to meet his gaze. "My grandmother and your mentor are below. We should talk to them before we retire."

She plucked at the folds of her gown. "I assumed that was why I dressed." Instead of changing into a night rail and robe.

He nodded. "Indeed."

They went down to the drawing room. Phoebe had been in this house, in the elegant reception room before, but not as its duchess. Would the older lady resent her? But relief surged through her when she saw her friend.

As soon as she entered, Angela was there in a swirl of silk, her arms around her. "My dear, I'm so glad! You will make such a wonderful duchess!"

Phoebe doubted that, but she could hardly say so. She had transgressed by not going immediately to the other woman in the room and making her curtsey, but she made up for that now. When she rose, the shrewd old lady was watching her carefully. "Sit, my dear. Tell me the truth. I have heard a mass of stories today, and I need to know."

So Phoebe told her. Like Leo, the two women did not try to finish her words for her or interrupt her impatiently. Because of that, Phoebe could relate the story, and because Leo sat next to her, clasping her hand, she could finish it.

Although when she was done, she was wrung out. Relating the story took her through the emotions once more, and she doubted this would be the last time she did so. Somehow she would hold her head high through all the gossip.

"So, we have a new duchess," Leo's grandmother said. "And I am again a dowager. I have been looking forward to returning to the Dower House. I was happy there."

Phoebe's eyes opened wider. She had not expected the lady to say that.

The dowager nodded. "Oh yes. When my son became a roué, I thought it was a stage of his life. Instead, he found a wife as reckless as he was, and they proceeded to ruin the estate and its reputation. If they had not died when they did, they would have succeeded. I have no such doubts about my grandson. If you are who he needs by his side, then I welcome you."

In any case, the job was done. "Thank you."

"I will help you through your first months, but I have every intention of returning to my hard-earned retirement." The dowager paused to pick up a glass of red wine from the table by her side. She took a delicate sip and replaced it on the silver coaster. "I feel confident leaving the dukedom in your hands. And of course, if you have need of me, I will be there to help you."

Her face was still, calm. Perhaps that was the way she always looked. Phoebe had expected recriminations at best and outright disdain at worst, but she had not received it.

"I-I will d-do my best, ma'am."

"I know you will, my dear. You must make the role the one you want it to be. Never copy the way anyone else filled the position. I made that mistake for the first five years after I married, but my husband tired of my trilling laugh and utter misery, as he put it. My mother-in-law was a brilliant, beautiful, witty woman. I am not."

No, she was stately, tranquil, and haughty.

Phoebe would be shy, silent, and reticent. Not a very good pattern for a duchess. "I w-will do what I c-can."

"I'm sure you will, and you will have my grandson by your side."

She glared at Leo, who gave her a smooth nod.

"She will indeed." He pressed her hand. "I am considering traveling to the country early."

Angela made a strangled noise in her throat, to which Leo directed a raised brow.

"You have something to say?"

"I hate to remind you, Leomore, but there's the matter of the necklace."

"That will die," the dowager said. "A new scandal will come along any minute."

Angela flicked the skirts of her gown, then smoothed them in a pointless gesture that gave her time. "Lady Latimer will not let it die. She is adding more scandalous talk, and to further it she is attending at least one ball every night and, in between, making appearances at the theater. If you leave the stage for her now, she will take advantage of it."

"That seems unnecessarily spiteful," the duchess said, having recourse to her glass of wine again. "What does she have to gain?"

"She hates us," Leo pointed out.

"Her family always has detested ours. This is her chance to wreak her revenge. I have received notes from several anxious creditors today, including the ship that has just docked from the East Indies. I have naturally reassured them all in your absence, Leomore, although you must also do so. She is using that necklace to create more trouble for us."

Angela nodded. "I have my suspicions on this affair, and I am making enquiries. Pray give me a little time if you can."

Leo tipped his head against the back of the chair, his mouth flattening in exasperation. "The woman is a menace."

"And the death of that woman?" Angela said. "The one killed for a copy of the Latimer necklace?"

Leo frowned. "Not a matter to be discussed in the presence of ladies."

Phoebe laughed. "D-Don't be so stuffy, Leo! You t-told me yourself."

Angela gave a delicate snort. "Phoebe is not a delicate flower to be protected from the world." Having rebuked Leo, she turned her attention fully to Phoebe. "Neither, I'll be bound, is the duchess. The dowager, I mean," she added with a laughing glance at Phoebe.

Phoebe was startled into saying, "Isn't that in extremely bad taste? T-To g-give a woman like that a c-copy of a family p-piece?"

Beside her, Leo broke into startled laughter. "Yes, my dear, it is in bad taste."

Angela glared at Leo. "Tell her everything, or I will."

"Everything?" Phoebe turned an enquiring gaze to her new husband. Leo closed his eyes. "I saw her. I was about to question her on her copy of the necklace, but I was too late."

"You found her? Oh no!" Reaching for his hand, Phoebe clutched it tightly, trying to convey her sympathy.

"Did you rush off to m-marry me because of this?"

"No. I came to you because you were abducted by a man who would have forced you to marry him."

"Altruistic, then?"

He had the grace to drop his gaze. A tinge of color touched his cheekbones, then was gone. "Not exactly. You were mine, Phoebe. Nobody would take you away from me."

"I am not a p-p-parcel." She was not, and her anger was bringing her stammer back. She felt the constriction in her throat and stopped to take a mouthful of the wine, and let it ease her tension away.

"You are not, and now you are my wife. I will not have you disturbed in that way. I do not think that my old connection with the woman had anything to do with her murder. She had a copy of the Latimer diamonds, and I have no doubt she was killed for them. Someone thought they were real."

"So Lord Latimer gave this woman the copy." The dowager drummed her fingers on the arm of her chair. "Or did he?"

"I am sure of it," Leo said firmly.

"It's a family piece," Angela said, as if that explained everything.

Would Leo stray from her side? Oh, not immediately, but what did she have to offer a man like him? Even the thought pierced her to the core, so that she gasped and closed her eyes.

Beside her, Leo got to his feet. "Enough for one day," he said firmly. "Miss Childers, you are welcome to stay, if you wish. Grandmama, we will wish you a good night. Evidently Phoebe and I are fixed in London for a little while longer, but we have taken matters as far as we can for one day. Come, my dear."

Phoebe opened her eyes to see he was holding his hand out to her. Wordlessly, she took it and got to her feet.

Angela smiled at her warmly. "I will take my leave." Getting to her feet, she flicked her elaborate gown into place. She did not seem to be a woman who planned to have an early night. "I'm due at Ranelagh Gardens, and since I have lost my companion in the most felicitous circumstances, I have dragged Miss Helmers from her sick bed. Much to her disgust. I must collect her from my house and then tow her along to the pleasure gardens, where we are to join a group of music lovers. Mr. Handel has promised us a new piece tonight."

If she was still at Angela's, Phoebe would have accompanied her. Guilt suffused her, but at least Angela would not miss her treat.

* * * *

Outside her bedroom, Leo clasped her hands and brought them up between their bodies. "I'll come to you in an hour."

Then he turned and left her. An hour. Goodness. She would have believed he was completely in control, planning a kind but dispassionate act, were it not for the fire in his eyes.

Phoebe opened the door to her bedroom with hands that trembled. Her new maid waited within.

She had to admit that getting ready for bed was less stressful with a mostly silent woman helping her to undress, wash and don the night rail. Tying a pretty cap over her brushed-out hair, Hatch left her with a nod and a smile, just like it was any normal night. Which it would be fairly soon, although to Phoebe this night felt completely out of time. She had persuaded the maid to call her "ma'am" in private, much more comfortable than all the Your Graces. She had to get used to it, but not in her own place.

Leo entered after a short knock. He wore a colorful banyan over his clothes; otherwise he seemed fully dressed. But as he entered, he pulled off his neckcloth and threw it aside, revealing his bare throat. His air of calm left him as he closed the door, and she realized that was for anyone lurking outside, and probably his valet. He reached her in a few quick strides, and then she was in his arms.

Her nerves settled, and she smiled up at him, expecting his kiss.

Instead he gazed down at her, and her smile faded. "I'm a lucky man."

Then, before she could ask him what he meant, he kissed her. His hands spread over her back, claiming her, drawing her into him with a surety that made her melt. He slid his palms slowly down as he plunged his tongue into her mouth, tasting her deeply. Already she knew his flavor, that essentially masculine spice that belonged to him alone. When she wasn't kissing him, she craved it.

He made a small sound, a low groan, and she responded as he sent it down her throat, to enter the heart of her. Claiming her. Although they stood in a luxurious chamber in a Mayfair mansion, they could have been in a cave, with the fire crackling at the entrance to keep the wild beasts away and straw for their bedding.

With her eyes closed, and his body pressing against hers, nothing else mattered.

She recognized the power he had over her. Not the rights of a man over his wife, but a man over a woman. But he had also shown her the reverse. Although she was not sure about that. Tonight she would learn.

He covered her buttocks, pressed her into his erection. Although he wore breeches under the banyan, the fabric didn't prevent her feeling it or gasping in response. Tonight she would know its power and enter into the world forever closed to lonely spinsters.

She could not count herself among that number anymore. Or ever again. And she couldn't wait for it to be gone.

On the other hand, he didn't seem to be in any hurry. He kissed her for long minutes, holding her close, until she moaned into his mouth, sucked his tongue and tried to push the mood further. He drew away, gazing at her with sultry eyes. "I want you so much, sweetness. Knowing you are mine and yet keeping away nearly killed me. No more waiting."

Enough to push her body into preparing itself for him. She knew it now. If he could do that by just looking at her, she was lost.

But she wasn't the only one. He felt it too.

"Come." Taking her hand, he led her to the side of the bed. Then faced her again and scanned her, his gaze so hot he made prickles ride up her spine. "How can I want you this badly?"

Admitting his need freed her. She could express her own, although she had never told anyone her inner thoughts, never been so frank with a single soul before. "I want you too. So much."

When she licked her dry lips, his gaze tracked the movement until she stilled. Then he put his hands around her waist, so slowly, and drew her closer for another kiss. But only a taste. He was smiling when he lifted his head. "Shall we take this to bed?"

"Oh yes."

"Lie down. I'll join you in a moment."

When she touched her night rail, he shook his head. "I'll do that."

So she lay on the crisp, clean sheets, so different to the rough ecru sheets of their night in the inn. They had scratched. These were smooth, ironed, finely woven. The texture enticed her as her senses sharpened and she lay down, not pulling the covers up and over herself. What would be the point? They'd be gone in a few moments.

He stripped. When he unhooked his robe, it was with clear and slow deliberation, one by one, teasing her. Tossing it behind him, he started on his breeches. He had already removed the buckles. But this wasn't a repeat of the night at the inn. It was the continuation.

This time she wasn't as panicked, as distressed, as she'd been then. Smoothly he'd taken over and made everything right for her. And him? She still wasn't sure. He was not a forthcoming man. Knowing his early history, she suspected there was a lot more to his character than anyone knew.

Looking at him now, she could understand why he would incite that kind of emotion. Because he was beautiful. Tonight he was hers, and that was all that mattered until dawn broke.

Golden light from the candles that ringed the room, from the branch on the dressing table to the pairs in the sconces on the wall opposite, to the ones set in shielded stands high up on the bed, delineated his body. He was strong, his shoulders broad, his arms bulging with muscle. "Do you enjoy exercise?" she asked before she could stop herself. That was getting to be a habit when she was with him.

"Yes." He smiled. "What a strange question! Do you?"

"I like riding. With my p-parents, I had to."

Completely comfortable in his own skin, he sauntered to the bed and leaned over her. "Your turn. Sit up."

Her heart in her throat, she did as he bade her, rucking up the night rail and unfastening the buttons at the cuffs. He pulled the tapes at her throat free, the one tying the nightcap to her head and the other at the neck of her night rail.

He pulled the bows free with a finality that she was only too eager to help him with. He tugged the garment over her head, obscuring her vision, her hair falling over her face. Impatiently she shoved the dark locks back behind her shoulders, smoothing them automatically. Then she met his eyes.

Chapter 20

Leo's gaze passed over her. Any hint of coolness, of planning, had gone. Her throat went dry. She swallowed. "It cannot be a shock to you. You've seen plenty of women before. You s-saw me last night. I'm…"

He caught her hands. "Beautiful. You're beautiful, Phoebe."

Her heart went out to him even as she wondered if he was only saying these things, looking at her like that, to make tonight easier for her and to put their marriage on a good footing.

Not because she didn't trust him, but because this was new territory for her. She had no experience, no idea how to behave, what to do. So she had to lean on him more than she would like. But only in the near future. She would learn.

And tonight she would enjoy.

Slowly he leaned over her, easing her to lie on her back. The sheets were smooth and cool, but his body heat warmed her. Pressing his hands either side of her head, he gazed at her, lowering his head to claim another kiss, fierce but brief. His taste and his scent surrounded her, the heady potency making her glad she had a solid surface beneath her. "Touch me," he demanded.

At first tentative, she stroked his shoulders, his skin hot and smooth, then cupped them to feel his strength, then slid her hands down his arms, enjoying his leashed power. He watched her, his dark eyes sparkling with fire and need. Were hers the same? Because she wanted him so badly she could barely think straight.

He remained still, propped above her as she grew bolder. When she spread her hands over the expanse of his back, a muscle twitched, and he flexed as he shifted position slightly. The silence between them crackled and popped with anticipation. He would take her tonight, make her his. She longed to reciprocate, but she didn't have the power, or the knowledge. "I don't know what to do," she confessed, but she continued to caress him, bringing her hands to his front and tracing the powerful muscles of his torso.

"Exactly what you're doing now. This is perfect."

Hot breath washed over her when she touched his nipples, tugged on the tips. His teeth snapped together, and he sucked in air. "No more. I want you too much."

With an ease that spoke of suppleness and strength, Leo lifted one hand, his body rebalancing as he held his upper weight on one arm. He slid his free hand under her breasts, tracing each, watching her response. Her nipples, already tight, pulled further, became even more sensitive as he lowered his head slowly, so slowly, to kiss around them and lick them.

His hand stroked her, across her belly and down to her thighs, until he pushed one finger between them. "Open your legs, sweetheart."

Eagerly Phoebe did so, and he rewarded her by caressing her, stroking down to her opening. Only this time, he did not skirt it. Lifting his head, he met her gaze. "I want to see every second of this. Keep your eyes open, Phoebe, watch what I do. Let me see what it does to you."

Phoebe had never known such intimacy existed. She watched him as he pushed one finger gently inside her. He took his time, easing his way past the partial barrier to her body. She tensed but didn't say anything. He continued, but even slower.

She had not realized she was so sensitive inside. As he breached the place nobody had gone before, not even Phoebe herself, he smiled. "Good. Now another."

"Oh!"

Another finger joined the first. And still she watched him. As he touched her, she discovered places of sensitivity, places that sent shocks through every part of her, little thrills feathering through her body. He began to ease in. Discomfort made her squirm, a sense of pressure she didn't know how to react to.

A sound came from the powder room. Phoebe jolted and broke their visual contact, her cry of shock forcing him to pull out of her. He cupped her cheek to bring her attention back to him. She smelled herself on him, an intimate scent she had never felt so close to her before. "They won't come in. They are strictly forbidden to do so. They are merely setting up a bath."

"I need a bath?"

He smiled. "You might, later. I won't have you in any discomfort, Phoebe. This should be a night of pleasure."

"Or a twenty minutes." She smiled at her feeble joke, inviting him to join her.

He didn't. "I said a night, and I meant it."

Goodness! Could she do it? She had read that the first time hurt, and sometimes after that, too. The library at Angela's house was most informative. Between the financial tomes lay an eclectic collection of reading matter. But that only told her what went where, which she already knew. After a few poems extolling the physical union between man and woman were hints that the first time wouldn't be pleasant. Words like *ripped, torn,* and *blood* did not sound like the pleasurable experience the poets promised.

But she had to do this. And after, she would enjoy it. He had made their one night together pleasurable in the extreme. She had no fears tonight, or that he would deliberately hurt her.

"Lift your knees, Phoebe."

Doing as he told her, she hugged his flanks with her thighs, keeping him close. His shaft nuzzled at her center, slid into the wetness and along the folds. "You feel good." His voice was shaky. "I can't remember anything this good before."

That had to be a positive sign, didn't it? "But you—"

With a small shake of his head, he bent to touch his lips to hers, then straightened once more. "Only us tonight, sweetheart. I don't want anybody else in my bed but you."

She felt obliged to remind him. "But this is my bed."

The smile widened. "So it is."

The rounded tip of his manhood pushed in firmly, nestling just inside her opening. Gently he rotated, but kept his movements barely there, shallow. Lifting her hands, she grasped his shoulders for support.

That's it," he crooned as he brought a hand between them and guided his cock closer, until he had notched it more firmly against the opening to her body. Tension pulled her tight as he contacted the barrier blocking his way, and the sense of pressure returned. "Hold me tight, sweetheart. Let's do this together."

He teased her opening, making her sigh. Already she felt better, her body slick and ready. So ready. He removed his hand and put it back on the mattress, supporting himself once more. "Ready?"

She nodded.

He withdrew a little, the tip barely inside her and then thrust hard.

He braced himself, the tip of his cock barely touching her and then thrust hard. "Ah!" Her wordless cry marked her passage from virgin to wife. A sharp pain arced through her as he pierced her and drove in deep.

No amount of reading could have prepared her for this, such a deep connection with another person. Lowering himself, he pressed against her, his chest hard against the softness of her breasts. His heart pumped against her, the throbbing echoed by the movements of his erection inside her.

Tiny movements as he explored her intimately, a little at a time. "It's done," he said, and his smile returned. "I didn't want to hurt you, and I will never do so again, but that was necessary."

The pain receded, and a sense of wonder replaced it. "You might."

"Sweet Phoebe, never knowingly."

Physically, at any rate. Her grip on him tightened as his movements grew more determined, increasing in strength. Beads of sweat popped out on his brow. He couldn't be nervous, and this could not be taxing his strength, surely. "What is it?"

"I'm trying to be gentle. But I want you so much." His tones rumbled through her, enriching and broadening what she was experiencing.

"I want you, too." But she had a vaguer idea of what that meant. She was learning fast. Experimentally she pushed against him, tilting her hips to bring herself in closer alignment to him. His balls nuzzled her buttocks, the furry surface tickling her sensitive skin.

His responding groan delighted Phoebe. "Very well, madam. Prepare yourself."

She was still chuckling when he pulled nearly all the way out and thrust back in.

Suddenly everything made sense. Her body knew what to do, even if she didn't, and she gave herself up to her instincts. As he thrust into her, she met him, their bodies clashing together, then pulling back and in again.

Sensations built inside her. He kissed her, taking her mouth in time to the rhythm of their bodies, his tongue thrusting in, caressing and withdrawing. Holding on tight, Phoebe entered the dance, letting him take her where he would, eagerly following, responding and finally initiating.

She roamed his body, his muscles moving under her hands, sweat-slicked as both increased their exertions. Crying out into his mouth, she pulled away, gasping for air, refusing to stop. A tinge of rawness remained, but only served to drive her further, toward the peak that lay just beyond her reach.

Chasing it, forgetting everything else, Phoebe's body blossomed and came to life. Heat swelled and burst, numbing her thoughts, forcing her into the present, where the past and the future could not exist.

Tilting her head back, she cried out. If servants lurked next door, who cared? She could not have stopped herself if they were standing at the bottom of the bed watching. The notion was so real that she turned her head. But of course they were alone.

Leo groaned. The tendons on his neck stood out as he gave a sharp cry, his cock pulsing out its release deep inside Phoebe's body.

He slumped over her, but even then, after a brief time when she could only breathe lightly, he forced himself up, using his elbows and forearms to support his weight. And she could breathe again.

"Ohhh."

The low groan came from him. Phoebe lay there, recovering her breath as he hung over her for long moments. Then, after kissing her shoulder, he hoisted himself up and off her, until he was standing on the floor. His gaze was just as hot, but lazy satiation lurked there now.

A gush of liquid left her body when he did, and she felt uncomfortable, but before she could clamp her legs together, he was there, hauling her up to join him. "Let's take that bath," he murmured, swinging her up into his arms.

"I can walk." Even though she loved his arms around her, she had to point that out.

"Let me pamper you. You will be surprised at your responses." He kissed her, his lips firm against hers. "I was right. You're a sensual creature, my wife."

The tub in the powder room was considerably larger than the one at the inn, and already filled, a cloth draped over it to keep the water warm. This time he stepped in and sank down with her still in his arms. She let him settle her between his legs, her back to his front. "It is done. We can't go back now."

"Do you want to?" When she would have turned to face him, Leo held her firmly in place.

"No. Not one bit. I couldn't be happier. You're lovely, Phoebe, and so responsive you take my breath away."

"Oh." Try as she might, she couldn't think of a response or a way to express her doubts. What had just happened had shaken her to the core, far more than a mere physical act should have done. As if he'd penetrated through to her very soul and claimed it. But had he left anything in return?

Those doubts plagued her even now. Uncertainty filled her until she shoved them aside and relaxed into his arms in the warm water.

Now she heard footsteps next door. "What are they doing now?"

"Bringing us food. And probably changing the sheets."

Her flush heated the water around her, at least it felt that way. "You mean they will see?"

His chuckle did not reassure her. "In the old days they'd take the sheet and hang it out of the window to prove that you're a wife in truth. I had not planned to change the sheets myself, and if they don't remove the old ones, we'll go to my room after we've eaten."

"I'm just not used to this level of attention. Besides, how did they know?"

"If nobody heard your scream outside, I would be surprised."

"Oh no!"

He dropped a kiss on her shoulder, then another on her neck before urging her face to one side so he could kiss her lips too. "I love it," he told her when he lifted his mouth from hers. "I love that you are mine, that everybody knows it. Never hold back, Phoebe, not in bed, I beg you."

"You don't have to beg."

His smile melted her. "I will if it gets me what we just shared. I'll go down on my knees every night for you."

Chapter 21

They had three days. Nights filled with sleepless glory, days filled with social events. Phoebe attended balls, accepted felicitations and watched society gossip about her. She saw the caricatures in the print shops, the scandal-sheet sellers bawling her name and pretended to ignore it all. She was a duchess. The numbing ceremonial aspects intimidated her until the dowager firmly took her in hand and told her what was expected of her.

"Be yourself, my dear. Nothing else. If you do not want to do something, don't do it. And don't explain, just walk away." They were standing in the small parlor, a sunny room overlooking the garden. One of the pleasures of being a duchess was her beautiful surroundings, Phoebe was learning.

Sharing tea, drank from delicate china dishes, Phoebe was wearing one of her new gowns, hurriedly assembled for her by Her Grace's mantua-maker. With more to come. The dowager had encouraged her to make her own selections with the same advice, but now Phoebe gave voice to her fears. "B-But who am I? How d-do I know when something is right?"

"Difficult." The dowager's tones softened. Although a formidable lady, of a decided and dazzling style, she was giving Phoebe access to the woman inside the gloss, something Phoebe appreciated more every day. "We are to a certain extent made by our pasts. Take your husband."

She raised a brow. Phoebe nodded for her to continue. She was hungry for information about Leo.

"You know his background, of course. His parents were undisciplined. They would have called it wild or something equally romantic. But the truth was, they disrupted on purpose. They cared for nothing but themselves. I say this even though I loved my son. But I could never control him, because he was the only child and my husband indulged him. By the time my son married, he had no control. They bled the estate white, and if my husband had not left a few properties in trust and the entail was so extensive, they'd have ruined us."

She took another sip. "Leo saw it all. They kept him with them as a pet, dressed him in the best French lace and silk, then chastised him when he did what boys do and got grass stains on his coat, or tore his breeches climbing trees. I could do nothing, or I thought not. The day I took him away from them was the day when I accepted my part in my son's ruin. I refused to allow it to happen again, to let Leo turn into the kind of wastrel my son was. They died shortly after."

She paused and gave Phoebe a sharp look. "You are the duchess. You must *be* the duchess, in spite of events or disappointments or even admiration. I was adored." She grimaced, her fine-cut lips, so like her son's, turning down. "Not by my family, but by society. I was considered a beauty, a wit, and I started to believe what I was told. They wanted a repeat of my mother-in-law." She wagged her finger in warning. "Never follow the role society wants to slot you into. Discover who you are and then live up to it."

"They will not adore me. Half of society believes I'm a thief."

The dowager shrugged. "What if they do? What does that matter? You are the Duchess of Leomore. Behave like it."

Yes, yes she was. And the dowager was right.

"About those gowns," she said. "I would like to cancel the olive-green one and go with the ultramarine one instead."

"I knew you'd see sense."

* * * *

Her husband having gone about his business, Phoebe went to visit the Society for Single Ladies, because they always met on Thursdays. And she wanted to see her friends again. But this time she arrived in the carriage her husband had assigned to her, with two footmen and a driver in attendance.

Angela met her at the door. "Goodness, aren't we grand!" Before Phoebe could stop her, she swept into a deep curtsey. "Your Grace is welcome," she murmured and rose steadily, to meet Phoebe's eyes. She was smiling.

Phoebe shook her head. "Please, Angela, this is all so f-foolish!"

Angela led the way into the cool hall that Phoebe knew so well. The footmen bowed to her. "Not at all. Don't worry, in no time at all you'll come to expect it."

Phoebe couldn't imagine that happening. But she followed Angela to the rooms set aside for the club, feeling a sense of coming home to a place she belonged. Except she would not belong for too much longer, because she was a married woman. She did not belong here anymore.

A dozen women sat there, the informal arrangement conducive to conversation. All got to their feet and curtseyed. Phoebe gave them the same obeisance back. They deserved it. These women endured what was sometimes miserable lives, and they did it cheerfully. But for the twist of fate that threw her into Leo's arms, she would have been of their number.

"Thank you, ladies." She drew out the reason for her visit. "I know I don't belong here anymore, s-s-so I've brought this b-b-b-back." She handed Angela the silver pin, her fingers lingering on the polished surface.

But Angela pressed it back into her hands. "No, it is yours. We have been talking, and we've agreed that we should institute honorary membership. This is yours to keep, Phoebe."

Tears in her eyes, Phoebe closed her fingers over the pin. This small piece of jewelry meant so much more to her than the diamonds and rubies she now owned. In the four days of her marriage, Leo had shown her some family pieces and given her jewels of her own, overwhelming her. "Th-thank you."

"Not at all." Angela's bright blue eyes twinkled. "In any case, with our new occupations, we need the help of people in high places."

Phoebe laughed aloud, and the ladies joined her. Soon, apart from her fine new clothes, she felt as if she'd only been away a short time and had come home. Talking and listening, she moved between the tables and found a seat next to Miss Collinge.

Naturally they discussed the Latimer diamonds. "I understand there were copies," the lady said.

Phoebe nodded. "There usually are." As she'd learned to her surprise. Even Leo had copies of the family pieces, though he used them to distract thieves, hiding them in badly concealed strongboxes. "So the thieves went after the copies." Then a notion burned into her brain. "Why would they do that?"

Miss Collinge, a young lady who'd had her season and not snagged a husband, nodded, her dark ringlets bouncing against her neck. "Exactly."

"Perhaps the thieves fell out," Miss Manners suggested.

"And La Coccinelle was involved with the theft?" Phoebe was quick to add.

The room fell silent, but only for a second. Phoebe glanced around. "What? Am I not supposed to know about my husband's one-time mistress?"

"Not at all." Miss Manners covered her hand briefly, and Phoebe caught sympathy in her gaze. "Every man needs a mistress, at least that is what I've heard."

Lady Dorothea Rowland, who was sitting across the room, snorted. "Gentlemen have no more excuse than ladies do. Why should they continue to behave after their marriages how they did before?"

Miss Manners was quick to defend Phoebe, when all eyes turned in her direction. "We have no proof of anything. For all we know..." Her voice trailed off.

Seated next to Lady Dorothea, Angela shot Phoebe a sympathetic smile. "Indeed, we know nothing. But we will always stand your friend."

"Let us speak plainly," Lady Dorothea said. "I believe that dissimulation causes more hurt than the truth. Better to face the truth, however painful it is." Her voice tightened, rose a little in pitch. "We know your husband has not suddenly reformed," she told Phoebe, "indeed, he has changed. Your handsome but boring duke had turned into a positive roué."

"I beg your p-pardon?" Heat rushed to Phoebe's cheeks. "Who told her that?"

"Nobody. We have seen it." Miss Manners touched her hand again, but Phoebe shook it off. "I am sorry, my dear. Before you left for the country, the duke was seen at the worst hells, but people assumed he was sowing the last of his wild oats." She brightened. "I'm sure that was the case."

But Lady Dorothea wasn't done. "No we are not. I'm sorry, Phoebe, but you probably know this already. He was out yesterday, and the day before. I assume you know about this? He is hardly making a secret of his proclivities." Getting to her feet, she came over to Phoebe in a swish of amber silk. "You do know, don't you?"

"Of course," Phoebe said, chin high. "Do not concern yourself with the business." She had known about La Coccinelle. Not about Leo's nocturnal wanderings.

"Except for your health," the woman said quietly. "Please ensure he is not risking your health as well as his."

In the dead silence she returned to her seat. Phoebe's head spun, but she had her pride intact. Certainty returned to her. She wasn't sure what Leo was doing in the gaming hells and the brothels, but he was not gambling his fortune away or spending time with whores. Marcus's spiteful words returned to her, enforcing her resolve. "He is n-not b-betraying me. He did not b-betray me b-before we m-married." If he proved her wrong, she would look a fool, but she knew it would not come to that.

Last night she could have sworn Leo was about to tell her he loved her. He treated her tenderly, passionately, listened to her opinions. Her own struggle not to fall for him had ended with her recognition of her state. Of course she loved him. She doubted that would ever change. She loved him more each day.

The meeting ended soon after, and the ladies filtered out. Unlike Phoebe, their time was not their own, but each lady swore she would do her best to discover whatever she could.

Phoebe sighed and closed her eyes, tipping her head back against her chair. She had not realized she'd fallen asleep until she felt a touch on her shoulder. She started awake. Angela hovered over her, her smile gentle. "You are tired, my dear." Gently, she traced a line under Phoebe's eye. "You need to rest. I will not ask, but I daresay you haven't been getting a lot of sleep."

Recalling last night and the night before, and the one before that, Phoebe dropped her gaze. "I'm f-finding adjusting a little d-difficult. Everybody is so c-considerate."

Angela laughed harshly. "No, they are being normal human beings." She straightened. "Stay here tonight, in your old room. Your father has gone to stay with your brothers in the City, since he doesn't want to encourage gossip now he is here alone. And he dislikes society. I believe they will enjoy themselves with pursuits other than balls and routs."

Reminded of the stories she'd heard about Leo, Phoebe shuddered.

"That is enough," Angela said, her mouth firming. "Come with me. Write one of your notes to your husband, and tell him you will remain here tonight. You need a good night's rest."

Although she disliked orders, Phoebe was sorely tempted. After all, why not? "Yes." As soon as she agreed, relief swept through her. Who would have thought that her new role was so exhausting? Assuming that the life of a duchess was all tea and gossip was extreme ignorance, and she had been complicit.

To sleep in her room, alone, to be Miss North for just one more night would be wonderful.

Angela sent her to her room to prepare for dinner. "Just Miss Helmers, you, and me for dinner," Angela assured her. "I'll send someone to call you, so if you want to rest, you need not fear you'll miss it."

Phoebe relished the time, but before she removed her outer clothing and lay thankfully on the bed, she sat at the writing table to contact her husband.

Here she'd sat writing a letter every day to him and reading his to her. This was truly where she had fallen in love.

A pity he didn't love her. He'd never said so, in fact he avoided doing so. She would cope with that one day. But not tonight. Tonight she had the luxury of being herself. A period of quiet reflection.

Dipping a fresh quill in the inkpot, she paused. She could tell him Angela needed her, or that she was indisposed. But lying went against the grain. Eventually she decided to tell him the truth.

"My love,"—why not start with the ultimate truth?

"I am staying with Angela tonight. Although I know you have the right to demand I return to Berkeley Square, I beg you do not. I'm tired, and I need to be me one more time before I turn into a duchess for good and all.

"I will still be me, I know that. Without your help and your grandmother's advice, I would have been lost. I will become someone else, someone new, and I am finding the process tiring.

"But I will return. I do not intend any insult to you or your grandmother."

She bit the end of the pen. Her other concern? Should she keep that until she could speak to him directly? Yes, probably for the best. But no. A hint would pave the way. Something was not clear to her yet.

She was too tired to think properly. Dinner and a quiet night. Unless her husband turned up to claim her.

Chapter 22

Phoebe blinked and came awake. Staring at the canopy above her head, its familiar pleated lemon-colored fabric greeting her like an old friend, she waited for her senses to return to her, and idly considered going back to sleep.

She was at peace with herself and the decisions she'd made. The dowager was right. She would cope and become the duchess she was, not force another mask over her face. Leo had written back to her, telling her to rest well, and he would see her on the morrow.

She let the events of the past few weeks roll past her eyes, as if they were merely events in a play and not reality. The clock chimed, striking the hour. Ten o'clock. Goodness, she'd almost missed the morning.

From the night she'd met Leo in the grotto to now, she let the pictures stroll past. She watched them as if she was an observer rather than the main participant. The sting when she'd cut her hand, then he'd come up behind her and claimed her.

Wait…

Her recollections came to a screeching halt. Phoebe thought back and went through the events of that fatal night again. The cut had been trivial and had healed cleanly. Lifting her hand before her face, she looked at the place where it had been. It had been a slice, clean with no snags, as a clasp or a claw setting might have delivered.

Phoebe slammed her hands onto the mattress and forced herself up, vaulting out of the bed, reaching the door in a few strides. Careless of her appearance, she tore open the door.

A footman stood outside, dressed in the Leomore livery. Aware of her state of undress, her voluminous nightgown and her hair in untidy braids because she'd done them herself, Phoebe clutched her hand to her chest like a distressed maiden. Something she most definitely was not.

Linton bowed. "Your Grace. His Grace sent me to watch over you."

"I see," she said, tight-lipped. "P-Please s-send someone up with tea and bread and butter."

"Your maid has arrived, Your Grace." The man kept his gaze averted, staring at the wall to one side of the door. "She is waiting at your convenience."

"Send her b-back. I w-will d-dress after breakfast."

Picking up the can of hot water before he could do it for her, she closed the door. The effrontery of her husband! Sending a footman so she could retain her state? That was all it could be, because she was safe in Angela's house, more so after the break-in, since Angela had increased vigilance in the house as well as outside. She stamped her foot impatiently before pouring some water into the washbasin and beginning her toilet. Before, she'd have hurried straight to Angela's room to share her revelation, but since at this hour Angela would either be downstairs in her office or at the bank, that would have been foolish.

Half an hour later, her hair neatly brushed under a plain cap, wearing a dark blue gown that she'd bought when she first came here, Phoebe swept out of her room and headed downstairs.

Fortunately Watson was there. At least Leo had not filled the house with his staff, even though Linton was trailing after her. Or rather, following her like a shadow. A stubborn shadow at that. "I n-need to speak with Miss Childers, Watson."

"She is at home, Your Grace. Should I tell her you wish to speak to her?"

"N-No. I know where she is."

Phoebe was one of the few people with permission to interrupt her cousin at her business. After tapping on the door, she slipped inside and closed the door firmly on her footman.

Angela, dressed as simply as Phoebe was, looked up from her work. They were not alone; a man leaning over the desk by her side also met Phoebe's gaze. In the corner, Miss Helmers sat, working on a shapeless piece of tatting. She nodded to Phoebe, flicked a glance at her over the top of her spectacles, and went back to work. Until recently Phoebe had taken that duty on herself, but she preferred reading to tatting.

Phoebe had held back long enough. "I've worked something out," she said.

The man quietly gathered a few papers and left the room.

"Good morning, Phoebe," Angela said.

"Yes, indeed, it is." Not the response required, but the one most appropriate.

A smile curved Angela's mouth. "Do tell," she invited. "I can see you are bursting."

"I am." Excitement filled her. "D-Do you recall the n-night the Latimer necklace was stolen?" She didn't wait for more than Angela's nod. "I received a c-cut on my hand." She held up the hand in question. "A long cut, not too d-deep, b-but it was straight and clean."

Angela raised a brow in query.

"A cut from a shard of glass."

Phoebe's statement had its desired effect. Angela sprang to her feet. "You mean that the necklace Lady Latimer claimed was stolen was a paste one too? The one she claimed was real?"

Phoebe nodded.

"Wait." Angela raised her voice. "Carson!"

The man she had been with before came back into the room. He couldn't have gone far. "Ma'am?" He shot a glance at Phoebe and nodded. "Your Grace."

Phoebe found the way perfect strangers knew who she was unnerving. She would no doubt get used to it in time.

"Do we have the Latimer file?" Angela asked. "I am about to share certain details with the duchess."

Carson gazed at Phoebe, clearly startled, his eyes wide and his mouth partially open. "But you never…"

"Her Grace has an interest in this matter." Angela twitched a file from Carson's hands. "Here it is."

She opened the file and pushed it across the desk so Phoebe could see it.

Phoebe studied the columns of figures, not much different from the household accounts she was used to, except the figures were larger. She followed the numbers down to their inevitable conclusion. "The Latimers are c-close to b-bankrupt," she said numbly.

"Indeed." Angela folded her arms and glanced at her employee. "The decline has been steady, mainly due to gambling. Lady Latimer's, mostly."

"Why didn't you t-tell me before?" Phoebe burst out, her attention still on the figures. The numbers advanced by the bank had increased steadily. She was looking at a summary page covering the last five years.

"This summary was only completed a day ago. I ordered it done this week, after Lord Latimer came to us for another loan. We could not oblige this time without security, and as a result, the bank has mortgages on his estate."

Phoebe gasped. "It's that b-bad?" She had no idea how much the Latimers were worth, so the sheet before her showed serious inroads, but not the final result. Now she knew. "They are b-bankrupt?"

"The estate is entailed, so they can't sell it, but they can mortgage it," Carson put in. "When an estate is mortgaged, it is customary to let others in the same business know, so that the estate cannot be remortgaged to someone else. No doubt the news will leak out." He sighed. "It always does. But the loans were not public knowledge."

"Ah." Angela must have found herself in a bind, but Phoebe still admired her. She kept the confidences she had to, despite her friendship. "You c-could have told me in confidence?"

"If I'd known. But the full extent of the loans didn't become apparent until this week. The Latimers have been borrowing all over town. Only when I saw her ladyship at the tables last week did alarm spark. I saw the feverish desperation and knew." She sighed. "The major banks meet occasionally to discuss mutual business. No doubt we will discuss the Latimers and how much credit we can extend them. They are close to disaster."

"So she likely s-sold the jewelry m-months ago."

"Months," Angela agreed. She took the file back, briskly tidied the papers, and closed the leather portfolio, handing it to Carson, who tied the red tapes. "The real stones are probably part of several new pieces by now."

Phoebe sighed. "All that n-nonsense for pieces of g-glass." Understanding sparked in her mind. "But by claiming it was s-stolen, she could c-claim the insurance money. And wearing that c-copy, people would not assume they were b-bankrupt."

The woman in the blue gown who had snatched the jewelry from Lady Latimer most likely didn't exist. Instead, she'd probably handed the pieces to Chapman, who had run off with them and handed them to his accomplice.

Angela exchanged another glance with Carson. She had obviously come to the same conclusion, since she was not surprised by Phoebe's revelation. "We must contact the people involved, naturally."

"I have sent a runner," Carson said, as if that was a normal act. It would ruin the Latimers.

"She'll deny it."

Angela got to her feet and went to the door. "I have an idea. That night, you were at the edge of the grotto, were you not? And you collided with the thief?"

"Y-Yes, that's r-right."

"I think I know what happened. Come to the grotto. Let's see if we can find anything."

They wasted no more words.

Rain had made the garden soft, drops sprinkled over the budding roses in the garden. Phoebe and Angela sped through, careless of their gowns and soft indoor shoes. By the grotto, they paused.

Ten minutes later they had found nothing and stood staring at one another, wondering what happened next. "Where were you standing?" Angela demanded.

Phoebe climbed the two shallow steps and then dropped down one. "One foot was on the path and the other on the edge of the bottom step. Like this."

"Stay there." Angela crouched and peered around the base of the steps. "Oh my goodness."

"What?" Phoebe bent and nearly pushed Angela out of the way in her haste to see. "Oh my word."

Leaning in, careless of her lace ruffles and silk gown, she reached into the gap under the small pavilion, to where a freshly dampened piece glittered and gleamed. Carefully, she drew it out.

It was covered with mud, as was her arm, but the shape was unmistakable. As they examined the piece, the rain started up again, pattering down and clearing the dirt from the magnificent necklace in her hand.

"Stop right there."

A stranger stood before them. Dressed in a rough frieze coat, a man glared at them. Dark hair was drawn back into a rough leather tie, and an unadorned cocked hat was crammed on his head.

In each hand he held a pistol.

"I'll take that."

Phoebe lifted her chin. "Mr. Forrester, I presume."

The man narrowed his eyes. "Maybe."

Phoebe glanced down at the glittering string in her hand. "It's not real."

"It has to be. That's what Chapman did that first night. You and him, you were in it together from the start, weren't you? Well, you don't get to trick me twice. Give it here."

Two pistols. One ball each. Phoebe's thoughts raced. If she gave him the necklace, he'd undoubtedly kill both of them. Or maybe he'd kill her and leave Angela to cope with the mess. Neither solution worked for her.

What on earth could she do?

* * * *

Leo turned the letter from Phoebe over in his hands. He'd written a brief note back, giving her the night. He had asked too much of her, but the obsession to clear her name and thus prevent any danger had taken hold, and he'd chosen to remain in town. Doing that had forced Phoebe to take on the mantle of duchess in the full sight of the whole of society. She was failing, wilting before his eyes, and it was his fault. All his fault.

He would leave the task to other people and take her to the country, where she could ease her way into her new role. Where he could concentrate on her.

If she agreed. The letter revealed absolute exhaustion. Guilt swept over him. He had put her through so much in the past few days: pursued her, married her, and brought her back to London to face her critics. After her quiet country life, he should not have expected so much. She should be cherished, and he would make sure she was. He'd kept her awake at night, unable to keep his hands off her, finding fulfillment in her body he'd never experienced before.

Opening the drawer in his writing desk, Leo tucked the letter away on top of the pile he had received from her, and fastened a black velvet ribbon around it, one of his hair ties that he had put to better use. He pushed a gold key into the gilt lock and secured the correspondence, so precious to him. That was when he'd truly fallen in love with her, when she was nowhere in sight but he could still hear her voice.

Of course he loved her. What a fool he'd been to deny it! The kind of love his parents had for each other wasn't the only kind. Society was full of loving couples, did he but look. He'd assumed too much. Phoebe was the love of his life.

He would call on her this morning. If she was not ready to return to him, he would not fuss, but give her more time. Of course he would, he assured himself, although the notion had all his senses rebelling against the decision. He wanted her in his arms again, curled against him, their hearts beating in time. But he would not allow his deepest desires to control him. Everything must be as she wanted.

Having steeled his resolve, he stood before the mirror over the mantelpiece and tugged the edges of his green cut velvet coat into place. His small sword was by his side, and the pearl pin firmly tucked into his neckcloth.

Fortunately his grandmother was still in her room when he quit the house, otherwise she would have taken him to task, as she had last night. As he walked the short distance to Grosvenor Square, he recalled her words, ruefully acknowledging that he deserved every one of them.

"Phoebe will make you an excellent wife, if you would but let her. She is not a grand lady, but she will be. Give her time, Leo. Do not rush her into the position, as you have been doing. At the beginning of the season, you told me you wanted a partner, not a servant, someone not afraid to stand up to you. She will, Leo, if you do not overwhelm her. If she chooses not to return to you, she may join me in the Dower House. I intend to repair there later this week. See to the arrangements, will you?"

Although he adored his grandmother, her autocratic manner annoyed him at times, but that did not blind him to the truth of her remarks.

He would give up searching for the necklace and take Phoebe away, if she would have him. He had not felt so nervous since facing his grandmother after climbing the largest oak in the park and falling out of it. Looking at it with the eyes of an adult, he knew her stark scolding and the excoriating words she had used were as much terror as anger. That oak had been at least twenty feet high. To her credit, it still stood, although she had threatened to have it felled.

Before that, his terror when his mother had ranted at him, because she had made no sense and she had appeared to forget his name. At five years old, he should not have been in the presence of an outrageously drunk woman.

Swinging around the corner, he strode to the house and took the broad white stone stairs leading to the shiny black front door. The footman opened it on his knock, and the butler sent to see if Leo's wife would see him.

If she would see him. What would he do if she refused? Slink away, tail between his legs, and come back the next day? Surely she would not refuse to see him?

The footman hurried back. This man looked as if a gust of wind would blow him over. "Your Grace, Her Grace and Miss Childers—they're in the garden by the grotto—there's a man—he has a gun…"

Leo needed no more prompting. To hell with correctness and holding back. His wife was in trouble. As he raced to the back of the house for the best view of the garden, he did some swift calculations. The grotto was where they had met. Where the thief had confronted her.

She was searching for something, and so was the man with the gun. The necklace? Had it been there all the time?

Two footmen stood by the open window. Fortunately better built than the one in the hall. Linton shot him an apologetic shake of his head. Cautiously Leo stepped forward and to one side of the window. "What is happening?"

"He is waving a pistol around, and he has at least two more stuck in his belt," one said. "We have sent for help."

By then it would be too late. He would not stand by and watch the woman he loved suffer. "Do you know him?"

The footman shook his head. "We were debating what to do."

Leo was afraid he knew. This must be Forrester. In that case the man was dangerous. He had to get to Phoebe.

"Stay here. Do not make a sound until I tell you to. Do not approach until it's safe."

Under no circumstances would he let his beloved wife face the ruffian alone. He would not watch. Slipping off his coat, he draped it silently over a nearby chair, keeping his attention on the scene outside.

The small group stood about twenty-five feet away, beyond a rose garden, before the artfully concealed grotto. A fine drizzle made the going soft and the day overcast. No shadow. Good.

He moved until he could sneak a glance at the man. He was dressed plainly, even roughly, black cocked hat and russet coat. Leo took in what the man was wearing, judging every aspect of how he could deal with this. He was a reasonable shot, but the man facing a totally still Phoebe and Miss Childers had his pistol aimed at Phoebe's head, and one in his other hand. Leo could not guarantee that if he shot now, the man would not take his first. Or on his way down. He needed to get closer.

"How do I get behind him?"

"The back door," Linton said. "It's the door we use to get to the mews or the garden. If you avoid the gravel path, you can walk across the garden."

Leo patted the hilt of his sword. He'd love to feel that bastard on the end of it, but he would take the man threatening his wife's existence any way he could. "Do you have pistols?"

Linton stepped back, without turning around, a movement that might attract attention. He drew out two pistols, elaborate dueling weapons, very fine. "They're the late Mr. Childers's. I loaded them, sir. They were the only weapons to hand. I would shoot that man, but I can't be sure I'd hit him."

"I can once I get closer," Leo said grimly. "Stay here until I tell you otherwise." He glanced at Linton. "Keep watching and come up behind me when you can. I don't want him to see me until I'm close enough to be sure of my shot."

Grimly, Linton nodded his agreement and picked up a pistol lying on a side table.

Thrusting a weapon into each of his breeches' pockets, hilts turned out so he could seize them quickly, Leo left the room on stockinged feet and followed Linton through a job door to a small, terracotta-tiled hall. Muddy boots stood there, testament to the rain and the morning's heavy fall of dew. For a big man, Leo could move very quietly when he chose, and there had never been a better moment for it.

Would Phoebe betray his presence, let her gaze go to him when she saw him? He would have to take the risk.

He stepped out, onto the grass, avoiding the path Miss Childers's footman had advised him. The women wouldn't see him until he emerged from behind a few ornamental trees, presumably planted to hide the servant's entrance. Very useful now.

Now he'd removed his coat, the better to move silently, he would be more visible in white shirt sleeves and an ivory waistcoat. His cut-steel buttons would catch the light, but he didn't have the time to unfasten the long row. Although the day was overcast, the sun shone through a thin layer of cloud, enough to mark Leo, should the man turn around. He needed to get closer, to be sure of his quarry. With the hilt of his sword and the butts of the pistols easily accessible, he took his first step out.

The women would see him now. He was not close enough to be sure of their expressions, but neither moved or gave any indication of his presence. But they must have seen him. The man stood with his back to them. He wore a rough frieze coat and held a black pistol, pointing it unerringly at Phoebe.

He took another step. Slowly, taking great care where to place his foot, he moved across the short grass area, then over a flowerbed planted with clusters of primroses and forget-me-nots. Sweet peas sent their perfume floating in the air from a nearby trellis as he passed. All was normal, even the drizzle, were it not for the man with the pistol pointed at Phoebe's head.

As he approached, she lifted her hand, and spoke. "Here, take it. This is paste, just like the other one." Something glinted and sparkled in her hand.

"I knew it would be here. It just took me a while to work it out. Chapman said he didn't have it, then he said it was paste." He paused and jerked the gun. His lip curled. "He's at the bottom of the Thames now, but he didn't have any money. It's my turn. Come over here and give it to me."

She ignored his demand. "What about the earrings?"

"Sold 'em. They're long gone. Now I want the main prize. Come. Here. Now."

No! Their attacker would kill her, once she'd served his purpose. She was half a dozen short steps away from him.

She must not get closer. She *would* not.

Leo was close enough now to leap for the man, if he could be sure he wouldn't fire his weapon. Another step, that was all he needed to be sure of the villain.

As Phoebe hesitated, Leo heard an ominous click. The man had pulled back the hammer. Damn, if he'd known the bastard hadn't cocked his weapon, he would have taken that chance. But now the weapon was ready, and if Phoebe made one wrong move, the man wouldn't miss at that range. She was barely three feet away.

"Here!" Drawing back her arm, Phoebe hurled what she was holding at her attacker. Miss Childers looked directly at Leo, and the man turned around as the jewels fell to earth behind him. For all the good it would do him.

Forrester's eyes blazed when he saw Leo. He fired his weapon at Leo, the report crashing through the preternaturally still air, the flash of powder igniting. But Leo was forewarned by that click. Throwing his body to one side, he let fly with his own pistol. He landed, rolled and pulled out his sword, ready to finish the job, as he sprang back to his feet.

Shouts rent the air, and someone screamed.

Not Phoebe. Please God, not Phoebe.

Everything happened at once. One shot, then another. The man standing before them opened his eyes wide, staring at them, and then slowly fell forward. His weight hit her, and she fell under her attacker.

In an instant she'd kicked herself free and scrambled to her feet, heading to where her husband stood. "Oh you foolish, foolish man!" she cried, launching herself at him.

He caught her, flinging his sword aside. "Phoebe! Oh my love, I am so happy to see you unhurt!" Grasping her waist, he eased her away. "You are unhurt, aren't you?"

"Yes, you idiot! I was never so worried as when I saw you. Angela and I were k-keeping him busy, trying to distract him long enough for s-someone to come. Because we were in s-sight of the upper windows, so obviously someone would come."

Dragging her close again, he kissed her. Before he crushed her lips against his, she detected a fine tremor in them. Then, as always, she forgot everything.

"We're going home," he said as soon as their lips parted. "Tomorrow."

Chapter 23

That afternoon, Leo and Phoebe received Mr. Cocking of Bow Street in their drawing room in Berkeley Square. Not the large, grand one where Her Grace was busy entertaining a few friends, but the one Phoebe preferred, the less formal, comfortable one with the view over the gardens.

Cocking sighed heavily. "It was a clear case of self-defense, Your Grace. Think no more of the unfortunate incident. The body has been removed. There were plenty of witnesses to attest to your story. It was Forrester. I remember him from his appearances in court."

The lock around Phoebe's heart opened. Although the footman had obviously brought his death on himself, she wanted it spoken aloud.

She bade Mr. Cocking sit, and poured him a dish of tea, which he thanked her for but did not touch.

They gave him all the information they had. Cocking drew a glittering string out of his pocket. "This is what he had on his person. It's paste. Probably the one he took from the other woman." The central stone was intact.

On the table at his side sat the other necklace, its central stone shattered, a broken shard of glass that had cut Phoebe that fateful night.

Phoebe nodded. "When I c-collided with the man—Chapman—I grabbed the bracelet, b-but the central s-stone on the n-necklace shattered. I cut m-myself on that. I should have realized the jewel was not real then."

Cocking leaned forward, resting his bony elbows on the silk arm rests. His eyes narrowed. "How many necklaces were there?"

"Two." Leo plucked the necklace from Cocking's hand. "This will be the one La Coccinelle was killed for. The other has a shattered central stone. If you have no objection, we will retain this one. We have plans for it."

Cocking shrugged. "Since there's no value in it, you may keep it. The principals are dead, so there will be no trial. Before he died, the murderer confessed as much to you."

Leo nodded. "Forrester refused to believe Chapman and killed him. His body is probably at the bottom of the Thames. Then he set out to discover the jewels for himself, first searching my wife's room, then going after La Coccinelle."

"Neither had the real diamonds," Phoebe said sadly.

"Tomorrow we will be traveling to Leicestershire and then to my main house in Derbyshire, so we will not be available," Leo put in.

Cocking's sharp gaze went down to where Leo and Phoebe were unashamedly holding hands, but he said nothing.

"Miss Ch-Childers asks you to p-pay her a visit," Phoebe said. "She says y-you may work with the SSL in the future, if you wish."

Cocking sneered. "You expect me to work with some amateur organization of ladies?"

"If you wish for answers," Phoebe told him, "you will work with them. You w-will receive a sh-share of the reward, if you do." Bow Street men worked for the rewards offered by the victims of burglary, or the families of the murdered. They received no other remuneration. If nothing brought Cocking to work with Angela, the promise of rewards would.

The Bow Street man sighed. "Very well. So we have been chasing…nothing?"

Leo nodded. "We believe the real necklace was sold some time ago, when Lady Latimer's gambling got out of hand. She has been using a paste version since then. That was stolen on the night of the ball, probably at the lady's instigation in a scheme to claim the insurance for the piece. The lady set about accusing my wife in an attempt to confuse anyone looking for them." His lip curled. "But I would not allow that."

Cocking grimaced. "I was counting on the reward for the diamonds."

"You will get it," Leo promised him. "She only offered it for the return of the necklace, and though this is undoubtedly a copy, it is still identical to the one stolen. We will return it to her, but I will ensure you receive the reward. This affair will come to an end."

* * * *

Leo had treated Phoebe tenderly, made her rest, but she had insisted on attending the meeting with the Bow Street man.

When she had gone for her rest, she found him waiting.

This time when he held her, he did not let her go. Dismissing her maid, he undressed her, and she performed the same office for him. When they were finally naked, standing by the bed, he gave her the last truth.

"I love you."

Gazing into the depths of his eyes, Phoebe saw nothing but honesty. "I was torn apart when I thought you did not. But I swore to myself I would learn to live with it. Many women do."

"You don't have to. I will tell you every day, lest you forget." Smiling, he kissed her, and they lost themselves to passion.

"I should leave you. You must rest."

"I d-don't want to rest." She would not bear him to leave her. "Please stay. M-Make love with m-me."

Laying her on the bed, Leo prowled over her, his erection huge and needy. The heat of it scorched her as she lifted her knees and made room for him at the heart of her. He slid into her welcoming heat, their movements practiced but no less wondrous. Fully embedded inside her, he paused, lifted up on his elbows and gazed at her.

"I was a fool. I should have come for you the week after we met. I loved you then, but I didn't recognize it." He gave a wry grin. "I thought it was lust."

"Wasn't it?" She teased him, rotating her hips for the joy of feeling his hard length inside her.

"Partly," he admitted.

"For me, too. I love you, and I always w-will. I c-can't believe we are here and doing this."

"Oh, you can believe that."

He moved with purpose, withdrawing and then driving deep, finding the angle that nudged her most sensitive spot with every stroke. Throwing all caution away, Phoebe arched up to him, encouraging him, no longer shy or reluctant to show him how much she wanted him. How much she loved him.

Leo didn't stop until her screams echoed around the walls of her bedroom, and then he joined her, his cries joining hers.

They lay in complete contentment, kissing and caressing, fully open to one another. "I'm snatching a few days for us. Just us, alone, together. No pomp, no ceremony," he told her.

She threaded her fingers into his hair. "How?" Because she was learning that a duchess was rarely her own mistress. She had duties. This was the best one, though.

"My grandmother has agreed to go ahead to the main estate. She'll set the servants to preparing the inevitable house party and ball to celebrate our marriage. But I have a hunting box in Leicestershire. No doubt your parents will enjoy its hospitality before too long, once they discover its existence, but it will be ours from tomorrow. We'll start in the morning, if you feel you can travel. Shake the dust of London and diamond necklaces away. Learn more about each other and spend far more time naked than dressed."

"That sounds wonderful."

"It does, doesn't it? I'm so glad you agree. I should have taken you there from the start." He caressed her breast.

She twined her fingers into his hair. "I know what you were doing at nights. People kindly told me."

He frowned. "Told you what?" He'd stiffened.

"You were walking around C-Covent G-Garden and the stews. V-Visiting the g-gaming hells. People t-told me you were doing that and c-claimed you were visiting mistresses and g-gambling your fortune away. Even my f-friends were c-concerned for me. What f-fools! I knew you b-better than that. I d-did not know what you were up to, but I knew you were n-not b-betraying me with whores or gambling in places where you c-cannot win."

Unlike her friends, and her enemies for that matter, she had trusted him. Because she knew him. Her honorable, orderly husband would never disport himself with whores and thieves. This morning, after her first good night's sleep in a long time, a flash of intuition had told her what he was doing, and when the ladies of the SSL expressed their concern, she was sure in her reasoning. Her honorable husband with the rakish parents would never dream of doing that. The only mistress she'd known about had been from the top tier, the courtesans with wit and taste who had more to offer than a quick ten minutes against the nearest wall. Therefore, there could only be one answer. "Y-You were t-trying to find the necklace, weren't you?"

"How well you know me!" He rolled onto his back, taking her with him, so she ended sprawled on top of his big body. When she tried to lift up, he clasped her close, claiming her with a mock growl. "I will never be able to keep secrets from you, will I?"

Smiling, she shook her head, her curls tumbling over his chest in disarray.

When she tried to roll off him, he held her tight. "I enjoy feeling you here. We will not sleep in different beds, my love. Ever."

"Aren't men supposed to keep their d-distance?"

He pressed a kiss to his finger, and then to her lips. The sweet gesture disarmed her. "The only person who can decide that is you. Phoebe, I cannot believe my good fortune. When I think of how we might not have met, I shudder. But you are here now, and I love you, and I'm not letting you go."

"Good, because I don't intend to g-go anywhere." Love had enlivened her, and the fatigue she had felt yesterday was no more. Even the lack of sleep that their lovemaking brought had not made her as pulled-down as yesterday.

* * * *

Phoebe dressed for her last London ball of the season with a sense of bemusement. She had expected—well, not this. She was adored, as Leo had demonstrated twice this afternoon. Touching him, watching him, sharing laughter and a few tears, when she recalled her fears, all was precious and unforgettable.

One more task and they were done in London for this year. By next year she'd be better prepared to cope with it.

Phoebe took more care than usual, choosing frivolous pink with ruching and flounces. A triple fall of lace caressed her forearms, and she wore a necklace of pearls that Leo insisted on giving her. Her earrings were huge pearls.

"They are supposed to have been owned by Queen Elizabeth," he told her when she'd touched them gingerly. "A match to the one on my pin. But they always say that about pearls. I do not think these are so old. Wear them, my love. You will dazzle."

Tiny brilliants were scattered over her gown and petticoat, the latter delicately embroidered with summer flowers and birds. Knowing Leo's preference, she went without hair powder, but she was no longer a stranger to the haresfoot, although she applied her face powder sparingly.

Feeling more joyous than ever in her life, she filled her pockets, picked up her gloves and fan, and went to find him.

The way his eyes lit up when he saw her went to her very soul. He took her hand and kissed the back. "Ready?"

She nodded. The dowager, who rarely attended balls, had decided to accompany them. Resplendent in silk and velvet, the two Duchesses of Leomore strode forth in perfect harmony. Although she didn't think she was supposed to hear, the dowager's comment to Leo warmed her and gave her the confidence to accept who she was now, and what she would become.

"You made the best choice possible, my boy. Look after her well."

"I intend to."

The ball, at another of London's great houses, was well attended, but noticeably the crowds had begun to thin as society, having done the business it had arrived for, had begun to slip away to the country. Tomorrow she and Leo would join the exodus.

The girls who had not snagged a match in their first season were there, and the women who would never find one. Phoebe went to them first, sweeping a curtsey. She was much better at those now.

Miss Manners's blue eyes sparkled. "You are so fine, Phoebe, I declare I hardly know you. How will you bear it when you become the latest toast?"

"W-we are leaving town t-tomorrow, so I won't care." Phoebe flicked out her fan, enjoying the snapping sound, and held it high, fanning herself with exaggerated boredom. "Indeed I d-do n-not know *what* we are to do in the c-country."

Which sent the ladies into whoops.

Miss Manners's merriment stilled, and her expression slipped into distant repose as she looked past Phoebe. "It's that blasted woman."

Phoebe didn't need to turn around to know who her friend meant. "G-good. Just the p-person I have c-come here to see." And to show society that she and Leo were one. She didn't have to hear the rumors to know they were beginning. Her night apart from her husband would have done the rounds. But not this afternoon, or the days to come. She wouldn't miss the gossip.

Turning in a swirl of pink froth, Phoebe pasted on a society smile and went forward to confront Lady Latimer. This task had to be done here, in the full view of society, so there was no confusion.

Delving into her pocket, she retrieved the pouch. Lady Latimer shot her a glare, then her eyes widened in alarm when Phoebe kept on her path. From a few feet away, Leo strolled across to stand by her side. Boxing her ladyship in nicely.

Phoebe kept her smile firmly in place. "My lady, I have s-something for you."

After undoing the gold cord that held the pouch closed, she upended it and poured the contents onto her ladyship's open palm. "We were f-fortunate to t-track down the wicked man who stole this from you and retrieve the object. No doubt you have heard some of the s-story f-from Mr. C-Cocking, the Bow Street Runner."

Her ladyship swallowed. The diamonds—or rather, glass stones— dripped from her open fingers. An earring dropped to the floor, and her husband, who was standing silently by, hastily snatched it up.

Lady Latimer found her voice. "How do I know that for sure?" Tears stained her voice. Understandably since her last chance of retrieving her fortune had gone. The worthless gems she held in her hand saw to that.

"Friends set about solving the mystery, and eventually the Bow Street man became involved," Leo said, his tone bored. "We can furnish you with all the assurances you might need."

The thief and murderer was dead.

Leo continued to speak, in a voice loud enough for all interested parties to hear. "We retrieved the gems from the man who stole them. He was a footman in your service."

Mr. Cocking had been assiduous in identifying Chapman, who had been a footman in Lady Latimer's service. Once they had discovered his identity, the rest fell into place. Lady Latimer had paid him to steal the gems, so she could claim compensation for their loss. But she had not told Chapman the jewelry was fake. Chapman was to pass the gems to Forrester, who had contacts who would break up the necklace and sell the result.

"You blamed my wife for the theft," Leo said to the woman before them. The room had fallen silent, nobody even trying to pretend not to listen. "That sent the thief after her. He abducted her in the street, before her mother's horrified eyes. You put her in danger." His voice hardened, became dangerous.

"How was I to know?" her ladyship wailed, tears pouring down her face.

"The man abducted my wife. You know about that. Half of society knows. I was forced to pursue them, but at that time the man got away. I was too eager to comfort my wife than to chase him down. By accusing her, you set the thieves after her."

"When did you marry?" His Lordship demanded.

"The day before she was abducted."

Phoebe's mouth dropped open. Leo had just changed the scandal of Marcus's abduction of her.

If he blamed Chapman instead, that made it less of a scandal and more of a crime. The whole nature of the adventure had swiveled. Of course that made Leo a complete hero for chasing after the carriage and rescuing her.

Marcus would escape scot-free, but she couldn't have everything. If he ended married to Lucinda, that would be punishment enough.

She didn't need Lady Latimer's stammering apology, but the words flowed over her, like soothing balm.

"Come, my love."

As she laid her hand on Leo's arm, finally, Phoebe felt like a duchess.

Author Biography

Lynne Connolly was born in Leicester, England, and lived in her family's cobbler's shop with her parents and sister. She loves all periods of history, but her favorites are the Tudor and Georgian eras. She loves doing research and creating a credible story with people who lived in past ages. In addition to her Emperors of London series and The Shaws series, she writes several historical, contemporary, and paranormal romance series. Visit her on the web at lynneconnolly.com, read her blog at lynneconnolly.blogspot.co.uk, find her on Facebook, and follow her on Twitter @lynneconnolly.

References

For a list of references and books I used, check my website, or contact me directly.

CPSIA information can be obtained
at www.ICGtesting.com
Printed in the USA
BVHW031705020919
557367BV00001B/20/P

9 781516 109555